F
HAR
Discard

Harington,
Donald.
Butterfly
weed : a
novel

Butterfly Weed

Books by Donald Harington

The Cherry Pit

Lightning Bug

Some Other Place. The Right Place.

*The Architecture of
the Arkansas Ozarks: A Novel*

Let Us Build Us a City

The Cockroaches of Stay More

The Choiring of the Trees

Ekaterina

Butterfly Weed

Butterfly Weed

A NOVEL BY

Donald Harington

Harcourt Brace & Company
New York   San Diego   London

Library of Congress Cataloging-in-Publication Data
Harington, Donald.
      Butterfly weed: a novel/by Donald Harington.—1st ed.
           p.   cm.
      "A Harvest Original"
      ISBN 0-15-100164-2 (hardcover).—ISBN 0-15-600219-1 (pbk.)
      I. Title.
   PS3558.A6242B87   1996
   813'.54—dc20   96-4686

Text set in Clearface
Designed by Kaelin Chappell
Printed in the United States of America
First edition
F E D C B

For Larry Vonalt

All lies and fantasy, but true as God's gospel.

    —Vance Randolph on *The Architecture of the
    Arkansas Ozarks,* in his *Ozark Folklore,
    Volume II*

To him the men of Stay More are still gods.

    —Martha Duffy on *Lightning Bug* in *Time*

Give a cock to Asclepius.

    —Socrates, last words

Butterfly Weed

One

Good of you to drop by again. Pull you up a chair, sit on your fist, and lean back on your thumb—but I see you're already seated. Can you hear me? I may mispronounce a few words, and the way I pronounce others may strike you as mispronunciation. I've had all of my teeth taken out, not like the old codger who could boast, "I never had no trouble with my teeth. They just rotted out naturally." What with my missing choppers and the stroke I had a while back, not to mention my chronic stammer, it's a wonder I can still hear myself talk. Yes, I may misunderstand myself now and again. So don't hesitate to ask me to try to repeat myself if you don't catch it the first time. Now if you'll be so kind as to reach down beneath my cot and feel around, you'll find a near-full bottle of Chivas Regal, the last of a whole case of the stuff that Gershon Legman—you know the great bawdy bibliophile?—arranged to have sent to me last Christmas. Fetch it up here and we'll have us a snort. I'm a badly backslid alcoholic, you know. But I can tell you, I don't never consume more than a half a pint a day. I'm not one of these fellers who just can't stop once he gets started. I was sorry I couldn't offer you a shot or two when you came to visit me last, that winter I was in the VA hospital—when was it? two years ago?—but the VA people are really tight-assed and by the book, unlike these here rest homes where they look the other way or pretend the janitor's broom didn't mean to knock over your bottles a-cleaning under the bed. But that visit you paid me to the Veterans hospital, you must've already had a lot to drink, a whole bladderful: I haven't forgot how you went outside on the hospital grounds and there in a snowbank took out your tool and urinated the letters V-A-N-C-E into the snow. I couldn't see it, but a nurse told me about it; she told as how that hard January cold kept the snow on the ground for weeks more, and those letters stayed there, yellow on white! You know, there's been some talk, probably just a joke, about the University is going to build me a monument and put up a statue in front of Old Main: a heap of white marble imitating a snowbank, with a bronze figure of me a-hunching over it with one hand aiming my tool. But back to that VA visit, before you went out and pissed my name in the snow, you told me your dad had just passed on, and you said to me, "Vance, I've just lost my actual father, so you'd better get yourself well, because if I was to lose my spiritual father too, it would just finish me off." And you recall what I said to that? All I could think of at the time to say to that, choked up as I was? All I could say was, "Bless you, my boy, I aint about to cash in, just yet."

But I've thought a lot about that. Me, who never had a son, who never fathered a child, leastways not that I know of. There's

2

not much I can give you in return for those kind words. This here scotch won't even repay you for that splendid review you wrote of *Pissing in the Snow* for the local underground paper. I won't pretend that anything I could say, running on at the mouth the way I do, could scratch your back the way you've scratched mine. No. But I've thought a lot about it, and I've decided that one little thing I could do for you would be to confess to you that I've actually been to your Stay More myself, once, a long time ago, and I could tell you the story about it, if you'd care to hear it. Might be you could even make a novel out of it, for it concerns your Doc Swain, God rest his soul. I haven't told anybody this, not even Herb Halpert, my diligent annotator, but Doc Swain is the model, or simply the source, for "Doc Holton," who appears in so many of my folktale collections, particularly *Sticks in the Knapsack* and *The Devil's Pretty Daughter,* to name just two. I reckon you know, though you hardly gave a clue in those novels of yours in which he briefly, all too briefly appears, that Doc Swain was quite the raconteur! He believed in the power of laughter to help the healing processes, and he rarely visited a patient—and I suppose you know, or ought to, that in those days he always went *to* the patients instead of having them come to him—he rarely visited a patient without telling a good joke or a real funny story, which helped many a nervous patient to relax and feel good enough to start getting well. Why, I myself was present once during a difficult childbirth, what they call a breech delivery I believe, when Doc Swain told the mother such a hilarious yarn that her shudders of laughter helped expel the baby! But I'm getting ahead of my story, which begins not with Doc Swain but with myself and how I happened to find myself in Stay More in the first place.

Mary Celestia hasn't heard this story herself, have you,

Mary? No, all these years she's been obliged to hear me rambling on, sometimes just a-talking to myself, sometimes telling her stories, sometimes just arguing the damn fool things that show up on TV or in the papers. She just sits there sweetly on her own cot, or lays on it, and she doesn't interrupt me except when I've got my facts badly wrong, as occasionally I do. She's blind now, you know, so I have to describe to her what's showing up on the TV or what the papers say, and I have to read her mail to her. Hers is not the blindness of Homer or Milton—though she could tell you some tales of her own— but of Tiresias, who accidentally gazed upon the naked beauty of wisdom and lost his eyes for it, but had the power of soothsaying in recompense. Oh yes, Mary Celestia could tell you everything that's going to happen. She could even tell me, if I asked her, how much longer she and I will have to live in this miserable little room before we move on, or pass on, or whatever. Mary. Mary Celestia! Now listen, love, I'm a-fixin to tell a story to this clever novelist, and you aint never heard it afore yourself! It is a story about myself when I was about this gentleman's age, about half of what I am now, long before you met me, but I've told you how I was one for drinking all the time in those days, and I wasn't too happily married to Marie, my first wife, and used ever excuse I could think of to get away from her. This is the story of how I got away from her one summer and wandered around the Ozark Mountains of Arkansas, looking for the wildest parts of the country where progress was still unknown and I might find and collect some rare old folkways and stories and superstitions and sayings that I hadn't never heard before. This is the story of how I come to find myself in a lost, lost place called Stay More, which happens to be the name of the village that this gentleman has written so much about. But this is mainly the story of a strange, remark-

4

able backcountry physician named Colvin Swain, and how he come to hide his heart from the world, but finally revealed it to me. I ought to have written this into a book myself, but now it's too late for that. So, Mary, listen in, if you've a mind to, but some of it aint pretty, at all, and some of it may make you think I'm just sawing off a bunch of whoppers to see if I still know how to lie convincingly, but I swear, if there's any lies in this story, I didn't make 'em up myself.

Now son, maybe you should just shut that door. People are a-hollerin too goddamn loud out there. Don't you hear 'em? No, I reckon you caint. Some old bat is screeching, as she constantly does, "MEDICINE! MEDICINE! MEDICINE!" It's the only word she knows. And there's this feller a-going, "It's time! It's time!" When me and Mary Celestia first moved in, I thought he was just trying to answer the old lady that it was time for their medicine, to quiet her down, but he doesn't even know she's there. Later I opined he was just complaining that his supper was late, or something, but I honestly don't know what he thinks it's time for. He makes such a racket, we can't help but get to wishing it was time for him to pass away. And there's this real old lady in her wheelchair, older'n me, and she's always screaming, "Tell me another'n, Grampaw! Tell me another'n, Grampaw!" as if she was still six years old wanting a bedtime story. You'd think some of these people belong in the loony bin, not just a common old rest home. And there's this real witch out there, I'm told she has Tourette's syndrome, who's uttering obscenities that would shame a sailor. I wish you could hear it. If you could hear it, you'd realize what I long ago did: the nastiest language loses all its power once it gets frequent. But the loudest mouth belongs to this old gent who keeps saying, again and again, "About that time, six white horses flew over." Did you ever hear that expression? It's what smart-alecky kids used to say if they didn't believe something you're saying. I met the old cuss once, when he wheeled his chair right into this room and looked me in the eye and said, "About that time, six white horses flew over," and if I hadn't already heard him hollering it a hundred times in the hall I would have thought he was making a personal accusation about my untruthfulness. I raised my cane over his head to get him to back off, and I said, "Yes, and all six of 'em bombed you with their turds." He gave me a look like he'd actually been hit with a horse turd, and he got out.

So just push that door to, if you will. I declare, the one big advantage, if it may be called that, of being confined to this godforsaken stinking pesthole is that it makes me appreciate that I may be sick and crippled, and I may be eighty-six years old, and I may be poor, but goddamn it I aint yet senile, nor about to be, and there's lots of old folks much worse off than me. When I was just a young man, going off to graduate school, my I.Q. measured out at 180, by God, and I don't honestly believe it has shrunk at all since then. And as I think you're about to discover, I can still tell a story.

This here tale begins in the summer of that year, whatever year it was—I've got a bad head for dates—let's say I was about the same age you are now, and you're what?—forty-two or forty-three?—so figure it out if you want to take the trouble to add up from my birthdate in 1892. The year don't matter. The national situation don't even matter, because even though we were smack dab in the middle of what we've been told was the Depression, folks in the Ozarks was so poor to begin with that they scarcely noticed. No, that's not right, because poverty's so relative. A better way to put it is that folks in the Ozarks still had everything they needed to subsist and endure, and they didn't want for nothing. So they didn't even know that people elsewhere all over the country was suffering from want.

It was a summer I couldn't make up my fool mind just what to do with myself, devoting my energies either to finishing up a novel that I'd been fooling around with, or else, if I made up my mind I couldn't write fiction, to a book that I'd had in the back of my mind for years, which I aimed to call *Recreational Sex in the Plant Kingdom*. Did you ever know there was such a thing? Plants are like people—why shouldn't they be?—they "get together" oftentimes not just for propagation but for the sheer pleasure of it. But even Haldeman-Julius, the publisher for whom I'd written so many popular Little Blue Books, a nickel apiece, wouldn't touch a book on that subject. So finally I decided just to continue thenceforward the work in which I had been engaged for a dozen years: the sympathetic seeking out and collecting of folklore, trying to record it before it was all gone, as it seemed in constant danger of going. But I was not—I kept saying, and I'm still saying—I was not a *folklorist*, whatever the fuck that is, possibly an academically trained pedant with a Pee-Aitch-Dee and a patronizing attitude toward the backward bucolics of the hinterlands. I wasn't getting paid much for the hard work I did, but I never earned a penny as a *folklorist*. These here modern-day folklorists don't even study folklore anyhow; they call it "folkloristics" to make it sound even more academically respectable, and they fill up their fancy journals with words like "paradigm" and "parameter," which I've got just a vague notion of the meaning of, and they talk about "etics" and "emics," which I don't know what the shit they're saying. I have never had anything to do with the folklorists. All right, Mary. Miss Mary Celestia wishes to remind me, and inform you, that she herself was, until her retirement, the

University's only professor of folklore. So all right, I married a folklorist, and I've known a whole bunch of 'em, I've met the great ones, I've corresponded with and talked with the likes of Stith Thompson and Archer Taylor and Richard Dorson and George Corson, and I've even developed friendships with some of them: there's a young Ph.D. of folklore over at the University, name of Robert Cochran, who replaced Mary, and who comes in to see us from time to time and tells me he's working on my biography, and then of course there's Rayna Green, a brave and sweet girl who annotated and introduced my *Pissing in the Snow*. No, there are several bona fide "folklorists" that I can not only tolerate but admire. But don't never call me one! Call me a collector, or call me an antiquarian, or just call me a shiftless bum who never had nothing better to do than mingle with and observe the forgotten cordwood folks of the hollers and hills.

I knew that the gods of the mountains are not the gods of the towns. And I knew that the young people of the mountains, given half a chance, would choose to ape their city cousins and abandon the old ways of their heritage, including enchantment with stories and tales. Television was just a distant fantasy, but radio was coming in, and talking motion pictures were being shown in the country villages as competition, if not replacement, for the old storytelling tradition. Along with it, movies and radio were attempting to establish new standards of "correct" English that would soon leave the Ozark hillfolk trying to mouth a homogenized "acceptable" English as it was spoken elsewhere in the country, and they would start discarding the old Chaucerian and Shakespearean and Spencerian language that had been in their safekeeping for generations, and they would lose completely what traditional memory they still had of the actual stories told by Chaucer and Shakespeare and Spencer.

I wanted to find the most inaccessible parts of the Ozarks, cabins on ridges at the end of crude trails, and talk to the oldest of the old-timers among those lost and forgotten people, and I wanted to write down what they had to remember. I wanted to befriend old shut-ins, and interview granny women and yarb doctors and old horse traders. I wanted to shack up with berry pickers under the ledges, and sit on the porch of a gristmill while the corn was a-grinding, and around the fire of the still while the corn was a-making, and listen to the stories told around midnight campfires on the stream banks and high ridges while fishing or coon hunting. I wanted to kick up my heels at square dances and play parties and other backwoods frolics, and write down the words the caller spoke and the tunes the fiddlers played. I wanted to sit in brush arbors under the boiling sun and listen to the preachers exhort the sinners to their salvation. I wanted to loaf on the courthouse steps and the steps of crossroad country stores and listen, and listen, and listen!

I wanted, in short, to make my most concentrated investigation of the distinctions between mundane "reality" and magical if untrue story. Without planning it or knowing it in advance, I would also be collecting material for one of my major books, *We Always Lie to Strangers,* on the distinction between exaggerations meant to deceive and to entertain.

So I went. I ought to have told Marie what I was planning to do, but I didn't. I just up and went. I left her a letter, apologizing for sneaking off before daybreak, and making it clear that my intentions were no different from that sort that had allowed her to say to her friends on several occasions, "Oh,

Vance has just hit the road again, to see what he can see." You recall that old folk tune, "The bear went over the mountain, to see what he could see"? In fact, I had spent most of the decade of the twenties, perhaps secretly driven by the coming of the Jazz Age, living hand-to-mouth in my rambles all over the Ozarks. This time I had a *little* money, and I was leaving Marie more than she needed for groceries and such. The year before I had been invited to put in a stint as a screenwriter in Hollywood—just like Fitzgerald and Faulkner and all the rest—and they had paid me a couple hundred dollars a week for nearly three months before they discovered that I couldn't write movies. That was the best money, the most money, I had ever earned.

Except for a sizable wad of cash, I was traveling light. I had everything I needed in a canvas knapsack, including plenty of scraps of thin newsprint, on which I would jot down my recordings of stories and jokes and old sayings and odd words and their meanings, and superstitions and whatever else I needed to collect and record. I had one change of clothes in the knapsack, and the clothes on my back, which I had carefully selected to make me look as much like a hillman as possible: a well-worn chambray shirt, frayed and faded denim pants, scuffed brogues on my feet, and on my head a crushed, floppy, sweat-stained black felt fedora. I had debated with myself whether to wear a felt hat or a straw, and had decided the latter might make me look like a farmer, which I wasn't.

Even in such old clothes, I cut quite a figure in those days, if I say so myself. You wouldn't guess it to look at me now, but I was a handsome man in my forties. I had a neat, nearly a dapper, mustache, not as full as I wear now nor as gray but dark, and in contrast to this shiny smooth dome, which looks like I'm a-clearing ground for a new face, I had a full head of

10

dark hair, just beginning to thin. During my ephemeral stay in Hollywood, I had more than once been mistaken for a movie star.

Much of my traveling was by shank's mare—on foot, but I got plenty of rides too—by wagon, by occasional auto, sometimes by truck or other conveyance, and thus I gravitated toward the remotest part of the Ozarks, that selfsame Newton County which has been the private purlieu of your fictions. As soon as I crossed the county line, I began to lose track of time, which I suppose was my intention anyhow. I spent the nights in a variety of accommodations: in the crudest, dirtiest log cabin, sleeping with a whole family of twelve in one room; in the "guest room" of a rather prosperous valley farmer whose wife came perilously close to sharing my bed; in an abandoned house that must surely have been inhabited by ghosts, who kept me awake most of the night; in a barn, on the straw, not once but twice; in the shelter of a moonshine distillery, whose owner and I both passed out sampling the product and slept on the hard ground; and in a house of sorts in the mouth of a cave, three of its four sides the natural rock of the cave.

Everywhere I went I was warmly received and invited to stay, and sometimes almost forcibly prevented from leaving. My business, to anyone who inquired, was simply that I was wandering the countryside, a vagabond in search of adventure and occasional work—and I had occasional work, being put to good service helping out around the farm or the house. Often I earned my keep. I was a good woodchopper. I was a good haymower. I could hoe a patch of corn with the best of them . . . although my hands, unaccustomed to manual labor, easily blistered and became quite raw, but I dared not ask for a pair of gloves, lest my hosts suspect that I was not the native hillman I was pretending to be.

One of the finest storytellers I encountered not only had a repertoire of the very best old folktales as imaginatively reconstructed or retold by herself but also was a fantastic teller of "local history." She was an old woman, a fortune-teller, name of Cassie Whitter, and she lived in a dogtrot cabin on a mountaintop in the most isolated spot I ever reached in all my travels. I sought her out on the advice of some of her distant neighbors, who assured me that the old lady could not only accurately predict my future, or tell me the location of anything I had lost, but could "keep ye up all night long with stories, ever one of 'em true." I had heard several references to the "Widder Whitter," an utterance which sounded like a birdcall, before I figured out that the first part was merely a title of honor: she had been widowed for many years. Climbing the steep and rugged trail to her place, hardly more than a pig's path, I felt such a fatigue and malaise, which couldn't be blamed on the arduous trek, that I wondered if I was coming down with something.

She received me hospitably, and sensed that I was not well, and, as was the custom everywhere I went, insisted, no, *demanded* that I spend the night. After I drank the coffee she gave me, she took my empty cup and studied the coffee grounds clinging to its sides, and "read" my fortune from those dregs, in the manner of other fortune-tellers reading tea leaves. The things she predicted would happen to me actually did happen to me eventually—in fact so many of her predictions did come true that I was convinced that all the stories she told me as "truth" must also have been true. Among her predictions, for example, was that I would spend all my later years in a nursing home, a concept of an institution that was unknown to me at that time and could not possibly have been known to her, and I thought her notion of it was a form of madness. I truly suspected that she was a little loony, and possibly even dangerous, and that is why, when I began to get honestly sick during the night, my first thought was that she might have poisoned me. She had fed me a dish I recognized because I'd had it elsewhere among those people—stewed squirrel with new potatoes and poke greens—it was very tasty, but after she had put me up for the night in "t'other house," that is, the opposite wing of the two-pen dogtrot cabin in which she lived, I grew desperately ill, and despite the warm June night, I had severe chills that shook me so violently I needed extra quilts, but the shaking served to distract me from a very severe headache and an even more severe backache. Several times during the night I had to get up and go out to "the brush." I had diarrhea, and used up several precious sheets of the newsprint I packed for keeping notes. At dawn of that sleepless night my nose began to bleed, and I lost more newsprint trying to stanch it.

When the Widder Whitter discovered my condition, she offered to bring me my breakfast in bed, but I had no appetite whatsoever. She put her hand on my brow for a moment and declared, "Wal, I may be able to read yore future, but I caint tell what ails ye in the present. We need Doc Swain, if he didn't live so blamed fur away. Too fur for me to fetch 'im. Why, he could fix ye up in nothing flat. Doc Swain could jist take one look at ye, and tell what ye needed to do to git well. He could . . ."

Sick as I was, and enfeebled, I did not realize that Cassie Whitter had begun to tell me the long, long story of Doc Colvin Swain of Stay More. It is the story that I am going to be telling to you, for as long as it takes me. It is the story that I heard again in part from various people I interviewed in Stay More itself. It is the story that, finally, Doc Swain himself was going to confirm to my satisfaction before I was done with him. Probably no one told me the story better than Cassie Whitter, but I could not appreciate it, nor even listen closely, those days and nights of desperate illness while she seemed to drone on and on. In fact, it was horribly tantalizing, listening to the exploits and the cures of this fantastic country doctor when I needed him so frantically myself. But I had the presence of mind to realize that the story she was telling me was so important, so fabulous, that I had better make some notes to jog my memory of it, and while I was so sick I could scarcely hold a pencil, I managed to write down a kind of outline of the story as Cassie was telling it to me. So I was sacrificing half of my newsprint as wipes for my diarrhea, and the other half was going to summarize Doc Swain's story, and sometimes I couldn't tell the difference!

One other thing I realized: being a woman, Cassie Whitter out of verbal modesty was censoring a great deal of Doc's story; she was obviously omitting or euphemizing the sexual parts of it, and if I wanted to learn those, I'd have to search them out from somebody else.

Nor did she reach, in her telling of the story, the crucial part, concerning his "affair" with a beautiful young girl. That most dramatic part of the story, which I would have to learn primarily from Doc himself, had just commenced when my illness became so severe that she was prompted to abandon the story and announce, "I had best see if I caint fetch Gram Dinsmore fer ye, or else you're not long fer this world." Then she disappeared, for the better part of the day, as I grew progressively sicker and felt hopeless that I was alone without anybody handy to help me. Late in the afternoon she finally returned with another woman, older even than she, who carried a bundle, an assortment of some things tied up in what looked like a gingham dish towel. Gram Dinsmore, I was told, was a "yarb doctor," and she proceeded to prod and poke me while asking various questions about me and my condition. How old was I? On what day of what month at what hour of day was I born? Through which nostril had my nose bled, and at what hour of the day? "Have you got the flux?" she asked.

"Flux?" said I.

"Yessir, are yore bowels loose and runny?" she inquired. When I admitted that I did indeed have diarrhea, she asked several embarrassing questions about the composition and color of the excretion. Then she opened her bundle and took out a small sheaf of green leaves, which she gave to the Widder Whitter, asking her to brew it up into a tea. She explained to me that it was simply ragweed, and the ragweed tea would cure me of the flux, but the flux, she said, was just a symptom of something far more serious, and she wanted me to take a strong dose of some oozy concoction she kept in a quart Mason jar. When I refused to take it until I knew what it contained, she recited the few ingredients, primarily the boiled-down residue of the inner bark of the slippery elm tree, *Ulmus fulva*. She gave me a tablespoon full of it, and it was nippy but not unpleasant. She forbade me to eat any solid food, and told me to drink lots of the ragweed tea, then she asked me for a dime, but I protested I ought to pay her much more than that.

"Jist let me borry a dime iffen ye got one," she said, and I gave her a dime and she inspected it closely and declared, "Hit aint shiny enough." I searched my pocket for a shinier dime, but had none. She gave the dime to the Widder Whitter. "Could ye rench this in some vinegar and lye soap?" And when this was done, she took the now-shiny dime and inserted it between my upper lip and teeth, and declared, "Now thet thar will stop yore nose from a-bleedin."

And sure enough it did. I wish I could report that her other prescriptions healed my afflictions as quickly as that dime cured me of nosebleed, but no. Gram Dinsmore accepted from me a half-dollar for her services, but left without telling me what her diagnosis had been, and my diarrhea and chills continued un-abated despite my regular consumption of the slippery elm ooze and the ragweed tea. The Widder Whitter attempted to resume telling Doc Swain's story, on the threshold of the appearance of the young heroine, but I could not listen attentively. Finally I interrupted her in desperation, "Just how fur away does this Doc Swain live?"

"He lives all the way over to Stay More," she said. "That's six mile at least."

"Miz Whitter," I said, "you've done gone and predicted I'll most likely spend my old age in a home under the care of nurses, so that means I aint about to up and die of what's ailin me right now. But if you can read the near future jist as good as the far future, can you tell me how long I'm gonna be sick and how I'm gonna get well? How long am I gonna have to stay here?"

"Yo're welcome to stay here, long as you like," she said. "And I can finish tellin ye Doc Swain's story."

"Well, yes, and I'm obliged," I said, "but can you tell me how long before I get well enough to travel again? At least the six miles to Stay More so's I could see Doc Swain myself?"

"Drink up yore ragweed tea," she told me, and I drank it, and she took the cup and peered closely at the small bits of ragweed clinging to the sides. "Hhmmm," she hummed, more than once, and I began to understand that perhaps she was as adept at reading tea leaves as reading coffee grounds. At length, she said, "How about that? It's Doc Swain hisself who's a-comin to fetch ye and take ye to Stay More and fix ye all up, and cure the ailments of yore soul while he's at it!"

So. We come at last to our hero, the main character of her story, and of mine. You've been patient to sit through this long preface. Okay, here he is: one afternoon during my second week at Cassie Whitter's, the door opened, and in walks this man who is the everlovin *epitome* of the old-time country doctor! Black bag and all! Steel-rimmed spectacles and all! Christ A-mighty, he was so much right out of a Norman Rockwell cover that I *knew* I was having a delirious hallucination (although that wouldn't come until a week later): that I had just invented him in my desperate need, out of my urgent fancy, that I was just *wishing* he was there.

"Why, howdy, Doc!" the Widder Whitter said to him in surprise, as if I was inventing also her confirmation of his reality. "I was jist a-talkin about ye. How'd ye know we've got a customer fer ye?"

"Gram Dinsmore tole me," the man declared, setting down his bag and opening it and taking out his stethoscope. I suddenly realized that in her long story about him, Cassie Whitter had made no attempt to describe his appearance. Was that in order to universalize him, to let him represent *all* physicians? He was not tall, and inclined to stockiness, and I guessed he was about fifty, maybe midfifties, about right for a skilled, well-practiced physician. I don't think Norman Rockwell could have given him a better face: as kind and benign as you could hope for, and even a little handsome. The only missing touch was that he was not wearing a doctor's coat and vest: he was not even wearing a necktie: he was not even wearing a white shirt.

I can't honestly recall *what* he was wearing; I just remember that although it was not at all *professional,* he still somehow looked very proper and official.

The Widder Whitter was chuckling. "Now what'd she go and do thet fer? Aint you her rival?"

The man laughed. "Yeah, and we was both up at Elbert Sizemore's place this mornin, a-tryin to cure him of a bad case of the hives, me with my magnesium sulfate and her with her maple-leaf tea. I had a little fun, askin her if her tea was made from rock maple or soft maple, and shore enough she'd used the soft, and I tole her that rock always beats soft when it comes to hives." The doctor paused to pick from his eyes some tears of laughter. "That shore did frost her gizzard! But anyhow, when we got done a-fussin around with ole Elbert, Gram tole me about this here feller here, said he most likely was ailin with something that was 'beyond her powers,' is the way she put it, 'beyond her powers.' Never heared her admit that of ary a case before. She tole me what she thought it mought be, but I'll jist have to see fer myself." All the time that he was speaking these words, the doctor was doing things to me: running a thermometer into my mouth, placing his stethoscope on my chest and back, squeezing my stomach and my sides, and peering into my ears, my nose, my mouth. At length he pulled up my shirt, inspected my stomach carefully, then let my shirt fall and said, "I don't reckon I've met ye afore. I'm Doc Swain," and offered me his hand.

"I'm Doc Randolph," I said, shaking his hand. In those days everybody around Pineville called me "Doc" just as a nickname, which had nothing to do with medicine nor with the Pee-Aitch-Dee that I'd never succeeded in finishing, but was just a common Ozark nickname for a gambler. So I added, "But it's jist what they call me, it aint but a nickname."

"Please to meet ye, Doc," he said. "You don't live here-abouts, do ye?"

"Nope, jist a-passin through."

"Wal, you shore caint pass on through if we jist leave ye a-layin here. It's too fur and a hard climb for a old man like me to come up here ever day and see you. And besides you couldn't afford my rates of twenty-five cents a mile for the distance I'd have to travel. So I need to git you down whar I can give ye a blood test, and keep a eye on ye."

"What seems to be wrong with me?" I asked.

"I caint be a hunerd percent certain, jist yet. I don't believe it's malaria, but it could be meningitis, or trichinosis, or abdominal Hodgkin's disease, or several other things. Whatever it is, it's serious. Gram Dinsmore thought it mought be typhoid, and that's what she prescribed fer ye, although she gave ye one thing to loosen yore bowels and another'n to stop 'em up!" Doc Swain laughed. "The way I learnt it, if the slippery elm bark is peeled upwards, it'll make ye puke, but if it's peeled down'ards it'll give ye the flux. She must've peeled it the wrong way!" He laughed again, then grew serious. "But do ye reckon ye could git up, and me and Cassie will help ye down the mountain to whar I had to leave my auto?"

So with no small expenditure of effort and finesse, the doctor and the Widder Whitter supported me between them as we made our way slowly and carefully down the steep trail from the widow's cabin. The doctor had to carry his bag in one hand and the Widder Whitter had to carry my cumbersome knapsack in one of hers, and the three of us had to stop whenever we came to a fallen log and sit on it for a moment to rest. Going downhill in my condition in that manner was a worse ordeal for me than any uphill hike I'd ever made. It seemed it took hours to reach the place where the trail met a graveled road, and the doctor's car was parked. Through the mental fog that was settling down on me, I tried to thank the widow for her hospitality and tolerance of my infirmity and her help and her food and her . . . but she put her fingers on my lips to hush me. "Come back and see me again when you git to feelin better," she said. "I never did finish tellin ye that amazin story. But maybe ye can git the ole hoss to tell you the rest of it hisself!"

As we drove off, the doctor glanced at me and asked, as if he knew the answer, "What ole hoss? What amazin story?"

"It seems that there womarn knows yore entire life," I observed. "And she's been a-tellin me most of it."

Doc coughed. "Wal, heck, Doc, I aint so sure she knows the past as well as she knows the future. Didje git yore fortune tole?"

"Yeah, I reckon I did, Doc," I allowed. "But it was kind of strange." I didn't feel much like talking, but maybe I could just let him do all of it. So I asked, "Does she really know the future?"

"Myself, I've never permitted her to mess around with my fortune," he declared. "She seems to know such fantastic tales about my past, I don't *want* to know my future. Tell ye the honest truth, if half of what she told ye about me was true, my past has done already had enough problems to last me plumb through the rest of my future!" I managed to join in his laughter over this. He went on, "So I couldn't tell ye if she knows *my* future, but she's either an awful good guesser or got some special knowledge of Fate, because she's never been known to be wrong in one of her readings. And I know fer a fack that she's 'specially good at tellin whar lost things is at—she can locate strayed animals and anything else that's been misplaced." Then, as the car—a Model A Touring Sedan considerably dented and dusted—bucked and jerked down the terrible road off the mountain, the doctor, speaking loudly over the noise of the car's rattling and bumping, told me the story of how the Widder Whitter had once located a dog the doctor had lost, or rather had had stolen. "I had me this great big ole hound, named Galen—after the olden-time Greek physician, you know?"—he cast me a glance to see if I did indeed know, and there must have been something in my smile which told him that I did— "and one day ole Galen turned up missin, and was gone more'n a week before somebody suggested it wouldn't do no harm for me to ask the Widder Whitter to tell me if he was lost for good, or dead some'ers, or what, so I hiked up to her place and tole Cassie what I come fer, and she started in a-conjurin around with some little sticks and buttons and what-all, and talked a lot of damn foolishment, but finally she says my dawg is tied up in a corncrib over to Spunkwater, some miles due east of my place in Stay More, and she even described the feller who stole 'im, and I knew right off it was ole Bib Ledbetter, who'd been bearin a grudge again me ever since I'd treated him fer syphilis and he'd wanted me to tell his old lady it was jist measles, but I'd had to warn her not to lay with him, and she'd done guessed that he'd been cheatin on her. Wal sir, I drove on over to Bib's place, and shore enough thar was my dawg Galen, big as life and twice as natural! Ole Ledbetter claimed he'd jist seen a stray dawg around the last couple of days, and didn't pay it no mind. He says some of the childern must of shut him up in the corncrib, maybe. So I couldn't prove nothing, and didn't try to argue with Bib—I jist took my dawg and drove him home. But there aint no doubt in my mind that I'd of never got Galen back if it hadn't been fer Cassie Whitter. So maybe we'd best not dismiss anything the widder says."

I managed a smile at his story, but I couldn't make any

comment. Eventually he coughed again, and cast me a sharp look, and asked, "Did she tell you about that time she predicted the future for a gal named Tenny?"

I tried to remember. "I think she was just getting around to that part of your story. Wasn't Tenny your wife?"

"Maybe not legally," he said, and did not elaborate, so I left it at that. The bouncing of the car was hell on my stomach, and after another mile of the rugged highway I searched for something to say just to keep my mind off my miseries. "Have you ever heared tell of a 'nursin home'?" I asked him. And when he pondered a moment before shaking his head, I told him that Cassie Whitter had predicted I'd spend my last days in a nursing home.

He meditated on that prophecy for a while longer before declaring, "Wal, it sounds to me like yore last days won't befall ye fer a many and a many a year to come. Forty year from now, maybe they'll conjure up some kind of house whar ole folks jist go to be took keer of in their feebleness and senility. A house filled with nurses."

Once we hit a rut so deep that my stomach got the better of me, and I frantically signaled for him to stop so I could open the door and puke into the road. He watched me with interest and sympathy and expressed regret that he couldn't give me anything on the spot to help. "We'll be home directly," he said.

My condition was such that I could not appreciate how close we might have been to our destination, nor could I even absorb the gorgeous scenery en route. To this day I have hardly any memory of how we got into Stay More. Sometimes in my dreams I seem to have relived that route, and caught glimpses of strange turnings in the road, streams forded, mountains rising up to enclose me or hug me, but I couldn't have mapped the route to save my soul, and much later I would realize that there was no way I could escape from Stay More, because I had no idea how I'd got there.

Haven't you remarked on this phenomenon in your novels? You've made it clear that Stay More is not simply remote and hard to get to, if not inaccessible, but that it's even harder to *escape* than it is to *find.*

Late in the afternoon we came to a clearing at the top of a hill affording a broad view of the valley below, and the doctor pointed at the small village there, a sleepy, decaying, almost storybook hamlet, and said, "Yonder's Stay More."

Are those tears in your eyes? From nostalgia, I trust, not from boredom. What can I tell you about Stay More that you don't already know?—except perhaps to assure you that although you must have allowed yourself occasionally to doubt its existence except in your novelist's fantasy, it does indeed exist! Or rather, it did; it doesn't anymore. You told me in a letter once that you took the name for your "mythical" village right out of the chapter "An Ozark Word List," in the back of the book I wrote with George Wilson, *Down in the Holler: A Gallery of Ozark Folk Speech,* wherein I had reprinted an item I'd originally published in a 1926 issue of the journal *Dialect Notes:*

> stay more: *v.i.* To remain longer. This is a polite expression, used when a guest is preparing to depart. "Don't be drug off, Jim! *Stay more!*"

But the simple, wonderful truth, Donald, is that it may be only a common polite expression in the Ozarks, but it is also the name given in the first half of the nineteenth century to a burgeoning community of hillfolk in Newton County, and while it may no longer exist, it most certainly did exist that summer of which I am telling you! My own name for my own mythical village, whenever I had recourse to mention it in my various collections, or in my book of stories, *From an Ozark Holler,* was "Durgenville," which I fabricated from the word for an awkward, uncouth hillman, "durgen." That's a hard "g." I can assure you that nobody ever named any actual Ozark village Durgenville. But I can also assure you that somebody, even if it was, as rumored, an Indian, did indeed name the village of which we are speaking Stay More.

Although the village had begun to decay, its essential architecture was still intact: there was a schoolhouse, a pair of doctor's offices, a sawmill and a wagon-bow factory, an inoperative but still impressive gristmill, and a couple of general stores. Doc Swain pulled up at the lone gasoline pump beside one of the stores, a large, three-story mercantile with a faded sign over it, INGLEDEW'S GEN. STORE, and in one of its grimy plate-glass windows a pasteboard sign, POST OFFICE, STAY MORE, ARK. The store appeared to be in operation but had no customers at the moment. The gasoline pump was one of those old tall, slender types where you pump the gas up into a glass cylinder before gravity lets it down into your tank. Doc said, " 'Scuse me, but I'd best fill up now, or it'll slip my mind, and I'll find myself called out in the middle a the night without any gas." While he was filling his tank, the storekeeper came out onto the porch, a white-haired but still-handsome old gent, and they exchanged greetings, "Howdy, Doc," and "Howdy, Willis." Doc Swain tried to pay for the gas, but Willis waved the money away, saying, "I still owe *you,* Doc, and probably forever will."

Driving on, Doc pointed out the towering gristmill behind the general store. "Been shut down fer some years." He pointed to the opposite side of the road. "But that's still runnin, sort of." There was a small hotel, or rather actually a large house, two stories, three front doors, which had a little HOTEL sign over its entrance. We passed an abandoned house next to it before Doc turned the car into his own yard, before a modest cottage with a sign out front, C. U SWAIN, M.D. DOCTOR OF HUMAN MEDICINE. The house's porch was practically right on the road, and what yard there was clung to both sides of the building and was littered with free-ranging chickens. As Doc got out of the car, he was greeted by a large, slobbering, black-spotted hound dog, and, ruffling the dog's neck, he said to me, "This here's Galen, not the one I was tellin ye about, not the original Galen, who, come to think of it, wasn't the original Galen hisself. No, this here's Galen Four or Galen Five, I forget which." Then the doctor directed my attention to a house across the road, where another shingle was posted on a stake: J. M. PLOWRIGHT, M.D. FAMILY MEDICINE. "There's my competition," Doc said, "jist in case ye need a secont opinion. But I was you, I'd shore hope I don't." Then he pointed at two more buildings: next to his house was an abandoned shop, flat-roofed, constructed of stonemasonry. "That there used to be the money-bank," he said. "Got robbed back in twenty-two. Remind me to tell ye the story." Then he pointed again, one last time, at a building up the road, across another branch road from the bank, which was not abandoned but had wagons parked in front and a couple of horses tethered at its post. "Stay More 'pears to be still big enough to support two physicians, more or less, and it's also big enough to support two general stores. That'un there is run by the nicest gal ye'd ever hope to meet, name of Latha Bourne."

Doc Swain helped me rise up out of the car and climb the porch and into the front room of his house. "This is what passes for my office," he said, indicating the room, which indeed looked professional enough and equipped enough to be a rural doctor's clinic. He supported me onward to an adjoining room containing a narrow bed, a bedside table, and a player piano. The walls and ceiling were covered with tongue-and-groove boards painted a not unpleasant shade of tan. "And this here is what will jist have to pass for my hoss-pittle," he said. "Let's jist plunk ourselfs down right here," and he helped me down onto the bed, which had a mattress stuffed with goose down and was infinitely comfortable. In my condition, which seemed to be growing worse despite the prospect of medical attention, I was grateful for any little thing that eased my pain.

"Now, Doc, I'd better go feed my livestock and milk the cow," Doc Swain declared, "unless there's anything else I can do fer ye right now."

"Doc, you don't suppose," I managed to request, "you could let me have a little drink of somethin?"

"Water? Sody pop? How about milk? You're gonna have to drink two quarts of milk ever day, but I'll have to get some from Bess first." I realized the female he referred to was his cow.

"Somethin hard to ease my misery," I suggested. "A drap of corn, maybe?"

He smiled his kindly smile. "Wal, I'll tell ye," he said. "Gener'ly it wouldn't make no difference nor do ye no harm, but I'm a-fixin to give ye somethin to he'p ye sleep, and they don't mix. When ye wake up, I'll see if I caint let ye have a drap or two of Chism's Dew, best corn on airth."

Doc Swain filled a hypodermic syringe and injected me with something that indeed put me into a deep, deep sleep. But when I woke up, it was still daylight. I figured I must not have slept very long, because it had been getting on to suppertime when I'd arrived. I waited for a good while to see if the doctor would check in on me, and then I hollered, "Anybody home?"

Instantly Doc appeared, and said, "Wal, you shore had a good sleep, now didn't ye? How you feelin?"

"It's still day," I observed.

"It's still day all right," he agreed. "But it's midday of the day after I put ye under." He reached beneath my bed and drew out a thunder mug, or chamber pot. "Use this if ye need it, and I'll give ye a snort of Chism's Dew, lessen ye'd keer fer some breakfast first." He went away while I used the chamber pot, into which I was able only to urinate. He noticed this on his return, and said, "Wal, Gram Dinsmore's ellum juice seems to be a-wearin off. You aint got the trots no more." He took my temperature, my blood pressure, and ran me through the routine of assorted palpations and reflex-checking taps with his little silver hammer. "You know, Gram Dinsmore did the right thing, I reckon," he said. "And even her diagnosis was correct. Blame if ye aint got the typhoid fever. I took some of your blood while you was asleep and ran a test on it. Wal, Gram Dinsmore aint such a bad ole yarb doctor, such as they come. 'Many an old wife or country woman doth often more good with a few known and common garden herbs than our bombast Physicians with all their prodigious, sumptuous, far-fetched, rare, conjectural medicines.' That's what ole Burton writ, in his 'Natomy of Melancholy." The doctor paused, then fixed me with a keen look. "You know ole Burton, don't ye?"

Certainly I knew Robert Burton, although, as I was eventually to confess to Doc Swain, I had never managed to read the entire thousand-odd pages of *The Anatomy of Melancholy*, into which I had first dipped when I was working on my master's in psychology at Clark University. But at the moment I was rattled: not because it surprised me to discover his familiarity with that seventeenth-century forerunner of Freud, but because he seemed to be casting suspicion upon my disguise as a mere backwoods durgen. It was a disguise of which I was proud, and which I wasn't ready to drop, and I pretended innocence. "Burton who?" I said.

"Oh, let's not fool ourselfs, Doc," he said. And when I continued attempting to maintain my look of ignorance—not very successfully, I suppose—he took one of my hands and turned it over, palm up, and called my attention to the blisters and abrasions on it. "Yore raw paws was the first thing I noticed about ye," he said. "You aint no simple farmer nor woodsman, now air ye?"

He had me there, but I stubbornly clung to my imposture, and even said some fool thing like "Now what on airth gives ye sech a notion as *thet?*"

"Wal, Doc, I hate to tell ye," he said, "but last night while ye was deep asleep, I took the liberty of lookin through yore tote sack, and I seen all them scribblins on all that paper in thar, with my own name mentioned frequent. Main reason I done it was I suspicioned ye might be a revenuer in disguise, and we've had some problems lately with them bastards. You shore aint no revenuer, neither, air ye? You wouldn't be writin down my name, because I aint never distilled any corn myself, nor had any dealins in it. So do ye mind tellin me jist what it is yo're after, writin my name all over those sheets?"

I decided to cease trying to deceive him. "Okay, Doc, you've got me, I reckon," I said. "I've just been a-wanderin around the country, tryin to pick up a good story hither and yon. Those sheets you seen was jist some notes I made on what Cassie Whitter told me about you."

He studied me quizzically, then smiled. "Kin ye earn a livin jist a-gatherin up folks' stories like thet?"

I laughed. "Jist barely."

"How? You aint one of these here *novelists,* air ye?" He pronounced the word with disparagement, as if he might have had an encounter or two with the products of a novelist.

"Nope," I said. "I aint published no novels."

"Do ye write it up fer the newspapers and get paid fer it?"

"I've written some books that weren't fiction," I declared. "Although I haven't been paid much for them. Most recently, I wrote a pair of books called *The Ozarks: An American Survival of Primitive Society* and *Ozark Mountain Folks.*" I felt pretty strange, telling him my titles, as if I were Roger Tory Peterson trying to tell a bird that I'd written a field guide in which the bird was included. "I don't suppose you've heard of 'em?"

Doc shook his head. " 'Survival of primitive society,' d'ye say?" he repeated. "I never thought of it thataway, but I 'low as maybe yo're right. I reckon we're pretty primitive compared with the rest of the world. I reckon we're still a-livin the way our forefathers had to live 'cause they didn't have any better, nor know any better." Doc Swain produced a demijohn and a pair of glass tumblers, into which he poured a liquid that was not clear and white like conventional moonshine but yellowed as if aged in a cask. He handed me one, and clanked his against mine: "Here's lookin at ye. See if ye think this here whiskey aint a survival of primitive society."

It was indeed the best whiskey I'd had in a long, long time, and I told him so. In return, he told me a little about its origin: a family named Chism, living up in the mountains east of Stay More (he had pointed out their house on the trip from Cassie's), had for generations been producing a superior moonshine which . . . but what am I doing?—trying to explain "Chism's Dew" to *you,* who practically invented the name for it. You'll just have to stop me whenever I get to telling this story in such a way I forget who I'm talking to. Sometimes I'm inclined to think I'm just talking to gentlepeople in general.

Anyhow, Doc and me had more than one glass apiece, and I told him a little of my background: born in Pittsburg, Kansas; first visited the Ozarks at the age of seven; taught biology at Pittsburg High School after getting my M.A. in psychology at Clark University in Massachusetts; served as a private in the infantry during the World War but got medically discharged without seeing any action; moved after the war to the Ozark village of Pineville up in Missouri and started my first experiments in collecting backwoods lore; interrupted by an attempt to get a legitimate Ph.D. in psychology at the University of Kansas, gave it up, and moved back to Pineville and lived there ever since, except for those months I lived in Hollywood the previous year. I concluded this capsule autobiography by declaring, "Now my throat's getting sore. Am I talkin too much, or do ye suppose the liquor is causing it?"

"That's jist part of yore disease," he said. "But the liquor ought to be he'pin yore appetite. Are you hungry yit?"

Sure enough, my appetite was returning, for the first time in several days. When I acknowledged this, Doc cupped his mouth and called, *"Ro-weener!"* A woman came into the room, a fortyish woman in a simple flower-print dress tight on her sturdy but shapely frame. She was not a homely woman but she wasn't exactly pretty. I assumed she was the doctor's wife, but he introduced us, saying, "This here's all I've got in the way of a nurse, and I can only keep her part-time, but she's the best there is. She'll be takin keer of ye most of the time. The thing about typhoid is, recoverin from it depends more on good nursin than on doctorin. Rowener can hep ye a good sight more'n I could do."

"Right proud to meet ye, Doctor Randolph," Rowena said, and sized me up, or, since I was still reclining, sized me sideways.

"He aint a *doctor* doctor," Doc Swain said to his nurse. "They jist call 'im Doc as a nickname, maybe on account of he's sort of a perfesser."

Rowena sniffed. "Have you boys been drinkin?"

Doc Swain coughed. "Wal, uh, I figgered it mought hep his appetite, ye know, and shore enough, he feels like eatin, first time in days. Do ye reckon ye could skeer him up some grub?"

"What about *yore* appetite?" she said to him, but disappeared and began banging things around in some distant kitchen.

"I'm fixin to mosey over to the store to get my mail," Doc said. "Wouldje like fer me to send a postcard to yore wife or sweetheart or anybody out thar in the world of society?"

"How long am I gonna be laid up in this bed?" I asked.

"Hard to say," he said. "Yore spleen is enlarged, and we'll have to see if it shrinks back to normal. Any day now, you may jist have a touch of delirium or stupor that could last awhile. But iffen ye don't git complications, like a hemorrhage or perforation, you mought jist be up and about in a week or two."

I sighed. I debated with myself whether to send a note to Marie, but decided against it. I hadn't sent her anything since leaving home, and I doubted that she was expecting anything.

I took advantage of my doctor's absence to examine the contents of his little "hoss-pittle" room, which would be my home for the next week, or more: the few pictures on the wall, a moonlit landscape painted on glass with some kind of garish pigment, a chromolithographed still life of wildflowers, and a glass-enclosed framing of pinned butterflies of various shapes and colors, none of them rare, just chosen and captured for their variety of color. There were stray pieces of furniture: a cedar chest, a rocker with splint-woven seat and back, and a birch washstand with stoneware pitcher and basin. But the dominant piece of furniture was a player piano. Its lid was closed, and dust covered, and the dozen or so rolls that were needed to make it play were stacked atop the piano and also collecting dust. The floor of the room was covered with a cheap Axminster carpet in a floral design, and my bedframe had cast-iron foot- and headboards.

Rowena brought me a tray with a plate of scrambled eggs and toast, and a large glass of milk. She removed my unfinished tumbler of Chism's Dew. "When ye git done eatin that," she declared, "I aim to give ye a shave."

Doc returned from the post office, leafing through his only mail, the local county weekly newspaper and the latest issue of the *American Medical Association Bulletin*. Then he began opening a large bottle of castor oil and poured into a tumbler a larger amount of it than he had of the Chism's Dew. "There aint no medicine specific fer typhoid," he said. "The most I can hope to do is clean out yore system and keep ye comfy 'til yore strength comes back."

"I'd druther drink coal awl than castor awl," I declared, truthfully. And then, as if to get under his skin, I said, "Gram Dinsmore's slippery elm juice would do me a sight more good and be easier to drink."

"Iffen it was peeled the right way!" he said. "Here, let's take a big swaller of this." He held the glass to my lips.

I took a small sip of the thick liquid and tried to swallow, but it was truly awful, and brought back some of the most unpleasant memories of my childhood, when my mother would regularly make me take the stuff, and I had thought that it was some kind of vicious, viscid machine oil for the purpose of

32

lubricating casters, those little wheels under furniture. "What do they make this stuff out of, anyhow?" I said, more rhetorically than because I wanted to know.

"The seeds of a plant called Palma Christi," he said. "Hit aint but a harmless purge. Hit's the best thing fer loosenin up yore bowels without aggervatin 'em. Here, let's have another big swaller," and he held the glass to my mouth again.

After I got another swallow down, I asked, out of curiosity about his knowledge, "How does the stuff work? What does it do to you?"

"Hit's got a toxic sustance called ricin in it," he said, trying not to sound pedantic. "The ricinoleic acid will give yore intestines a fierce peristalsis. I reckon ye know what peristalsis is." When I nodded, not so much because I really did know as in a kind of surprise at his use of the word, he continued, "Wal, that will liquefy and soften yore stools."

"But I've already got diarrhea!" I protested.

He smiled, and shook his head. "You did have," he said. "But you don't, no more. And anyhow, the good thing about castor oil is, it's also a cure for diarrhea!" He held the glass to my mouth. "Come on here now, my friend. Let's drink up the rest of this."

"Couldn't we mix it with some Chism's Dew?" I suggested.

"And spoil good whiskey?" he demanded.

So I had to finish off the glass of the stuff and I surprised myself by not vomiting. And I actually got to feeling some better. That, as I recall, was the time that Doc Swain told me the little anecdote, which I would later borrow for my 1965 collection of jests, *Hot Springs and Hell,* and which you borrowed five years later in your novel *Lightning Bug,* having your hero Every Dill tell it to your heroine Latha Bourne. I forget just how Every told it, but this was the way I told it: Doc Swain gave an old woman some medicine and he told her, "Keep a close watch, and see what passes." Next day he came back, and she was feeling a little better. "Did anything out of the ordinary pass?" asked the doctor. "No," says the old woman, "just a ox team, a load of hay, and two foreigners on horseback." The doctor just looked at her. "Well," says he, "it aint no wonder you're a-feelin better."

I guffawed despite my bodily aches, and I thought that tale, which I believe actually happened, was one of the most hilarious anecdotes I'd ever heard, and I asked on the spot for my writing materials, so I could copy it down. And afterwards there developed a kind of routine between Doc Swain and me, in which each morning he would ask me, "Did anything out of the ordinary pass?" and I would come back with something like "a mule team hauling logs," or "a girl rolling a hoop," or "a shepherd and eighteen sheep." And he would always wink and say, "Well, it aint no wonder you're a-feelin better." And I actually was feeling much better, day by day.

But right now, I'm commencing to feel a mite weary, and too hoarse to talk more, and the nurse is gonna bring our supper in just a little while. Maybe I'd best wait and tell you some more of this tale tomorrow. You will come again tomorrow, won't you? I haven't bored you yet, have I?

Two

I thought you'd come back. Tell me if I'm wrong, but you came back not just out of friendship, or politeness, or even a desire to hear what I have to say about your patented exclusive real estate, the world of Stay More, but because I still know, after all these years, how to tell a story, and to tell it in such a way that you can believe it.

But in all truth, if anything did pass in the road, I couldn't have seen it from where I lay. The world of Stay More surrounded me without my awareness of what, if anything, was going on out there. The one window of my small room afforded a view chiefly of the ruin of the stone bank building just to the north of Doc Swain's house. Doc told me the story of how the bank was robbed in 1922, when the same Every Dill who . . . but you know that story and have told it so well yourself. Now the bank had lain empty for over a decade; and its wooden timbers, encased within the rustic stonemasonry, were beginning to decay. The wooden door at the side facing my window had rotted and fallen, but it was only after several days of glancing at the bank that I noticed I could see through the open door to the window on the other side of the interior, and through that window I could discern the front porch of Latha Bourne's general store, where that woman, whom you have called the demigoddess of your world of Stay More, was often sitting.

It is funny how we all have the habit of not noticing what is visible beyond the immediate vista, how, for example, you can look through that window yonder and see nothing but a bunch of nondescript houses across the way from this nursing home, and you wouldn't even notice, until I call it to your attention, that the towers of Old Main at the University are rising up in the distance. See? Had you noticed before? Well, I was a little embarrassed at myself, that there had been so many hours, so many days, when I just lay on that bed in that room with nothing to do but stare at the blank stone wall of that bank building without even noticing that I could see *through* the wall, or rather through that fallen door and the window on the other side, and catch a clear glimpse of people on the porch of Latha's store over two hundred yards away, including Latha herself.

Shall I describe her for you? You, of all people, who have, by your own declared intention, granted her eternal life? The Latha I first saw was the Latha who existed in the year before you were even born, and whom you never knew. The Latha you fell madly in love with at the age of five-going-on-six was perhaps beginning to discover a gray hair or two in her dark hair, and perhaps was even beginning to thicken at the middle, or to develop wrinkles here and there, or maybe even a skin spot or two, and of course if she already had any of this six years before, I couldn't have detected it from a distance. All I could tell, from that distance, was that she was most beautiful creature I'd ever seen. And I was overwhelmed with desire for her, to the extent that she became my reason for wanting to recuperate and get out of that bed and go meet her.

Did you know that Doc himself was in love with her? Alas, the story I'm going to keep on telling you as long as you come back to hear it does not really involve Latha Bourne. I wish I could tell you a story about how I finally got out of my bed and went over and met her and we became lovers and lived happily ever after, or at least spent a wild night together. Could you accept that? No, nor could you accept the story of how Doc finally persuaded her to become his lover. Because you are "saving" her for Every Dill. As perhaps she was unknowingly saving herself. So she is not going to be the heroine of this narrative. She is incidental to it, and indeed during the time of which I shall be mainly speaking, she did not live in Stay More at all, but was in a kind of exile, either at the state hospital for the insane in Little Rock or, after Every Dill kidnapped her from that awful place and she subsequently was parted from her rescuer, in Tennessee, trying to find her way home but not succeeding until . . . but that is another story which you must tell us yourself one of these days, perhaps when you have no other stories to tell or you cannot do a fair job of telling whatever story you're trying to tell.

Anyway, from my window I could not only see through that bank building and catch a glimpse of Latha in her rocker on the porch of her store but also, at least once a day, Doc Swain himself sitting beside her, talking with her. As I'll probably have to show you, it was an unrequited love he had for her, or maybe even an unexpressed love.

You'll have to decide for yourself, when I'm all done telling my story, whether or not Doc Swain even understood what love is. And making that judgment of him, you may also have to make it of me, because I'm not sure, even yet, that I know. Mary Celestia yonder accuses me to my face of not knowing, don't you, Mary? Yes. Could be that she, like some women, just suffers from the insufficiency of my speaking of it. I don't tell Mary Celestia every blessed day that I love her. That would turn it into a routine, like eating or breathing or taking a shit. There's nothing routine about love, and it's not something we do *all* the time, or even most of the time. I don't love Mary every day. Some days it hits me all of a sudden in a way I can't express that I love her more than anything ever got loved in the history of mankind, but other days I don't even think about it.

You know, I tried to point out in my folk-speech book, *Down in the Holler*—sizable parts of which I collected in Stay More that summer—that among the euphemisms and prudish taboos of the Ozarker even the word "love" is considered more or less indecent, and the mountain people seldom use it in its ordinary sense, but nearly always with some degrading or jocular connotation. If a hillman does admit that he *loved* a woman, he means only that he caressed and embraced her.

And as far as I know, or was ever able to find out, Doc Swain never caressed, nor embraced, nor even *touched* your Latha Bourne. There was a woman—and also a girl—that Doc Swain had caressed and loved, over ten years and more previously, and this is going to be a story about them.

So I lay there looking through that window, watching Latha's store porch and watching her and whoever was on the porch talking to her, and whatever fantasies I could fix up in my idle mind involving myself and her or whoever. But that wasn't all I did, of course. Rowena would bring me my breakfast of scrambled eggs or oatmeal, biscuits or toast, and make sure I drank a whole quart of fresh milk. Then she'd lather my jowls and shave me expertly with a straight razor that she kept keenly stropped, all the while keeping up a running palaver of chitchat. She even contributed to the story of Doc Swain by adding a few anecdotes and more interesting items that she had learned about him.

Then she'd give me what the doctor prescribed as "a Brand bath." Like my youthful misunderstanding of castor oil as a lubricant for furniture casters, I misunderstood this name to mean that it would permanently brand me, like cattle, but Doc eventually explained it was named after a German doctor named Brand who'd invented it as a therapy for typhoid. It was a lot harder to take than the "enemers" that Rowena also administered. It involved getting into a galvanized tub—I think it was just a sort of oval-shaped trough for watering livestock—and having Rowena dump buckets of fresh well-water over me, cold as a well-digger's ass. Colder! Colder than a preacher's balls! 'Scuse me, Mary. That water would make me scream, and then my teeth would start a-chattering, and my fingernails would turn blue. Doc called the Brand bath "a cardiovascular tonic," but it near about gave me a heart attack. A wonder it didn't give me pneumonia. But just when I'd got colder than I could stand, Rowena would commence a-rubbing me, like a massage only real hard, on my arms and legs and back and sides and all, until my blue skin had turned red as roses, and then, without drying, I'd get wrapped in an old linen sheet with a double blanket over that and put back to bed. All that rubbing Rowena done, especially around my lower stomach, would give my ole ying-yang a bone, and if I hadn't been so sick I would've begged the gal for a little relief. Mary Celestia, it's time for your nap, sweetheart, you don't have to listen to this.

But all of my "commerce" with sweet Rowena was limited mostly to friendly banter, sometimes off-color, and to her answers to occasional questions of mine, for example, Was Doc ever married? "Still is," Rowena said, and when I tried to get her to elaborate she told me, as if I didn't know, that there was no such of a thing as divorce in these here parts, and Doc had had a wife a number of years previously, whom he hadn't seen in many a year, and *another* wife who died. "But you'll jist have to git him to tell you his own self about all of that," Rowena said.

What with all that therapy and attention from Rowena—I don't know if I was her only patient but she gave me the impression that I was—I was getting better day by day and reaching the point of wanting to get out of bed. "Doc," I requested one morning, "how about lettin me sit in the rocker 'stead of layin in this bed all day and night?"

"We aint out of the woods yit," he declared.

I sighed. "Tell me, Doc," I said with a little exasperation, "how come you always say 'we' as if you're the patient too? 'Time for our breakfast,' you'll say even if you've done et. 'Now let's take our temperature,' you'll say, but you aint takin your own. Yesterday you said, 'We wanter watch out we don't git ourselfs a intestinal perforation,' but there aint a bit of danger that *you* will ever git one!"

Doc looked a little bit crestfallen. "Wal, don't ye know, I reckon hit's jist plain ole *empathy*," he observed. "I aint never had a patient that I didn't feel like everything happenin to them was happenin to me too. Ever baby I've delivered was birthed by me. Ever time anybody died I died too."

There was such a melancholy in his speaking of these words that I softened my annoyance. "Okay, I get the drift. But don't 'we' get pretty goddamned itchy and on edge when 'we're' confined to bed all the time?"

"Yeah, I reckon we do. That's how come me and Rowener tries to keep ye beguiled."

I was charmed by his use of that word, which can mean either to cheat, to deceive, or to amuse, to entertain, the latter meaning carrying the connotation of whiling away the hours and diverting one from one's problems. It set me to pondering how the latter meaning could have grown out of the former, as if the ways we really entertain ourselves involve some kind of deception. A good story *beguiles* us: by deceiving us it entertains us. Maybe it's even necessary to make some kind of corollary: a story is successfully delightful in proportion to its deception.

But although Doc Swain had both beguiled and regaled me with quite a lot of anecdotes, jests, and tall tales that I had not heard before, he hadn't yet got to the stage of telling me real stories, that is, extended narratives with plot development running through beginnings, middles, and endings. And despite my occasional promptings, he had not yet begun to tell me the most important story: his own. "Doc," I would prompt, trying to get it out of him, "is it true that you were once a basketball coach?"

"Basketball?" he would put me off. "I never knew nothing about basketball." And, as I would eventually learn, that was quite true: he never knew nothing about basketball. But he had coached it.

Maybe I'm giving the impression that Doc didn't have anything better to do, when he wasn't killing time chatting with Latha Bourne on her store porch, than to sit around telling me tales and windies. My picture of him might run counter to the traditional idea of the overworked, underslept physician who had to see a hundred patients a day or night at all hours. In truth, Doc Swain was not the slave of his job . . . but he was the slave of his research, which he was keeping private. I knew that he spent a great number of hours each day in a back room of the house that he called his "laboratory." He explained that of course he was his own pathologist, but that wasn't all he was doing back there in that room. For all I knew, he was creating a monster, like Frankenstein. I can remember a few occasions when Rowena said to me, "Colvin caint see you this mornin"—she never called him "the doctor" or "Doc" or anything but his first name—"on account of he was up all last night hard at work in his laboratory." Eventually I came right out and asked him what kind of research he was doing, but all he would say was, "Oh, I've jist been foolin around with some pathogenic microorganisms, tryin to see if I caint come up with an antibiotic."

He had very few office calls. Whenever somebody was sick, Doc went to them, at their house. And usually that was only after they had exhausted every other possible means for a cure: home remedies, patent medicines, superstitions, visits from Gram Dinsmore or some other "granny woman." Doc was just the expedient if nothing else worked.

"I am the last resort," he declared to me one day, in a kind of self-deprecating way. But there was not only a poignant seriousness to the declaration, there was also a kind of symbolism in it.

And he scarcely made enough income to meet his expenses. He had practically not one cash-paying patient . . . except me, whenever my time came to settle the bill for my treatment. His patients paid him through a kind of barter. The storekeeper

Willis Ingledew gave him free gasoline for his car. Other patients gave him produce from their gardens, or fruit from their orchards, or cordwood from their woodlots, or corn whiskey, or even livestock: pigs and calves and chickens, and a horse. Later, after I became ambulatory, Doc showed me his pantry, crowded with Mason jars of canned fruits and vegetables, blackberry preserves, jams, honey, and molasses, and he showed me the little smokehouse behind his home, where he had hanging a great collection of hams and side meat. "The pay in this line of work aint nothin to mention," he declared, "but the eatin is sure dandy."

He was a good doctor, too. My first and most vivid impression of his talent occurred early in my second week there, a morning after my Brand bath when I began feeling worse, after a steady improvement. I wondered if the Brand baths were taxing my system or giving me pneumonia, but they wouldn't have given me the stomach distress I was feeling.

Doc was customarily easygoing, relaxed, slow moving, and deliberate in everything he did. But that morning he took a good look at me and became suddenly brisk. He popped his thermometer into my mouth and could hardly wait to read it, and when he did, he yelled, "Git the morphine, Rowener!" I began to get dizzy even before he administered the morphine; I was scarcely conscious of his busy movements and what he was doing, and I barely heard him say to Rowena, "He's a-hemorrhaging." He worked me over, then said to her, "Fetch me some thromboplastin."

The last thing I remember of that episode was his telling Rowena to run up to Latha's and see if she had any ice in her icebox that she could spare, and to fill an ice bag to keep on my stomach. That was, incidentally, my first awareness of Latha's use of that modern convenience which you would note in your first book about her: that she ordered from Jasper, the county seat and depot for it, an occasional block of ice, manufactured in distant Harrison, the nearest large town. The mail truck brought the ice wrapped in canvas. Latha had the only icebox in Stay More; and a few years afterwards in her general store she would have the only soda-pop cooler in that part of Newton County.

I am not certain that I avoided the delirium that he had predicted might be a sequela of my disease. For a long time I thought it was just a dream, but it could have been a delirious dream. I am reluctant to reveal it, except that it casts some light on what we are going to learn, later on, about Doc Swain's early career as a physician. Rowena was in the dream too, the player piano was in the dream, in fact there was so much from "life" included in the dream that I did not understand until I "woke" from it that it had all been a dream. It was, frankly, the most vivid, the most real dream I had ever had. I do not remember what Doc said to me, nor I to him. He was holding in his hand that ice bag that he had supposedly obtained from Latha, and he applied it to my stomach and successfully induced the clotting of my blood, so that a transfusion would not be necessary. He then manipulated my abdomen, lay his hands on my chest for a while, and finally put one hand on my head and pronounced me cured. I remember only one thing I said: "Just like that, huh?"

And then I found myself in exactly the same position, in relation to the other two people who had been in the "dream," except that I understood that I was "awake," and that whatever I had been experiencing must have been a dream or a delirium. I felt wonderful. I felt, at least, much better than I had in weeks. "I reckon that ice bag worked!" I observed.

"We couldn't use it," he said apologetically. "Latha was all out of ice."

"But didn't you just put an ice bag on my stomach?" I asked.

He and Rowena exchanged looks. "Nope, I'm sorry," he said. "But somehow the blood clotted anyway, so I reckon we won't have to give ye a transfusion after all. I could've given ye one from my own arm," he declared, "since me'n you has got the same blood type, but I'd shore of had to charge ye a good bit extry for *that!*"

I was sitting up, I was ready to get out of bed, I was all well, but I was puzzled that Doc did not realize what he had done to me. "I must have been just dreaming," I said, "but whatever it was, you healed me! You appeared to me in the dream and fixed me up just fine!"

He smiled his benevolent smile, and said, "Wal, it's been a good long while since I did the dream cure on anybody, but if you think that's what it was, and it worked, then we're sure enough in good health again."

"Dream cure?" I said, snared by the possible mythology of it. "Doc, you are just going to have to tell me about the dream cure."

He let me get out of bed. He invited me into the adjacent room, his office, where there were a pair of comfortable chairs. He pulled out his pocket watch, looked at it, and declared, "Rowener's taking off in a minute or two." Then he opened a drawer of his desk and brought out a cigar box which contained, I was surprised and delighted to discover, a few cigars. He handed me one and began unwrapping one himself. Those weren't nickel cigars, either. Hell, they weren't even dime cigars, but two-for-a-quarter Antonio y Cleopatras. You know, I can't hardly ever smoke anymore, mostly on account of consideration for Mary Celestia but also because this nursing home don't allow smoking in bed and I aint allowed to get out of bed! But there was a time, many and many a year of my earlier days, when I truly appreciated a good cigar.

After Doc lit my cigar for me, and lit his own, and we commenced a-suckin and a-puffin and actin like a pair of pigs who'd got into the corncrib, pretty soon Doc got up again to fetch the demijohn and poured us both a good helping of the Chism's Dew, saying, "Don't worry, ole Rowener won't be back 'til after suppertime." Then Doc put on his storytelling face. I had learned to recognize it: the slight upturning of the corners of his mouth as if he was getting ready to be amused himself; the twinkle in his eye, the wrinkling of the crow's-feet at the eye corners. But the gaze in his twinkling eyes was far, far away, and he said, "I aint quite ready to tell you my own story. Not jist yet. I reckon I could do it, by-and-by, but I'd better warm up first on somebody else's story. I'm a-fixin to tell ye about the first physician of Stay More, who was my paw, and if you can swaller his story, you jist might be ready for mine."

Then he began. He wound himself up and went all the way back to when his father, Gilbert Alonzo Swain, first arrived in what had become Stay More at the age of two or three. You have already told the beginning of that in your *Architecture of the Arkansas Ozarks:* how the first white settlers of Stay More after Jacob and Noah Ingledew was a family from North Carolina, the widow Lizzie Swain and her thirteen children, the "least'un" being Gilbert, who would later prefer being called by his middle name. You have told how tiny Gilbert played a crucial part in the matchmaking of his oldest sister, Sarah, with Jake Ingledew, thereby starting the Ingledew dynasty. Doc told me all of these stories which I recalled when I read your book, and I learned from him also of the annual visits of the legendary peddler from Connecticut, Eli Willard. I don't want to bore you with what you already know, so I suppose I'll begin, myself, with Gilbert's acquisition of his knife from that peddler. The knife would later serve as his scalpel. Eli Willard sold to each of the Swain sisters a pair of scissors and to each of the Swain brothers a knife, which would fold up to be kept in one's pocket.

Gilbert did not have a pocket but he became inseparable from his knife, carrying it closed in his hand at all times except when he slept and placed it under his pillow. He noticed there were letters on the knife, and he asked his mother what they meant, and she said they said, "Prince," so he decided that would be his knife's name, and sometimes he would even talk to it, saying, "Prince, I have got to find me some way to raise four cents' cash money to pay for you."

His brother Murray showed him how to rub Prince on a piece of Arkansas whetstone, which is the best there is, and he always kept Prince sharp enough to slice a hair in two. His brother Virgil tried to show him how to use Prince to play a dumb game called mumble the peg, but he did not like sticking Prince into the earth, which was dirty. He did not mind sticking Prince into things which bled, because blood is not dirty. With Prince he carved up birds and frogs and squirrels, and he got into bad trouble with his mother when he carved up a cat that she cherished. His mother took Prince away from him for two months.

When she finally let him have Prince back, he took Prince and stuck him into the largest snake he could find. The snake writhed and twisted and flopped for a good long spell before it finally died. Gilbert wanted to hang it on the wall of the house, but his mother would not let him, so he took it back to the spot where he killed it and told it, "You can jist lay there and rot, for all I care." Then he had to scrub his hands with lye soap to get rid of the snake's blood and stains. Gilbert's childhood ended not when he learned that death is an escape nor even when he learned that we must confront the meaning of death but when his well-meaning sister Bert tried to teach him what death is like. Elberta did not try to kill him, and what she did was not even meant to hurt him. She did not even understand perhaps that a six-year-old boy was not old enough to feel the kind of death she was contemplating. Many years afterwards he was to ask her, "How come ye didn't pick Boyd or Frank or Virgil or one of yore other brothers?" and she was to answer only, "They was too big and besides they wasn't handy." He assumed she meant that they weren't sleeping with her, as he was.

Being the "least one," Gilbert Alonzo had always been required to sleep in the bed that contained all the females of the family, where every night there was usually a right smart of constant whispering and giggling amongst his sisters, which kept him awake and went on until Gilbert's mother told them to shut up and skedaddle for the Land of Nod. Sometimes Gilbert listened to the sounds of the dark: the snickers and titters and tee-hees, and sometimes he heard a fragment of their whisperings, which had to do with girly stuff that either didn't interest him or, more than likely, was too tough for him to figure.

Although they had customary places in the bed—Gilbert usually sleeping between his mother and Esther, the youngest girl, who was less than a year older than Gilbert and, being so small, not as encumbered with protruberances as the older girls—the place a body went to sleep in was not necessarily the place a body would wake up in, and sometimes before morning Gilbert would find himself at the opposite side of the bed from his mother, and not be able to remember how he had managed to climb over or roll over or be shoved or lifted over all the sisters.

The night his childhood ended, the night he decided henceforth to "go by" his middle name, Gilbert Alonzo woke perhaps an hour after going to bed to find himself face-to-face with Bert, who was the fleshiest of the sisters, and being so soft, not so troublesome to be face-to-face with, although you usually didn't get face-to-face until you were in deepest slumber. Bert was awake too, and she commenced whispering into Gilbert's ear. All he could make out in his grogginess was the question "Does that feel good?" which she would repeat in several variations during the course of the next hour or so. She was doing something that not even his mother had ever done, as far as he could recall. She was holding him by his handle, which had swole. He had never touched his jemmison himself except when he had to go to the bushes with it, and he had been taught that one goes to the bushes for a good reason: because the bushes are private, shielding. Sometimes one of his sisters had to go to the bushes in the middle of the night, but she didn't actually go outside where the real bushes were, she just squatted down over the slop jar that was kept beneath the bed, and apparently didn't even have to aim her jemmison, an accomplishment which led Gilbert to the eventual realization that girls don't even possess jemmisons, and now Bert was taking his hand and making him touch her to confirm that she did not possess a jemmison and asking him, "Does that feel good?" He didn't know for sure if it felt good or not but it sure felt funny, just a damp crease where a jemmison ought to be. And next thing he knew she was saying, "Let's us mash our things together and see how that feels," and they did, and when she asked the next time, "Does that feel good?" he was compelled to speak the only word that he uttered that night: "Some."

Bert squirmed and shifted her legs and tried to arch her back without knocking the next sleeper out of the bed, and she grabbed him and pulled him and tugged him, and pretty soon he knew that his swole jemmison had been tucked into her. "Don't that feel good!" she said, but it was not a question. He studied the feeling. It was not quite like sticking Prince inside of something. Prince would slice or tear to get inside. But still it was a kind of insideness. A disappearance. He was only mildly troubled to discover that Bert, and by implication all other girls, had all of that slick tight warm interior space, which his jemmison could not quite fill.

The movements that Bert began making seemed intended to make him fill her better or fill her repeatedly or fill her deeper or fill her faster. Bert was getting so busy that the mattress, which was stuffed with corn shucks, began to utter and grumble. Whoever was sleeping on the other side of Bert was jostled awake and said "Huh?" and then "Who?" and then "Hee," and then rolled the other way and dropped back into sleep. Bert was making the whole bed shake. It was a wonder she didn't wake everybody. But then she asked, "Don't ye feel good enough to die?" and she declared, "I'm a-fixin to die!" and then she gasped and hollered, "I'm a-dyin!" and Alonzo tried to break loose from her but she grabbed his bottom and mashed him even harder against her, and she went on dying for a while and then, to his relief, she quit dying and came alive again, and let him go. He got his jemmison out and backed off from her as far as he could, up against whichever sister was behind him. Bert said, "Wal, I reckon ye aint old enough to die yet." And she went to sleep.

Five more years went by before Alonzo was able to die himself, and discover why dying was so important to Bert and also to his sisters Octavia and Zenobia, who, once they discovered what Bert had done with Alonzo, had to try it themselves. Tavy and Nobe were both older than Bert. Two of the sisters younger than Bert, Nettie and Esther, also wanted to give it a try, but although they managed to do everything with Alonzo that they were supposed to do, with some difficulty because of their virginity, they were not able to die yet. For four years Alonzo was passed around from one sister to another, usually in bed in the dark, but sometimes elsewhere around the place in daylight too. He greatly enjoyed "the funny feeling," as he called it, the mild sting or buzz or whatever it was that was almost but not quite dying.

Then when he finally did die for the first time, it wasn't with a sister but a pretty little girl who lived up the creek a ways, name of Mellie Chism. But while this death was the best feeling that he'd ever had, two things troubled him about it: the very fact that Mellie wasn't any sister of his, and the fact that Mellie herself didn't die as his sisters so readily did. Studying this problem, he decided that you aren't supposed to do it with your sister if you want to die, but if you're a sister you have to do it with your brother if you want to die. Since he wasn't a sister, it didn't matter to him whether Mellie died or not, and he went on doing it with her whenever they could sneak off somewheres private together.

For a year all of his deaths were dry deaths. Mellie got right damp and creamy but he never did. A few times at her suggestion because she wanted to see if it might make her die, he had taken a piss while he was inside her. It had felt funny to him and given her a thrill but it didn't kill either one of them. The time when finally he had his first true wet death he thought at first that he was only pissing again, but it wasn't. Whatever it was, it stayed inside her.

Alonzo Swain was fourteen years old before he ever saw

what his own jism looked like. It happened one time when Mellie took a notion to remove her dress. Alonzo had never seen a girl naked. All his sisters slept in nightdresses that came down to their ankles and besides it was dark, usually, and the few hundred times that he had lain with a sister in the daylight she had kept her day dress on, just raising it to her waist. But one time Mellie and Alonzo were way off in the woods and it was hot July and she suddenly took her dress plumb up off over her head. He already had a very stiff jemmison in anticipation of what they would sooner or later do and because they hadn't done it in over two months, and now the sight of Mellie without a stitch just caused his mind to run away with him and then his glands ran away with him and before he knew what had happened he was squirting jism all over creation, even hitting Mellie in the face, which for some reason she thought was the funniest thing that had ever happened to her. The stuff had no resemblance to piss. It was much thicker, and white, and runny. Using his hand to wipe it off her face, he asked, "Is this yere what I've been a-fillin ye up with all along?"

Even though Mellie never died, she craved to have him fill her up, and he filled her so often he had nothing left for his sisters. When Mellie started getting pooched out in the stomach, Alonzo figured that those Chisms must be eating high off the hog in harvesttime. But the rest of her family stayed as skinny as ever. Then one day he never saw Mellie, and the next day neither, and when he finally did see her, months later, she was holding a baby to her breast.

That was the first of Alonzo's seven sons. Nobody, perhaps not even Mellie herself, ever really understood that Alonzo was the father of the boy. The boy was given "Chism" as his last name, and, because he had difficulty pronouncing it, so that it came out as "Ism" if anyone asked him what his name was, that is what he was called for the rest of his life. As Ism grew older, he clearly inherited his father's good looks: the golden blond hair and the broad brow and perfect nose and strong jaw. In fact, Ism was going to be as popular with the ladies as his father was, and, as I'll have to tell you by-and-by, Ism ended up competing with his father unknowingly for one of the best of the ladies.

Alonzo, as he grew into manhood, was irresistible to females, and before he was eighteen he left both Cora Plowright and Sirena Coe with woodscolts, both boys. In all of Newton County there was only one girl who wouldn't come a-running the instant Alonzo crooked his finger at her, and that was Lora Dinsmore, who lived out toward Butterchurn Holler on Banty Creek. Lora had made up her mind to stay a virgin, and she didn't want some boy chasing after her who'd already knocked up three girls, even if he was the handsomest feller in all creation. Maybe because she was so hard to get is why Alonzo Swain made up his mind that he had to have her, or die trying. He lost interest in all other girls, even his sisters. He spent all his time for two years trying to get himself fixed up with Lora. He even promised her he wouldn't even try to lay with her. Then he promised her he wouldn't even touch her. Finally he promised her he wouldn't even try to kiss her. He stopped just short of promising to marry her, and he gave serious consideration to promising that, but he wasn't the marrying kind.

Lora turned him down flat. She didn't want anything to do with him. She begged him to leave her alone. " 'Lonzo, you jist leave me *be!*" But she was such a pretty thing, the cutest girl any feller could hope for, and Alonzo spent all his time for two years hoping for her, and doing everything he could to get her to notice him, and trying everything he could to persuade her to step out with him.

When it finally became obvious that she wasn't going to listen to reason or any kind of cajolery, not even with him down on his knees, he decided he'd just plain and simple have to ravish her against her will. So he commenced laying low for her and watching for a chance to grab her alone. The longer he waited, the hornier he got, and he began to mutter to himself, "If ever I catch that gal, I'll give her a fucking she won't never forget, like nobody never had!" And he meant it, too. He was storing up his jism, and he'd give her a gallon of it in one dose.

So then one day he happened to catch up with her along a lonely stretch of the road to Butterchurn Holler, which was only a deer path in those days. She saw him coming, and took out for the woods as fast as she could run. He was gaining on her, and she commenced yelling and begging, but she wasn't begging him. It was like she was begging for God or somebody to help her.

He finally caught her and flung her down in a patch of butterfly weed. That's just a kind of milkweed, fit for nothing and even the cows won't eat it because it tastes bad, but those big orange butterflies, some folks call them monarchs, like to lay their eggs on it and have their caterpillar babies grow up on it. Maybe that's what gives the butterflies their bad taste, so a bird would think twice before eating another one after getting a taste of one of them. Anyhow, the butterflies were a-hovering over it when Alonzo threw Lora down there.

The way some folks tell this story, those butterflies were going to try to protect Lora, but the truth is more likely that they just sort of distracted Alonzo from what he was doing, maybe they even got in his eyes or leastways tickled the back of his neck as he started taking down his pants and whipping out his jemmison and yanking up her dress. It doesn't matter, because the butterflies didn't really have anything whatever to do with what happened next.

Alonzo woke up lying atop a big clump of butterfly weed as if he'd been a-fucking that clump. Lora was nowheres in sight. The back of Alonzo's head hurt as if he'd been hit with something. He wondered if maybe Lora had conked him with a rock or a big stick, maybe. He got up and pulled up his pants and spent some time looking for Lora, but never could find her. The next day he discovered that he wasn't the only one looking for her. Couldn't nobody find her. Sheriff Jim Salmon and a couple of his deputies came out to Stay More, and they took Alonzo and asked him a whole bunch of questions, because it was widely known that he'd set his hat for her. He wouldn't admit to what he'd done, or tried to do. The sheriff and them looked all over creation, and even dug a few holes looking for a body.

Some years later, about the time of the War, a couple of fellers claimed they'd run into Lora working in a whorehouse down to Little Rock, but it was just a rumor. Nobody ever saw Lora again. Of course Alonzo was very sad, and he realized he probably was really in love with that girl. Sometimes he'd go back up the hillside to that place where the butterfly weed was, and he'd stand there a long time, thinking, and watching the butterflies if they were there, and each summer whenever the butterfly weed burst into bloom, with its bright orange flowers that was almost the same color as the butterfly, Alonzo would have the peculiar notion that Lora had turned into a butterfly weed, or even into a butterfly. But folks were a lot more superstitious in those days, and inclined to have such fanciful ideas.

His sad experience with Lora didn't stop Alonzo from fooling around, and pretty soon he had got Clara McKinstry with child, the boy Phil, and also had got Samantha Tennison with the child Linus. He even knocked up one of his sisters (it was a wonder it took him so long), Esther, who was so ashamed of the baby that she'd hardly given him a name, Milo, before taking him up the mountain to the deepest woods, where she left him to die, but the baby was discovered by a she-wolf, who suckled him and raised him and taught him . . . but Milo Swain is another story unto himself and I don't have time for it.

I don't have time either to tell of how Alonzo was recruited to join the Rebels during the War by the brazen whore Virdie Boatright, the only woman ever to lay with him so many times that he had not a drop of jism remaining, although the three gallons of it he left in her did not leave her with any babies. I can't stop to tell the sad story of Delphie Bullen, another girl like Lora who tried her best to keep Alonzo from taking her cherry, and, when she couldn't escape from him in whatever way Lora had, drowned herself in that spring up on Ledbetter Mountain, which to this day still gives water that aint fit to drink. I'd like to tell you the story of how Alonzo became a bushwhacker during the last part of the War, and in that renegade capacity seduced girls hither and yon wherever he found them, including a sweet young thing named Cassie Sizemore, who, like Lora and Delphie before her, tried to resist him, and did a pretty fair job of keeping him off, until he finally begged just a single kiss, which she let him have, to her undoing. But Cassie Sizemore didn't get knocked up by Alonzo. She later married Tom Whitter and had a respectable life which lasted until the next war, the First Big One, where Tom was killed, leaving her alone as a widow in their cabin on a mountaintop, which is where I met her as an old lady, that time I had the typhoid and she took care of me until Doc Swain arrived. I had no idea on earth that she'd once been kissed by Doc Swain's dad, Alonzo, nor did Doc himself know this. But she told me the whole story without mentioning Alonzo Swain by name. I just figured out, from the way she described him, that he was the same feller. And I also figured out that when he kissed her and breathed into her, it gave her the power of telling the future.

No, that story too has to go by the wayside in order for me to get on to the main story, which didn't take place until many years after the War, when Alonzo was already nigh on to middle age and was restless because the whole business of catching women and filling them with jism and fathering woodscolts was beginning to bore him somewhat, so in his listlessness he took up the study of medicine. Next to Jake Ingledew, who had become governor after the War, Alonzo was the smartest feller in Stay More if not all of Newton County, and folks thought it was a shame he never done anything worthwhile with his brains, he was too pussy-struck to have time for serious matters, or rather he considered the pursuit of women the most serious matter there is. But as he approached middle age and maybe his glands begun to give him a moment's peace, he decided that the best way to make a living was to study medicine and become Stay More's first physician, because Stay More kept on growing and getting bigger without one. In fact, the only doctor in that part of Newton County was a feller lived in a kind of cave-house over toward Spunkwater, name of Kie Raney, and Doc Raney was the closest thing to a friend that 'Lonzo Swain had in all this world. Gilbert Alonzo had been so busy all his life a-humping gals that he hadn't had time for buddies. As he told it to Kie, who'd been able only to dream of having sex with a female, "Women has got three holes but men has got only two, and they aint neither one as good a fit. No offense meant, Hoss, but given my druthers I'd as lief not spend so much time here with you." But Doc Raney had treated him for blue balls or the clap so many times that he practically lived at Doc Raney's cave-house the way I was to live at Doc Colvin Swain's, and both of 'em was bachelors so Alonzo and Doc Raney had spent a good deal of time running around together, hunting in the woods and just a-settin on the creek bank drowning worms, and they were good pals. At least Doc Raney didn't mind one day when Alonzo said to him, "Hoss, how long would it take fer ye to teach me everthang ye know about this yere doctorin business?"

"Half a year, at least," Kie Raney said.

"What would ye charge me fer it, or swap with me fer it?" Alonzo asked.

Kie Raney thought about that. He did not answer right off, but a few days later he said. "Wal, 'Lonzo, I'll tell ye. Next time ye sire a woodscolt, if nobody wants it, you could jist give 'im to me. I aint never gon fine me a womarn, but I'd shore like to have me a kid of my own."

So Alonzo said that oughtn't to be no problem because the country was already full of his woodscolts and he'd see if he couldn't get the next one away from its mother and give it to Kie. And so Kie commenced that day to teach Gilbert Alonzo the solemn study of medicine.

Doc Raney himself had learnt pretty near everything he knew from studying with granny doctors and witches and yarb doctors and such, and experimenting around on his own with all kinds of mixtures of yarbs to find out what they were good for, and it didn't take Kie too awful long to teach all of that stuff to Alonzo, but Kie had also mastered a big thick book called *Home-Study Guide to Materia Medica, Pharmacy, Therapeutics, and Surgical Procedures,* and he helped Alonzo spend a few months reading his way through this book, and gave him quizzes on it, to help. Finally he said to Alonzo, "I've taught ye all I know, but there aint no teacher near as good as experience, so it's time ye started practicin. Jist don't practice in my territory. And don't fergit that baby you owe me." Of course that word "practice" has always had two meanings that would seem to be different but they aint. On one hand, it means to do something over and over until you learn how, but it also refers to a doctor's general line of work. Doc Colvin Swain said to me, "In his practice, a physician never stops practicing," meaning even when he's supposed to know what he's doing, he's still just trying to learn it.

Alonzo went back home to Stay More to get out of Doc Raney's territory and set up his own practice. He was Stay More's first physician, but for the longest time, the only patients he could practice on, apart from the mental defectives who loitered around Ingledew's store, were older women with imaginary complaints who just wanted Alonzo Swain to visit with them, because he was still the sightliest-lookin feller in Newton County although his golden blond hair was beginning to gray. Some of these women he treated and some of 'em he "treated," if you know what I mean. Because Alonzo never did lose his rollicking lust for the fair sex.

The last of the seven boys he fathered happened like this. There was a keen-lookin dark-haired gal named Corinna McKinstry, the prettiest of the six daughters of old Vester McKinstry, the horse rancher and squire of Sidehill, some ways west of Stay More. One day Alonzo happened to be out that way, fording a creek on his horse when he spied her a-washing her pretty feet in the stream. The first glimpse of her made his jemmison stand up in the saddle and nearly poke its head above his waistband. She was so pleasant to behold that Alonzo was afraid he'd fall in love with her the way he had loved Lora Dinsmore and thus he might lose her as Lora was forever lost.

Once a year at least Alonzo still visited that little stand of butterfly weed, to pay his respects, or try to figure it all out, or whatever. He didn't want to force Corinna to turn into a flower clump. So he was real careful with her, and courted her for a long time without trying to spark her or woo her or even touch her; he just talked to her, sweet as he could, and was even sort of like a father to her. He sure was old enough to be her father, him in his late forties at that time and her not yet twenty. And with all them other daughters, old Vester hadn't paid Corinna much notice, so she was probably real happy to get all that attention from "Lonzie," as she took to calling him.

Well sir, this went on for a right smart spell of time, months and months, even though it was a good day's ride from Stay More to Sidehill, because Alonzo was determined to make a conquest of her in his own sweet time. Then the poor girl came down with pleurisy. This is a trouble with the lungs, where the lining of the lungs gets inflamed, and if it isn't cured it can lead to consumption, or tuberculosis. Alonzo hadn't ever even touched Corinna, but now he had to massage her chest and strap her chest, which is part of the treatment for pleurisy, and in the process he got a pretty good feel of her breasts, and her nipples were swollen, and he couldn't tell if she was breathing so hard because he was getting her aroused or because of her lung trouble. Of course this was happening right in her house, in her bedroom, with her mother somewhere in the next room and her father not far away. For a whole week, he came every day to Sidehill to massage her chest and strap it and dose her with creosote and a bit of laudanum which was for her pain but which also seemed to calm down whatever excitement all of that stroking of her titties was causing. But she wasn't getting any better, and in fact her pleurisy had worsened from dry to wet, meaning it had abscessed and was getting runny.

Alonzo went back over to that cave-house medical school for a "consultation" with his friend and mentor, Doc Kie Raney, saying, "Hoss, ye never taught me how to handle wet pleurisy," and Kie told him how to use pleurisy root, which is one of the many names given to nothing other than these here big fat roots of the butterfly weed. Now of course the stuff grows all over creation, but Alonzo knew that there was only one patch of it that would suit him, and that was the patch up on the hillside where Lora had disappeared so many years before. So he went back up there and found the place and talked to that butterfly weed, saying, "Lora, sweetheart, I've got to dig up your root and use it to heal a pore young gal who's got pleurisy. You won't mind, will ye?" He didn't get any answer, but he went ahead and dug up a clump and took its big root and brewed it into a tea for Corinna McKinstry, and it cured her, or leastways it arrested the disease so that pretty soon she was feeling normal again. One day she smiled and said, "Lonzie, sometimes I wish I was still sick, so's you would feel my bosoms again the way ye done."

"Aw, hon," said Alonzo, "you don't have to be sick for me to do thet! Would ye like to take a little stroll up to see the butterfly weed that cured ye?" And pretty soon they were heading for the woods, where he showed her the patch of butterfly weed that had included Lora, and still did, for that matter, for he hadn't dug her all up. Of course he didn't tell her about Lora, and they lay down beside Lora, and Lora watched them while Alonzo closed his eyes and pretended she was Lora, and got on top and unloaded his jism and got off.

Naturally she had soon stumped her toe, as they used to say of an unmarried girl who has a cake in her oven. She knew what had caused it too, and she tried to get her Lonzie to make it legal, but all he could say was, "Why, chile, I caint be yore man. I'm old enough to be yore paw!" And it looked as if poor Corinna would have to have a woodscolt like all those other girls that Gilbert Alonzo Swain had unloaded his jism into.

Having a woodscolt wasn't all that uncommon in those days, and it happened even in the best of families. But Corinna had some pretty set ideas about what was right and proper, and she made up her mind that she wasn't going to have a baby out of wedlock. So she said to him solemnly, "Lonzie, if I caint have ye for my man, I'll get me a man who looks jist like ye!"

He laughed, because he knew that there wasn't any feller anywhere as well-favored as he was. So he wasn't worried that she'd go and take up with some other feller.

But she actually commenced looking around for a likely feller to become her husband. She searched high and low for anybody that favored Lonzie, knowing that as pretty as she was, she shouldn't have had any problem latching onto him if she found him, so long as he wasn't already married. She knew if she found him, she'd better not never tell him about the cake in her oven. She knew she'd have to find him soon enough to persuade him that he was the father when the baby came along. She didn't have an awful lot of time.

And who do you think she latched onto? There was a certain son of Mellie Chism, grown to manhood, who had inherited from his father not only his handsome features but also his conviction that the only purpose of life is chasing women. The one way that Ism was different from his daddy was that whereas Alonzo was a confirmed bachelor, Ism had always believed that once he found the prettiest girl on earth, he would marry her and settle down and stop chasing women.

When Ism and Corinna met, they knew they were made for each other. He looked almost exactly like his daddy, but not quite so much that Corinna would know that Ism actually was the son of her Lonzie. And she was the loveliest creature that Ism had ever beheld, with her hair as black as a crow and her skin fair as a swan. He used all his skills, practiced with dozens of women, to talk her into laying with him, and she only pretended to be hard to get, and pretended to be a virgin, because laying with him was exactly what she wanted. Ism even practiced the same method of fucking as his daddy, quick on and quick off, hard in and limp out, and she should have guessed who he'd inherited that tendency from, but she didn't. She let him do it to her every day for several weeks, and even pretended like she enjoyed it, even took on each time as if she was having one of those deaths. After a couple of months, she told him that all that fucking had put her in a family way, so they had best think about starting a family, and did he reckon he might see his way to becoming her man? He didn't need to be asked twice.

So Corinna and Ism got the JP to marry them, just in the nick of time, because she was already swollen out more than Ism could have been held accountable for. When Alonzo found out that Corinna had went and got herself married, he nearly went crazy. He thought of her as *his* woman, even if he would never have married her himself. He still wanted her, and he hoped that she would go on making herself available to him, because after all he was still the best-looking feller in the country and nobody knew how to titillate her bubbies the way he did. But once she was married, Corinna told her Lonzie that she was a respectable woman and did not intend to sneak around and cheat on her husband, so Lonzie had just better go and find himself another bed partner.

Now Alonzo did not know, and he never knew, that Ism was his own flesh and blood. He never even got a good look at him, or he might have recognized himself in the young man. He just knew that Corinna's husband, whoever he was, was the lowdown misbegotten suck-egg dog who had stolen away all that good first-rate nookie. Alonzo couldn't stand this. The more he brooded about it, the more it drove him balmy and boiling. It makes you understand why a simple word like "mad," which in the old days always meant insane, or deranged by violent emotions, came to mean angry or resentful. Alonzo was foaming at the mouth and pissing puppies.

Ism took to married life like a duck to water, and just as he had planned, he gave up the pursuit of women and settled down to being a good husband. He built a sturdy little cottage for him and Corinna to live in, and to raise the baby in, when it came, and then he took to clerking in a store all the way up to Jasper, to make ends meet and be a good provider. Of course, Ism being gone all day presented an opportunity for Doc Alonzo Swain to drop by that new cottage to visit with Corinna. He leered and told her he was going to be her obstetrician as well as the baby's pediatrician, and he wanted to make sure everything was okay with the baby in her womb, but even that excuse wouldn't get him permission to lift her dress and have access to her twitchet, and pretty soon he had a full-blown case of frustration to go along with his madness.

And then it was too late, too far along in the advancing of the pregnancy, for him to lay with her even if he could talk her into it.

Nobody knows just how the fire started that burned down that new cottage. It happened in the middle of the night, the dark of the moon, and there wasn't any thunderstorm that would allow lightning to be the cause. It could've been a coal-oil lamp knocked over, or maybe Ism had got careless with the pipe he smoked, or who knows? maybe it was some kind of spontaneous combustion in the corn-shuck mattress stuffing.

But whatever it was, it happened so fast that Ism and Corinna must have both been deep asleep, and a good many folks were said to speculate on that and ask how could a fire have burned the house down before they even noticed it and got away? The sheriff reckoned maybe they were both dead before the fire started, but both bodies was burnt to a crisp and there was no way of finding out if they'd been killed by some means other than the fire. There wasn't anything at all left of the house or of the newlyweds except a pile of ashes and a few pieces of charred bones.

What must've happened, at least according to one or two of the folks who tell this story, and who weren't even living at that time, was that Alonzo, regardless of whether he started the fire himself or maybe even killed both of them before he started the fire (and nobody ever accused him of it), somehow got into the cottage while it was still a-burning, and found Corinna, whether she was dead yet or not, and took his trusty knife Prince and performed a Caesarian section on her right then and there amidst the flames, and grabbed the baby out of her, and took off. That's what must've happened.

Then, directly or soon after, Alonzo must've taken the baby up to that cave-house where Doc Raney had his home and his office, and gave the baby to him, saying, "Here, Hoss, here's that little misfortune I promised ye."

I notice you have glanced at your watch, and more than once. I trust you're just curious about what time of the afternoon it's getting to be, or perhaps you've got an appointment somewhere, or maybe even you're timing my story to see if I'm pacing it properly, the way a runner gets paced by somebody on the sidelines with a stopwatch. I do hope I'm not boring you, but I'm going to have to call it quits for the day pretty soon anyhow. Dr. Gilbert Alonzo Swain's story has taken a lot out of me, and I don't mean it's taken a lot of effort for me to make it up, because I've been telling it to you more or less the way I heard it from various folks, primarily Colvin Swain himself, but also from Cassie Whitter and, in variations, assorted Stay Morons lounging on the store porches of Willis Ingledew and Latha Bourne.

Who named our hero? Well, one story about that is this: Alonzo and Kie sort of did it together. They sat around and studied the problem and studied the baby, who was yelling bloody murder—excuse the expression—the infant was of course very desirous of a lactating teat, which neither of the men could provide. Pretty soon Kie Raney would summon a granny woman accomplice of his, who happened to know a young lady from Spunkwater—her name doesn't even matter, though it is known—who could wet-nurse the baby for a while until Kie could get ahold of one of them nursing bottles, one of them flasks with a long rubber tube and a rubber nipple on the end of it.

Kie was a learned feller and he wanted to name the baby something with "vin" in it, not for wine but from the Latin *vincere* for conquer, because Kie hoped that the boy would grow up and become a doctor who could conquer all the ills that the flesh is heir to, maybe even cancer and consumption and the common cold. So Kie wanted to name him Vincent, but Alonzo thought that was too Frenchified and he suggested instead they name him Irvin, but Kie thought that sounded Jewish so he proposed Melvin, but Alonzo thought that was rather unmanly and timid, so he opined they might try out Alvin, but Kie said, "Aw hell, 'Lonzo, that's even less manly than Melvin." So they considered Marvin and Kelvin and Gavin and a bunch of others, and finally Alonzo said, "Wal, Hoss, let's us jist name the boy Steven," and Kie agreed that was a right manly name, and he dipped his goose feather into ink and wrote it out on the birth certificate, and they studied it and admired it for a while and even called the baby that name a few times, but it suddenly dawned on Kie Raney that the name didn't really have a "vin" in it unless they had misspelled it, and somehow changing it to "Stevin" didn't look right. "Shit," Alonzo said, "we may as well change it to Spavin." But Hoss Raney knew that "spavin" was a hock-joint disease in horses, and he wasn't about to afflict the boy with a horse ailment for a name.

They got to babbling, and tried Tomvin and Dickvin and Harvin and Carvin, and Halvin and Gilvin and Colvin, and Alonzo snapped his fingers and said, "That'un'll do her! *Colvin.*" Little did either of them know that Colvin is a perfectly good Teutonic name, meaning "black-haired friend," appropriate since the baby had inherited not his father's golden hair but his mother's raven hair.

I like to think that Alonzo instinctively selected Colvin because it had a certain Ozarkian ring to it, a country sound; it seemed appropriate for a black-haired country doctor who would be a friend to everyone and would conquer, if not the common cold and cancer, at least consumption.

They never gave him a real middle name, only an initial, "U." That wasn't too uncommon in those days, that a feller would have a middle initial that didn't mean anything, it was just for looks. Harry S Truman for one. Another example is . . .

Hark! You can't hear him, but that old fool out in the hall is yelling, "About that time, six white horses flew over." He's been at it for the past hour, and it's a wonder he hasn't wakened poor Mary Celestia from her nap. Surely you can hear the sound of his voice even if you can't hear the words? Well sir, it's been hard enough for me to remember Alonzo Swain's story and get it straight and try to rehearse it to you, without listening to *him* and that blather insinuating that I might as well have flying horses in my story! Have I told you a single blessed thing yet that was impossible, like flying horses? There may be some aspects of Alonzo Swain's story that really stretch the blanket, but there isn't anything inconceivable about it, now is there?

Maybe I need Herb or Ernie around to annotate for me. You know how Herbert Halpert, the great academic folklorist and my dear friend, took the trouble to write commentaries on each of the tales and stories in my collections, all of 'em except *Sticks in the Knapsack,* for which Ernest Baughman supplied the notes, and *Hot Springs and Hell,* which I annotated myself, because it aint nothing but a joke book, and *Pissing in the Snow,* which Frank Hoffman annotated because he's a specialist in dirty tales. But the main purpose of all those notes is to show that likely the story I'm relating, even though I'm telling it exactly as I heard it in the back brush, is just a rehash of some ancient tale that goes all the way back to Chaucer or Boccaccio or even the Bible. Hell, them academic annotators has even got a thing called the *Motif Index* and another thing called the *Aarne-Thompson Index,* and they can probably take any story you tell 'em, even if you think you're a-making it up, and scribble all over it their numbers, like Motif D 420.1.6.7., and Incident VIII in Type 1542, which shows that there aint no such thing as an original story.

So I'd hate to see what the academic annotators would do with Alonzo Swain's story. They'd probably all shake their heads and say, "About that time, six white horses flew over," and then they'd say, "This comes out of Hesiod. Or Pindar. Or Homer hisself."

I'm tired, and I'm gonna let you go.

Three

Oh, I just switched you on. It's good to see a welcome face again. I've discovered a new power lately, although it could just be a sign I'm dying. You know the excruciatingly commonplace observation that when you die your whole life story flashes before your eyes? Well, I don't know about that, leastways nothing like that has ever happened to me. But here's what really is happening to me: whenever I don't like who I'm looking at, I just close my eyes and then reopen them, and it's like flicking a switch—I get rid of whoever was here. Works like a charm. Just now I switched you on, after switching off the most obnoxious preacher I hope I ever have to meet. Mary Celestia and I are visited, biweekly on the average, by one or another of the local ministers, Pentecostal Holiness and Assembly of God and Jehovah's Testicles and Whoever, all shapes and sizes. I don't suppose anybody at the desk gives them any information about us, letting them know that Mary is a retired full professor of English and Folklore at the University, and I aint so dumb myself even if I look like a bald-headed old citereen in the last throes of Alzheimer's. A few of these preachers are friendly and almost respectful, but most of 'em patronize us and talk down to us like we were helpless babies. "Have y'all finished your lunchie?" this feller who was just in here asks us. *Lunchie,* for God's own sweet sakes! Nearly as bad as the nurse who brings us our *brekkie.* Or the goddamn attendant who has to come in and change my *di-dee* because the other attendant who was supposed to bring my bedpan didn't get here in time and I had to take a shit. Anyhow, this preacher was one of the worst. He sways back and forth in front of Mary and waves his arms in her face because she's blind, and he hollers at me because I'm a little hard of hearing. "Did y'all have somebodee read the Bible to y'all this weekie? Did y'all get a nice big bitey of the Holy Wordie?" Ooh, lawsy mercy 'pon my soul!

But as I say, I've discovered that I can just shut my eyes and make 'em go away. The trouble is, I can't have any more control over who I'll see when I reopen my eyes than I could control my bladder or my bowels. Just now I reopened my eyes and there *you* were, and I'm mighty glad to see you, but this morning I shut my eyes to get rid of Dr. Bittner—remind me sometime to tell you about him, he works over at City Hospital and comes around once a month to check up on us—I closed him out of my consciousness and when I reopened my eyes, flicked that switch, it wasn't him I was looking at, nor you, but Colvin Swain! I swear. "Lord love a duck, Col!" I exclaimed. "I heared tell you had up and died back around the late fifties, wasn't it? Some old boy told me you'd got hit by lightnin."

He smiled his benevolent reassuring smile that was always so good for making his patients feel like they didn't have any cause at all for feeling bad, and he said, "Wal, Vance, I reckon that's true enough, as far as it goes. But jist recollect what I told you about how I learnt to cure folks in their dreams. And ask yoreself if you're not jist dreaming."

But I knew I was wide awake, and he was just a-sitting there right where you are, plain as you are . . . unless I'm only dreaming *you* too, and only you can decide that for yourself. But if you *know* that you are really there beside my bed and I'm really here, then you'll just have to believe that he was there too. "Mary Celestia, sweetheart!" I called to her. "Don't you see this doctor feller here?" And then I remembered that she is blind.

What's that, Mary? Oh, yes. But this isn't the doctor, and I wasn't calling to you again, I was just quoting to him the way I called you this morning. This is my good friend the novelist.

Mary just said she wanted to remind me what she answered this morning, that of course she couldn't see the man, but she could hear him, and he sure did sound like Doc Swain!

So maybe both of us are in our second childhoods and we deserve to be spoken to like babies.

Babies. How does one properly speak to a baby? Which brings us right back to our story, next installment of it, because I have to ask you now to picture a cave-house on a mountainside near Spunkwater, Arkansas, oh about 1886 or so, and a middle-aged bachelor ex-schoolteacher turned self-styled physician and medical preceptor, name of Kie Raney, trying to talk to this baby named Colvin Swain.

If Colvin had grown up in a "normal" household with a "normal" family, especially a mother and all, or even one brother or sister, he would have been nicknamed something like Butch or Spike or Pug, or leastways maybe Collie. But Kie Raney never called him anything but Colvin, always sticking that "vin" on the end of it as if to remind 'em both that he was going to conquer. Sometimes just for emphasis Kie might use his middle initial too, and call him Colvin U, but maybe that sounded like he was saying, "Colvin, *you,*" and as far as Colvin knew he never had a last name. He grew up without a mother and without a last name. Alonzo didn't want him to use the name Swain and Kie didn't think it would be right to use the name Raney, since he wasn't really Kie's son, just his foster son, so as far as he was concerned his name was just Colvin U, with that middle initial able to stand for anything his fancy might dream up, like Ulysses or Usher or Unthank, although his favorite was Underwood, because that was usually where he was.

From the earliest time that Colvin seemed to be paying attention, maybe around half a year old, Kie always addressed him just as he would an adult, never talking any kind of baby talk to him, and never talking down to him. "Colvin," he would say, "it would appear that you have done gone and taken a shit on yore blanket and I am a-gorn have to clean it up and git ye a fresh 'un." Or he would say something like, "Wal, Colvin, don't ye reckon thet thar bite of oatmeal would sit better on yore stomach than it would on top of yore haid and all over yore face?" He'd sound just like a doctor discussing a patient's problems, and later, when Colvin would overhear his foster father talking to various patients of his in the same mild, polite tone, he probably understood that that was the way a feller ought to talk to anybody, and that was the beginning of the calm, soothing way of speaking that grown-up Colvin Swain would have with his own patients.

Not even in their games would Kie use anything approximating baby talk or child talk. From earliest memory, Colvin's favorite amusement was to be bounced on Kie's knees in that popular little surprise sport called "Ride a little horsie down to town. Whoa, little horsie, don't fall down." Only Kie didn't say it that way; he would call the imaginary animal "a stout steed" or "a prancing stallion" or "a plunging mustang" or "a trotting colt" or "a winged palomino" even if the meter wasn't trochaic and thus the horse's bounce was out of rhythm.

Being bounced on Kie's knee, by the way, was all the holding and cuddling that little Colvin needed, that he might've got from a mother if he'd had one. He didn't need more of it. But Kie would hold and cuddle him if he hurt himself or was afraid of something.

Kie was a talented guitarist and a pretty good singer of old songs, and he sang for his foster son every ballad, ancient and modern, which concerned horses.

Later when Colvin had outgrown the knee-horsie, or rather graduated to being able to ride Kie's back as Kie got on all fours to become the horse, Kie taught him to recite such things as "Ride a cock horse to Banbury town," and such old rhymes as:

> One white foot, buy a horse;
> Two white feet, try a horse;
> Three white feet, look well about him;
> Four white feet, do without him.

. . . Or the Ozarkian variant on this last: "Four white feet an' a white nose, / Take off his hide an' throw him to the crows." And later, such things as: "Dear to me is my bonny white steed; / Oft has he helped me at pinch of need." And even these lines from Shakespeare's "Venus and Adonis":

Round-hoof'd, short-jointed, fetlocks shag and long,
Broad breast, full eye, small head and nostril wide,
High crest, short ears, straight legs and passing strong,
Thin mane, thick tail, broad buttock, tender hide:
Look, what a horse should have he did not lack,
Save a proud rider on so proud a back.

And later still, Kie taught him Latin: *Tum bene fortis equus reserato carcere currit, Cum quos praetereat, quosque sequatur, habet,* which is from Ovid's *Art of Love* and means: "The valiant horse races best, at the barrier's fall, when he has others to follow and o'erpass," or, to translate it into the way folks would talk in those parts, "A good horse runs better if he's got other horses to beat out." But by that time, Colvin was too old to ride the playlike horse of Kie or even the various broomstick horses that he outgrew one by one. He was ready for his own real horse. When a Spunkwater mule skinner named Felix Amidon got blinded by his own daddy for fooling around with the daddy's kept woman, Kie went to him and treated him with a combination of large doses of thiamine and the singing of a special magic song in countertenor, which restored his eyesight, and Felix Amidon paid Kie for this cure with a broomtail Indian pony, which Kie presented to Colvin, who named the pony Pegasus but called him Ole Peg. I doubt if Kie ever told him the old tale of how Pegasus sprang from Medusa's neck when her head was cut off, but possibly he did tell him about how the nine Muses took care of Pegasus and maybe even how Bellerophon tamed him and rode him off to fight the Chimera.

What the knife Prince had been to his daddy at that age and later, the pony Pegasus became for Colvin. He took to riding it all over creation, especially westward to Stay More, which somehow seemed more like a hometown to him than Spunkwater did. Even though he didn't know it, Stay More was a-swarming with his own kinfolks. He had first cousins and last cousins all over the place. He liked to tie Pegasus at the porch of Isaac Ingledew's gristmill and sit on the edge of the mill porch with all the other loafers of Stay More. Because his hair was black and his features favored the McKinstry side of his family, nobody suspected that he was another son of Alonzo Swain, who had his doctor's office on Stay More's Main Street and sometimes came to the mill to loaf around. Colvin had learned to call him "Uncle 'Lonzo," because that is what Alonzo had requested that Kie tell the boy he was: not his father, but his uncle. If any of the Stay More boys his own age asked him who he was or where he was from, he would just say he was Colvin and he lived in a cave-house over toward Spunkwater with Doc Kie Raney. He never told anybody that he was Doc Raney's son. We don't even know if he believed that himself, but leastways he never gave out that he was Doc Raney's son; he just said he lived with him, in a cave-house. The other boys were curious to know about that cave-house, what it looked like, how it was built (or rather how the boards and windows and door covered the mouth of the cave to form one wall of a dwelling whose other walls were the natural stone of the cave), and how it felt to live inside of it. When Colvin explained how cool it was in hottest summer and how warm it was in coldest winter, the boys went home to their parents and demanded to know why everybody didn't live in caves. Most of the parents could only reply, "Beats me," or, "I don't have the first idee," or, "You've got me there, boy."

One day Colvin noticed that the Stay More boys were missing. He waited around the mill porch for them to show up, but they never did. He went over to the Ingledew Store to see if they might be there, but they weren't. So he went back to the mill and waited some more, until somebody asked him, "How come ye aint in school?" Now the only school he'd ever heard tell of was once when Kie Raney had showed him a school of fish in the creek. So he figured that the other boys were all off a-fishing somewheres. He got back on Ole Peg and rode up and down Banty Creek a ways without finding any boys fishing, so then he rode up and down Swains Creek a ways, and it just so happened that when he come to the Stay More schoolhouse, the boys was all outdoors for recess, and there was a bunch of girls too! Colvin had hardly ever seen a girl. Riding Pegasus all over the countryside, he had sometimes spied a girl standing on the porch of a house or maybe even working in the garden, but he'd never seen one up close. He wanted to talk to one of them, to see if they sounded like human beings.

Colvin got down from his pony and stood there admiring the girls, and admiring the schoolhouse, a handsome structure with a little bell-tower cupola on top of it, and big glass windows, and a couple of twin doors—"bigeminal," as you say. Colvin went up to one of the boys and asked, "What are y'all up to?" The boy replied, "We're a-playing Dare Base." Colvin watched them run around for a while, and then the bell up on the roof went BOMB-DOOM one time, and all the kids quit running around and went into the building, the girls through one door, the boys through the other, with Colvin joining the latter. He found a seat at a desk in the back and sat there watching as a old feller got up and took a piece of white chalk and used it to make some letters on the wall, which was painted black. The letters said GEOGRAPHY, LESSON 6, and STATE CAPITALS, and then the feller turned around and said, "All righty, what's the state capital of Arkansas?" and some girl held up her hand and the feller said, "You, Sarey," and the girl said, "Little Rock, Teacher!" And the man said, "Keerect. Missoury?" and somebody said "Jeff City, Teacher." This went on for some time, with the feller naming all the neighboring states, but then he began to name far-off places, and when he named Virginia nobody knew its capital, except Colvin, who did as he had observed the others doing and held up his hand.

"You thar," the teacher-feller pointed at him. "I don't believe I recollect yore name."

"Colvin, Teacher," he said. "Richmond."

"Colvin Richmond, huh? I don't know any Richmonds hereabouts. Are you new to this country?"

"Nossir, I meant Richmond is the capital of Virginia."

"Is that a fack?" the man said, and consulted his book, and said, "Why, yes indeed, Richmond is the capital of Virginia. What is the capital of North Carolina?"

Nobody else held up their hands, so Colvin said, "Raleigh, Teacher." His ability to answer apparently amused some of the boys, who began giggling and making remarks among themselves, which appeared to anger the teacher, who took one of the boys, Oren Duckworth, to the front of the room and used a hickory switch to flog him unmercifully. Colvin had never seen anybody flogged before, nor considered that one human might do this thing to another human, so despite his sympathy for Oren he considered this experience more educational than learning the state capitals, which he already knew anyway. And since nobody except Colvin knew that Pierre is the capital of South Dakota and Montpelier is the capital of Vermont, the teacher gave up on Geography and went on to Reading, where it turned out that Colvin was the only one who could read a page of the McGuffey Reader without using his finger as a pointer or screwing up his face and reciting the words in a singsong; to 'Riting, where it appeared that Colvin alone could use script instead of block letters; and to 'Rithmetic, where

Colvin was able to do higher sums without counting on his toes.

Then school let out for the day. Colvin had been looking for a chance to talk to some of the girls, especially since he'd already learned from the classroom that they sounded pretty much like any other human being. But before he could approach any of the girls, he was surrounded by a group of the boys, and Oren Duckworth said, "Aint you a big sprout?" Colvin was not sure which of the various buds or shoots of young plants he was referring to, and before he could answer, Oren put both hands on his chest and shoved, throwing Colvin off balance so that he landed on his buttocks, and before he could get up the other boys began kicking him, in his ribs and stomach and even in his face. It was very painful. He tried to cover himself with his arms. "Git on back to yore cave, Smartypants!" Oren said. "Jist crawl on home to yore hole and don't show yore face around here again!" They allowed him to get up, and he made a dash for Pegasus, leapt atop the pony and took off, but the boys pursued him, throwing rocks, some of which hit both him and his pony, before they could make their getaway. Riding home, he meditated on the irony that in a place called invitingly "Stay More," he was told imperatively, "Git Out."

He did not tell Kie Raney about being banished from Stay More, but he told him about the school. "You never told me there was such a place as a school," he mildly complained, because Kie had tried to tell him about everything under the sun.

"Yeah, I used to run a school myself," Kie said, and he told about his years as schoolmaster at the Spunkwater school, and how he'd been the preceptor of some kids who grew up to be some of the finest people in this part of the country because he'd tried to make them interested in some subjects that would otherwise have been boring. "Did ye git bored at the Stay More school?" Kie asked him.

Colvin allowed as how he hadn't particularly enjoyed it, nor learned anything worth knowing, except his two lessons, one as an observer and one as a participant, in the way the human species gets pleasure from inflicting pain on one another. "But I don't see the point," he declared, "in a teacher standing in front of a bunch of kids who all face the same way and sit at the same kind of desk and have to learn the same kind of stuff . . . unless maybe that was my *third* lesson, if a teacher has fun making learning painful."

Kie laughed and said he suspected that there was a streak of cruelty in many teachers that was not expressed only in the corporal punishment of the hickory switch but in the pleasure of exposing ignorance and provoking feelings of stupidity and worthlessness. "Don't ye fret, Colvin," Kie said, "I won't let anybody *make* ye go to school if ye don't wanter."

"Suits me," Colvin said, but then he thought of something, and added, "I reckon all I'd miss would be the chance to git a good look at some of them gals. I don't never see ary gal hereabouts, and maybe I'll git to missin 'em." He pondered this prospect, and then, having been encouraged all his young life to ask *any* question that he wished to ask of his sage and kind mentor, he asked, "How come gals has got long hair and dresses?"

"There's always two reasons for everything," Kie reminded him, "a practical reason and a purty reason. The purty reason is the same as the reason gals gener'ly look sweeter in the face than boys do, and the reason the grown-up gal is the only female in all creation who has swollen bubbies all the time. A gal gits a feller to notice her by all these things: the long hair and the nice dress and sweet face and the shapely bubbies let on that she's a *she,* jist in case his weak nose and his weak ears didn't let him know. That's the *purty* reason, and ye know, of course, why it's necessary for fellers to want gals, to propagate the species like all other critters and livin things. Now the practical reason is this: the long hair keeps the gal's head temperature more even and reg'lar and helps her think better, and she shore needs to use her wits and her brains to git along in this world; the sweet face makes fellers want to protect it and help her git along in this world; the dress makes it more handy for them to lift it up so's they can propagate the species, you know? And the swollen bubbies make a nice soft piller fer babies and menfolk alike."

"Pillow or pillar?" Colvin sought to clarify the pronunciation.

"Both, like I say," Kie said.

Doc Kie Raney was all the teacher that Colvin ever needed, and there were so many things to teach him that perhaps it was just as well that he wasn't distracted by long hair, dresses, sweet faces, and bubbies. If Colvin inherited any of Alonzo's legendary appetite for the pleasures of the flesh, he would not really have an opportunity to express it for years to come.

Man's first sublimation of the sexual urge was hunting, a necessity, and that is what all sublimations are, if I may use Kie's theory: there is both a practical reason and an aesthetic reason for everything, and the sexual urge is sublimated, on one hand, the practical hand, to make man hunt, to feed himself, to destroy life in order to nurture life, and on the other hand, the aesthetic one, to make man create: to build, to paint, to compose, to tell stories.

Kie and Colvin spent a lot of time hunting. Although Doc Raney's patients paid him off with produce and livestock, and Kie never lacked for a larder, he and Colvin had a taste for game, and they'd rather eat a rabbit than a chicken, a deer than a beef, a wild turkey than a tame one, and they were crazy about bear meat. Kie taught Colvin marksmanship not only with a variety of firearms, side arms, and shoulder arms alike, but also with bow and arrow, crossbow, and even, in emulation of the Bluff Dwellers who had lived in their cave before them, the *atlatl*. Kie spent a great deal of time teaching Colvin about knives: not just the common jackknife like his daddy's old Prince, but real hunting knives, Bowie knives, carving knives, daggers, frog stickers, and, of course, scalpels, with which Kie taught him the anatomy of everything in creation, animal and plant alike. Once, an indigent, homeless patient of Kie's died, and Kie brought the cadaver home and used it for months to teach Colvin the anatomy of the human body. Colvin's keen mind was too fascinated to be frightened or disgusted by the cadaver.

Living in the near-wilderness gave Colvin a better understanding of nature than most physicians could ever learn. Just as Kie and Colvin preferred the wild meat of the forest to the tame meat that Doc Raney's patients offered in payment, they preferred the wild plants to the produce from the vegetable garden. They foraged not just for the delicious things like muscadines, dewberries, wild blackberries, and walnuts but also poke sallet, lamb's quarters, dock, and sorrel. As long as Kie had him in the forest teaching him how to tell a possum from a coon or an edible boletus from a deadly amanita, the wise and good doctor thought it was time to begin Colvin's education in the finding and preparation of medicinal herbs, and even their naming by Latin botanical name, for example *Hydrastis canadensis* for goldenseal, *Digitalis purpurea* for foxglove, and *Podophyllum peltatum* for mandrake. He took especial pains to show Colvin how to find, dig up, and make a tea from the stout taproot of *Asclepias tuberosa,* called variously silkweed, white root, orange milkweed, wind root, chigger weed, pleurisy root, Indian paintbrush, and, most commonly, butterfly weed. It is tops for curing any of the various diseases that are generally called "lung trouble." Even when it fails, butterfly weed is still the most powerful placebo known to man. Kie taught Colvin all of the magical incantations that are meant to accompany the administering of each herb, but he pointed out that butterfly weed is the only remedy which doesn't need a verbal incantation to go with it.

Incantations, Kie had to point out, did not work in veterinary medicine, because animals could not understand our language. Kie made Colvin into an expert veterinarian before allowing him a chance to treat a human being, even including himself. Kie taught him never to kill a snake, especially not a poisonous snake, and most particularly not a particular poisonous snake who has bitten someone, because an essential part of the cure for snakebite, the exact details of which I was never able to pry out of any of my informants, was to find the actual snake who had bitten the victim, do something or the other with it, but release it unharmed afterwards. Colvin himself was bitten once by a deadly copperhead, cured of the bite by Kie with the help of the reptile itself, who, instead of being released, became Colvin's pet. Colvin called him Drakon and fed him and talked to him, and, for some years, even slept with him. Drakon and Pegasus did not like each other, however, and Colvin had to learn to enjoy the company of one without the other.

When Colvin turned fourteen, and demonstrated to his master's satisfaction his ability to cure rinderpest in cows, glanders and staggers in horses, bluetongue in sheep, and swine fever in pigs, Kie got out a big book and blew the dust off it, *Home-Study Guide to Materia Medica, Pharmacy, Therapeutics, and*

Surgical Procedures, the same book Kie had used to teach Colvin's daddy the rudiments of human medicine. Alonzo had required six months to master the book with the help of daily quizzes from Kie; Colvin was able to commit the book to memory in one month. Then, because Kie fortunately had a little cash on hand, from tending a rheumatic widow who couldn't pay him in produce or livestock and had to use real money, he was able to send off and order such additional books as Boenning's *A Textbook on Practical Anatomy,* Buret's *Syphilis in Modern Times,* Eisenberg's *Bacteriological Diagnosis,* Edinger's *Twelve Lectures on the Structure of the Central Nervous System,* and Hare's *Fever: Its Pathology and Treatment.* Since these new books contained all kinds of stuff that even Kie himself didn't know, he and Colvin read them together and quizzed each other on them, and by the time he was fifteen, Colvin was accompanying Kie on his rounds and assisting in surgery and obstetrics. Eager to please, Colvin offered to take over the management of the disorderly office accounts, and began riding Pegasus around to collect the livestock and produce that patients owed. All of this activity brought him occasionally into contact with, or at least in sight of, a female, and he enjoyed this.

Colvin used money he had saved from trapping furs to buy for four dollars his own copy of a big medical dictionary, and when he had stored it in memory within two months, to order for one dollar a year's subscription to *Medical Bulletin: A Monthly Journal of Medicine and Surgery,* and for three dollars a year's subscription to *Journal of Laryngology, Rhinology, and Otology,* and his faithful perusal of each month's issue of these magazines made him even more knowledgeable and au courant than Kie himself. It was through these magazines that Colvin discovered two rather astonishing facts about medicine: first, that in order to practice the profession legally, you have to have something called an M.D., and secondly, that the only way you can get an M.D. is by going off somewheres to something called "medical school." Colvin was appalled. Ever since his brief attendance at the Stay More institution of lower learning, he had had a poor opinion of "school," and he couldn't quite understand why it was necessary to sit at a desk facing a teacher in order to learn medicine. His memory of the one afternoon at the Stay More school came back to him, and he tried to conceive of sitting at a desk and raising his hand to name the parts of the gastrointestinal system. If he left one out, would the teacher flog him?

But the more he thought about this business of medical school, the more it bothered him. Finally he asked Kie, "Did you ever go to medical school?"

Kie looked around, from left to right, as if there might be somebody else within earshot, and then he raised his index finger to his lips. "Colvin," he said, "maybe they's some fellers down to Little Rock has been to medical school, and maybe you'd even find a doctor or two in Harrison who might at least have walked down the hallways of a medical school, but most Arkansas doctors learnt their trade the same way I'm a-learnin you: they just apprenticed theirselfs to somebody who had already learnt it."

Colvin tried to forget the matter, to bury it in the back of his too active mind, but over the years it would occasionally creep up on him again. On Colvin's sixteenth birthday, Kie discovered that there was not one single question he could ask of Colvin, on any medical subject, which he could not answer, not even something like "How do you induce spontaneous remission of cancer?" or "How do you restart a heart which has stopped?" So Kie presented Colvin with that most delightful of all treatises, the fourteenth edition (carefully revised and greatly enlarged) of Dr. D. W. Cathell's *Book on the Physician Himself and Things That Concern His Reputation and Success.* Kie declared that he had nothing whatever left to teach Colvin; that the Cathell book would instruct him in all the matters of behavior, conduct, ethics, and other subjects above and beyond the acquired science that he had already learned.

There were tears running down the wise, kind instructor's face, the first time that Colvin had ever seen him weeping, and Kie wrung his hands, the first time that Colvin had ever seen him wringing. "Son," Kie said, although he had never called him that before and really didn't mean it in a paternal so much as a sociable way, "I'm a-gorn have to send ye out into the world, all on yore lonesome. You'll jist have to set up yore own practice somewheres, anywheres so long as it aint in my territory. There's jist a few things you've got to promise, and I want ye to recite these after me."

And Kie had Colvin raise his right hand and put the other hand, lacking a Bible, on top of the Cathell book, and repeat after him:

I swear that

1. I'll be a-thinkin on my ole teacher the exact same way I'd think on my own daddy, and I'll be a-helpin him out if he ever needs it.

2. I'll be using everthang I learnt to make folks well, but not never to hurt 'em or wrong 'em.

3. I'll not never be giving no man nary drug that would harm him even if he baigs me fer it, nor will I never be giving no womarn a abortion even if she baigs me fer it.

4. I'll not never be a-gorn inter nary a house except

to go in thar and heal the sick. I'll not never go inter nobody's house to do nothing wrong or seduce some pore gal or feller neither one.

5. I'll not never be a-blabbin nothing I hear or learn that aint nobody else's business to them or nobody, so help me ye gods.

When Colvin had finished swearing this oath, Kie said, "Now you go on and git out of here. You are the seventh son of a seventh son, and any durn fool knows what that means: it means you are a doctor in spite of yourself, it means you couldn't never *stop* being a doctor even if you tried. And it means you can cure any ailment under the sun; you can heal any complaint that ever was or ever will be."

Colvin could not budge. He just stood there, with his mouth open, and his own eyes a-watering up like Kie's, and finally he asked, "Whose seventh son am I the seventh son of?"

"Ole Lizzie Swain's, rest her soul," Kie said. And even though he had ordered Colvin off the premises of the cave-house, he relented long enough to tell Colvin the complicated story of how Elizabeth Hansell Swain had come from Cullowhee, North Carolina, with her thirteen children, arriving in Stay More not long after the brothers Jacob and Noah Ingledew had already founded it and named it, and the youngest of her children, her "least'un," Gilbert, grew into rambunctious manhood impregnating females hither and yon all over the goddamn county, and later opting for his middle name, Alonzo ("I hope ye don't never choose to be called by *yore* middle name, U, which sounds like an Englishman pronouncing 'Hugh' "), under which Alonzo became a doctor after training with Kie— "So you'd best not never practice in *his* territory neither."

"Uncle 'Lonzo is my actual paw?!" Colvin asked, dumbfounded. "But how d'ye know I'm his seventh son?"

"Aw, hell, Colvin, he jist might've had seventeen sons, fer all I know. And maybe fer all he knows, either. But I'm jist a-tellin the story the way she ort to be told. Now go on and git out of here." Kie turned his back so that he would not have to watch Colvin leave, because there is a wise and venerable belief, which has both a practical and a pretty reason, that you should never watch anybody go out of sight.

Colvin packed a few of his belongings—his Cathell book and back issues of his medical journals and his clothes, and his copperhead Drakon wrapped in a burlap sack—into the saddlebags of Pegasus, and headed west. His initial intention was to keep going west until he got to California. He had heard many marvelous things about California, what a great land of opportunity it was, and his medical journals had led him to know that it desperately needed some good doctors. Isolated in the cave-house as he had been, Colvin had never heard the legendary Curse of Jacob Ingledew, which doomed any Ozarker who dared venture into California, doomed him into a bad life of ill luck, sickness, poverty, even death.

It was just as well, because the closest Colvin ever got to California, on his journey westward, was the village of Stay More, where, the first evening into his journey, Pegasus came down with what veterinarian Colvin correctly diagnosed as encephalomyelitis. He could have prevented it by immunizing Ole Peg for one season with a chick-embryo vaccine, but he had not, and there was no cure once the virus had taken over. Pegasus died.

Afoot, Colvin was stuck in Stay More . . . not a bad place to be stuck, come to think of it, in fact the best place on earth to be stuck, but Colvin still remembered too vividly the beating at the schoolhouse and the injunction never to return. That was the third factor giving him pause, the other two being the presence on Main Street not only of the office and clinic of Uncle Alonzo, the man presumed to be his father, but also, directly across the street from it, *another* office and clinic, that of John Mabrey Plowright, a Stay More native who had done gone and apprenticed himself to an actual M.D. up at Harrison, and after a year's apprenticeship and perhaps some mail-order lessons from a St. Louis diploma mill, had erected a stake in his front yard with a shingle hanging from it: J. M. PLOWRIGHT, M.D. FAMILY MEDICINE." Colvin stood on Main Street for a while, staring at this shingle, trying to determine how "family medicine" was any different from any other kind, unless possibly it meant as opposed to medicine of individuals who didn't live in families, and also thinking about the circumstance whereby the population of Stay More had now grown to the point where it could support *two* physicians—not a bad idea, because it meant the two would keep each other in line, provide healthy competition, offer second opinions, and ideally assist each other in complicated operations, not to mention being "on call" when the other had gone fishing or something.

Then Colvin turned, climbed the steps of the other doctor, knocked, and when the man appeared, said, smiling sweetly, "Howdy, Paw."

Alonzo said, "Why, howdy there, Col boy," and then he coughed and inquired, "What didje call me?"

" 'Paw,' Paw," Colvin said, like naming the *Asimina triloba* tree, which was overabundant in the woods and fields of Stay More. "Kie threw me out, Paw. I reckon he's done already taught me all there is to know about doctoring."

"Is that a fack, now?" Alonzo said. "You don't mean to tell me." He coughed again, and Colvin, detecting that the breath was also bad, realized it wasn't merely from nervousness or discomfort; his father likely had a bronchiectasis, but damned if Colvin was going to write prescriptions for lipiodol and iodide of potash for a man capable of writing his own. "So where are you off to?" Alonzo asked.

"I was thinkin about Californy," Colvin admitted. "But my horse broke down. You could either give me another horse, or you could move over and make room for a third doctor in this town."

"Hellfire, boy, didn't Kie warn ye to stay out of my territory? He tole me to stay out of his'n, and I don't aim to let ye practice in mine. I've already got all the rivalry I can handle from Jack Plowright across the road yonder."

"Tum bene fortis equus reserato carcere currit," Colvin began to recite, because doesn't any kid want to impress his daddy? *"Cum quos prætereat, quosque sequatur, habet."* And when Alonzo failed to look impressed, only annoyed, Colvin offered the translation, "A good horse runs better if he's got other horses to beat out."

"I caint afford to give ye a new horse," Alonzo said. "You'll jist have to find some other way to git to Californy."

"That aint what I'm talkin about," Colvin said. "I'm talkin about maybe you and Jack Plowright both would be better doctors if you had a real thoroughbred to have to run against."

"Shit on a stick!" Alonzo grew red with anger. "Sonny boy, you aint but a little spadger still wet behind the ears! You caint be more'n what? Fifteen? Sixteen year old? You think anybody would trust their life to you? Hell, you couldn't even—" Alonzo coughed, gagged, spit up some blood into his handkerchief, and then had another paroxysm of coughing. Colvin was sure it was generalized bronchiectasis, but he wanted to be able to discount emphysema in association with it.

"Dad, what are you a-takin for that there cough?" he asked.

"Jist horehound, and a bit of tea from butterfly weed root," Alonzo said.

"Could I see yore hand." Colvin took his father's hand and checked it for clubbed fingers and hypertrophic osteoarthropathy, apparently negative. "Doctor," Colvin said respectfully, "if ye don't mind, I'd like to do a bronchoscopy."

"Say what?" Alonzo said.

"Doctor, we need to rule out any furrin bodies in yore trachea and bronchi," Colvin suggested, "if ye could lend me the borry of yore bronchoscope."

"Aint got ary of them newfangled gadgets," Alonzo admitted.

"Do ye reckon Jack Plowright might have one?"

"Maybe, but I aint about to ask 'im fer it."

"Then I'd best do it fer ye, Paw," Colvin said. "I'll be right back." And before his father could stop him, he had gone out and crossed the road and knocked on the other doctor's door, and when the man answered, the man who would become his lifelong competition and his nemesis, Colvin squared his shoulders and said, "Doctor Plowright, sir, I'm Doctor Colvin Swain, nephew of the good gentleman across the street, who, I'm a-feared, may have contracted dilatation of the bronchi with secondary infection, most likely unilateral bronchiectasis of the lower lobes."

"Serves that bastard right!" Jack Plowright exclaimed. "Jist what he needs!"

"My bag is missin its Hampton bronchoscope," Colvin declared. "Could ye see yore way to lendin me the borry of your'n, fer jist a secont?"

"Wal, I don't rightly know as I've got ary," Doc Plowright said. "What do they look lak?"

Colvin described the instrument and offered to help Doc Plowright search among his apparatus for it, and sure enough, there it was, although it wasn't the Hampton but the Crowell model, which would do. "I don't reckon it's been sterilized, if ye aint never used it?" Colvin asked, and then he said, "Thanks a load. I'll be back with it lickety-split, afore ye even notice it missin," and he took the instrument to his father's and sterilized it, and said, "Doctor, if you'll be so good as to open wide, and hold real still . . ." and he performed the bronchoscopy, ruling out foreign obstructions. He borrowed his father's microscope to examine the sputum and determine which organisms were involved in the infectious process. Then he mixed up a dose of wild cherry syrup with potassium iodide in it, administered a teaspoon to his father, and told him, "Now, Doctor, I'm a-gorn to have to put ye into a position for postural drainage."

And he showed his father how to hang over the side of the bed with his head on the floor, so that gravity would drain the pus from the dilated bronchi. "How long've I gotta stay this way?" Alonzo asked.

"Months, even years maybe," the young doctor prognosed, and although he did not mean that his father had to stay constantly in that awkward upside-down position, he did honestly mean that his father might have to carry out the procedure every morning and evening for a very long time.

While his father was hanging upside down over the edge of the bed, Colvin took over his routines, borrowed his black bag and his horse, and successfully treated a variety of Stay Morons for a variety of ailments: sigmoid diverticulitis, tetany, mercury poisoning, gout, scurvy, hookworm, whooping cough, asthma, diphtheria, and rabies. Although there was much skepticism among the citizenry over Colvin's qualifications and credentials, owing largely to his extreme youth, a singular fact of his practice was soon noticed and widely voiced: he never lost a case. Not one of his patients ever failed to be cured, not even those suffering with renal failure, anthrax, snakebite, general paresis, and gunshot wound.

So famous and popular did Colvin become that the only way Doc Jack Plowright could hope to compete with him was by attempting to beat him to the patient. This became literally a horse race in which Doc Plowright would jump atop his nag, Lucifer, and try to reach the patient's house before Doc Colvin Swain, riding his dad's sorrel mare, Sadie, could get there. Stay Morons took to pari-mutuel betting on which of the two would win. Lucifer actually was the better animal, and often Doc Plowright arrived first, but just as often he made the wrong diagnosis or prescribed the wrong treatment, so people who sent to the village for a doctor learned to instruct the messenger to be sure and give Doc Swain's mare Sadie a good drink of coffee mixed with corn whiskey in order to speed her up. Doc Plowright began to hate the younger Doc Swain as much as, or more than, he had ever hated the older Doc Swain, and he would spend the rest of his life dividing his time between his patients and his attempt to sabotage his competition. Indeed, the only way he managed to keep any patients was by charging only half as much as the Swains did, whatever they charged, even if it was produce or livestock. If you had to give one of the Doc Swains a whole hog to get your appendix removed, Doc Plowright would do it for you for only a piglet.

Over the years, Doc Plowright became known as the poor folks' physician, and the Doc Swains were viewed as limiting their practice to "quality."

Socially, no such distinctions existed. Socially, Colvin Swain saved the life of Oren Duckworth and thereby earned his right to free mingling with those who had originally driven him away from the Stay More school yard. Oren lost the ability to breathe, and while Doc Plowright treated him for pulmonary disorders and the older Doc Swain attempted to treat him for hemolytic anemia, Colvin's stethoscope told him that it was congestive heart failure, specifically left ventricular, and taking the patient's history, deduced that it was associated with syphilitic disease of the aortic valve. Colvin sedated Oren with chloral hydrate, and then he addressed the assembled family: "Do any of y'uns know what foxglove looks lak?" Oren's sister Dulcie was sent out to gather a quantity of the leaves of the foxglove flower, from which Colvin extracted the glucoside digitalin, and administered it to Oren along with one of Kie's favorite incantations, with pronounced beneficial results. Oren, recovering, said, "Doc, I shore am sorry fer that time I whupped ye at the schoolhouse." And Oren's pretty sister Dulcie walked him to his horse and told him, "If ever you'd like to have a sweetie, I reckon I could step out a time or two."

But "stepping out," in Dulcie's view as well as that of the typical Stay More girl, did not necessarily mean leaving the house. For all of the still-told stories of how the older Doc Swain had cajoled hordes of females into the back brush and the hayloft and even the creek bed, the younger Doc Swain was to discover, when he finally had a spare moment to experiment with courtship, that the best he could hope for was a usually chaperoned situation in which some member of Dulcie's family was nearby, possibly in the same room, while Colvin and Dulcie attempted to make conversation. They had little to talk about. After discussing the weather and the chances of rain or continued drought, they would attempt to tell the latest joke that they had picked up, but most of Dulcie's jokes were silly or simple, and most of Colvin's were somewhat risky, and neither of them laughed at the other's jokes. Dulcie, having observed that her mother and her mother's friends loved to discuss their illnesses and physical problems, tried to get Colvin to talk about his patients, but he never forgot Kie's fifth precept, namely, that the good physician never discloses any information about his patients, so Colvin would not even tell Dulcie who he had been treating, let alone for what. Usually, Colvin and Dulcie sat in silence until it was time for him to go.

"Paw," Colvin asked Alonzo bluntly one day, "how did ye ever sprunch a gal in the old days?"

"The *old* days?" Alonzo said indignantly. "Why, I'll have ye to know that jist last night I shagged Bessie Mae Murrison *two times!*"

"How d'ye do it? How d'ye talk 'em into it?"

"Aw, I don't rightly do a whole lot of talkin. There aint that much to talk about. I jist sort of gentle 'em down into a laying position."

But when Colvin attempted to gentle Dulcie into a horizontal, or even a reclining position, it seemed to ruffle her dignity, and she snapped upright like his very manhood had been snapped upright by the thought of what he was hoping to do.

After many months of an unexciting and uneventful romance, Colvin finally gave himself a strong dose of veronal, a barbituate good for relaxing the inhibitions, and he said, speaking in that same calm, soothing way he addressed all his patients, "Dulcie, honey-bunch sweetums, I sure would like to interduce my membrum virile betwixt yore nymphae."

"Where is my nimfy?" she inquired, but he had not taken enough veronal to give him the courage to say, let alone to point out.

Dr. Colvin Swain spent a few years palpating the breasts and manipulating the vaginas of many females, but always only in a professional manner that may or may not have gratified the patient but did nothing for his own biological urges. He was ever mindful of Kie's fourth precept, namely, never to seduce a patient, but Stay More, not to mention adjacent areas of Newton County, was teeming with females who weren't his patients. He was nineteen years old, and still a virgin, when he blurted to his father one day, "Dad, did you ever commit rape?"

Alonzo tried to recall. "Wal, I reckon it 'pends on how ye'd look at it. Who did you have in mind to do it with?"

"Anybody!" Colvin said. "It's either got to be a she-person or a sheep!"

"Son, you don't mean to tell me it's been *that* long since you done it last?"

"I aint never done it!"

When he had recovered from his shock, Alonzo Swain began to feel great pity for his son, and to realize it had been a mistake to have raised Colvin in the household of an old bachelor like Kie Raney who never had any women around the place. Forthwith, he arranged for Colvin to meet up with Della Sue Kimber, who lived with her sister Rosa up toward Parthenon. Both sisters had reputations, but it was Della who had not only put out for Alonzo on occasion but had done so in such a way that he knew poor Colvin wouldn't have to do the talking, or the gentling, or any kind of work whatsoever. "Just don't tell her you're my boy," Alonzo requested. "And I guarantee ye, you shore won't even need to think about raping her."

So Colvin went to see Della, who was maybe nine or ten years older than he was, but still right sightly and shapely for a woman of her years and experience. "You git yourself right in here and give me a big kiss!" she hollered, like he was her long-lost boyfriend, and she took him in and held him real tight and gave him such a kiss as would even revivify the jemmison of an old invalid like me, and for a young feller like him he had one on him that could've serviced a giraffe. It didn't need any excitation, but she put her hand right on it and commenced squeezing and rubbing, and said, "My, my, my, let's us have a little peek at thet thar whopping sockdolager!" and next thing he knew she was unbuckling his belt and taking down his pants, and hollering over her shoulder, "Rosa, there's enough for both of us!" In nothing flat all three of 'em was naked as jaybirds and they had Colvin spread out on the bed. "You kin go first. You're oldest," Della said to Rosa, but Della couldn't wait herself, and while Rosa commenced climbing atop that flagpole, Della went on kissing him and putting one of his hands onto her twitchet.

Colvin was admiring how white Rosa's legs were, but then just as she was about to lower herself atop his jemmison, it occurred to him that the whiteness of the legs might be caused by a clot in the outer veins of the thigh, or thrombophlebitis. He ought to get Rosa's legs elevated onto some pillows, paint them with some ichthyol, put a hot-water bottle over them, maybe even give her a shot of whiskey. "Pardon me, ma'am," he said in that maddeningly polite physician's voice of his, just at the instant he was about to lose his virginity, "but I'm afraid you might have phlebitis." Withdrawing his hand from Della's groin, he took a sniff of it and then a sharp glance at Della's twitchet, and declared, "And *you*, ma'am, it appears you may have caught yourself a case of trichomoniasis. Do you have any itching down there? Or a kind of greenish yeller discharge? It aint nothing too serious, like some of the poxes. Nothing to worry about, but it *is* catching, you know."

Colvin was able to clear up Della's disease in just two weeks with sitz baths and a vaginal application of gentian violet and vinegar. But Rosa's problem required six weeks of treatment, and he nearly lost her to a pulmonary embolism, since he lacked anticoagulants . . . but he never lost a case, and he stuck with it, although she had postphlebitic symptoms for quite some time thereafter, and didn't feel like joining her sister when the time finally came for them to pick up where they'd left off, or been interrupted, in that bed. Della tried to go it alone, but discovered that she somehow was not able to induce that "whopping sockdolager" that had equipped Colvin earlier on. She played with it and even put it in her mouth, but the only excuse Colvin could offer for its refusal to stand up and become useful was that he was possibly working too hard, although he privately surmised that he'd developed some kind of aversion to sticking it into a postvulvovaginitic orifice.

Alonzo Swain, learning of his son's continuing virginity, told Colvin that he ought to grow some upper lip hair in order to make himself more desirable to women. At twenty, Colvin still looked like a teenager. He was handsome. He was tall and dark. But he looked like a kid. All of the other men of Stay More, without exception, had full mustaches. It was the vogue of the day, perhaps inspired by the nation's current president, Teddy Roosevelt. Alonzo's own mustache covered his entire mouth and often got chewed up at mealtimes. And women could not resist him.

So Colvin obeyed his father, and gave up shaving. He tried to be a dutiful son. The two Swain doctors lived together in the house on Main Street, and they had to accommodate each other, as bachelors must. (Since Alonzo did not like Colvin's snake, Drakon, Colvin did not let Drakon have free run, or free slither, of the house, but kept him confined when Alonzo was around, and only took him out for walks, or slithers, at night.

In return, Alonzo agreed to stop using the unsterilized Prince as a scalpel, toenail cleaner, and stirrer of medicine.) Both Swain doctors belonged to the Ingledewville Lodge, No. 642, of the Free and Accepted Masonic Order, and they attended meetings together in a back room of the Ingledew store, and they studied their Masonic texts together, making of Masonry a religion in substitute for any other beliefs they lacked. Like so many physicians, they found it difficult to subscribe to the notion of a Supreme Being, although, as I'll have to tell you later on, Colvin did finally come to believe in God, in a way. At the age of twenty, however, all he believed in was the gods of medicine. And he believed in the goddesses of the Fair Sex, and kept on hoping to find one that he could do it with.

Alone of the Masons, alone of the men of Stay More, Colvin grew not just a mustache but a full beard, a thick, black, luxuriant, and somewhat curly beard, which indeed made him look like an older man, and a physician, and even a classical physician, or at least a classical American horse-and-buggy (though he did not yet have a buggy) doctor. And he became suddenly exciting to women.

It was Dulcie Duckworth herself, who had given him so much trouble in his efforts to tear off just a little piece, who seemed to be the first to notice his newly acquired virility, although she wasn't able to determine whether it emanated from his beard or from the snake she observed him playing with, one evening on the porch of the Swain clinic. "Oh, my," she said. "I shore have missed you, Col hon boy sugar. Oh my oh my. You better jist put down that there sarpint and take a little walk with me."

By coincidence that was the twenty-first anniversary of the night Alonzo had ripped him from his mother's womb in that fire. So Colvin lost his minority and his virginity at the same time. Neither is recoverable.

It never rains but it pours, as they say. Feast or famine. Almost as if to make up for all those years he'd done without, he now found himself with more women than he could handle. But just as a drought is often ended by an uncontrollable flood, Colvin's sexual drought was followed by an uncontrollable flood of his jism. Try as he might, he could not regulate it. It came fast and furiously without warning, as if it were happening to somebody else, not to him. From his lodge brethren in the Masonic Order, he received plenty of advice on the sundry ways to postpone the outpouring of the jism: you can review your financial accounts in your head, you can imagine trying to catch a fly ball during a game of baseball, you can pretend the woman beneath you is actually a revolting witch, you can try to make your mind a total blank, you can drink enough Chism's Dew to get yourself into a stupor, you can play with yourself beforehand until you shoot off, or you can try smearing any of a number of natural desensitizing substances on your pecker. Colvin tried all of these things, to no avail, and finally decided to ask the one lodge brother who was actually his father, but he chose to do it in a clinical manner. "Doctor, from your considerable experience, what method is best, during the act of coitus, for prolonging excitation in order to intermit the ejaculation?" Alonzo gave him a look as if he had asked what's the best way to fly to the moon, and then he said, "What in tarnation do ye need to do *thet* for?" To make the woman happy? Colvin suggested. Alonzo snorted. "Boy, if it takes a gal one minute to chew and swaller a nice big slice of apple pie, she aint gonna feel no better if it takes her fifteen minutes to do it."

Colvin was twenty-three before he learned how to take fifteen minutes instead of one. And that was with the help of an exceptionally intelligent girl named Piney Coe. It was not a nickname and had no allusion to pining or yearning; she was the youngest of seven sisters all named after trees; anyone pitying her name should have had more compassion for Hickory, Dogwoody, Redbuddy, Persimmony, Chinquapinny, and Sycamoria. They belonged to a very poor family living in hard circumstances on the far side of Ingledew Mountain, and all of them were victims of pellegra, hookworm, impetigo, and scrofula. All of them stank of the asafedtida the mother made them wear around their necks in futile treatment of their various afflictions. Piney was required to consult Doc Plowright (not being able to afford the doctors Swain) for shortness of breath and heart palpitations. Jack Plowright diagnosed an aneurysm, specifically a syphilitic aneurysm, although Piney did not have any of the other symptoms of syphilis nor did she have difficulty swallowing; on the contrary, she was ravenously hungry all the time and would eat anything. He told her that if the heart medicine he gave her didn't do any good, he might have to cut into her artery. This prospect scared her into crossing the road to seek a second opinion at the Swain clinic, where she critically examined the walls, noting the calendar from a Harrison feed store, the chromolithograph of *September Morn*, and an embroidery of the words "Patience is the best medicine." She asked of Colvin Swain, "Why do you charge twice as much as Doc Plowright if you don't have one of those certificates on the wall?" Colvin pleasantly and politely asked her what sort of certificate she meant. Piney described it: an impressively framed (behind glass) piece of paper which proclaimed that the St. Louis Royal Academy of Physicians and Surgeons had awarded to John Mabrey Plowright the degree of *Medicinae Doctor* and all rights and privileges pertaining thereto.

"Wal, I don't know about that piece of paper," Colvin said, "but I'll show ye why we charge twice't as much. Let me see the bottoms of yore feet." That was no problem because she, like all her family, wore no shoes. And he looked at her feet (whose soles were pimply) and then asked her about her appetite (ravenous) and her stools (black), and he said, "Doc Plowright ort to leastways have given ye some peach-leaf tea 'stead of that heart medicine, because the only thing wrong with yore heart is that its blood is gittin stolen away from it by a bunch of worms in yore duodenum. And if I caint cure ye, you don't owe me nothin." He gave her half an ounce of magnesium sulfate, a saline purge, and told her to come back at sunrise the next day without eating breakfast.

Then he crossed the road and told Jack Plowright he was a fool for scaring the daylights out of the poor girl and misdiagnosing her besides. "Did ye plan to cut open her chest to get at her aorta?" he demanded. "If you'd cut her open a foot lower down, you'd find a washpan full of hookworms." Colvin took the opportunity to examine the diploma on Plowright's wall. It was impressive, but Colvin had never heard of the St. Louis Royal Academy of Physicians and Surgeons, and he knew that "royal" was supposed to be reserved for things British. "Where'd you get this?" he wanted to know. Jack Plowright said he'd sent off to St. Louis twenty-five dollars in good cash money for it.

Piney Coe came again the next day just as the sun was rising over the top of Dinsmore Mountain, and it was a beautiful day, a lovely day, a most pleasant and fragrant day, and Colvin noticed she wasn't so bad-looking herself, in fact right admirable, hair as black as his own and a smile as if she knew and understood most of what was wrong with the world. "Tell me exactly what you're going to do," she requested, and he described the treatments as he administered them: two 15-grain capsules of thymol, which he had compounded himself from thyme growing in his herb garden, and he would repeat the dose in two hours, followed two hours after that with another dose of magnesium sulfate. Did she want something to read while she waited, or what? "Could we just talk?" she asked, "Or do you have a lot of other patients to see you?"

Colvin and Piney discovered that they got along just fine. In contrast to Dulcie and some other girls he could mention, she never ran out of things to talk with him about. In the course of the weeks it took him to eradicate every last worm and worm's egg from her duodenum, they became practically best friends, a marvelous circumstance because Colvin had never had a friend before, if you didn't count Drakon, who couldn't talk. It even got to the point where, one day when Piney asked, "Don't doctors themselves ever have any problems?" he broke down and confessed that indeed doctors are human beings like anybody else and they get sick and they have disorders and malfunctions and demons. "Tell me about *all* of yours," she requested, so he told her eventually about the evanescent aches or stiffness he felt in some of his finger joints upon awakening, a possible arthritis—which made her want to hold his hand; his labial frenulum was missing, the tiny band of skin that holds the upper lip to the gum, which made his upper lip rather too full—when he showed her, it made her want to kiss it, so she did, their first; and finally he told her blushingly about his difficulty in the act of sex, explaining that it was not technically *ejaculatio praecox,* which implies emission before penetration, but rather it had no precise medical term for it, the inability to hold back the ejaculation more than a couple of minutes after penetration. "Aren't you going to show me?" she requested.

One day, while he was showing her for a second or a third time, she stopped him during the process and said, "Let's just hold still for a little while," and she waited until he'd calmed down and stopped breathing so hard before starting up again, and then after a while more she said again, "Let's just hold still for another minute," and this went on, several times, until she said, "All right, just keep on going as long as you want," and he discovered that minute after minute flew by as he kept on a-going, all he wanted, for a right smart little spell, maybe twenty minutes all told, before he finally detonated like a keg of gunpowder.

By-and-by it got to where they were spending just about all their spare time together, and doctors don't have a whole lot of free time, or they oughtn't to, if they do. Colvin was beginning to have thoughts about having Piney around the house *all* the time, and that would sure have suited her.

Then the state of Arkansas passed something called the Turner Law, which said that you had to have a license to practice medicine and the only way you could get a license was to have a diploma. There was a "grandfather clause" in it, which said that if you'd already been practicing for twenty years or more, you were exempt from the new regulations, so Alonzo Swain wasn't affected by it.

But Colvin had to have a diploma. He asked Jack Plowright for the address of that St. Louis Royal Academy of Physicians and Surgeons, and he sent them his twenty-five dollars, which was a lot of money in those days. They wrote back to say that the rising costs of medical education had necessitated the elevation of the fee to fifty dollars. So he sent them another twenty-five of his hard-earned dollars, but they never answered.

He waited as long as he could stand it, getting madder and madder, and then he decided he'd better just run up there to St. Louis, wherever it was, and get his diploma or his money back, one.

Piney offered to feed Drakon while he was gone.

You can be sure this will be continued.

Four

After you left yesterday, Mary Celestia fussed at me a little bit for the way I'm telling this story. Oh, yes, you can bet she's listening in. Even when she appears to be nodding off. You'd think she'd be embarrassed by the bawdy elements of my story, but those are her favorite parts! Sometimes when I get into the short rows, as they used to say—that was an old Ozark allusion to the brief interval just preceding the orgasm, derived from plowing in odd-shaped fields, where the last few rows to be plowed are the shortest—in other words, the exact time when Piney knew to make Colvin stop and take a little rest—sometimes when I'm getting into the short rows of telling a story, I'll glance over at Mary and the woman is practically drooling! Unless it's just geriatric slobber, or whatever Colvin would have called it.

She tore into me, some, after you left, because of a couple

of things. One was, she wouldn't "buy" that Piney Coe was all that smart. Growing up in a dirt-poor ridge-runner's shack, Piney would've talked the same way as everybody else. Even Colvin, smart as he was, too smart sometimes for his own good, used incorrect grammar and tautological sentences and mangled syntax like any other Ozarker who's comfortable with that easy, folksy dialect. Hell, I aint always so proper myself. But Mary, she says there's no way on earth that Piney could've talked as much as she did without ever committing a single little mistake in the speaking—or misspeaking—of the King's English. "Vance," she says, "you can make her special without making her so all-fired perfect." All I could do was try to remind her that I'm just showing Piney Coe the exact same way that she was shown to me . . . and let me tell you, when I'd had enough of Mary's criticism, I closed my eyes to get shut of her and when I reopened them—did I tell you last time about this talent I've discovered I've got, or this magic, or this transcendence of mundane reality?—when I reopened my eyes, Mary was gone, and there on that bed sat Piney Coe, real as life and twice as natural! I kid you not, son. Even though I'd not ever seen her before myself, even though she's been dead for half a century, even though nobody ever showed me a photograph of her or anything, I knew it was her! That sable hair and those bottomless eyes and that cute little mouth that so often began a-beaming at some private knowledge of how funny and wondrous life is showing itself to be, and she was looking at me not as if I was this shrunken, wizened, bedridden old duffer but as if I still was the charming, presentable smoothie that I used to be. You have to believe it was the first time I'd ever seen her. And you have to believe it was love at first sight! But I knew that I could keep her there only as long as I could go without blinking my eyes, so I had to keep 'em open long enough to

106

hear whatever she had to say. Which was, in that sweet and proper voice that Mary'd just been criticizing me for giving her but which she honestly had, to ask me, practically to beg me, to let her become my heroine.

I commenced a-weeping, and it was hard to keep from blinking with tears in my eyes but I kept my eyes open long enough to tell her that I was awfully sorry she couldn't be the heroine, because that was just the way things was, I was only telling what had been told to me, I didn't have the power to let her and Doc Colvin U Swain live happily ever after. She got real sad herself then, and I knew I was going to have to blink my eyes or wipe 'em or both, and I had just enough time to say, "But Piney, child, I promise I'll try to keep ye as long as I can." Then I had to blink, and she smiled again one last time as if to leave me with the memory forever of that special smile, and she disappeared, and there was Mary again, just Mary.

So. Piney is keeping the home fires burning while Colvin gallivants off to St. Louis to see what he can see. When he went to St. Louis, that time, he might have stayed there. As I'm about to show you, he was *urged* to stay there. He could've become a prosperous St. Louis physician, or had a big-city practice elsewhere. But then of course we wouldn't have any story, would we?

The Ingledews prepared Colvin for St. Louis. Actually he knew roughly where it was located, up in eastern Missoury, and for several years now he'd been listening to people sing, "Meet me in St. Louis, Louie, meet me at the fair . . ." Most all of the Ingledews had gone to the Louisiana Purchase Exposition, or the St. Louis World's Fair as it was known, back in 1904, and they still remembered how many thousands upon thousands of people they'd seen, and they warned Colvin that the roads in St. Louis were filled with horse shit from all those strange conveyances called trolleys that carry all those thousands of people constantly to wherever they seemed to want to be going. Colvin discovered the Ingledews were wrong about the horse shit, or, rather, the horses had been replaced by electricity, which now powered the trolley cars. Colvin had never seen electricity before, and, of course, he didn't actually "see" it now, but he saw all of the things that were being operated on it, like streetcars and street lamps. In fact, Colvin had never seen a street before, which is a kind of tamed road, held hostage by cement sidewalks, a road which doesn't go anywhere but endlessly crisscrosses other streets at right angles. Beneath the street lamps of St. Louis were streetwalkers, one of whom offered herself to him for three dollars. He discovered more interesting and attractive specimens of life in the St. Louis Zoo, where a whole house was devoted to snakes, which both fascinated him and made him homesick for Drakon.

There were big buildings all over town called "hospitals," all of them named, like the city itself, after saints: St. Luke's, St. John's, St. Mary's. Of course Colvin knew what a hospital was, from reading his medical journals, but he could not imagine what one was like. Curious, he entered St. Matthew's and spent an hour wandering around, astonished to discover that all of the doctors were female and they were all dressed identically in striped dresses and little hats. And these lady doctors didn't seem to be curing anybody; they were just feeding 'em and changing their bedpans and their sheets, and trying to keep 'em comfy. All the patients looked sick. Colvin could tell just by looking at 'em what was wrong with most of 'em, but he didn't think it was his place to go around telling those lady doctors what ought to be done.

He assumed that the St. Louis Royal Academy of Physicians and Surgeons would be connected to one of these hospitals, if not right next door to it. But the address given him wasn't a big building at all. It was just a little shop on a side street, not much bigger than you'd find in Jasper, and the sign over the door said AJAX JOB PRINTING. Colvin figured he had the wrong address, but he went in anyway and told the feller, "I'm tryin to find the Royal Academy of Physicians and Surgeons." The feller gave Colvin a kind of shifty, beady look and asked him why he was trying to find it. Colvin said, "Wal, I ordered me a diploma but it never come." What was that name? the feller asked, and took his name, and wanted him to spell out what the "U" stood for, and Colvin had to explain it didn't stand for nothing, so then the feller went over to one of his tables and commenced collecting bits of type which he stuck into this printing press, cranked it up, and let her fly, and then he handed Colvin his diploma.

Despite whatever pride he felt in seeing his name in fancy lettering on a lavish piece of paper which awarded him the degree of *Medicinae Doctor,* Colvin was just a little disappointed. "Is this all I git for my fifty dollars? Seems like the least ye might do is ask me some questions to see if I know beans about medicine." Take it or leave it, the man said. So Colvin took it, hoping that it might satisfy the state of Arkansas as far as getting a license went.

But Colvin Swain, as I hope we have seen, was nobody's fool, and his good conscience bothered him. As long as he had gone to all that trouble to make a journey to St. Louis, he thought he would look into this whole matter of "medical education." So he went to the trouble to locate and to visit the city's actual institutions of medical training, the St. Louis University School of Medicine and the Missouri Medical College. Since the former was Catholic and the latter Protestant, he decided to enroll at the latter, not that he was Protestant, but he certainly wasn't Catholic, and besides, "college" was probably a better place than "school." But at the Missouri Medical College, the admissions officer was confused in his attempts to determine how and where to obtain Colvin's high school transcript, so Colvin was passed along to an assistant dean, who spent an hour trying to determine how Colvin expected to be admitted if he'd never been to school, and then passed him along to an associate dean, who received from Colvin a rather frank, extensive biographical sketch of his preceptor, Dr. Kie Raney, which he found most interesting but conceivably irrelevant. At the end of the day, Colvin found himself in the office of the dean, a very wise, kind, and learned gentleman, an M.D. himself, who did not snicker at Colvin, as his assistant and associate had done, but examined Colvin's diploma and took down the address of the Ajax Job Printing Company, declaring that he would love to see to it that the place was shut down. Then he asked, not with sarcasm as his assistant and associate had done but with genuine politeness and curiosity, "What do you know about medicine?"

"Ask me something," Colvin suggested.

The dean smiled benignly and started off with a few simple questions, like naming the bones of the chondrocranium of a human embryo and describing the functions of the lymphatics of the thorax, but he discovered these were child's play to Colvin, so he graduated to more complicated questions, such as microscopic identification of slides of *Coccidioides* and *Neisseria intracellularis,* but these too Colvin answered so quickly and effortlessly that the dean began asking him what he would prescribe for prolapsed rectum, hepatitis, and pancreatitis.

The dean began to hand instruments to him and to ask him what they were, and Colvin successfully identified various retractors, curettes, clamps, and forceps, as well as a vaginal speculum, an anal dilator, and a tonsil snare. Then the dean picked up an instrument which Colvin could not recognize, and his heart sank. It looked kind of like an anal dilator but was much too large for that purpose. Instead of handing the instrument to Colvin, however, the dean held it to his own mouth and said, "Henry, could you and Clarence drop whatever you're doing and come down? I have someone I'd like you to meet." Soon they were joined by two other fellers, whom the dean introduced to him as the professor of physiology and the professor of pharmacology. "Gentlemen, I've ordered supper sent up," the dean said. "This may take awhile."

It was nigh on to bedtime before the dean finally dismissed those other fellers. They were all worn out from thinking up questions, and Colvin was getting kind of tired of answering them. "There is one more ordeal I should like to submit you to," the dean said, "if you could return early in the morning and meet me at the hospital. And may I suggest that you trim your beard?" So Colvin came back the next morning after spending the better part of an hour snipping around at his beard and mustache. They gave him a white smock to wear and a brand new stethoscope. Two dozen other fellers in white smocks and stethoscopes joined them, and not a one of them was a lady doctor like he'd seen in that other hospital. This hospital did contain a lot of those women in their neat uniforms, but Colvin heard a doctor order one of them in a bossy way, "Nurse." Before long, Colvin had figured out that these women weren't really doctors but some kind of white slave. Although they were constantly commanded, "Nurse," not one of them was actually giving suck to the newborn.

The dean-doctor and the other couple dozen doctors took Colvin around to all of the beds on six different floors, and at each one of the beds the dean-doctor would look at him and say, "Well, Doctor?" and wait for Colvin to examine the sick person and say what ought to be done, and maybe even do it. In the course of a long day, Colvin U Swain drew out poisons, killed microbes, corrected deformities, made the lame walk, the blind see, the deaf hear. He come mighty nigh to resurrecting the dead, but the patient, who had an advanced brain tumor, was already clinically dead when Colvin got to him, and although Colvin restored heartbeat, breathing, and other lapsed functions, the patient remained alive only long enough to say, "No, thanks, Doc," before resuming final demise. Colvin was upset and apologetic, because he had never lost a patient before, but the dean-doctor explained that the patient had actually been dead for three days and they were simply curious to see if Colvin would concur in that diagnosis.

"You were wrong," the dean-doctor said, "but it's the only time you've been wrong so far." Then he took Colvin back to his office and gave him a cigar and some honest-to-God sippin whiskey and said, "Well, Dr. Swain, I am prepared to offer you a position on our faculty. Would you like to locate in St. Louis?" When Colvin hesitated, because he had never even given a thought to locating anywhere except maybe California in that long-ago idle fantasy, the dean said, "Of course, you could maintain your own practice in association with our hospital, and your teaching duties would not greatly distract you from your patients."

"But I don't even have a bony fide diploma," Colvin pointed out.

The dean laughed, but nervously. Then he coughed and said, "Let me see if I can't do something about that. Come back tomorrow." And when Colvin returned the next day, the good Dean presented him with an actual Missouri Medical College diploma made out of lamb hide, with *Medicinae Doctor* in gold letters, and a fancy red leather cover and all. It didn't even matter that they'd misspelled it "Calvin" and put a period wrongly after "U."

"Much obliged," the newly legitimate Doctor Swain said, "but last night I took me a walk down by your creek—what do you call it, the Miss'ippi?—I went down there and thought for a long time about your offer. That creek is too damn big and deep, just like this city. These here hospitals are too big and have too many people in 'em, and it's a sin to Moses the way you work them pore women that have to run the hospitals. But the roads—them streets out yonder—are filled with people walkin around who ought to be in the hospitals. I reckon I'd be a whole lot happier if I jist stayed put, in Stay More."

"This 'Stay More,'" the dean said wistfully, "it must certainly be a special place."

"It shorely is," Colvin said. "Come see us sometime."

When he got back home, Piney asked him, "How was St. Louis?"

"Porely," he said. And then he said, "Piney, darlin, what do you say me and you git hitched?"

"I say I'm game if you are," she laughed gaily. "Did you obtain your diploma?"

He showed her his diploma, and then he took it and made for it a frame out of spare boards from the corncrib and a windowpane from a back window where nobody would notice it missing, and he hung his diploma in his office and even invited Jack Plowright over to see it. "Mine aint printed on a animal skin, is the only difference I can see," Doc Plowright observed.

Alonzo Swain, who had been elected justice of the peace of Swains Creek Township for several years running now, officiated at the nuptials of his son and Piney Coe. The wedding was held under the shade of Stay More's lone pine tree, which towered over the intersection of Main Street and the Banty Creek Road, and it was attended by fifty-six Swains and forty-three Coes, plus an assortment of Duckworths, Whitters, Plowrights, Dinsmores, and even a bunch of Ingledews, including old Isaac, who played on his fiddle, accompanied by Doc Kie Raney on guitar, such things as "Black Is the Color of My True Love's Hair" and the wedding part of "Lohengrin." Drakon was permitted to attend, kept in his cage. The bride was radiant and beautiful all in a white dress and an armful of white flowers: Queen Anne's lace, common yarrow, fleabane, and hedge parsley. The groom stood up straight and tall and looked like he was mighty glad to be home, or mighty glad to be getting married, one, or maybe both.

Even if Colvin and Piney were not destined to live happily ever after together, they sure started off living happily enough to beat the band. And if I was you, if I had a smidgin of your talent for writing novel-books, I'd sure do one in which Piney is the *only* female, a heroine like she asked me to make her. I'd start off by reminding my readers that she was the seventh daughter in the family, just as her mother, Minnie Potts Coe, had been a seventh daughter. Now it's well known everywhere that the seventh son of a seventh son is foreordained to be a physician, even in spite of himself, and there was no way on earth that Colvin U Swain could have *not* been a doctor. But did you ever know what the seventh daughter of a seventh daughter is fated to be? Of course, like any other woman in that day and age she was fated to be a housewife, or a spinster, one or the other. She wouldn't have a career, like doctoring.

And I aint even going to say that the seventh daughter of a seventh daughter is ordained to be a doctor's wife. No, that's not it. What it is, is this. She is fated, or doomed, however you look at it, never to be told anything. I mean, you can't tell 'em *nothing!* They already know it all. Before, we've had a notion of Piney's fate through the way she talked, as if she knew exactly the way the language ought to be spoken, and wouldn't hear of any other way. Now a woman like that, if Colvin told her the house was a-burning down and it actually was, she'd say, "You are mistaken." Or if he tried to point out that the sun rises in the east and sets in the west, she'd say, "That is not the case at all."

Their house never burnt down (Alonzo moved in with the Widow Kimber and left the house on Main Street to the newlyweds, although he kept his office next to Colvin's in the front), and the sun just went on rising and setting the way it always had, but Colvin and Piney had some problems. You'd think they might have sort of complemented each other: since he knew everything there was to be known about medicine, she knew everything there was to be known about everything else. Whenever somebody died and they sang that funeral hymn "Farther along we'll know all about it, farther along we'll understand why," it didn't apply to Piney, because she already knew all about it; she already understood why everything was. Between them, Colvin and Piney were totally omniscient. But Colvin was too strong-willed and opinionated to allow some woman, even his beloved Piney, to get the upper hand. They argued. If Colvin tried to point out that the Republican Party had always been the traditional party of the people of Stay More, all the way back to the Civil War, and was therefore the *right* party, Piney (and in those days women weren't even supposed to *care* about politics) would likely come back at him with the information that the Democratic Party was the only *just* and *valid* party, and that Woodrow Wilson was the only person who could keep us out of another war. Never mind that she might be proved wrong; never mind that Wilson didn't keep us out of the next war; never mind, goddamn it, that the Republicans are right, or wrong, just as often as the Democrats are. If Piney said the Democrats were *the* party, then they were. There were no ifs, ands, or buts to Piney. She knew everything.

The seventh daughter of a seventh daughter can tell you what beliefs are "true" and which are just superstitions, and not just about the Republican Party. Piney could tell you that it's just an old notion that if you find a pin in the road and pick it up, it'll bring you good luck, but she could prove that it's true that if you find a pin in the road and don't pick it up, it'll bring you bad luck all day long. She'd also let you know that it isn't true that singing at the table will bring misfortune on the whole family, but it's certainly demonstrable that if you sing before breakfast, you'll cry before supper. She was an expert on beliefs having to do with marital relations: she knew in her bones that it's true that two persons using the same towel at the same time are sure to quarrel, but it's only a superstition that you can "take the cuss off'n it" by twisting the towel between the two of you. If Colvin was helping her do the dishes, as he often happily did, and they accidentally dried the dishes or their hands on the same towel, there was nothing for them to do but go ahead and wait until some bone of contention came along and then have a real bad quarrel over it and get it out of their system. And usually the quarrel was over something she *knew* she knew, and he had the temerity to challenge her belief.

But as often as not, Colvin for the sake of harmony would let her have her way, or concede she was right. She was a real good cook, and if she insisted that fish had to be baked although he liked his fried, he didn't raise any objection. If he liked his sweet potatoes mashed but she kept them in the skins, that wasn't the end of the world, as far as he cared. Even when it came to okra, which he'd always had sliced and fried in corn-meal, he wasn't going to raise a fuss if she served 'em whole and slimy. When Piney started in to redecorating his office, putting up curtains and moving things around, he never even protested that he couldn't find anything anymore. When she ordered from Sears Roebuck a fancy dark gray cheviot suit of wool for him to wear, he protested that there wasn't another man in Newton County who had long *tails* on his coat. Piney just smiled and said there wasn't another man in Newton County like him, period. But when she tried to get him to wear this new felt hat she'd ordered with it, a kind of homburg to replace his old floppy fedora, and he couldn't persuade her that he didn't want to look *that* genteel and swellish, all he could do was try a bit of psychology: the dent in the crown of the hat, he pointed out to her, was like an advertisement (she would have understood "symbol" better) for the dent in the crown of his penis, and he even yanked out his tool to show her the exact same resemblance, saying, "Now damned if you want me to be Old Peckerhead, do ye?" Piney just replied, "As long as men are going to personate their peckers anyway, by having *heads,* what does it matter whether you personate it with the dent in your hat or the part in your hair?"

And speaking of matters sexual, we may as well reveal that as often as not, Piney *knew* that the best place for the female in the process of coitus was woman-on-top. This was not be-cause she wanted to dominate, or prove her obvious superiority, but because in her absolute certainty about everything, she *knew* that this position allowed both of them more control over the hiking to climax: she could let go, he could hold back. True? But it worried Colvin somewhat; man is, after all, a depositor, while woman is a receptacle. Man stashes; woman seals. He argued that gravity alone should be the determinant, and he tried to win the argument with his medical knowledge: "Sperm can swim upwards, but semen can only flow downwards."

"Do you want to have fun," she asked, "or do you want to have a baby?" Dr. and Mrs. Swain had a lot of fun, and, knowing everything, she let him go on believing that all the ways they did it, every time they did it, they were just dead-level set on having the time of their lives, when in fact she had decided to have a baby. She never asked him if they could. She never discussed raising a family with him. They never talked about times of the month or taking precautions. As far as Colvin was concerned, there ceased to be any connection between what they were doing and the existence of sperm and ova. Piney not only continued to believe that a woman can regulate and control the steady rising to climax in both herself and her partner, but can also control her conception and her contraception, and when she was ready, she conceived. She knew the exact moment, the exact instant, that one of those upward-swimming spermies, an audacious little scamp she'd already given a name, met up with her ripe fat lucious egg and said, "Howdy sweetheart, let's cuddle up and multiply!"

She didn't tell Colvin. She *knew* that the sex of the fetus was male, and she *knew* that the baby would be named after her father, McKay Coe, and the boy would be called Mackey Swain, and she *knew* that "Mac" means "son of" in Scotch-Irish, and that Mackey means virile or manly in Irish, and she *knew* that Mackey Swain would grow up to become a virile doctor like his father, and she *knew* that Colonel McKay Swain would serve with great distinction as a surgeon in some future national war, and that great stories would be told about his heroism on the battlefield, where, however, he would be mortally wounded.

"How come you're a-weepin, darlin?" Colvin asked her one day, when she was thinking about Mackey's tragic death, for indeed it was the first time Colvin had ever known her to cry. People who know everything do not cry. Crying is the result usually of not understanding something, of being unable to deal emotionally with a situation because it is not understood, and if you know everything you have no reason to cry. Piney was terribly embarrassed over her tears, which were not necessarily the result of a mother's inability to grasp the reason why her beloved son will have been taken from her prematurely, because she fully *knew* that in order to serve his country and his fellow man as he will have had to do, Colonel Mackey Swain will have had to be willing to give up his own life, which he will have done, so it will not have been his death, nor the absolute foreknowledge of it, that made her cry, but rather the sudden fear, the overwhelming fear, that when the moment will have finally come that she will have been informed by telegram of her son's death, she will lose control. And she had never lost control. In response to her husband's question, she could only shake her head, wordlessly, and continue shaking it until he grew bored and left the room.

But Colvin's magical physician's fingers detected, in only the second month of her pregnancy, that she was with child, and he was as happy as he was mystified that she had not told him nor asked for his knowing collaboration in the happy event. When he confronted her with his findings, she confessed that she had known the exact moment of the conception, and that she had already named the child McKay "Mackey" Swain, and that she had been secretly sewing the layette ever since. She knew that the boy would be a brunette, that he would have a slight left clubfoot, that he would speak his first word at the age of eight months and take his first step at the age of eleven months, and that he would be toilet trained before his second birthday. She knew he would marry a Dinsmore at the age of eighteen. She knew everything about him, and she was happy to have the chance, now that she had confessed his conception, to tell Colvin everything that she knew about Mackey's entire life and heroic death.

Piney made such a project out of Mackey that Colvin was forced to get himself a dog. This was Galen the First, although of course Colvin didn't call him that, because he didn't realize that the dog would be only the first of many, many dogs to whom he would give that name. He just called him Galen, after the ancient Greek physician, whom Colvin admired because he'd founded experimental physiology, and Colvin owned and read with pleasure his *Corpus Medicorum Graecorum,* and considered himself in many ways a Galenist. Galen was just an ordinary bluetick hound dog, scrawny and gangling and smelly, but he was devoted to Colvin in ways that Piney was not (although it is hard to imagine anything deeper than her devotion to him), and Galen went everywhere with Colvin, on every house call he made. I would like to discount as mythical the stories I heard that Galen sometimes licked the wounds of injured persons and thereby effected the healing. Surely that is stretching the blanket! If one is a collector of folk narratives, or "oral history" as they're calling it these days, one learns to distinguish between the colorful, extravagant, but factual retellings of remembered events, and the embellished reshapings or reimaginings of "reality" which sacrifice truth for the sake of charm. Lord knows, Colvin's entire story is shot full of the latter, but I think I'm doing a good job of not foisting upon

120

you anything incredible or inconceivable, and that is because I'm editing the story as it came to me, and I must exercise the editor's prerogative to stand up and say, No! it is not likely that Colvin permitted Galen to lick anybody's wounds! Why, there's not any more truth to *that* than there is to the story of Sukie Ledbetter, who claimed that Colvin cured her of her "barrenness" by permitting her to have intercourse with Drakon!

Where was I? Yes: Piney was so absorbed with that little Mackey in her womb that Colvin needed a dog to keep him company. Piney might have known everything, but she didn't perhaps know that the reason Colvin and his dog were gone from the house so much was to escape from her constant recital of the life story of Mackey Swain. This was the period when Colvin became involved in the story of Nail Chism, the Stay More shepherd who was convicted of raping young Dorinda Whitter and sentenced to the electric chair in Little Rock . . . which is a story you'd admire to put into a novel at some future time, before or after this one. Remind me to tell you how Colvin helped hide Nail when he escaped from the prison, and how Nail used to could hear the trees singing, and all.

Well, I wish I could also suggest for one of your future novels the World War II story of the heroism of Colonel McKay Swain, but the sad truth is that Mackey Swain was stillborn. Piney may have known everything, but she was wrong about that. When she started gaining a lot of weight, she *knew* that pregnant women were supposed to do that, and not even Colvin realized that she was gaining a lot more weight than pregnant women usually do, and when she had some terrible headaches she *knew* that pregnant women are supposed to get headaches. But one day she discovered that everything was growing dim to her sight, and there were spots before her eyes, and she began violently throwing up, and she *knew* that these things

121

weren't supposed to be happening. Colvin wasn't home or in his office. Just the week before, old Alonzo Swain, seventy-eight, had taken down his shingle, turned the office over to his son, and retired, for good, and was spending his days in the Widow Kimber's bed, so he was not available in this emergency. Piney waited for as long as she could stand it, hoping Colvin would return to the office. Waiting, she began taking her own pulse, which was very rapid, and she was growing drowsy and dizzy and blind. Finally, she decided that she'd just better try to get across the road to Doc Plowright's. She could hardly stand up and felt she would faint, and she was so dizzy she had to get down on all fours and crawl, out onto the porch, down the steps, across the dirt road into Doc Plowright's yard, and up his steps. Piney, knowing everything, *knew* that there isn't any such thing as "God," but she prayed, anyway, prayed that Doc Plowright would be home. From what we know of Jack Plowright, she ought to have had the sense to have prayed that he would *not* be home. He was home, though, and he helped her onto his examining table and asked her a bunch of questions in an effort to find out where she hurt and what was a-troubling her. But there was nothing he could do because he had no idea what diagnosis to make.

Fortunately, Colvin came home, having been out on a call setting a broken leg, and after noticing that his wife wasn't anywhere around the premises, and that Galen was acting kind of peculiar, he asked Galen, "Whar's Piney?" and Galen did two or three complete turns and then headed across the road to Doc Plowright's, and Colvin had the sense to follow him.

"I jist don't rightly know what the trouble is," Doc Plowright confessed to his colleague. "Aint it too early for her to be a-birthing?" By this time, Piney had begun to flail. That is, she was thrashing her arms and her legs wildly, and it took both men to hold her down to keep her from breaking a bone, and Colvin had to put a spoon wrapped in cloth into her mouth to keep her from biting her tongue. Colvin took her blood pressure, which was way up, and he tested her urine for albumin, which was present. He shook his head sadly and told his colleague that his wife was having eclampsia. "Ee-which?" Doc Plowright asked. Colvin explained "eclampsia" was from a Greek word meaning "I explode."

Piney was exploding. Her convulsions kept both doctors busy for the next several hours, and Colvin was mighty glad to have the help of Doc Plowright, even if the man didn't know the difference between eclampsia and eczema. Colvin injected Piney with magnesium sulfate to control the fits and gave her both morphine and chloral as sedatives, and he kept a close watch to see if the seizures would induce premature labor. Piney went rigid and lost consciousness. She twitched in her face and limbs in such a way as to make Doc Plowright ask, "She aint a-dying, is she?" Not yet, Colvin said.

All night they stayed with her. When Colvin could no longer detect the fetal heartbeat, he decided to induce labor. He saved the mother, but lost the child. Outside, Galen began to howl like a wolf. Across the road, Drakon escaped from his cage and tried to slither his way to the Plowright place, but was run over by an automobile, a Phantom Phaeton, and died, age twenty-one. Colvin discovered his corpse when he was carrying Piney home in his arms. He kept Piney in a darkened room of their house for several days. He buried the stillborn infant and the squashed snake in the Stay More cemetery and attempted to conduct a simple ceremony for each. He decided not to say anything to Piney about the loss unless Piney asked. He did not understand that Piney did not need to ask, because she knew. He was puzzled that she never even wanted to know if the baby had been a boy (it had), or that she never asked what the matter had been, so that he could have explained eclampsia to her. He began to have problems communicating with her; for example, if he asked her what she wanted for breakfast, she would likely respond, "I just don't know." If he inquired how she was feeling, she might answer, "Land knows," without explaining who or what Land was. If he became specific with something like, Does your stomach hurt? she would more than likely reply, "It beats me," leaving him to puzzle out whether she was trying to explain that her stomach was beating her. Once he asked her, *Where* do you ache? but she only told him, "Search me," and he searched her pretty thoroughly without being able to determine if anything was dysfunctional that would cause her any pain.

He began to notice that she no longer was so all-fired stubborn in her opinions about everything, and he gently inquired, "Do ye reckon maybe you don't know as much as you thought you knew?"

To which she could only reply, "You've got me." Yes, he had her, and she was all he needed to have (there had been moments during her coma when he feared he'd lost her forever), but what was he going to do with her?

In the fullness of time, when she seemed to be pretty much back to normal, he noticed subtle changes. She began to fry fish instead of bake them, skin the sweet potatoes and mash them up, and even to fry the okra in cornmeal. And the very first time after her confinement that they were permitted to have intercourse again, she lay back down beneath him instead of clambering atop him, and the novelty alone of the position made him shoot off too soon, but she didn't seem to mind. She just waited an hour and wanted to do it again. And then again after another couple of hours. And yet twice more in the wee

124

hours. At dawn, when he was called out to tend a patient, he could hardly walk. But as soon as they'd had supper the next night, she yanked him off to bed again. In no time at all, after several nights of this, he had nothing left to deposit, he was plumb dry, but she kept on coming, sometimes before they got out of bed in the morning, sometimes during his noon dinner hour, and oftentimes on the table in his office whenever she could catch him without a patient. He developed blisters on his penis, and eventually a bend in it. Finally he decided to try satisfying her with other devices: his fingers, or even his mouth, but when he attempted this, she protested, "I want your thing in me! I want you to fill me up with your seedjuice!" He tried to explain that he was totally drained of seedjuice, that there was no way his system could manufacture enough of the stuff to keep up with her desires. She thought about that, and, although she no longer seemed to know everything, she understood that in order to be filled up with seedjuice she would just have to abstain from sex for a while, particularly during the days preceding her ovulation. Having made a habit of coitus a dozen times a day, it was difficult for her to taper off the habit, but she took up quilt making as a substitute and managed to go for days at a time without even thinking about seedjuice.

But each month, regular as the calendar, for the whole length of the calendar's year, and more, she let Colvin go without any sex for an entire week in the middle of the month, and then, when she *knew,* as she sometimes still knew some things, that she was ovulating, and that Colvin's system had replenished its store of seedjuice, she'd drain him dry with a succession of acts at all times of day and night.

This went on for another year before she finally had to admit to herself that she did not know everything, and therefore she was forced to ask Colvin a question. It was one of the few times that she ever asked him a question. "Why am I not getting pregnant?"

Gently he tried to tell her that while he wasn't one hundred percent certain (he was the first to admit that in medicine there is never, ever anything like one-hundred-percent certainty), it was quite possible that the eclampsia had left some permanent damage to her interior organs of reproduction.

Secretly Piney had been planning the life and career of her second son, Potts Swain (named after her mother's family, the Potts). Although she could not be certain that she *knew* this, she *thought,* or at least *hoped* that Potts, like his late lamented brother, Mackey, would follow in his father's footsteps as a physician. Maybe Potts wouldn't be a heroic army surgeon in some future war, but he'd be a good doctor, she knew. No, not *knew,* but *thought,* or *hoped.* Now she found it hard to believe, no, impossible to accept, that poor Potts couldn't even get his medical diploma because the eclampsia had ruptured her reproductive system. Not sure any longer that she knew anything, she *wondered* if perhaps making Potts into a gynecologist, and a famous one, might make it possible for her to *hope,* if not to *know,* that her gynecological apparatus could be repaired so that Potts could be born.

Brooding on this puzzle, Piney isolated herself with her quilt making. She gave up sex entirely. Like the consumption of alcoholic beverages, quilt making is something that ought not be done in private; as long as drinking and quilt making are social activities indulged in the company of one's friends and kindred, they are relatively harmless, but once you start drinking or quilting in private you are in a trouble. Colvin missed Piney. It was almost like finding himself without a mirror to look into and see his own image, because in so many ways Colvin and Piney were mirrors of each other. Not physically, although her hair was the same black as his and there were enough other similarities that they could have passed for twins. Not even emotionally, although being seventh son of a seventh son and seventh daughter of a seventh daughter gave them depths of temperamental kinship that transcended whatever "magic" powers they had acquired (and perhaps lost) from such a lineage. But probably mentally, because they remained each other's best friend, and would always be, even when Piney withdrew so deeply into solitary quilt making and into her sadness over her infertility that she no longer talked to him or to anybody.

The years passed. Although America belatedly joined the world's first great war, only two Stay Morons volunteered to become soldiers, as you have noted. Another great event of that time affected the town more than the war, and that was the outbreak of Spanish influenza, which presented Colvin with the first disease for which he could not prescribe a cure, because there was none. I myself as a young infantryman stationed at Camp Pike in North Little Rock had a bout with the flu, which later became an epidemic killing dozens of soldiers there. Nationwide, 548,000 victims of influenza died that year. Of those, only one was a patient of Doc Swain, but that was too much for Colvin, who had never lost a patient before. He ought to have been consoled by the survival of the 189 folks that he treated successfully for the flu, doing whatever was necessary to help them get over it. He'd given up his saddle horse in favor of a horse-drawn buggy, and his horse, Nessus, always knew the way home, so that after Colvin had been out all night tending the flu victims, he could go to sleep in the buggy and Nessus would take him home. Even Doc Plowright too was exhausted from treating, or trying to treat, the flu. It ought to have consoled Colvin that Jack lost six or seven of his patients, to

Colvin's one, but that one haunted his sleep and gave him bad dreams, in which he kept trying to resurrect the dead man. Never mind that the man was old Willis Dinsmore, who wasn't so far off from dying of natural old age anyhow. Colvin began to have dreams in which he tried something different on Willis and saved him. Before long, he was "visiting" more flu victims in his dreams than he was in his buggy, and the funny thing was, the ones that he visited in his dreams got well! At least, more of 'em did than the ones he visited in his buggy.

There were two things Colvin couldn't admit to Piney. One was that he had a touch of the flu himself. The other was that he was going around in his dreams curing people. The first was no problem: he just stayed away from Piney until his own contagion could no longer infect her. But the second was a big problem, because they had always shared their dreams, and Colvin couldn't admit to her that he was going around curing all of these sick people in his dreams. Knowing everything, she knew he was up to something. She asked him where he'd been in his dreams, and he had to make up lies: he'd just taken a trip to Harrison, or he'd gone off fishing or whatever. Finally she accused him, "You're seeing a girlfriend, aren't you?"

Like all healthy, normal, even happily married men, he sometimes dreamt of women he wasn't married to, but he wouldn't admit this to Piney. As a matter of fact, he was visiting a patient in his dreams who was both a friend and a girl, a second cousin of his named Lorraine Swain, who was a dizzying redhead. In his dreams she came down with an awful case of the flu, and he was trying everything he knew to help her.

One day he happened across the girl's mother, who was his own cousin, and just out of curiosity he asked her how Lorraine was, and the mother replied that Lorraine had had a real bad case of the flu but seemed to be completely over it now.

Weeks passed, and Lorraine came to him one day, saying, "Doc, you shore fixed me up jist fine when ye came in my dreams. But now I've got something else, and ever time I try to see ye in my dreams you're out on a call."

Apparently as a consequence of the flu, or even a slight pneumonia accompanying it, Lorraine had developed empyema, which is where an accumulation of pus builds up in the pleura, the lung coverings. Abscess is what it is, and Colvin had to spend a lot of time with her, treating her with various measures to avoid having to operate, which is often necessary to drain the cavity.

Colvin found that his daytime, "real," unasleep treatment of Lorraine was not as effective as his nighttime, dreaming treatment of her, so he continued the latter to the point where, one night, Piney woke him up and accused him of being with another woman, and he simply tried to explain that he was treating a patient, Lorraine Swain. He was abashed because he'd actually had normal, healthy fantasies of getting into bed with Lorraine, but he had refrained from doing it, even in his dream. "For Godsakes, Piney," he complained, "I'm jist a-doing my duty as her doctor!" Haven't you been holding her hand? Piney asked, feeling the return of her old omniscience. Colvin blushed and had to admit that he had been holding Lorraine's hand in the dream, not just for her comfort but to check her circulation and nerves. Haven't you been feeling of her breasts? Piney asked, surprised and pleased to discover that now she *knew* what he had been doing. Colvin did an inadequate job of explaining that it was necessary to palpate her bosom in order to examine the state of her thorax. Haven't you kissed her a time? Piney wanted to know, *knowing* as well as if she could see them doing it. Poor Colvin was really clumsy in his attempt to explain that he was trying to determine if the pus was odorless or infected and had put his nostrils right up against her nostrils in order to smell her breathing.

"You had better just keep that girl out of your dreams, you hear me?" Piney told him. And just to be sure that he had stopped seeing Lorraine in his dreams, each morning she would ask him if he'd dreamt of her. Now you may wonder if it was unethical for a doctor to be so henpecked by his wife that he'd neglect one of his patients even in his dreams, and the truth was that Colvin had discovered he was doing something he'd never have suspected himself of doing: lying to Piney. He was *still* seeing Lorraine every night in his dreams, but only to treat her condition.

Before he knew it, Lorraine was up and around and just as good as she ever was. One day, he was riding his horse up the road to see another patient when he came across Lorraine picking blackberries along the road, and he figured it wouldn't be violating any of Piney's restrictions if he just stopped and passed the time of day with her for a minute or two. In the course of their talk, Colvin learned that not only had he visited her every time she'd gone to sleep and dreamt, for a week or more, but in her dreams he'd told her what to take, and—get this—he'd even "opened her up" in her dream and removed a portion of her rib in order to drain the pus from the cavity and had injected some medicine into the cavity as well as into her chest muscle.

"Hold on, gal!" Colvin exclaimed, astonished because the treatment she was describing was exactly what he dreamt he had done. But how do you operate in a dream? "Show me where ye claim I cut ye open." And right there in the road Lorraine unbuttoned her shirt to show him the incision. Bertha Kimber happened to be coming down the road at that moment, and word got back to Piney that Lorraine Swain had popped one of her boobs into Colvin's face right in the road in broad daylight, and there was hell to pay when Piney got onto Colvin about *that*.

But the worst thing was, Lorraine Swain had told her best friend, Ella Jean Plowright, about how she had been cured in her sleep by dreams of Colvin Swain, and Ella Jean, who had been visiting her uncle, Doc Jack Plowright, for treatment of her nausea and vomiting, decided to give it a try herself, and sure enough, she went to sleep and had a dream where Colvin Swain appeared and assured her that her nausea was not morning sickness, as Doc Plowright had diagnosed it (a faulty diagnosis in view of the fact that Ella Jean was still a virgin) but was actually uremia, not nephritic but treatable by an injection which he gave her; the pain of the injection woke her from her dream, but within a few hours the vomiting had stopped, her appetite returned, and she was well enough to visit Lorraine and compare notes on how nice Doctor Swain had treated them in their sleep. Naturally, they couldn't keep it to themselves, either, and before long everybody in Stay More knew about it, and ailing folks were going to sleep right and left in order to have dreams of Doc Swain.

Yesterday I asked your friend and mine, Bob Besom, who works over in the Special Collections department at the University Library, to look into the Swain papers and check on this matter for me. You know that they've got over there nine ledgers that Doc Swain kept during his years of practice, including several "calendar diaries." According to Besom, there's nothing of particular interest in this material, mostly just accounts of charges made and collected, accounts receivable but never received, et cetera, but Colvin did have the habit of jotting down all of his visits to patients with a notation of what he used to treat them, and the record is fairly complete. There's even the record of how he treated me for typhoid that summer I was confined in Stay More for a few weeks. No commentary. He doesn't say whether he liked me or not, or how we became friends. Just what medicines he used and that the treatment was successful and I got well . . . and, under "Amount due": *N.C.*

But that was in Ledger #6, years later, and we're concerned right now with Ledger #2, and Bob Besom was good enough to make photocopies of a few pages in that ledger for me, if you'll hand me my reading spectacles from the table there.

> *June 3* Lorraine Swain Empyema following influenza. Clear yellow serous fluid. Tea of butterfly weed t.i.d. Dover's powder for pain.
>
> *June 9* Lorraine Swain Fluid thickening. Irrigated cavity with hypochlorite. May try injection of gentian violet.
>
> *June 17* Lorraine Swain Ambulatory, robust, and claims I treated her in dreams (!) including surgery for drainage (!!) but section of 6th rib actually missing (!!!). ???

According to Besom, there are no further entries in the ledger on Lorraine Swain's condition, but there is this:

> *June 30* Ella Jean Plowright, not my patient. Hardly know her, but had dream last night of treating her for uremia with injection, etc. Lorraine Swain confirms this is true.
>
> *July 3* Complaint from Dr. Plowright that I had "stolen" his patient and niece, Ella Jean. Swore to Jack I never touched her, nor spoke to her. "Don't matter," he said. "You cured her of uremia."

Besom says there's only one more entry, three months later, that is relevant to the matter:

> *October 4*   Haven't had an awake patient in over a
> month.

By "awake," we may suppose that Colvin Swain meant exactly that: all of his patients were now visiting him in their dreams. All over Stay More, and even in Stay More's "suburbs," sick people were attempting to see if they couldn't follow the examples of Lorraine and Ella Jean, and they were finding that it was easy, and they were rapidly converting skeptics by showing their evidence: a man proudly exhibited an enormous tapeworm which he claimed Doc Swain had extracted from him during his dreams; a woman showed a set of false teeth which she had swallowed and Doc Swain had extracted from her stomach in a painless dream surgery; several proud mothers displayed babies which Doc Swain had delivered while they were asleep and dreaming. There was even a case of a "vicarious incubation": a girl who was too embarrassed over her "female trouble" to permit Doc Swain to visit her in her dreams was persuaded by her mother to allow the mother to have the dream for her, and the mother dreamt that Doc Swain had come and corrected the girl's prolapsed uterus, and indeed the girl, who had been unable to walk because the womb had been protruding from her vagina, was now blissfully hopping, skipping, and jumping.

She was the most conspicuous advertisement for the Swain Dream Clinic, which nearly everyone was now patronizing. You didn't need an appointment. You didn't need to send somebody out in the middle of the night to fetch the doctor to your house. The Doctor Swain they met in dreams was if anything even nicer, gentler, more polite and easygoing than the "real" Doc

Swain. And if the "real" Doc Swain could never be "a hunerd-percent certain" about anything, the Doc Swain who came in dreams was infallible and omnipotent.

Best of all, you didn't have to pay! Not even in the barter of produce or livestock. But while that was considered a tremendous advantage from the patient's point of view, it was not putting any food on Doc's table. In fact, he was nearly broke. He had some savings, which he had deposited in a savings account in the Swains Creek Bank and Trust Company, the small financial institution that John Ingledew had erected on Main Street, and he hated to dip into his savings, but unless he could find some wakeful patients to treat, he was going to have to make a withdrawal. Poor Jack Plowright had already gone out of business and been forced to retire prematurely, after losing a court case in which he had unsuccessfully attempted to have his attorney, Jim Tom Duckworth, sue Dr. Swain for monopolizing the medical practice of Stay More. Colvin had had to go to Jasper for the trial and had testified that there wasn't any way he could be monopolizing the medical practice, because he hadn't had any patients himself lately, and he could prove it.

Then, as you well know, and have already told about in your *Lightning Bug* and elsewhere, the bank was robbed. A young Stay More man, son of Billy Dill the wagon maker, lover of Latha Bourne if not loved by her, came and raped her and robbed that bank and started one of the best stories that ever came out of the town, leaving Latha pregnant. There is no doubt in anybody's mind that Doc Swain would have gladly visited her in her dreams and performed an abortion, because even though the "real" Doc Swain had taken an oath never to perform an abortion, the Doc Swain of dreams wouldn't have let himself be stopped by such scruples or oaths. But she wouldn't visit the Swain Dream Clinic; for whatever reasons of her own, she went off to Little Rock to live with her sister and have the baby. Never mind about that, for now. Her rapist robbed the bank, and Doc Swain was penniless.

So we have here two good reasons why Colvin was forced to accept the job that he took, which brings us to the real heart of our story. Come back tomorrow and I'll take you on a tour of the "college" in Parthenon where Colvin Swain became medical consultant.

Five

How long have you been a-sitting there? How long have my eyes been closed? I closed my eyes to get a glimpse of Tenny, the gal who's the real heroine of this story, although we haven't laid eyes on her yet. How many times have you been here so far? I'm not keeping count, but I'm a little dismayed to realize that I've talked so much, and told you all that I have, but I still haven't really done nothing but a kind of prologue. Today we'll meet Tenny, if all goes well. We've waited so long. But so far, so good? How'm I doing?

I see you've got there a fresh bottle of Chivas Regal to lubricate my larnyx. That's real thoughtful of ye. We've run out of Gershon Legman's contribution. I've been meaning to ask why you only come in the afternoons or the evenings, never in the mornings, but I reckon it's because you're up late of a night, drinking and thinking, and you tend to sleep late of a morning.

That's what I was doing at Stay More, and Doc Swain was going to try to cure me of it, as we'll see. Anyhow, if you'd been here this morning, you wouldn't have missed the little excitement we had. There's precious little to keep us from getting bored to death, but this morning one of our fellow residents got raped. You know how you read in the papers sometimes there's a certain kind of punk kid who only lusts after old ladies? Well, there was a young feller working here, one of the orderlies, who fit in that category, and I could tell because of the way he was always buttering up to poor Mary C. You know that old woman I was telling you about, lived a few doors down the hall, who was always yelling, "Tell me another'n, Grampaw"? Maybe you never heard her, but she was always out there with her little-bitty voice like a child begging for another bedtime story . . . or, come to think of it, maybe that wasn't what she was doing. Maybe there was a kind of edge to her voice, maybe a touch of sarcasm, as if she was accusing her invisible grandfather of having lied to her. It troubles me, come to think of it. I don't take nothing personal from it, hell, she didn't even know I was here. But anyway that punk orderly crope under the covers with her early this morning, and it turned out she knows other words besides "Tell me another'n, Grampaw." She knows "help" and she knows "rape," and she knows "Will somebody please come and git this thing offen me?" It woke me up. I recognized the voice and wondered why the voice was not begging to be told another one. I nearly tried to get myself into my wheelchair so I could go out there and see what was happening. But I guess the nurse on duty had got to them, and she stopped it and called the police, and they come and got the feller, and then Dr. Bittner came and examined the old lady and sent her off to the hospital. The reason Mary C. is just a-sitting

138

there looking stunned is probably because she's thinking it could've happened to her. And it could've.

So there will be one less voice in the chorus of those dotards out there. Maybe it will even inspire me, as we approach the real thickening of the watery plot of our story. Son, this is where it commences to get exciting.

It may have been toward the end of my second week in Stay More—I wasn't paying a bit of attention to the calendar—when one morning Colvin came into my room and took my temperature and blood pressure and then asked, as he customarily did, "Well, Doc, did anything out of the ordinary pass?" and I replied with something like, "No, Doc, just six white horses a-flying over," and after he'd winked and said, "Then it aint no wonder you're a-feelin better," and we had our laugh, he asked, "Doc, do ye reckon you feel up to hoppin in my car for a little spin?"

Rowena shaved me and I dressed and had a big breakfast, and Rowena had packed a hamper with a fine lunch of fried chicken and potato salad and I don't know what-all. It just looked like we were going to be gone for the better part of the day. And we were. Doc explained he wanted to take me to Parthenon.

You've mentioned that village in each of your novels, but I don't think you have bothered to speculate upon the circumstance whereby some old settler, more literate and imaginative than usual, had chosen to name his town after a temple dedicated by the Greeks to their favorite goddess, Athene Parthenos, meaning Athena the Virgin, because she was practically the only one of those immortal Greek women never to lose her cherry. All over America people were naming their new towns after Greek towns, and this Newton County feller thought he was doing the same, but he was mistaken. The name of the town was Athens. There was a hill in Athens called the Acropolis, meaning "high town," and he might have used that name, as I believe you did in disguising Parthenon's name in your novel *Some Other Place. The Right Place.* But this feller didn't use "Athens" or "Acropolis." He used the name of the temple on top of that hill. For all he knew, he might as well have called the town "Innocence" or "Chastity" or "Maidentown" or "Virginville." But in his confusion over classical matters, he called it originally "Mount Parthenon," which could only be translated as suggesting that we get ourselves up atop a virgin. Hell, it took eighty years for the natives themselves to learn how to pronounce the place. They used to call it "Par-THEE-nun," and even corrupted that to "Par-THEE-ny."

But Colvin pronounced it correctly when he told me where we were going, so I asked him, "Are you taking me to a big stone building on a high hill?"

He smiled. "Yep, Doc, we're going up a hill to see a mighty fine big stone building, all right, the biggest stone building in Newton County, but that aint the Parthenon. I reckon strangers might think the town was named after that building, but the town has been there since 1840 and the building wasn't done much more'n a dozen years ago."

We drove northeastwards from Stay More a number of miles, the road mostly following along the east bank of the Little Buffalo River, and it was one of those gorgeous summer days with cottony tufts of clouds stuck hither and yon over the azure. I enjoyed that ride, especially in comparison to the last time I'd been in Doc Swain's car, when he was transporting me down the mountain from the Widder Whitter's. I paid close attention to the turnings and forks in the road, in case I needed to remember how to get out of Stay More, because as we've said before it's even harder to escape than it is to find. But I could also sit back and enjoy the scenery and the fine cigar Doc had given me. "Beautiful country" was all I could say.

Actually, and fortunately for that part of the tale, the road is mostly downhill from Stay More to Parthenon, and that "up" he used was just geographical, as we all tend to speak of places north of us as "up" from where we are.

Fording Hoghead Creek (and all streams in those days had to be forded; there wasn't a bridge anywhere in Newton County), I saw the godawfullest creature that I hope I ever have to see, and I thought for a moment we'd actually come across one of those gowrows or jimplicutes of legend. "What in *hell* was that?!" I said. Doc Swain laughed and explained it was just an oversize aquatic salamander, called a "hellbender." It had scarcely disappeared from sight when a huge bird swooped down as if to attack it, a bird with a very long and agile neck that must've given rise to the legend of the giasticutus. "Just a great blue heron," Colvin said, his "just" letting me know that there were more prodigious creatures out there.

We talked a lot, not just making chitchat or nature-study observations. It had not quite sunk into me yet that my companion, this mild-mannered, affable, folksy country doctor well into middle age, was actually *the* Doctor Colvin U Swain whose fabulous life and adventures had been captivating me (and, I hope, you) in recent days. Almost as if I were testing him to prove it, I asked, "Doc, what ever happened to Kie Raney?"

Colvin gave his head one shake of sadness. "Oh, he departed, some years back. Nobody knows for sure what he died of. I went over there, but just in time for the funeral, too late for an autopsy. Doc, sometimes"—Doc's eyes glazed up a bit—"sometimes of a night I sit on my porch and look up at the stars, you know, and think about him. If that old Archer is shining up yonder amongst the constellations, I'll recall ever word of that solemn oath Kie Raney made me swear." He gave me a sharp look and asked, "You haven't heard anything to give ye the notion I've ever violated a single one of those promises in that oath, have ye? Wal, Doc, before you've heard it all, you'll know how and why I had to violate ever blessed dang one of 'em." And he fell into a silence that lasted the rest of the way to Parthenon.

We came down off the mountain into this lovely village, about the same size as Stay More but with one considerable difference: in the distance, on a hill, rose a group of buildings that seemed somehow mysterious because they were so unusual. You're an art historian, aren't you? Didn't you ever observe how any pastoral landscape painting, filled with meadows and shepherds, et cetera, et cetera, generally has some old buildings rising up in the distance? That feller who did those pretty things with the thunderstorm and the half-nekkid gal nursing her baby under a tree? George E. Owney? Didn't he also do one of some fellers playing their guitars with a couple of nekkid gals hanging around? *Pastoral Symphony* or something like that? Well, you know in both those paintings of his there are these buildings in the background, not necessarily houses, though they could be, and not necessarily temples, though they could be, but *human structures* of some kind, as if to show that Nature may be pastoral but she aint wild, she's been tamed by man, and those buildings in the distance give you the awfullest urge to go and get inside of them, out of the rain, out of the sun, out of the country. It's like the buildings are a refuge against Nature, if Nature gives you any trouble.

Well, up on that hill was this cluster of buildings, and Doc Swain broke the silence that had come on him with thoughts of Kie Raney's oath in order to start telling me about those buildings, even before we got to them. The buildings were still being used as a public school, shut down now for the summer, but Doc explained they had once been a private school, the Newton County Academy it was called, although the local folks had referred to as "the college."

Back in the years after that first great war, the one that involved the whole world, folks were so poor in Newton County that there wasn't enough money raised from the taxes on their property to support public schools. Of course Stay More had had its own elementary school, first through eighth grades, for some time, and at one time Jasper, the county seat, had had a kind of high school, which is where your Latha Bourne went, riding in each day with Raymond Ingledew in his buggy, a long way to go for an education.

So a lot of Newton County people were willing to listen when the Home Mission Board of the Southern Baptist Convention proposed that a "mountain mission school" be established to provide some good education for the backwoods boys and girls of the hill country. If you know anything about the Baptists, you know how partial they are to "missions," either foreign or domestic. A mission is a kind of meddling. Its purpose is to convert. The Baptists came into Newton County—hell, they didn't come in; they'd already been there ever since displacing the unconverted Indians—and they decided to build their mission school to convert the older boys and girls from heathen illiterates into good Baptist Bible readers.

That was a period, just at the start of what the rest of the country knew as the Jazz Age, when the Baptists were somehow raising the money to build these schools in several places around the Ozarks and Ouachitas—at Blue Eye, Missouri, and in Arkansas at Maynard, Hagarville, Mt. Ida, and Parthenon. They chose Newton County because they considered it "the most destitute field in Arkansas," and they picked Parthenon instead of the county seat at Jasper only because Parthenon is closer to the geographic center of Newton County. With the help of "subscriptions" from some of the better-heeled upstanding Parthenonians, and a few Stay Morons, like John Ingledew the banker, who, although he had no use for the Baptists, being like all the Ingledews not so much an atheist as a nontheist, was willing to put up a couple hundred dollars as his share toward building the campus. The main building alone cost $15,000, the most money that had ever been spent on a single structure in Newton County. Even abandoned for the summer, with some windows broken and dust everywhere, as it was when Colvin took me through it, it was still impressive: the largest stone building anyone had ever seen or imagined, two whole floors of six classrooms and an auditorium that would seat two hundred. It had even had a library! Nobody had ever heard of one of them things before, and thought it was some kind of berry which would turn you into a liar if you ate it. Although the contents had not been considerable, maybe three hundred volumes all told, it was the only thing approaching a book repository in all of that country. But when the building had changed hands from the Baptists to the state of Arkansas after a decade, the library had disappeared.

The Baptists had sent a young flatlander lady, Miss Jossie Conklin, to be the head of what was officially named Newton County Academy. Naturally the locals considered her a "furriner," because she was from a "foreign country"—Texas. She had graduated from Baylor College, the biggest Baptist school in Texas, and she also had a "B.M.T." from one of those angel factories, the Southwestern Baptist Theological Seminary in Fort Worth, where she'd met the feller Tim James, who not only outranked her with a "Th.M." but would also replace her after a couple of years as principal of the Newton County Academy, which he accomplished by marrying her. But that's getting ahead of the story.

Shapely Miss Jossie just showed up one day at Colvin's door and commenced talking a blue streak. He had some trouble understanding her at first, because of her Texas accent, and he mistook her for one of those women homesteaders who had invaded the Ozarks a few years earlier. He kept waiting for her to reveal what her ailment was. He was mighty glad to have an awake visitor to his office, the first in a coon's age, and he suspected that she was such a foreigner she hadn't even heard about the dream cure that everybody else was freely availing themselves of. He hoped she had something really serious wrong with her, so he could make her into his first paying patient in over a year. But the longer he listened to her, the clearer it became that she didn't really have anything wrong with her, or, rather, she had a whole bunch of problems but they weren't medical. He offered her a drink of Chism's Dew to calm her down, but she managed to blurt out that she never in her life had ever touched a drop. Even without the Chism's Dew, he managed to get her to slow down and repeat some of the more difficult parts of what she was saying.

Finally he understood that this pretty gal in her ruffled blouse and smocky jumper was offering him a kind of job. She was fixing to start a school and wanted him to be the school's doctor. It wouldn't be a full-time job, since they had only 144 students to start with. It would only require that he make one trip a week to Parthenon, to check up on things, and to be available in emergencies at all other times. They could pay him twelve dollars and fifty cents a month, a pittance, but it was twelve dollars and fifty cents *more* than he had been making. Of course, if he were willing to conduct a class, one afternoon

145

a week, teaching hygiene to freshmen, they would add another seven-fifty on top of that, making twenty dollars a month. And if he could coach basketball . . . ? No? Well, coaching basketball was optional, and also voluntary, meaning no pay. Also voluntary was participating in the book drive for the library, if Dr. Swain might himself happen to have, or be able to locate, any suitable volumes?

He listened to her proposal with gravity. Now we know that Colvin didn't think much of "school." His brief experience at the age of eleven with the Stay More school, his memory of the tales Kie Raney had told about his years teaching at the Spunkwater school, and his brief experience at the St. Louis medical school, had pretty much soured Colvin on the concept of an institution of formal learning. He knew he couldn't coach basketball, and he wasn't sure he could teach hygiene, whatever that was, but he certainly was willing to be a doctor for the pupils if they needed him.

He had a question he wanted to ask. Why had she chosen *him?* Why not one of the doctors in Jasper, which was closer to Parthenon? "Everybody says you're the best doctor in the world," she said. "They tell me you practically invented the idea." He was flattered, and since he needed the money and could easily spare one day a week, or seven for that matter, he agreed to do it. "I have just one question for you," Miss Jossie said. "Of what persuasion are you? Not that it matters, too much, because we Baptists are tolerant of sects, but we'd just like to know which of the sects you follow."

He thought she'd said "sex," and he answered, "Why, the weaker variety, I reckon."

"I don't believe I know any such," she said, and he figured she was asserting that she wasn't weak, herself. "Do you observe Sundays?"

Colvin was not comfortable discussing sex with a stranger-lady, not unless it had to do something to do with her own condition. "Any day or night of the week suits me," he said.

"Well, then, I don't suppose it matters which day you come," she said.

He blushed and said, "Or night, one."

"How about Mondays, starting next Monday?" she asked.

She was a mighty feisty gal, and he wondered if she was making him a proposition. "Where?" he wondered.

"Just come to the Academy, to the main building, and you'll find me," she said.

That day we drove up to Parthenon, Colvin showed me, on the ground floor of the big stone building, the small room, now being used just as a storeroom for junk, old textbooks, and supplies. Mice had made a nest in one corner, and a broken window had allowed a free-ranging chicken to come in and lay some eggs. The chicken flew off with a squawk as we entered. The room had been stripped of whatever furniture it had held, but Colvin showed me where the desk had been, and, by the window, a kind of sofa, a lounge actually, a backless couch with one end curled up into a headrest, which had served as both the examining table and the infirmary bed for the occasional patient who had to stay, but, on Colvin's first visit to the room, had misled him into thinking that was where Miss Jossie intended to engage in sects, causing the both of them considerable embarrassment, which had ended with Miss Jossie patting her dark hair back into place, straightening her jumper, and saying, "It isn't that I'm not that sort of girl, I mean, well, I'm really *not* that sort of girl, you know, but we hardly know each other, now do we? Perhaps *after* we've had a chance to get better acquainted . . . but aren't you a married man? Not that I wouldn't even dream of being *with* a married man, I mean,

I never *have,* but it isn't inconceivable, you know, it's just that it makes it rather complicated, don't you think? Now please understand I'm not *rejecting* you, not totally anyway, I just . . ." She kept on a-talking like that until he interrupted her with a question: Why did she have this here sofa in her office? "*My* office?" she said, agog. "This is *your* office. Would you like to see the rest of the building?"

"Would you like to see the rest of the building, Doc?" Colvin asked me, and took me on a tour. Down the hall was the principal Miss Jossie's office, perhaps still being used as a principal's office and smelling of the body odor of one of the four Baptist men who had succeeded Jossie as principal during the school's decade of existence as Newton County Academy. Two of the larger classrooms were on this floor. An anti-goggling staircase rose to the second-floor auditorium, which still had all two hundred of its seats in place and remained the largest gathering place in the county, larger than the courthouse's main courtroom or any church. Up there also was the library, one room with two of its walls lined with bookshelves, empty. Colvin had been recruited to "volunteer" for the book drive and had canvassed his neighbors in Stay More for contributions of reading matter, discovering that only one of them had any books, the woman still living in the old Jacob Ingledew house, the lady you've chosen to call Whom We Cannot Name, so I will refrain from revealing my knowledge of her name. She contributed to the lie-berry of the Newton County Academy a set of the Brontë sisters, a set of Macaulay's essays and poems, and a set of Gibbons. From his own meager lie-berry Colvin was able to sacrifice a set of Bulfinch and Mary Olmstead Stanton's *Practical and Scientific Physiognomy; or, How to Read Faces.*

That first day, a most pleasant Monday in October, with the trees and sumac shrubs already turning every color of the warm part of the spectrum and the crisp air hinting of cool days to come, Colvin's first task was to examine everybody. Teachers first. There were six of them, and Miss Jossie introduced Colvin to his colleagues as she brought each of them to his office for examination: Miss Billie Hood, a high school graduate from downstate, would teach the primary department, first through sixth grades, and had postnasal drip, for which he could only prescribe that she attempt sleeping with two pillows under her head and drink butterfly weed tea instead of coffee. Miss Dulcie Best, a graduate of the big high school at Little Rock, would teach the intermediate department, seventh and eighth grades, and had herpes zoster (shingles), for which he gave his special lotion compounded of herbs. Next, a stunning creature, name of Mrs. Venda Breedlove, a graduate of Jasper High School and Shenandoah Music School, would teach music, and had Ménière's syndrome, with vertigo and deafness, for which she was under treatment by Dr. McFerrin of Jasper, so Colvin did not wish to intervene, even though Venda was the prettiest lady he'd ever seen outside of Stay More, and she flirted shamelessly with him during his examination of her. Nicholas L. Rainbird, a young possessor of the lone master's degree, from the same angel factory that had produced Jossie Conklin, would teach history and natural sciences, and would not accept Colvin's diagnosis that the chancroid lesions in his genital area were venereal; he insisted he had never, never, and would therefore get a second opinion from Dr. McFerrin. Miss Bee Leach, also from that angel factory but with only a "B.M.T." like her classmate, Jossie, would teach English and Latin (!), which prompted Colvin to offer both his diagnosis and his prescription (for an unmentionable "female trouble") in that language. *Nec amor nec tussis celatur.* And finally, Miss Jossie herself, who in addition to her administrative duties would teach arithmetic and something called "business," and who said, "I don't have to take off my clothes, do I?" All that he could find wrong with her, with her clothes still on, was that she had a very bad headache, treatable by his special neck massage and some aspirin.

The student body was much worse off than the faculty, and in the course of what remained of that first morning he was hard-pressed to see all 144 of them and give smallpox vaccinations to those who hadn't had them. By coincidence, 144 is a dozen dozen, or a gross, and he used up a gross of wooden tongue depressors examining their gross throats and finding some gross disorders and diseases. He also examined their gross anatomies. Those with hookworm he could recognize at once because of their "angel wings": protruding shoulder blades; those with pellagra he spotted because of their spots, distinguishable from the red dots of those with scarlet fever and the pimples of those with smallpox. There were cases of goiter, bone malformations, and assorted other abnormalities, including one lad, Russ Breedlove, son of the comely music teacher, Venda, who had diphallus (he possessed an extra penis), but did not realize his situation was irregular. Those who did not have a preexisting condition quickly were catching something from someone else, either infectious microbes or lacerations, abrasions, bruises, and punctures in the school-yard brawls necessary for boys to prove themselves to each other on school's first day, or the rope-skipping (and -tripping) contests the girls were conducting, and all of these wounded were coming to Colvin in droves and exhausting his supply of Mercurochrome, which they learned to call Doc Swain's "Cure 'em chrome" and wore proudly as a kind of war paint—or, rather, school paint.

One youth, refusing the antibiotic treatment Colvin tried to give him for his mastoiditis, declared he would just wait until he got home and "dream it off." Colvin grabbed him by the

150

collar and said, "What's your name, boy?" and when the young man answered Lum Dinsmore, Colvin said, "You're from Stay More, aint ye?" and Lum nodded. "Are they any more of ye?" Colvin wanted to know, and Lum told him that Dewey Coe and Opal Whitter were also from Stay More. Colvin got the three of them together in his office, closed the door, and gave them a stern lecture. Had any of them already told any of their classmates about the dream cure? Not yet, they said. Well, then, he said, they must promise him never, ever, under any circumstances, not for personal aggrandizement or gossipy inclination or even cash money, reveal, divulge, or betray, to any of their classmates, that the general populace of Stay More was no longer patronizing their doctors because they had learned how to use the dream cure instead. Their promises alone did not ease his mind, so Colvin threatened them, telling them that if they ever breathed a word of the dream cure to a soul, and then got sick with anything, he would refuse to let them into his dreams. He would stay up all night if he had to.

Few of the boys who attended Newton County Academy came daily from home, like Lum and Dewey. Most of them lived at such distances that they were boarded out at one of the homes in Parthenon, or they had rooms on the second floor of Casey's General Store, an impressive stone building in the village. But all of the girls, except the few who already lived nearby, were housed in a dormitory, one of the other big buildings on the hill, just a stone's throw from the main building. This girls' dormitory was a fine two-story wooden building, with a hipped roof like the main building and a general style of architecture resembling Jacob Ingledew's mansion in Stay More but three or four times as big. Colvin showed me the spacious empty room on the main floor that had been the dining room where everybody had their noon dinner together, but he missed his that first day, or rather was late for it, because he had to perform an emergency appendectomy on a student, Ora Casey, who had complained of "cute inner jestion." She had been his last patient of the morning, and, sitting down to have his dinner with the "help," the three girls who worked in the kitchen to pay their tuition (three or four dollars a month for those who could afford it), he was exhausted and realized he had only twenty minutes to eat before rushing off to meet his first class in hygiene, whatever that was.

But those twenty minutes were never forgotten by Colvin, because one of those three kitchen maids was Tenny. As a matter of courtesy, he asked the three of them their names, although he'd already inspected each of them earlier that day, finding asthma in Orva and scoliosis (a spinal curvature) in Olive, but nothing in Tenny, even though the young lady had insisted her right arm was killing her and her stomach really *ached* clean through all over down to the ground inside out slam to pieces. There were three things that struck him about Tenny: one, she was the only student at the Academy who, despite his thorough examination, was negative, negative, negative, not a thing in the world wrong with her; two, through one of those odd concatenations of circumstance or happenchance or whatever it was, she was the only girl at the Academy whose first name didn't start with "O"; and three, she was the prettiest little thing he ever laid eyes on. I mean, she was a knockout of a looker. She had plenty of here and there for her age, fifteen, and she might even grow up (not that she wasn't already fully grown) to look as gorgeous as that music teacher, Mrs. Venda Breedlove, who was a golden blond, but whose hair wasn't nearly as long and wavy as Tenny's light-brown hair. In addition to the almost-blond hair that came down nearly to her waist, and eyes that would put the sky to shame, and a mouth which seemed pouty because the lips were so broad and full and ripe, Tenny just had scads of taking ways about her. Oba and Orlena and Oma had eyes that were too far apart in their heads, while Odele and Orpha and Ona had eyes that were too close together, but Tenny's azure eyes were set just exactly the right distance apart. Olga was too fat and Opal was too thin, but Tenny was just right. A poor girl named Olma had acromegaly, with massive jaws; another one, Obedience, had exophthalmic goiter with a permanent expression of frozen terror; Odessa had an adrenal cortex disease which gave her a heavy beard; and Oneida had myxedema, a very puffy face. Oleta and Orena and Orela had faces that were too pear-shaped, while Omega and Ova and Oklahomy had apple-shaped faces. Tenny was a peach.

"How's your tunny, Temmy?" Colvin asked her as she started her second helping of custard pie.

"Huh?" she said, her full lips forming a perfect, tender, pretty-pink O, which struck him as ironic: of all the O-named girls, she alone could make her mouth into that exact pure shape. Ora and Olga and Orena had lips that were too fat and lopsided, while Oma and Olive and Opal had lips that were hardly visible, but Tenny's lips . . .

He realized his slip and wondered why he was nervous around her. "How's your tummy, Tenny?" he corrected himself. "You tole me this mornin it was a-hurtin ye bad, but I see it aint hurt yore appetite."

"Hit's a-killin me still, Doc," she said. "I don't reckon I can hardly walk, it hurts so bad, and probably I'll be dead before sundown."

"I misdoubt it," he tried to assure her, but, fishing out his gold pocket watch and opening it, discovered he was already late for class. " 'Scuse me, gals," he said. "I got to run."

His classroom was up there on the top floor of the main building, next to the auditorium, and its windows had a commanding view of the whole valley, now painted so nicely in autumn colors, a view that would provide his pupils with a relief from the tedium of the lessons. Jossie Conklin was waiting for him there outside the door, her arms full of books. "You're late," she said, as if he were a tardy pupil himself. Then she put the books into his arms and said, "The publisher, Mr. Henry Holt, is a good Baptist himself, and he donated a dozen of these to the school. Be sure the students take care of them." Then she led him inside and introduced him to the twelve members of the N.C.A. freshman class, although he'd already met all of them that morning during his inspections of them. As she was finishing the introduction, the door opened, and Tenny came skipping in, her long hair streaming out behind her, and took a front-row seat. "You're late," Miss Jossie said to her. "Tardiness will not be tolerated in this school." And she gave Colvin a glance to remind him that he was included in that intolerance. "Well, they're all yours," she said to him, and departed.

He cleared his throat. "Wal, howdy, folks," he said, determined not to call them "boys and girls," even though they were, ranging in age from fourteen to twenty. All he knew at that point about the course he was about to teach was that it was something you had to *learn,* and the only way you can learn something is to be treated as equally and civilly as Kie Raney had treated him. "Jist let me give each of y'uns a copy of this here book," he said, but discovered after distributing the texts that he didn't have one left for himself, so he had to look on with Tenny at her copy. The book was called *The Human Body,* and it was by H. Newell Martin, "Late Professor of Biology in the Johns Hopkins University and of Physiology in the Medical Faculty of the same." Colvin was somewhat relieved for several reasons. He recalled the professor of physiology he'd met that afternoon many years ago at the Missouri Medical College, a pretty decent sort of feller. This book had a subtitle, "Its Structure and Activities and the Conditions of Its Healthy Working," which suggested that the subject might be something that Colvin knew a few things about, since that was his line of work, more or less. The one thing he knew about "hygiene" was that it must have something to do with the ancient Greek lady Hygieia, who'd been the goddess of well-being. He'd once told Piney that if they had a baby girl he'd like to name her Hygieia, but Piney had made up her mind the baby would be a boy.

So this was simply a course in how to stay well, which all of them (except possibly Tenny) really needed to learn how to do. He ought not have too much trouble teaching these young people whatever they'd like to know about how the body works and what we ought to do to keep it running proper. He could use Kie Raney's system of teaching that there's both a practical reason and a pretty reason for everything. "I got a idee," Colvin suggested. "How about let's each of y'uns jist let yore book fall open to a page, and then you can ask me anything you like about whatever's on it. Let's jist go around the room, startin over here with you, Miss. What's yore name?"

"Ophelia," the girl said. "Folks call me Philly."

"Wal, Philly, jist let yore book fall open and ask me anything."

Philly took her book and let it fall open. Then she screamed, "AAAAAAHHHHHH!" and jumped out of her seat and tried to run away from it, as if a spider had landed on her. Colvin got her calmed down but he couldn't get her to go back to her book. "Thar's a *skeleton* in thar!" she said.

Sure enough, on page sixty-two was a walking spooky skeleton, looking as if he was a-coming to get you with a big grin on his face. "Folks, there's nothing to be a-feared of," he sought to assure them. "Hit's only a pitcher. The pitcher is jist a-trying to show how the jiants of the body are hinged together. Did you know you've got two hundred bones in yore body? Now who can tell me *why* critters have bones?"

The youth Russ Breedlove (he of the diphallus) raised his hand and suggested that critters have bones so their skin won't slide off, but another boy said, "A chaunk of meat has got to have bones so you could pick it up and carry it to the kitchen, and have something to gnaw on." Philly finally came timidly back to her seat and sneaked a peek at the skeleton, and said that bones are hard and rough so's to protect us from our enemies, or leastways scare 'em off. Finally Colvin resorted to the young lady he knew would be his star pupil. "You, Tummy," Colvin called on her, but added, "I mean, Tenny." *Why does that gal tie up my tongue?* he wondered.

"Bones is like the timbers that hold up a house or barn," she said. She poked herself in her lovely ribs. "My ribs hold me up the way the timbers hold up the building."

"Right," Colvin complimented her. "But do they do anything else for your pretty torso?" The class giggled, and he was as abashed at his adjective as she was.

"I reckon they protect my lungs," she said, "like the rest of my bones protect the rest of my innards. Bones is all we got to protect us from gittin squoze and scrunched by the cruel, mean world. But lots of times we git scrunched anyhow. I know a man who died of broken bones."

"Bones can break, shore," Colvin agreed. "But they're also springy and pliable. I could jump out that winder right chonder, and maybe not break a thing."

"LET'S SEE YE, TEACHER!" the thirteen of them chorused.

Colvin wasn't sure he could survive the drop with all his

bones intact and he realized he was getting off the track. "Wal now, if I was to break my fool neck, I'd not only fail of making my point, but I wouldn't be around for the next part of the lesson, which is this: there's both a practical reason and a purty reason for everything. The practical reason you've got a skeleton inside of you is to hold ye up and protect yore innards and get ye to moving around and about. But what could be purty about having two hundred bones? Anybody?"

The students stared at the textbook skeleton and screwed up their faces in concentration. They looked at one another. They examined their elbows and their kneecaps, their fingers and their toes; they poked their cheekbones and rapped their skulls. Finally Russ Breedlove offered, "Is it so's folks can be sure you're dead, if that's all that's left of ye?" Colvin suggested there were easier ways to determine if somebody was dead. A girl suggested that it's mighty pretty to know you can sit up straight and walk tall because your skeleton is a-holding ye up. Various other near-the-truth answers were exchanged before Tenny held up her hand and said, "Humans are the purtiest of all God's critters, and the reason they're the purtiest is because of the way their skeletons stand 'em up on their hind legs and let 'em move about so's they can do anything!"

"Except fly," Colvin said. "Some critters can fly. How do they do that?" Because they got wings, several students said. "But what are their wings made of?" Colvin asked. Feathers, of course, the students said. "No, feathers are just the skin. The wings are *bones*." He went on to ask them to speculate about the many ways that humans are indeed, as Tenny said, the prettiest of all God's creatures despite their inability to fly. He asked them to discuss the prettiness of the visible bones, but none of them were able to name any visible bones, until finally Tenny said, "Fingernails? Toenails? Teeth?" Tenny's fingernails were somewhat dirty from her kitchen work, but she had the best teeth Colvin had ever seen, if she would only smile, so he complimented her on her answer, which made her smile, and then he got them to talk about why we use our mouth bones—our teeth—to make ourselves more pleasant. Why do girls always show more teeth than boys? He also wanted to point out that the pubic arch in the female pelvis is also broader, to allow for births, and he wanted to talk about the articulations and ligaments that connect the pelvis to the legs. He wanted to talk about cartilage and foramina and vertabrae and marrow, especially about marrow, to ask if they (or Tenny) could figure out how hard bone can be alive like the rest of the body. And he wanted to talk about how diseases can hurt our bones as well as our tissues, how tuberculosis, for example, thought to affect primarily the lungs, can also attack the bones and cause their abscess. He wanted to talk about arthritis and bursitis and how drinking lots of milk might keep them from getting the osteoporosis that was stooping their grandmothers.

But Jossie Conklin came into the room and said, "This period was over fifteen minutes ago, and you have made these boys and girls tardy for English." Colvin had time only to say, "Well, see you next week," and make a wave of farewell.

None of his pupils made to leave. Moments passed, with Jossie glaring at them, her hands on her hips. Finally Tenny asked the principal, "How come he caint jist teach us English too?"

"Miss Leach is waiting to teach you English," Miss Conklin said. "She is waiting to teach you that you don't say 'how come,' you say 'why'; you don't say 'caint,' you say 'can't'; and you don't say 'jist,' you say 'just.' Now get out of here!" After they were gone, she said to Colvin, "You've got a number of patients waiting for you in your office."

Tired though he was, Colvin spent the rest of the afternoon setting broken arms and legs and meditating upon the fragility of bones. It was starting to get dark before he could put his horse, Nessus, into the buggy's harness and prepare for the long ride home. As he was driving off, a young lady came skipping down the hill, waving her arms for him to stop, and he recognized her long, flowing hair.

"Have ye got the fatty goo, Doc?" Tenny asked.

"The which?" he asked. He was delighted to see her again, but he was weary.

"I've been reading our hygiene textbook," she said. "The part on fatty goo, how a body gits 'accumulated lactates' in the muscles that makes ye give out and come down with fatty goo."

He was too tired to correct her pronunciation. So instead of saying fatigue, he said, "Yeah, Temmy, I reckon I've got the fatty goo purty bad. It's been a long day."

"Can somebody die of fatty goo?" she wanted to know.

"Wal, I aint never heared of nobody a-dying of it," he said, "although I reckon everbody when they get real old and worn out, if they haven't already died of something else, they'll jist die of fatty goo."

"But not while they're young?" she asked. "Because I think I'm a-dying of it, I'm so tard and beat out."

"Angel, hit's been a rough day for everbody but twice't as bad for you, having to work in that kitchen and all. You jist git you a good night's sleep, and them 'accumulated lactates' will go away."

She would not let him go. "My old heart is calling it quits. I jist don't have any pulse left." She offered him her wrist.

He held her wrist. The skin was like silk, and warm, and he'd rather have sniffed her pulse than felt it. He didn't need to drag out his pocket watch to know that her heart was beating perfectly normal. "That's a mighty purty pulse ye got, gal," he declared. "Purtiest pulse I ever seen. Not a bit slow nor fast, neither one. Now you jist go hit the hay." He raised his coach whip to send Nessus onward.

"Doc!" she said, urgently. "If I don't see ye again . . . or if I have to wait 'til ye come to that Other Place to see you again, in case I've gone to my reward when you come back next week, I jist want ye to know . . . I want to tell ye right here and now before I've quit this world, you were the nicest man I ever met!"

"Why, thank ye, Tunny," he said. "That's right kind of ye. But I 'spect you'll be a-sittin on the front row of class next week, answering all the tough questions that nobody else can answer."

She brought her other hand from behind her back. "I snuck ye a bite of supper," she said, and gave him, wrapped between two sheets of notebook paper, a nice ham sandwich. "Have ye got fur to go? Whereabouts do ye live at?"

He told her that Stay More was a number of miles up the road, and he'd better be gittin on. "Night-night, Temmy," he said. "Thanks for the samwich."

She stepped up onto the buggy's running board, as if to hang on there, threw her head at his, and gave him a big kiss meant for his cheek but landed half on his mouth, and then she was gone, and so was he.

Nessus knew the way home, and Colvin, as soon as he'd finished Tenny's sandwich, dozed off and let the horse take the buggy home, as he had done so many times in the long-ago days when he was returning from calls paid on patients in all hours of the night. Colvin not only dozed but dreamt, and in his dream he began to give Tenny a complete physical examination from head to toe. She was totally naked for it, and her beautiful body distracted him in the process of giving her a thorough stethoscopy, followed by a bronchoscopy, a pharyngoscopy, and a laryngoscopy. While performing the latter, he heard a repeated laryngeal sound and, paying closer attention, he determined that it was simply Nessus neighing. The horse was trying to tell him that he was home. He staggered into the house and in reply to Piney's "How was school?" he mumbled that it had given him a bad case of fatty goo. Then he hit the bed and resumed his dream, giving Tenny a fluoroscopy, an arthroscopy, and even a cystoscopy, following by a proctoscopy. In his comprehensive physical examination, he discovered that Tenny's hymen was intact, confirming his observation that the areolae of her breasts were virginal pink, and he mused upon this exceptional circumstance, rare for an Ozark girl, unless she has no brothers or an impotent father (which in fact was the case, but Colvin didn't know this yet).

Colvin's complete attention to Tenny's body was so meticulous that it prevented him from seeing any of the sundry Stay Morons who needed his attention for their ills and were trying desperately to mesh their dreams with his. The line of dreaming patients grew. The patients patiently waited for admission to his dreams, but the doctor was busy. All night long, and for several nights thereafter, the doctor was not available. People were beginning to worry whether they were dreaming properly or not. They tried catnip tea, taken warm just before bed, to help their sleep and dreams. Infusions of fresh alfalfa are supposed to help, but it was October and dried alfalfa doesn't do the job. Nervousness and restlessness inconducive to good dreaming can also be palliated by infusions of the roots of butterfly weed, hard to locate in October because if the monarch caterpillars hadn't chewed up the plants already, the first frost would've got it.

Then somebody came up with the brilliant idea that the only

way to get the doctor's attention in dreams would be to sleep in closer proximity to him. "Get up, Colvin!" Piney woke him on Saturday morning. "There are people sleeping all over our front porch!" He was irritated, being interrupted in the middle of his endoscopy of Tenny, but he got up, dressed, and went out to the front porch, and one by one began to rouse the sleepers, each of whom would blink, rub their eyes, and ask him if he was "real."

There were even more of them sleeping there Sunday morning, spilling over into the yard, and the spectacle of all those folks dreaming up a storm at Colvin's place caught the attention of old Jack Plowright, across the road, who, despite his spotty record of misdiagnoses and outright malpractice, was not exactly anybody's fool, and deduced that these were prospective patients, some of whom had been waiting so long for Doc Swain's attention in their dreams that they were now emergency cases. Doc Plowright stepped over there and invited them to come and see if he couldn't treat them just as well in the world of "reality" as Doc Swain was failing to do in the world of dreams.

Thus, the magical days of the dream cure came to an end. Maybe, even, there were other elements of the enchantment of the old-time Ozarks that somehow were also ceasing to exist at that moment. As a matter of fact, because elsewhere in the nation it was the beginning of what has been called the Jazz Age, perhaps the Ozarks were going to be dragged into it.

Doc Plowright had his hands full, so much so that Colvin understood it would be a violation of that old oath he had sworn to Kie Raney if he did not pitch in and offer to help. So he spent the rest of Sunday actually receiving actual patients into his actual office, curing them all, and cleaning off the porch. Sunday night he slept his first dreamless sleep in many a moon, having concluded his complete physical examination of Tenny, and thus he was moderately refreshed and eager when he arrived for work Monday morning at the Newton County Academy.

There was a long line of students waiting outside his office, and Tenny was at the head of the line. She was almost as beautiful in real life as she had been all week in his dreams. Perhaps, he reflected, in a way she was even lovelier, because she hadn't had on a stitch of clothes in his dreams, and somehow having all the secret parts of her body covered up with a pretty cotton floral-print dress gave her an allure that she didn't have nude.

"I've missed ye so, all week," she said, "even though I dreamt about ye ever night, all night long." Once she was inside his office and the door was closed, she fell upon the lounge as if using up the remainder of her strength to do so, and declared, "Doc, I'm afraid I've got a metabolism."

Colvin suppressed a chuckle and said in feigned seriousness, "I'm right sorry to hear that. What are the symptoms?"

"Jist like the book says," she said, holding aloft her copy of *The Human Body*. "There's a steady wastage of proteins from my cells. Also, I have faulty oxidations. I caint find the part where it says you can die of a metabolism. Can you?"

"Not me," he declared. "But jist the other day, I had me a feller who took down real bad with a metabolism and it killed him right off."

Tenny began to look happy. "Really? And there wasn't nothing you could do for it?"

"Metabolisms are tricky," he said. "You don't want to mess with 'em. But the best way to prevent a faulty metabolic reaction is eat a big breakfast. Have you done that?" She nodded. "Then eat a big dinner, is all I can tell ye. Will ye do that?"

"I'll try, but caint ye give me nothing for it?"

163

Colvin opened some bottles and took out both some yellow placebos and some green placebos. The yellow pills, he explained, were for the steady wastage of her proteins, and the green ones were for her oxidations. "Take one of each twice a day," he said. "I'll see you in class."

After he'd sent her on her way, he realized that his complete week-long physical examination of Tenny had not actually included a basal metabolism test, but all of his other tests had confirmed his earlier impression that she was the healthiest specimen he'd ever come across in his years of practice, so it was very unlikely that anything was wrong with her metabolism.

As the semester progressed, Tenny's alarms paralleled exactly the subjects covered in the textbook. Before they had finished the bones, she was convinced she had all the symptoms of multiple myeloma, and it did Colvin no good to inform her that usually the disease strikes only males above the age of fifty. As a consolation, when she thought she had spontaneously fractured her wrist as a result of the myeloma, he set it in a cast for a week, long enough to get them into the chapter on muscles. But when they studied muscular activity, she came down with all the symptoms of the Duchenne type of muscular dystrophy, and Colvin had to command her to take off her clothes, not so he could prove that she wasn't a male (because he'd already proved that many nights in his dreams) but to prove to her that she wasn't fooling him: she was definitely *not* a male, and only males get Duchenne's muscular dystrophy. "See," he said, and told her to get dressed, perceiving that she was more blindingly beautiful in the absence of her actual clothing than she had ever been in his dreams, and he had to turn his face away to protect his eyesight. After the chapters on the anatomy and physiology of the nervous system, she was sure she had multiple sclerosis. Colvin dreaded to introduce

164

the chapter on the structure and functions of the cerebrum, so he wasn't too surprised when she became convinced she had cerebral palsy. Colvin unwisely attempted to argue that she couldn't possibly have it because she was not exhibiting the spastic movements of a sufferer of that disease, and he demonstrated how the CP victim attempts to walk. Instead of convincing her that she lacked this behavior, he was unwittingly teaching her how to become spastic.

Tenny didn't need that. She'd already acquired a reputation on campus as dangerously different and difficult. She was strong-willed, outspoken, and viewed as a show-off, especially because in all of her classes she outshone everybody else. She didn't respect the rules (that very first night, when she'd run out to talk to the departing doctor about fatty goo, she had been punished for breaking the rule that you must stay in the dormitory after supper), and she had already accumulated more demerits than any other student. But perhaps worst of all, in a student body whose bodies and faces ranged the spectrum between grotesque and acceptable, she stood out conspicuously because she was so breathtakingly beautiful. Other girls sniffed and pouted with envy at the very sight of her. And boys, alas, were so dazzled by her looks that they could not even approach her, and kept their distance.

Now, all of a sudden, this smartest and loveliest of all the students was walking around—or attempting to walk around —with the terrible lurching dip-and-jerk movements of a sufferer of cerebral palsy. If anyone could have proved that she was just pretending, that might have been cause for confining her to the dormitory, but as far as anyone (except Colvin Swain) could tell, she actually had come down with the hideous affliction that strikes so many young people and is certainly no laughing matter.

Jossie Conklin summoned Colvin into her office. "What's wrong with Tennessee?" she asked him.

"Never seen it myself," he admitted. "Some of the old-timers of Stay More was actually born there, and I hear tell the east parts of it are real purty, but it got kind of overcrowded, is why they moved on to this part of the country."

"Ha ha," said Jossie. "I'm talking about your student, and mine."

"Oh," he said, and abruptly realized that he had never learned dear Tenny's whole name. "The gal, you mean?" he said, and attempted to measure her height above the floor, about five feet and five inches, and then even attempted to outline in the air her basic bodily configuration, exceedingly shapely.

"That's her," Jossie said. "Is she really dying?"

"Not on your life," he said.

"What about *her* life? She can hardly move. What is her disease?"

Colvin tapped his head. "She's got a real awful case of hypochondria, but it aint fatal." Abruptly he realized he had violated one of Kie Raney's commandments: don't never blab nobody's troubles to nobody else.

"Hypo what?" said Jossie. "Is it catching? Should she be quarantined?"

Colvin wondered if he had seen, heard, or read of any cases of contagious hypochondria. It was certainly hereditary, but not contagious. "I don't believe so," he said.

"What are you giving her for it?"

"There aint nothing much you can give for it," he said. "Just attention. She needs somebody to pay her some attention, and I'm doing my best."

"I need your assurance that she won't spread it."

"I guarantee you she won't."

But the student body of Newton County Academy, the girls out of deathly envy and resentment of Tenny and the boys out of their own shame at themselves for lacking the nerve to approach her, began to ape her movements, mocking and teasing her. All 143 of them, from first through twelfth grades, began to walk—or to attempt to walk—with the same stiff lurching scrape-and-kneel as Tenny.

It was a sight to behold, but Jossie Conklin, beholding it, came to Colvin and shrieked, "Now they've all got it!"

"But only one of 'em has got it real," he said. "All the rest of 'em is jist pore imitations." Having said this, he wondered just how "real" it was for Tenny.

He knew, and hoped, that the only solution to this mass hysteria was to move on to another chapter. I'm going to have to move on to another chapter myself and send you away for now, but I want to finish this one first, just as Colvin had to finish the chapter they were still bogged down in, on locomotion, the autonomic nervous system, fatty goo, sleep, et cetera. The very last of that et cetera was the thyroid, and that's where Tenny came to him in private to ask if hyperthyroidism is as fatal as cerebral palsy. Colvin hated to lie, but he did. He told her that her cerebral palsy might last another several years before it did her in, but her hyperthyroidism would kill her off before Christmas. That made her real happy. He knew that the worst sequelae of her new condition, Grave's disease, was simply eyeballs bugging out, like poor Obedience "Beady" Spurlock, one of the other girls in the class, who actually did have exophthalmic goiter, as I've already told you, with a permanent look as if she'd seen a ghost, and there was no way that Tenny could possibly imitate those pop-eyes.

But he underestimated Tenny. In no time at all, she was causing him infinite distress with her constant expression of huge eyeballs protruding from the front of her face as if they would fall out. At least, if it made any difference at all, she no longer walked like a CP cripple. So the other students gave up copying her. They just couldn't copy her eyes. Of course, Beady Spurlock already had it, and she began to think up ways to kill Tenny.

The odd thing was, even with her eyes all pooched out of her skull like that, Tenny was still so ravishingly gorgeous that all the boys were afraid of her and all the girls hated her guts. So she had not a friend in the world, except Colvin, and he decided to capitalize upon that circumstance in order to begin what was going to be a long, long treatment of her central disease. He knew that trying to cure hypochondria is like trying to shape a piece of flint into an arrowhead with nothing but your fingernail. But, to paraphrase that ancient Chinese saying about journeys, the longest carving begins with a single scratch.

So he did two simple things. He sent off for a copy of that fine old book, Burton's *Anatomy of Melancholy,* which I mentioned very early in my story. Then on his way to work he stopped at W. A. Casey's general store in Parthenon and bought one of those big circles of candy on a stick, I guess what you'd call a giant lollipop or an all-day sucker.

"Do you like suckers, Tammy?" he asked her nervously in his office and presented her with it. It was his first gift to her, and she was thrilled. "Jist git comfy and we'll visit a spell."

She plopped out on that lounge by the window, and he pulled the curtain to keep the sun's glare out of her bulging eyes. She commenced a-licking that huge lollipop, which would in fact take her all day. When she was as relaxed as she'd ever get, he said, "All righty, Angel, let's us start at the beginnin, and you tell me all the marvels of yore whole life long."

168

Six

Your champion and mine, sweet Miss Mary Celestia a-sprawlin yonder with that clever grin on her face, has taken it upon herself to correct me on another error, but I think she may be growing as deaf as you are, to go along with her blindness as a final withdrawal from this sorry world. She claims I said Tenny was the most beautiful gal on earth. Did I say that? Hell, you being so deaf yourself, you wouldn't know if I did or not, would you? I didn't hear myself say it. I didn't even say Tenny was the prettiest girl in Newton County, which she wasn't. Mary says she wants to remind me that you've already pointed out in more than one of your books that Latha Bourne was the most beautiful girl in the world. Didn't I tell you Mary knows your books? Well, so do I. In fact, there was a time before Colvin Swain was telling this story to me that he told much of it to Latha herself, a-sitting there on her porch with her the way they did so often, with nothing better to pass the time of day but talk about how the past was passed but had been so nice, and so mean, to both of them. So Latha knew almost all of the story about Tenny, and she would never forget the one afternoon that her dear friend Colvin got up his nerve and told her that he wanted her to know that Tenny may have been the prettiest little thing he'd ever laid eyes on, but she wasn't anywhere near as lovely as Latha.

To tell you the truth, Tenny wasn't even the *second* most beautiful female in Newton County, after Latha. She was *third*. Late today I'm going to have to bring Mrs. Venda Breedlove into this story, that music teacher at the "college," because if anybody had ever thrown a beauty contest like that one where the shepherd boy gave that golden apple as first prize, and Latha won it, then the shepherd would have had to give a silver apple to Venda, and poor Tenny would have had to be happy with the bronze apple . . . but I think we already know her well enough to know that she wouldn't have wanted any of them apples.

Anyway, I'll have a good deal to say about Venda later on, because if Colvin was the most important man in Tenny's life, Venda was going to become the most important woman, more important than Tenny's momma or her grandma or anybody else. That grandma was the one she was named after, Tennessee McArtor, who had been born in that state east of here and had twenty children but chose to spend her old age, and that of her husband, Grampaw Ray McArtor, with her favorite daughter, Tenny's momma, Jonette McArtor, who married Wayne Don Tennison. Both families went way back practically to the beginnings of Newton County. The Tennisons may have come originally from Indiana, not from North Carolina or Tennessee or any of those other mountain places that produced most of the settlers of the Ozarks. No doubt the family was related at one time to the same people who produced the great poet, Alfred Lord Tennyson, but they didn't know how to spell it. They could also have been related to the Tennisons that was already settled all over the Missouri Ozarks. But as Wayne Don Tennison said, "It don't matter where we come from. It only matters where we're a-gorn, and that's straight to Salvation."

He was a Holiness preacher, Tenny's dad. Some people call them Pentecostals, they themselves prefer to be called Church of God, I've always known them as Holy Rollers. Whatever you call them, they have some wild church services, with plenty of shouting and flopping around and speaking in tongues. And they handle poisonous snakes. When Tenny lay a-licking that lollipop on the lounge in Colvin's office and telling him her whole story, all fifteen years' worth, his ears perked up when she got to the part about the copperheads and rattlers and moccasins, because he'd been quite a snake handler himself. But Colvin had handled snakes as friends and pets, while Wayne Don Tennison handled snakes to convince the skeptical that he had the spirit and the power and the faith and the glory of the Lord in him, because the Bible says, "They shall take up serpents," and although the Bible doesn't say it, it ought to have said, according to Wayne Don, "You better take up snakes yourself if you want to attract enough believers to start a congregation in the Baptist back brush of the Ozarks." Wayne Don was the first snake-handling Pentecostal in Newton County, and he had the devil's own time trying to scrape together enough believers to fill a brush arbor, let alone a church house. He had started out a Baptist, like most of his neighbors, and in fact his wife, Jonette, never really quit being a Baptist, but Wayne Don had the "gift" for speaking in tongues and the Baptists wouldn't tolerate that, so he had to try to start his own church, and he'd been trying ever since, hardly ever making any money at it but convinced he was God's own appointed servant to convert the Baptists into Pentecostals.

Colvin sensed that when Tenny talked about her father, she was both embarrassed and angry. She had never quite recovered from her first attendance, when she was four years old, at a Pentecostal meeting held on the front porch and in the front yard of their house on Brushy Mountain in eastern Newton County. For pews, rough lumber had been spread across empty tomato crates to make backless benches in the yard, but hardly anybody remained seated once the services started. She had been required to watch her daddy, for whom she had a lot of natural affection, screaming and crying, jerking and jumping, whistling and hooting, swaying and swooning, strutting and stamping, twitching and falling, working up a sweat that completely soaked his clothes, and then sticking his hands into a box and bringing out a whole bunch of big writhing snakes that like to have given her her first heart attack. Afterwards she shunned him, couldn't bring herself to look him in the eye or listen to him, closed up her ears when he tried to demonstrate he still knew how to talk gently and rationally, and she transferred her affection to her mother's daddy, Grampaw Ray McArtor, a pleasant man who was always smiling and making Tenny laugh with his quips and his banter, and who wouldn't attend the Holiness services himself but would take Tenny fishing during them, or play his fiddle to get her to sing and dance, or otherwise entertain her despite eventual violent arguments with Wayne Don, who tried to tell her that she was going straight to Hell by avoiding church, and when his pictures of Hell failed to intimidate her, began to shake her, grabbed her by her shoulders and shook her and shook her, saying, "You wouldn't never of been born if it wasn't for me!"

What he meant was, ironically, not that his loins had sired her, which maybe they hadn't, but that it was his prayers and his gift of Divine healing which had cured his wife, Jonette, of her barrenness. Tenny had two older sisters—much older: Jonette at the age of fifteen had given birth to one girl, and at the age of sixteen to the other one, but both girls had grown up and married and gone away from home and even had children of their own before Jonette, at the age of thirty-seven, had, after years of fruitless attempts and even visits to some doctors, been able at last to conceive Tenny. Wayne Don claimed that it was his conversion to the Holiness faith and his acquisition of the gift of Divine healing and his many, many prayers for his wife to regain her birthing powers, prayers uttered fluently in "the unknown tongue," that had made Tenny possible. She was literally a gift from God, and Wayne Don had tried to name her Dove, as the bird of God, and because her older sisters had been named after birds, Oriole and Redbird, but Jonette felt it was her mother's advice that had made her fertile again, so she named the baby after her mother, Tennessee. And what had that advice been? Tenny couldn't be sure, but from some remarks that Grampaw Ray McArtor had made, she had suspected since the age of five that Wayne Don was not her actual father.

Whatever Jonette had done to become pregnant again, the pregnancy had not been good for her health, and while she adored and treasured little Tenny as the child she'd waited twenty-one years to have, she possibly also felt some hostility because, as she said to Tenny one day in a rare moment of anger, "I aint had a single blessit minute of feelin good since the day you was born!" Although Jonette and her mother were close, they argued over methods of treatment for Jonette's many ills. Tennessee McArtor in the best Ozarks tradition had a "natural" cure for everything (even for infertility!) and believed devoutly in the efficacy of superstitions and herbs, while Jonette, being much younger and much more "modern," believed just as devoutly in any number of patent medicines that were available. When Jonette was bothered with one or another of the "female troubles," her mother would insist on administering teas brewed from black snakeroot (*Cimicifuga*) or squawroot (*Caulophyllum thalictroides*), while Jonette would prefer taking large doses of Lydia E. Pinkham's Vegetable Compound (18% alcohol) or Watkins' Female Remedy (19% alcohol).

But Wayne Don Tennison did not believe in any sort of medicine except Scripture and speaking in tongues. "Is any sick among you?" he was given to frequent quoting of James 5:14–15. "Let him call the elders of the church; and let them pray over him, anointing him with oil in the name of the Lord; and the prayer of faith shall save the sick." Wayne Don was so opposed to both his wife's patent medicines and his mother-in-law's herbal remedies that he even omitted the oil from that Biblical prescription.

The same conflicts of opinion occurred over the little girl's ailments. Tenny remembered at the age of three receiving the devoted attentions of her whole family because she had croup. From her description of it, Colvin determined that Tenny had had *laryngismus stridulosa,* for which he would have put her into a hot bath with mustard, and blankets over the bath to make a tent so she'd inhale the steam, and then have steamed a kettle of tincture of benzoin beside her bed. But Tennessee the grandmother had tried dosing her with skunk oil—this stuff is rendered from the fat of skunks trapped in the winter, and makes a strong stinking mess. It made Tenny vomit, and then the grandmother rubbed Tenny's chest with a salve made of groundhog oil, turpentine, and kerosene. After this, Jonette the mother insisted on trying something called Campho-Rub on top of the groundhog mess, and having Tenny drink something called Dr. Sloop's Twenty-Minute Croup Remedy. The alcohol in the latter (15%) had given Tenny a pleasant buzz that partly took her mind off her paroxysmal cough, while the stroking of her mother's fingers in applying the former had done nothing for her larynx but had made her chest feel good. Then her daddy had spent a whole night chanting and warbling some gibberish over her bed, and shaking his fist at God. What Tenny remembered best about the whole experience, however, was the way one or another of them, including Grampaw and Daddy, kept sitting down beside her bed and looking at her with great concern. This, Colvin decided, may have been what kept the little girl from a blockage of the larynx which might have been fatal. But it was also, he knew, the beginning of the need for attention which every hypochondriac craves.

At a very early age, Tenny began to observe that her father and her mother argued loudly about everything but primarily about health matters, since Wayne Don rejected medicine and doctors but Jonette swore by her patent nostrums and remedies, and constantly complained of one or another disorder, disease, or emotional problem that could only be cured by Wine of Cardui or Carter's Little Liver Pills or Zymotoid, and tried to ignore Wayne Don while he was speaking in tongues she couldn't understand in his efforts to help her.

Tenny had the thrash at four. Did you ever get that when you were a kid? Maybe you called it thrush. It's an inflammation of the mouth with white patches on the tongue and lips and palate. Colvin knew it was caused by a fungus, *Candida albicans,* and he knew it generally affected babies and children who already had a serious constitutional weakness, and he usually treated it with applications of borax-honey and gentian violet but also did a lot of other things to improve the child's general condition and keep the infection from invading the throat and lungs. He listened with astonishment to Tenny's recital of the "cures" her family had tried on her. Her grandfather Ray McArtor was convinced that common creek water drunk right after a rain would do the trick, but if anything this just gave her a new set of germs. The grandmother called him a fool and said that the rainwater had to be drunk out of an old shoe, but it has to be a shoe that hasn't been worn by any of Tenny's kinfolks, so they searched all over that part of the country to find an old cast-off shoe that had been rained in, and dosed Tenny with the water, but it didn't seem to help too awfully much. The grandmother then tried various ointments made of crushed green oak leaves, and of garden sage, and while the latter seemed to help a little, it didn't remove the white patches. The mother took over and dosed Tenny's mouth with Dr. Philpott's Thrush Tonic and Mme. Yale's Antiseptic Syrup, but these had no effect. Finally, since Wayne Don's babbling of gobbledygook wasn't helping either, he was persuaded to try the old folk belief that the only cure for thrash is to have a preacher blow into the child's mouth. We may only imagine (Tenny was unable to say) what psychological effect it may have had on the child for her daddy to grab the sides of her face and squeeze her mouth open and press his lips up close to hers and blow and blow and blow. This was just a few months before the experience she would have of watching him go crazy in a church service. His ministrations gave her a headache and a bad taste in her mouth, but didn't seem to help the thrash, so Wayne Don had to just keep on doing it, day after day, along with intermittent recitations of the unknown tongues, plus the others' repeated doses of all that rainwater and sage ointment and patent medicine, until finally the thrash just cleared up of its own. Colvin considered the possibility, without sharing his the-

176

ory with Tenny, that something in her had held on to that thrash in order to continue to get all the circus of concern she was getting from all of them.

That experience of her father blowing air into her mouth was probably what set her to studying the whole business of breathing. The Tennison cabin had a great view toward the west, and Tenny could sit for hours on the porch, not necessarily admiring the view but watching it while she meditated upon the passage of air in and out of her body, through her nostrils, and between her teeth, wondering where the air went and what it did when it went there, deep down inside. Sometimes she would see how long she could hold her breath without passing out. For the longest time . . . in fact, until Colvin's course in hygiene finally got around to Chapters 23 and 24 on respiration, she believed that the air she inhaled went down into all of the parts of her body, even her feet, and that it went up inside her head, and that if she didn't breathe properly or allowed herself to fall asleep and not pay attention to her breathing, the absence of good air inside her head would cause the headaches that she often had.

Studying the way your own body breathes is a sure way to start feeling that your body doesn't belong to you, or, maybe a better way of putting it is that your body is also inhabited by somebody besides yourself, who never forgets to do your breathing for you, especially while you're asleep. Although they had given Tenny a doll or two of her own to play with, there wasn't any kind of doll that had a body as interesting as her own body, so she spent a good deal of time examining herself all over, inside and out, every inch, heart and soul, sometimes with the help of a hand mirror. She became her own doll. Does that make sense? She believed that she was inhabited by another entity, her breathing-doll self, and she even gave it a name, 'See, taken from the last syllable of her own name, Tennessee. Of course it must've sounded redundant even to herself when she addressed that doll and used the verb "see" at the same time, as in, " 'See, see what a cute nose ye've got," or "Let me see, 'See," or " 'See, see what I mean?" She did a lot of talking to 'See, more, by and by, than she ever did to her folks, except maybe Grampaw McArtor.

Tenny and 'See were not twins or clones or double-gangers or whatever you'd call them. There were differences. For example, on the matter of favorite things. Tenny and her 'See would sit "together" of an evening on that porch, watching the sunset, and studying its colors, and while 'See decided that her favorite colors were the bright red ones, crimson and carmine and scarlet, Tenny decided that she preferred the sunset's dark purplish colors, the deeper bluish shades. These colors did not exist anywhere around the house or in their clothes or anything Tenny and 'See could see except the sunset. Once, after watching the sunset until it got dark, Tenny and 'See tripped over a washtub and fell off the porch and cut her leg, which bled. When Grandma McArtor held Tenny in her lap while her mother stopped the bleeding and covered the wound, Tenny studied the color of the blood and decided it was 'See's blood because it was 'See's favorite color, and she told herself that if she ever bled herself, it would be deep purple, and it wasn't until a number of years later, when Colvin's class got to Chapter 17, on the Structure and Functions of Blood, that she finally asked, "Why is blood red instead of blue or some other color?" and received from Colvin an answer that satisfied her.

When Grampaw McArtor started dying, Tenny and 'See spent as much time with him as she could get away with, as if to repay him for all the time he'd spent with her when she was sick, or sad, or scared. Ray McArtor had consumption. He could only explain to Tenny that his lungs was bad, and he wasn't sure what had caused it. Nothing he ate. Maybe his cigarettes, he didn't know. His wife, Tennessee, and his daughter Jonette were doing everything they could, and Jonette had sent off for a whole bunch of stuff, a four-week supply of Addiline, a quart of Prof. Hoff's Consumption Cure, and a box of Dr. Hill's Systemic Wafers. Wayne Don was coming down with laryngitis from speaking in tongues on his father-in-law's behalf. They tried everything on Grampaw McArtor, but he kept on getting worse, losing lots of weight and coughing all the time. Tenny told 'See to see if she couldn't get down inside of Grampaw and see what was wrong with his breathing, and fix him up. When Grampaw began coughing up blood, Tenny was convinced the blood was a signal that 'See was sending up, to let them know that she was down in there finding the trouble and getting rid of it. For two months Grampaw coughed up blood and couldn't get out of bed. One day when nobody but Tenny was sitting with him, he smiled at her and said he reckoned it was time he told her good-bye. She asked where was he going. 'See was still down inside him and Tenny didn't want him taking 'See with him. He said he didn't believe in that Gloryland that Wayne Don preached about, but he was going somewhere that folks don't even have to breathe, nor eat, nor take a shit. That place was the same place that every bird and bug went when their time was over and the birds and bugs didn't have to breathe anymore, nor eat, nor take a shit. "Can I go too?" Tenny asked him. Not for many and many a year, he said, but he'd be waiting for her when she finally came, and maybe in that place folks could go fishing or fiddle and dance and sing even if they didn't breathe nor eat nor . . . Grampaw's voice faltered and his eyes closed and Tenny had to finish the sentence for him, ". . . take shits?" but he didn't hear her, because

179

he was already over there in that place amongst those folks and birds and bugs. He didn't take 'See with him, either. 'See came back into Tenny and helped to console her over Grampaw's departure, and they talked a lot together about how long they might have to wait before they could go to that place and visit with Grampaw.

One of the awfullest things about Grampaw's leaving was that Tenny would never get any answers to the many questions she'd asked him which he'd responded to by saying, "I reckon we'll jist have to wait until you're older before I can properly answer that fer ye." Now here she was, much older, but Grampaw was gone. If the McArtors and the Tennisons had always been oversolicitous for Tenny's health and well-being, they were even more overprotective when it came to shielding her from all the "nastiness" that exists in this world, and she remained ignorant of all things that were considered indecent or foul. They were determined that she remain "pure" until the age of sixteen, when she could get married. Her grandmother Tennessee had married at fourteen, and her mother, Jonette, had married at fifteen, but they were determined to keep Tenny "innocent" until she was sixteen, even if folks talked about her becoming a spinster at that age.

Not only did they *not* give her any sort of teaching that could've been remotely called "sex education," but they did their level best to keep her from ever finding out that there is any such thing as sex. Any kid growing up on a farm is bound to see *some* evidence of Nature's way of propagating the various species, such as a bull mounting a cow, or a boar giving it to a sow, or a stallion with a yard-long pecker trying to stuff it into a mare. But not Tenny. Her folks were not only very careful to use all those old euphemisms, like calling a bull a surly or a male-cow, and calling a boar a stag-hog, but they also were careful never to use even euphemisms if the connotation was sexual; for example, they couldn't even mention rhubarb or okra or horn or goober or even tool because of the suggestion of a penis, an item of the anatomy which they were determined to conceal entirely from Tenny's knowledge. Whenever the various male farm animals were displaying their penises in preparation for "service," Tenny would be kept inside the house with the curtains drawn. There was an old dog on the premises who had the habit of sticking his pecker out of its sheath so he could take a lick of it, but Jonette sewed a pair of pants for him to wear whenever Tenny was around.

Tenny did not know there was such a thing as the male organ until she was nine years old. Her folks were careful not to let her play with boys, for fear she'd find out, and they weren't happy about her playing with girls, for fear some girl would tell her. So she'd mostly had just 'See for companionship and Grampaw 'til he went away, and 'See didn't know anything more about penises than Tenny did, and Grampaw never could bring himself to say. When she was nine years old, her mother took her visiting a cousin who had recently had a baby. Babies, she knew from asking her grandmother, were born from women's mouths after being carried in their stomachs for three seasons. Both her grandmother and her mother agreed that women have to puke the baby out through their mouths (Tenny had spent many hours with her mirror studying her mouth and 'See's mouth and trying to make it open up enough to expel a baby), but her grandmother and mother disagreed on how the baby got into the woman's stomach in the first place, the grandmother insisting that a woman had to have a husband who could journey deep into the woods to find and bring home a mess of babyberries for the woman to eat, while the mother knew that all the woman had to do was drink enough Wine of

Cardui (20% alcohol) so that she was relaxed sufficiently to permit her husband to feed her some babyberries, which were hard to swallow. Tenny would just have to wait until she was sixteen and got married and could find out. Anyway, this cousin had recently puked up her baby, and was about to change its diaper, and before Jonette could stop her daughter from getting a good look, Tenny observed that the baby had some kind of growth between its legs. Too polite to call attention to it on the spot, Tenny waited until she was alone with her mother to ask about it. Her mother explained that it was a large wart. All boy babies have those big warts, Tenny was told, which was God's punishment on them for being descended from Adam, the first male, who was disobedient and smart-alecky and tough, which boys have been ever since. The warts could never be removed or healed; they just kept on getting bigger and bigger.

When Tenny was eleven, she happened to come across a seven-year-old neighbor boy who was standing in the path heeding nature's call, and she noticed that he was making water through his wart! He was even holding on to it! She drew nigh for a closer look. "Does it hurt, at all?" she asked him, because she had never had any kind of wart, not even a mole, nor boil, nor even a blister. She had seventeen freckles, was all.

"What hurt?" he said, ceasing his tinkling.

"Yore wart," she said, and pointed.

The boy laughed. "This aint no wart, you silly," he said. "This here's my doodle and when I git growed up I'll be able to stick it in ye." He gave it a shake and pointed it at her. "Wouldje like to feel of it?" She reached out gingerly and touched it. It began to swell, and she backed away, wondering if she'd caused it some strut by touching it. But he held it proudly as it plumped, and told her, "Girls don't git doodles. Too bad. Do ye want to show me where ye aint got nary un?"

When she showed him, he said, *"See!"* as if calling to her doll-self although she knew he wasn't. Then he said, "Well, that's jist what ye git for bean a gal. Nothing but a cut."

Not very long afterwards, her cut began to bleed. She thought it was 'See signaling again, 'See sending out her favorite color to let Tenny know that she was away up in there doing something, she didn't know what. This blood had a kind of tinge of purple, which was Tenny's favorite color, not 'See's. Tenny hoped it didn't mean that she had consumption like Grampaw, but maybe it did. She wanted to be able to ask someone, but she couldn't. If she had a stomachache or a bad headache, she wouldn't feel the least hesitation about telling her mother or her grandmother about it, so they would comfort her if not cure her, but somehow she felt that this profuse bleeding from her cut was just a personal matter between her and 'See, not to be shared with anybody. After five days, the bleeding stopped, and Tenny waited to feel 'See returned to the world of watching sunsets, but 'See did not return. Tenny began to think that all of that bleeding was 'See's way of saying good-bye, as Grampaw had said good-bye. She decided that 'See had gone to that Other Place where Grampaw had gone, and although people who had not yet gone there still called it by the ugly name, Death, Tenny knew that 'See was not dead but just roaming in that Place where Grampaw was. Tenny was very sad and lonely to lose her only companion, but she was happy for 'See, that 'See had escaped this terrible world where everybody has to breathe constantly, and eat all the time, and take many, many shits.

But while Tenny never heard from Grampaw again, every month Tenny got a message from 'See, and Tenny knew it was from 'See because it was in 'See's favorite color, addressed to Tenny in a tinge of Tenny's favorite color.

Colvin's class had to get away on along to Chapter 35, Reproduction, the last chapter in the book, the last week of school, before Tenny learned the name for that monthly message and learned that all girls get it and it didn't come from 'See. That was in the springtime, the middle of May, and Tenny had already passed her sixteenth birthday, the age at which her parents had told her she would get married. She had not met anyone she would want to marry, except Colvin Swain, and he was already married, and she was trying to decide how she would be able to tell her parents that she was not going to get married, because all she wanted to do with her life was to long for a man who was already married. But then when she got to page 622 and the explanation of what the book called "the monthly sickness," she grew angry at Colvin for the very first time. Despite her devotion to him (or because of it), she couldn't understand why he hadn't troubled himself to correct her ignorance when she was a-laying there licking lollipops on his lounge. She must have already consumed a couple dozen of those suckers (in fact, Colvin had told the storekeeper to order him a box of them, and there had been twenty-four to the box). So the next time she stretched out on Colvin's lounge, she refused the final sucker, saying, "My teeth are going to rot plumb out from eating them things." And she added irritably, "And you don't know yore ass from yore elbow about dentistry, do ye?" And then on top of that she said, "And apparently you don't even know enough about menstruation to tell me I'm wrong when I'm a-layin here spillin my guts about me and 'See." She let that sink in, and waited for his apology or whatever he had to say for himself.

Colvin was abashed. Dear Tenny had never been cross with him before, and he wasn't sure he deserved it. The school year was at an end now, and he might not see her again, because he'd decided not to return for another year to Newton County Academy. He didn't need the salary. Ever since the previous autumn, when his people of Stay More had abandoned the dream cure and returned to the good old ways of being treated in the flesh by him and Doc Plowright, he hadn't really needed the piddling pay that N.C.A. was doling out to him, although Jossie Conklin had offered him a raise to thirty dollars a month for the next school year, and thirty-five if he could see his way to coaching basketball. He didn't want it, and only two things had kept him from quitting before Christmas: he wanted to help Tenny, if he could, and he believed that anything you start you ought to finish. Well, he could never finish helping Tenny. He'd read Burton's *Anatomy of Melancholy,* all the thousand pages of it, and even reread the parts on the cure of hypochondriacal melancholy several times, but he hadn't really learned anything about curing Tenny, who, despite sometimes thrice-weekly sessions on the lounge with lollipops, remained just as hypochondriacal or hypowhateverall as she had ever been. When they had taken up Chapter 13, The Receptor System, she had been so impressed by the section on Pain that she had developed analgesia, loss of the power to feel pain (which had at least alleviated her headaches for a whole week). After Chapter 14, The Ear, she had become deaf, not responding to his tuning forks or voice and not hearing the class discussion of Taste and Smell, which had kept her from losing the sense of either. Colvin had dreaded Chapters 15 and 16 on The Eye, but had arranged with Tenny's classmate and only friend, Ozarkia Emmons, to spend a week serving as a kind of seeing-eye dog for Tenny, who had of course been excused from kitchen duty until she could again see the dishes. Colvin had decided to skip entirely Chapter 20, on the Action of the Heart, because he didn't want Tenny to acquire any of the symptoms of cardiac disease. It bothered his conscience, cutting out the heart, and Tenny had even asked him about it, "Why did you ignore the heart?" and he'd tried to explain that it was a very tricky subject, and the heart has things about it that we can't know, by heart. Ever once in a while, Tenny would say, "You left out my heart," and they both knew what she really meant. The day he ought to have taken up the heart was her sixteenth birthday, the beginning of the year in which she would get married. Colvin had a form of heart disease himself, which made him give her on her birthday a golden ring set with an amethyst, not because it was her birthstone (it was) but because it was her favorite color. The ring was the first jewelry she ever owned, but she had to tell her friend Zarky and anyone else who asked that it had come from her rich older sister Oriole who lived in a big city. Colvin tried to cure his heart disease by rereading what old Burton wrote in the chapters on "Love-Melancholy." But Burton hadn't been able to do any more for Colvin's love-melancholy than he had done for Tenny's hypochondria. There might not be any cure for it. Colvin had realized it might become incurable when he had learned that Tenny's childhood had been so much like his own: because they had both been reared in such solitude they had a special bond of lonesomeness that would always draw them to each other. On that day in February, with the very first signs of the coming of springtime, when he'd left from home with that amethyst ring in his pocket, Piney, who still knew everything, had asked him why he had got into the habit of going up to Parthenon on Wednesdays and Fridays also if he was only supposed to work on Mondays, and quite possibly she had not accepted his explanation that the students at N.C.A. were having the usual run of late-winter ailments that needed his increased attention. The painful truth was, Colvin still loved Piney. With all his heart, I was about to say, but then I remembered that he had omitted the heart, and I also remembered the sad thing about the old-time Ozark use of that word, "love," that I've already told you, as if you hadn't already found it out in your own life in the Ozarks: the word itself was considered indecent, so that if a hillman ever did admit that he *loved* a woman, he meant only that he petted her or screwed her. Piney, knowing everything, knew the word in all its meanings, and knew it in its sense of deep-down devotion as well as desire, and she *loved* Colvin in that sense even if she never told him so. And he fully reciprocated the feeling, even if he never told her so. Tenny hadn't known the word. It had never once been used in the house where she grew up. The first she ever heard of it was when Ozarkia Emmons, her seeing-eye dog during that spell of blindness, smuggled a copy of *True-Story* magazine into the dormitory, where such trash was strictly forbidden. Zarky was the only girl who was friendly with Tenny and didn't seem to hate her for her good looks and intelligence, even if she hadn't been appointed by Dr. Swain as Tenny's seeing-eye dog. Tenny's and Zarky's beds in the dormitory were side by side and when somehow Zarky got ahold of a copy of that lurid confessional magazine, she read parts of it aloud in a whisper to poor blind Tenny, who thereby learned about something called "love," a disease which is supposed to attack you during your adolescence and possibly continue for the rest of your life. Love is such an awesome disease it wasn't even mentioned in the hygiene textbook. As a connoisseur of diseases, Tenny was totally captivated. Love might or might not give you hot flashes and heart irregularities, but it definitely affects your brain and your whole nervous system. It makes you pick out another person and focus all your attention on that person, pretty much in the same way that Tenny had once focused all her attention on 'See. But 'See had been a girl, and love is supposed to make you want to spend every minute you can steal with a member of the opposite sex. Tenny supposed that perhaps this could have applied to her feeling for Grampaw, except she could not honestly remember ever wanting to get into bed with Grampaw, which is what you have to do. She had spent many hours *beside* Grampaw's bed but never *in* it. Zarky had actually spent a whole night in the bed of one of her uncles, and while she was too bashful to give Tenny all the details, she made the experience sound wonderful. "More fun than sending off a big order to Sears Roebuck," Zarky said. Tenny asked if the uncle had brought her a mess of babyberries. "*Baby*berries, you say?" Zarky said. "Well, if they was any babyberries, he poured so much cream over 'em I couldn't see 'em."

But what Zarky had had with her uncle could not have been this thing called "love," because the essential characteristic of love is not what you do with your bodies but rather what you do with your ears and voice, parts of the anatomy that Tenny was now an authority on, having spent countless hours on Colvin's lounge talking to him, and having finished the chapter on ears in her textbook at the cost of her hearing, now returned although she was blind. Love is blind, Tenny learned, but it sure aint deaf nor dumb, because the main part of love is feeling as if you could say anything that pops into your head to that other person of the opposite sex, and that opposite-sex person would hear every word you said and even tell you in return some of anything that popped into his head.

The only person that Tenny had ever felt this way about was her doctor. Learning all about "love" from Zarky and her copy of *True-Story,* Tenny realized with a shock of recognition that these were exactly the feelings she had for Doc Swain, even though he was twenty years older than her, and married, and a teacher, and everybody knew that teachers weren't allowed to "flirt" with students, and vice versa. Students could flirt with each other, and teachers could flirt with teachers, and in fact Mrs. Venda Breedlove was flirting something awful with Doc Swain. An essential lesson of *True-Story* is that love between two persons married to somebody else is very dangerous. It always ends in heartbreak, suicide, disaster, or gunshot wounds from jealous spouses. So Tenny knew that her great overwhelming passion for Doc Swain was hopeless, because he had a wife, and Tenny didn't understand why Mrs. Breedlove didn't leave him alone on account of it, especially since she had a husband herself, even though there was a rumor going around that Mrs. Breedlove no longer lived with her husband but had her own house in Jasper, right off the square, where she lived with her boy, Russ, who was one of the boys who rode a horse to school; he had a big white stallion he called Marengo, and each day he brought his mother to school riding sidesaddle in front of him. Supposedly Russ had to take Marengo and spend weekends living with his father and helping him in his blacksmith shop on the other side of Jasper. Zarky thought that Russ was awfully "cute," a word that Tenny was slow in learning because she associated it with "acute" in reference to diseases which are sudden and intense. Perhaps Zarky had a crush on Russ which was sudden and intense, but the way she and other girls used that word "cute" was as if it had something to do with looks, and there was no denying that Russ was the sightliest-looking boy at Newton County Academy, understandable in view of how pretty his momma was, and especially when Russ was mounted on Marengo with or without her. Tenny had Mrs. Breedlove for music twice a week and also Mrs. Breedlove was in charge of the Glee Club, which was an organization of students who were supposed to be devoted to merriment or joy but mostly just stood in rows trying to sing the school's song:

There's a school of learning
There our hearts are yearning;
    N.C.A. we love thee.
To thine ideals guide us
Lofty aims supply us.
In life's joys and sorrows
O'er land and waters,
Thy sons and daughters,
We will e'er to thee be true.

Although Tenny was the only member of the Glee Club who could sing all the words without forgetting one or making a mistake, she wasn't sure she could honestly say she loved N.C.A., because N.C.A. was not a member of the opposite sex to whom she could say absolutely anything that popped into her head, the way she could talk to Doc Swain. Whenever she sang the song, she always substituted "Colvin Swain" for "N.C.A.," same number of syllables and nobody noticed if everybody was singing.

There was one final thing she knew about love, and that is this: it always gets bigger. Sometimes like a little tree sapling, it may start out just as a seed, but it keeps on growing, and it never stops growing until it dies and goes to that Other Place where we don't have to breathe, nor eat, nor use the privy. Tenny was bothered by the thought that she could not say *everything* to Colvin that popped into her head, but she was confident that if love grows, then someday she would be able to say everything, including this, "Colvin Swain, I love thee."

But she had told him her whole life's story, had told him things she would never have mentioned to Grampaw, and had told him her deepest, darkest secret, about 'See, and about 'See's monthly message in red, and Colvin had just sat there with a pleasant smile on his face, saying, "That shore is real purty" and "How did that make you feel?" And then now at the end of the school term, by coincidence right at the time of a message from 'See, Tenny had read that textbook's shocking last chapter, Reproduction, and had learned about menstruation. Most of the chapter was just dull stuff about cell division and maturation of germ cells and heredity and chromosomes, but then all of a sudden there it was, a section on the Male Reproductive Organs with all kinds of stuff on *vas deferens* and *vesiculae seminales* and *spermatozoa,* and *penis.* Especially *penis.* She realized she had read the entire section of three paragraphs on the penis without once taking a breath, not once. *Erectile tissue,* enclosing cavities that filled with blood! *Corpora cavernosa,* two of those caves along the penis's topside, that swell with blood! *Corpus spongiosum,* that surrounds the pee-tube and culminates in the *glans,* a "terminal dilation," sort of like a mushroom, covered with a *prepuce,* soft, moist, red, to the *meatus,* the opening of the pee-tube, where some other stuff also comes out. The book didn't say a single blessed word about either a practical reason nor a pretty reason for all of that apparatus, except something about the spinal cord being the center of reflex excitation associated with sexual emotions. Since the book had already made quite clear that we experience emotions not in our heart or soul or guts or anywhere except our brain, Tenny wasn't sure how the spinal cord could be the center of sexual emotions, whatever those were, and she couldn't wait for the class to take up that chapter. She would ask Colvin in private, with or without a lollipop. But before she got a chance to see him again, she kept on reading, into the Reproductive Organs of the Female. Just as she suspected, girls are much more complicated than boys. The only illustration in the portion on the male was a cross-section of a testis that made it look like a slice of lemon, but the female portion had a bunch of pictures, including a poor girl's whole cut-away bottom end with all those tunnels and tubes and cavities up in there. Tenny had no idea that she was so deep, and in three different places down there, one for pee, one for shit, and one for . . . blood? She couldn't be sure what the middle tunnel was for, squoze betwixt the other two but running way up to a big-mouthed critter labeled *uterus*. She kept on reading, and was amazed to discover that women make eggs just like chickens, only they don't lay them or sit on them to hatch them, but hatch them up inside.

And then, the section with that big word, *menstruation,* and the explanation of 'See's message. Tenny reddened as she read, not from embarrassment but from anger and also perhaps because she was menstruating at the moment, and she came across this: "During menstruation there is apt to be more or less general discomfort and nervous irritability; the woman is not quite herself, and those responsible for her happiness ought to watch and tend her with special solicitude, forbearance, and tenderness, and protect her from anxiety and agitation." Tenny felt kind of cheated, thinking of all the wasted opportunities she might have had for solicitude, forbearance, and tenderness if only she had told her mother or grandmother about the message from 'See.

She also realized that it was her menstrual discomfort and nervous irritability which made her snap at Colvin, "And apparently you don't even know enough about menstruation to tell me I'm wrong when I'm a-layin here spillin my guts about me and 'See."

Colvin realized it too, and once he had thought the matter over, he asked her, "Are you getting the message right now?"

It didn't take her long to figure out what he meant, and she confessed, "As a matter of fact, yes, I am. Started yesterday."

"Didn't your folks ever use words like 'courses' or 'flowers' or 'monthlies'?" he asked. Tenny shook her head. " 'On the rag'? 'Unwell'? 'Period'?" Tenny shook her head. " 'Flying the red flag'? 'Falling off the roof'? 'Coming around'?" Tenny shook her head. "Well," Colvin tried one more, "surely you've heard of 'having a friend'?"

"I never had no friends except Grampaw and you," she said.

"And 'See," he reminded her. "Don't you see? Maybe that there's the purty reason for the menstruation, and I wanted to hear ye draw me a pitcher of it. The reason I never interrupted ye to set ye straight was because I thought the idee of 'See as a kind of soul who has gone to that Other Place but sends you a monthly message is a much nicer explanation of catamenia than anything us doctors could come up with. Or that textbook, either."

"But what about 'babyberries'?" she asked. "What about my stupid idee that babies are born from the mouth? How come ye never set me straight on none of them other dumb notions?"

"I jist wanted to git to know ye," he said, and then he went a little farther than that. "I jist wanted a glimpse of your soul."

"Why me and none of them other kids?" she wanted to know. "Maybe they've got some purty dumb notions too. But you don't spend any of yore time with *them*. I think Zarky suspicions that this purty ring came from *you*, and Zarky says there's a lot of talk going around that you are giving me private lessons in 'reproductive behavior.' I wasn't sure what she meant. Don't ye dare laugh, but until I read it in the book, I never heard of a *pennus!* "

Colvin blushed, but he corrected her pronunciation. "That's

'pee-nis.' Why do you think the textbook kept puttin off that chapter, till the very end? Since all the rest of the body is the result of what happens to it *after* it's been conceived by the coming together of the male and female, you'd think that chapter on Reproduction ought to come first instead of last, wouldn't ye? Why do you think they held off so long?"

Tenny thought. "No, maybe the whole reason that all of the other things are there—bone and blood and breath—is to make the coming together of the male and female possible. Maybe the book's trying to say that's all we live for."

Colvin smiled. "I never thought of it that way, but I reckon ye may be right. I thought the book put it off so long in order to give us time to get used to the idee. You know there's no way I could start off the first day of class talking about sex. I have to build up to it. I have to git to know ye first."

"Do ye know me now?"

"I know ye now." He reached up on the shelf and took down the lollipop box to show her that it was empty. "There aint no more, and I aint gonna git another box, and school's over, anyhow. I reckon I've learnt near about all ye have to tell me." Painful though the very thought of it was, Colvin was trying to work his way up toward saying good-bye. This was the last day of school, and she would be going home tomorrow, and it was quite possible he would never see her again. Even if her parents were not determined to get her married off, now that she was sixteen, she might not be coming back to Parthenon again, and, in any case, he had made up his mind not to return himself. But the closer he got to the moment of saying good-bye, the more he realized he wasn't going to be able to do it. He was in love.

"The last page in the textbook is about death," she pointed out. "I'm still a-dying, and you haven't cured me of that."

194

"We're all a-dying, Tenny," he said, surprised he'd been able to say her name correctly without messing up. "The textbook says, 'While death is the natural end of life, it is not its aim—we should not live to die, but live prepared to die.' You've been living to die, Tenny. I wush I could of stopped ye from doing that. I wush they was some way I could prove to ye what ye jist said: that maybe the whole expectation of us livin and havin bodies is not for dyin, let alone gittin sick, but the coming together of male and female."

"There *is* a way you could prove it to me," she suggested, although she had to catch her breath three times to say this.

And he knew what she meant, but he couldn't do it here, not in his office, not on that lounge. Not even with the door locked. He wasn't even sure he could do it if some magic enchantment could evacuate all the rest of the population of the campus and Parthenon too and leave him and Tenny the whole place all to themselves, with a big bed right in the middle of it, and it full dark with maybe just a nice moon to set the mood. Picturing such a scene in his mind's eye, he recognized a certain familiarity about the setting: you only see places like that in dreams. Thinking of dreams, he had a sudden bright idea, and he asked her, "Do you ever dream, of a night?" Of course, she said; doesn't everybody? "What do you dream about?" he asked. She reminded him how for example that whole week last fall she had a dream every single night of him, with all her clothes off, and him poking some instruments into every orifice of her body. It had nearly cost him her respect for him, because he had been totally unable to find anything wrong with her. "And was I really there in your dream as if you could reach out and touch me?" he wanted to know. It was more like him reaching out and doing all the touching, she said, but she sure could feel it, all over her body. "Well, then, Tenny, how about, tonight, let's—" He tried to make his suggestion, but he couldn't come right out with it. After all, she was a virgin, and he wasn't sure he had any right to take her virginity away from her, even in a dream, not in this year that she was scheduled to become married. He postponed bluntly suggesting, "—Let's me and you have a dream in which we lay down together . . ." by becoming gruffly pedantic and trying to explain to her certain matters which were not covered in the hygiene textbook, namely incubation, succubation, and masturbation. None of these were covered because all three of them were events in the mind's eye, and the textbook didn't even discuss the mind's eye, a supreme part of the anatomy even though it was invisible, like the things it observed. All three words came from the Latin root, *cubare*, to lie down upon, same root that gives us concubine, meaning a woman who lies down with a man without being married to him. *Incubatio* refers to the man lying down with the woman, in her dream; *succubatio* refers to the woman lying down with the man, in his dream; and *masturbatio* refers to anybody lying down with themselves . . .

Tenny yawned. She had to yawn, not because she was bored, but because she had understood very quickly what her lover was trying to suggest but wasn't able to, and the suggestion had taken her breath away, and when your breath gets stolen, according to the textbook, yawning is an involuntary respiratory reflex that returns your breath to you. But when Colvin saw her yawning, he assumed he was boring her, so he tried again, "How about, tonight when we go to sleep, you in your bed and me in mine, and we start to have dreams, how about let's—" Damn him, he *still* couldn't come right out and say it, and Tenny was about to become asphyxiated despite yawning.

So she used what little breath she had left to say, or ask, "I'll be your concubine and succubate you?"

"That's the idee!" he said. "Except of course a concubine is a lady with a lot of experience, and it will be your first time, so I'll have to be real careful and gentle with you."

She had no breath left, but she managed to utter, "I caint wait."

The really good thing about doing it this way, he explained to her, was that they were permitted to choose whatever location they wanted, just anywhere at all, and furnish it as they wished, and even decide what kind of fancy clothing they would be wearing when they took it off to get undressed So they were able to kill the rest of the long afternoon by discussing and determining the ideal setting for their tryst, adjusting the temperature, getting the moonlight just right, selecting the bedcovers, starting a breeze to waft the curtained canopy of the huge four-poster, and even deciding which platters the Victrola would play throughout, a mixture of soft and slow numbers in the beginning, and faster things later on.

They were all set. But one thing troubled Tenny, and she was brave enough to inquire about it. She reminded him that she was in only the second day of having a friend or flying the flag, whatever, and she was worried that might be messy, not a message from 'See. "I might could git blood all over ye," she warned.

He patted her hand. "My goodness, I'm a doctor, Tenny, and folks've been gittin blood all over me for years."

Trying to kill the rest of the day in her dormitory, she reflected that he hadn't even given her a good-bye kiss, which might have left her with something to help endure the rest of the dying but everlasting day.

Killing time in his barnyard and killing a rooster for Piney to cook for supper, he realized that he and Tenny had not agreed on a specific time to hop into their dreambed together.

Time, though, is just something you kill in your waking hours. In dreams, time is indestructible, undying.

But Tenny could not get to sleep. Away in the night, Zarky whispered, "You still awake, Ten?"

Long after bedtime, Piney said, "You still awake, hon?" but Colvin lay there feeling like a kid on the night before Christmas.

It must have been after midnight before Tenny and Colvin finally met, and joined hands and gazed together at the huge mahogany four-poster with a quilt in a Garden Butterfly pattern of velvet and linen broadcloth, and a canopy hung with long chiffon curtains a-wafting gently in the breeze to the tune of slow violins on the Victrola. Tenny was dressed in a royal purple silk nightgown that clung nicely to all the swells and buds of her young body. Colvin was dressed in a loose-fitting flouncy-sleeved white shirt such as swashbucklers wear to do their duels and adventures in. *Can you see me?* he asked her uncertainly, because the atmosphere was just a mite clabbered. *Naw, I'm blind of one eye, and caint see out th'othern,* she replied, but she was just teasing in response to his silly question, because of course she could see him, and he had never looked handsomer, even in her previous dreams. *Well,* he said, gesturing at the extravagant bed, *do you want to crawl in first, or you want me to, or both of us at the same instant, or what?* She put her finger on his lips, saying, *Oh hush, Colvin. Could you jist hold me real tight for a long time, first?* So they just put their arms around each other, and mashed their fronts together, and squeezed. Neither of them had any further doubt that they were "real." But just to be certain, she stroked the back of his neck with one of her hands, and he lay one of his hands alongside her cheek, and they spent a long moment assuring themselves that their hands were indeed touching live flesh that was warm, almost hot. Even that was not enough, so Tenny said, or asked,

Do you think we could kiss, now? and she raised her lips and after an awkward few moments of readjusting their noses to keep them from bumping into each other, they succeeded in getting their mouths to mash together. He reflected upon how the anatomical juxtaposition of two *orbicularis oris* muscles in a state of contraction can be felt in the soles of the feet, the spine of the back, and in every corner of the brain. She had tried to kiss him on the mouth that very first evening of that first day they'd met, last October, but her aim had been off, and she'd missed, and she'd waited all year for this second chance. Now her aim was pretty good, except for the noses. Each of them was thinking, simultaneously, in the same words, "I wonder how long a kiss ought to last," but neither of them did anything to remove their lips, and pretty soon Colvin realized that his *corpora cavernosa* were engorged with blood, while Tenny studied the sensation of a liquid seeping from her vulva that was certainly not blood but something else. *I'd better take a look,* she said, concerned, and stepped back, but Colvin misunderstood her, thinking she wanted to have her very first view of the male organ, and rather timidly he exposed himself to her view. It is possible that some things get exaggerated in dreams, and maybe the penis Tenny saw was larger than in "reality," but whatever the case that sudden materialization before her sight of an object the textbook hadn't even had the guts to illustrate distracted her entirely from her immediate objective, which was to determine the color and composition of whatever was smearing up her groin. *Hold on a second,* she told him, and nervous Colvin took that to mean she wanted him to handle his own part, so he got a good grip on it. But what she meant was that she needed a second to lift her own royal purple nightgown and run her hand up between her legs to find out what that substance was. She examined her fingers: it certainly wasn't blood, it wasn't even the least bit reddish. It was kind of like some clear ointment. Tenny had a quick mind, and if dreams exaggerate, then her mind was even quicker now, as she stared back and forth between her fingertips and his greatly distended penis, and realized the connection: what was coming out of her was an involuntary liniment intended to grease the passage of that big penis into her vagina. All year in hygiene she had studied the marvels of the involuntary system—heartbeat and breathing and glandular activity—the things that go without any effort on our part to keep them going, and now *this* struck her as the most marvelous involuntary doing of her whole body, and made her think again of 'See, as if 'See had returned once more to oversee the sweet ceremony of saying good-bye to virginity, and was bringing along the oil to do it with. This hard breathing she was doing was certainly as if 'See had resumed control of her lungs. Of course Colvin's mind was just as quick as hers, if not quicker, and he understood what she was doing, and thinking, and therefore he did not even need to say, as he was tempted to, *That there is jist the secretion of the greater vestibular glands of Bartholin.* No need to bring that Danish physician into their bower, nor that British surgeon William Cowper, who named the glands that were producing a big drop of dew on the end of Colvin's instrument. In just a little while, he might say something like, *Let's mix your Bartholin with my Cowper,* but before they did that he wanted to make sure that Tenny understood two important things: the rupturing of the hymenal membrane, which would mingle one kind of new blood with the older blood of her menses, and her possession of a tubercle at the top of her vulvar groove which was homologous with the penis and ought to be respected as the seat of the woman's pleasure just as the penis was the man's. All the textbook had dared to say about it was to name it, *clitoris,* and to say it was very sensitive. Colvin wanted to be sure Tenny knew how to use it, because it wasn't something a girl could wrap her fist around and jerk off.

In dreams it scarcely matters, or is even known, whether one is right-side up or upside down, so without even being aware of it they were no longer vertical but horizontal, stretched out together upon the percale sheets of that fabulous bed, and Colvin took Tenny's fingers in his own and guided them to the exploration of her vestibule, while he gave her a rather lengthy explanation of the structure and function of, as well as both the practical and pretty reasons for, the hymen and the clitoris. Tenny grew squirmy, not because she was embarrassed, nor because she was impatient, but because it was exciting her as she had never been aroused before, not the feel of her own fingers *there* but the thought that it was his fingers which were making her fingers feel. We all need to feel that others are making us feel. But I'm afraid there was one other reason for her squirming. All this time, the Victrola had somehow started a new platter; this was a good sixteen years before the first automatic changeable Victrola, but dreams don't know that, and it was playing not just the violins getting faster but a bunch of clarinets and oboes and flutes getting faster and faster, urgent and immediate, and Tenny thought she was approaching a glimpse of that Other Place where people and birds and bugs don't never have to eat nor breathe nor defecate. But she suddenly realized that here on the doorstep of Paradise she needed to go to the privy. They had not taken the trouble to furnish their dream with an outhouse, but there was a lush virgin forest all around their bower, and she could "use the bushes" just as well as she had back home on Brushy Mountain. *'Scuse me,* she said, *I'll be right back.* And she jumped out of that big four-poster and ran off into the forest, hoping she was not ruining the moment or the mood. Colvin sadly watched her go, and worried that his *corpora cavernosa* would release their blood and let his pecker droop and he might have an awful time getting it to rise again.

Now I hate to mention it, but I myself have got to attend to one of nature's subpoenas. Son, I'm going to have to ask you to excuse me while I summon the orderly to help me get out of this bed and into that potty-chair yonder. No, no, I don't want you to help me; I'm such a goddamned cripple I have to be lifted and carried. The whole process is so complicated and cumbersome that I'd appreciate it if you'd just run along now and hold your curiosity until tomorrow, when I'll be obliged to reveal the somewhat disturbing conclusion to that wonderful dream-tryst they were having.

Damn it all, I'm almost eager to get myself to that Other Place where people don't have to eat nor breathe nor

Seven

I don't mind telling you that yesterday after you left and I finished my interminable business, Mary C. and I got to talking about this matter of being able to take a roll in the hay in your dreams. Mary said she didn't think it was possible. Well, you'll recall when I was a graduate student in psychology at Clark, I did my whole damn thesis on dreams, and I must've read everything written on the subject, not just Freud, but Jung, Ferenczi, Brill, Abraham, all those fellers. Two things I learned pretty fast: one, all dreams are sexual, period. But two, there are very few dreams that are explicitly sexual. Dreams are filled with sexual symbols, but you hardly ever see a real pecker or a real twitchet in a dream, let alone such particulars as maidenheads or clits. I not only kept records of all my own dreams in those days but I went around talking to other graduate students, women as well as men, and getting them to tell me their dreams, and I almost never found a case of anybody actually getting their ashes hauled in a dream, and let me tell you this right now: I never once found a single case of any two people having the same dream at the same time, goddamn it!

So what are we to make of this story? This is what me and Mary got into an argument about that lasted till bedtime last night, and then she had the boldness to suggest to me that we give it a try, I mean, see if we couldn't "get together" in our dreams. Hell, maybe I shouldn't be saying it, but Mary and me haven't "got together" in the world of "reality" for many and many a year. We don't never even sleep together. I was already past seventy when I married her, and it wasn't no May and December marriage neither, more like November and December. But anyhow, just as an experiment, we agreed last night to see if we couldn't meet in our dreams. We tried our best, too. But the sad fact is, you don't have no control whatever over what you're going to dream. Among the involuntary systems of the human body, the dreaming system is the most involuntary of them all.

That don't mean the story of Colvin and Tenny is a bunch of hooey. Nor even a fairy tale. Any good story, in order to hold our interest and entertain us, *must* concern itself with things that never happened to us but which we believe could possibly happen to us. And I for one, even though I never met Mary nor anybody else in my dreams for the explicit purposes of un-ashamed and undisguised he'n-and-she'n, have the right to believe that what happened to Colvin *could've* happened to me!

So if you and Mary want to sit there and laugh behind your hands while I try to tell this, go right ahead, that's your privi-lege. If you don't want to believe me, you might as well just turn off that hearing aid, goddamn it, and I'll lay here and finish telling the story to myself, which is what I've been doing most of the time anyhow when you aren't here or Mary Celestia has faded off into whatever celestial realm she prefers to inhabit.

Anyway, excuse the interruption, and excuse my present dyspepsia. I hope you didn't get too impatient, being sent away right smack in the middle of the first really good sex that we've had so far, before it even had a chance to "consummate" itself, as they say. Maybe yesterday I didn't have the heart, nor the bowels, to reveal that this sex story didn't have a climax, but an anticlimax.

Because when Tenny, hurrying so fast to finish her visit to the bushes that she dampened her pretty purple nightdress, finally got back to the four-poster, rehearsing in her mind how the time had come at last that she could say, *Colvin Swain, I love thee,* she discovered to her horror that there was a naked lady in bed with Colvin! Being smart, she knew that sometimes in dreams we can step aside from ourselves and see ourselves as if we were somebody else, so she calmed down enough to attempt to tell herself that the naked lady in the bed was herself. But the lady's hair was blond, not light brown nor nearly as long as her own, and it was cut in the fashion of Mrs. Breedlove's. And she and Colvin were wrestling to beat all, something fierce, with Venda on top! Colvin looked over Venda's shoulder and saw Tenny and yelled her name, *Tenny!* but she had already turned and was running as hard as she could, trying to find her way out of there.

Zarky was shaking her shoulder, saying, "Wake up, Ten! You're havin a nightmare."

"I sure am," she said, and burst into tears, and cried so hard that Zarky had to hold her until sunrise, when she got up and began stuffing her clothes and books and things into a gunnysack to take them back home to Brushy Mountain.

"Who's Tenny?" Piney asked Colvin.

He stared at her while he rubbed his busted dream out of his eyes, and began to feel the intense frustration of not having achieved his expected joy. "Aw, heck," he said. "I was jist havin this dream of treatin ole Jim Bullen for his heart problem, and I asked his wife, Sarah, 'He took that there medicine I gave him, din't he?' And when she wouldn't answer, I kept a-saying, "Din't he? Din't he?' You must've jist heard me saying, 'Din't he,' not 'tenny.'" Then Colvin jumped out of bed, grabbed a quick breakfast, and told Piney he had to go back up to Parthenon to collect his belongings. Piney wanted to know why he hadn't just collected his belongings yesterday, on the last day of school, but he could only say that he'd overlooked a bunch of things.

He drove as fast as he dared without running the buggy off the road or wearing Nessus out, and reached the N.C.A. while it was still early day, and parents were arriving and departing with their wagons, and a few automobiles, to pick up their kids to take them home. Seeing him, his devoted students gathered around him to say good-bye and to wish him a happy summer and to beg him to please reconsider and come back in the fall to teach something else like psychology or basketball. Colvin, who was looking all around for Tenny, could only tell them that he'd sure had a lot of pleasure knowing them, and he hoped they'd have the best of luck in life and not forget to take real good care of their bodies and systems.

He couldn't find Tenny. He even entered the girls' dormitory and boldly marched up to the sleeping rooms, but Tenny wasn't among them. Thelma Villines, the housemother, grabbed him and told him that men wasn't allowed up here. He asked her, "Have you seen Tennessee Tennison?" but she could only say she reckoned that Tenny had done already gone. Colvin spotted

Ozarkia Emmons on the front porch, and asked her, "Have you seen Tenny?"

Zarky gave him a kind of frightened look and said, "Teacher, I don't know what ye done to her last night, but ye broke her heart. She cried her eyes out 'til daybust, then lit out fer home."

"Afoot?" he asked. And when Zarky nodded, he looked wildly around, as if he could see her, and asked, "Whichaway is Brushy Mountain, do ye know?"

Zarky pointed vaguely eastwards, then corrected her point to southeastwards. "Some'ers up in there way over round about beyond Mount Judy," she said.

He had no idea how far it was, but he thought he might be able to catch up with her, and he was getting back into his buggy when Venda Breedlove came up to him and put her hand on his arm and said, "Honey, I'm sorry about last night."

He stared at her. Rather than accept her apology, he replied, "You ort to be. That wasn't your dream. That there dream belonged to somebody else."

"Let me guess who," she said. "If you're aimin to catch up with her, you're way too late. She caught her a ride out of Jasper on the mail truck."

Colvin clenched his teeth, and glared at Venda. "Woman, you've done went and made an awful how-de-do of things. Tenny took a lot of trouble to git that rondy-voo set up jist right, and you come buttin in and spoilt it."

"That there was the purtiest bed I ever did see," Venda declared. "I jist couldn't resist it!"

"Hit was Tenny's four-poster, and quilt, and all, gosh-darn ye!"

"She's jist a chile, Colvin," Venda said. "Even in yore wildest dreams, she caint give ye the kind of lovin I could give ye, if you'd let me. You shouldn't have thrown me out." And Venda put her hand on his knee and began to scoot it along the inside of his thigh.

Colvin told himself that if all he was interested in was loving a woman, he couldn't do better than Venda. This gal had the old oomph oozing out of every pore of her body, and oomph was not in his medical dictionary but could easily be defined as *that,* or possibly *it,* with a lot of *these* and *those,* or *what it takes.* Venda Breedlove had what it takes to run up any man's pressure. All year long she had been so friendly with him, and made herself so available, that if he hadn't been completely absorbed with Tenny, he could easily have given in to Venda's obvious enticements. Even after he had thrown her out of the four-poster, he had had more than physical pangs of regret. Her naked body had felt so voluptuous during the moments it took him to disengage himself from her that even now, thinking of it, he felt the blood backing up in his *corpora cavernosa,* and for a long moment he gazed upon sweet Venda with a desire that erased Tenny for the duration from his mind.

The gossip about Venda Breedlove was almost as alluring as her seductive body, and Colvin had been tempted all year to invite her to lie on his lounge and tell him all about herself, if not with a lollipop perhaps with a soda pop and a sentence he had rehearsed in his mind but had never spoken to her, "I've heard so many stories about you, I'd like to know the truth." Nobody knows where she came from. She was said to be an orphan who was discovered one day floating in a johnboat on the Buffalo River, fully grown but as naked as she'd climbed into that four-poster, amnesiac but so lovely that she entranced the three sisters who found her, rescued her, dressed her, and took her home with them. These sisters, Aggie, Thalie, and Phrosie Grace, lived up toward Pruitt in northern Newton County, and they dutifully notified Sheriff J. C. Barker of their discovery, but he made an investigation without being able to find out just who she was or where she was from, or what she was doing naked in that johnboat. She had no memory of a mother or father, and wasn't wearing a wedding ring. Sheriff Barker wasn't about to let those Grace girls keep her, because everybody knew those girls were kind of "funny," if you know what I mean—it was a scandalous sort of Lesbian incest going on amongst them—and Barker was afraid they might turn the poor girl into one of them, so he took her home to his wife, figuring to give her a place to stay temporarily until she could find work or a husband, whichever came first. Pretty soon Barker himself was sneaking around with her, and Mrs. Barker was about to throw her out, so Barker fixed her up with his best buddy, Mulciber Breedlove, the blacksmith, who had once been living with Aggie Grace, one of those girls who found Venda.

Old Mulce was just about the ugliest feller in Jasper, and he was practically a cripple from a childhood accident that left him with twisted feet and dislocated hips, and a way of walking that made folks poke fun at him when they ran out of jokes about the fact that Aggie became a dyke as a result of trying to live with him. But he was a steady worker, the best blacksmith in the country, and a solid, peaceable, upstanding citizen, and he fell in love with Venda at first sight and became her devoted slave, willing to do anything for her. He made her a lot of jewelry out of horseshoe nails that was a sight to behold. Venda was so charmed by a wedding ring that he made out of a horseshoe nail that she couldn't turn him down, and became his bride. He was the happiest man in the Ozarks, having such a beauty for a wife, but he should've had the sense to know he couldn't hold her. When the baby boy Russ was born, Mulce became even more devoted as a father than he'd been as a husband, but he already had suspicions that he might not be the boy's real father, or at best only one of his fathers, since the boy had two peckers, a sign that maybe he had two daddies.

Rumors of Venda's infidelities were commonplace. She was not just the most beautiful woman in the country (your Latha was still a little girl at the time) but she was also the earthiest. Folks called her feisty and fleshy, the latter having nothing to do with her weight but with her devotion to the pleasures of the flesh. Feisty suggests *fast* and fleshy suggests *flashy,* and she was both of those too.

She had a lot of nerve accusing Colvin of picking a child when he took up with Tenny, because Venda's own most famous love affair was with a boy who was practically just a kid, a teenager from up around Gum Springs named Donny Kilgore. He was only fifteen when Venda was out in the woods one day trying to show her little boy Russ how to hunt with his "bone air," and she come across Donny also a-hunting, and was so smitten with passion for him that she left little Russ to amuse himself while she talked Donny into stepping over behind some boulders to hide them from sight. Venda didn't take Russ with her next time she went hunting. She was bringing home more rabbits than they and all the neighbors could eat, and Mulce complained she was hunting too much. The truth was, Donny was such a good shot he could bag a whole nest of rabbits in no time flat, and have all the remainder of the afternoon to shag Venda. But pretty soon she wasn't even bothering to bring home rabbits, nor even squirrels. She'd just disappear at all hours and didn't even care if Mulce fumed and hollered. Practically everybody knew she and Donny were off somewheres fucking like minks, and a few folks had even spied them at it, in broad daylight.

But Donny kept on hunting in the woods, because that's what he liked to do, next best to shagging Venda, and that was his downfall, because one time when he was a-chasing a bunch of wild razorback hogs, one of the big old boars turned and charged him and buried those sharp tusks in his side. Venda found him and took him to Doc McFerrin in Jasper, but it was too late to help him, and he died, and Venda was so heartbroken she didn't even think about fooling around with anyone else . . . except her favorite man, who was Mulce's brother.

I can vouch for that brother myself, from the time when I was stationed at Camp Pike in North Little Rock, during the First World War. My battalion captain in the infantry was a feller named Marty Breedlove, and he used to brag about going home on furlough to Jasper, where he'd "snitch a little twitchet" from a gal named Venda, who he'd been a-banging ever since she married his brother fifteen years before. This Breedlove was a stuck-up, belligerent dude with a real mean streak in him, and I never liked him. He was a right handsome feller, though, and claimed that Venda loved him because his brother was ugly as sin, and sin was a subject Venda was a foremost authority on.

Seems what happened was, his brother, Mulce, caught them at it, in his own bed, and he threw a minnow seine over them to tie them up together while he beat the living shit out of both of them. Marty came back to Camp Pike from the furlough all black and blue, and wouldn't say any more about it. Venda was forced to move out, and took the boy with her, and went off to Shenandoah Music School to study singing so she could get some kind of job. When she finally came back to Jasper, Mulce went to court and got an order that the boy had to spend weekends with him, and that was the arrangement that was still in effect when Colvin first met Venda.

When the Baptists hired Venda to teach music at the new Newton County Academy, they didn't know anything about her past; all they knew was that she had a certificate from the

Shenandoah Music School and knew a few tunes on the piano. But rumor grows faster than tumor, and pretty soon Jossie Conklin had heard enough about Venda to require a little meeting between them, during which Venda told Jossie that she had turned over a new leaf and wiped her nose, in order to bring up her boy Russ properly, and she'd even start going to Sunday school if they wanted her to. In fact, her and Jossie became real good friends, and it was Venda who taught Jossie how to get a man . . . but that's another story. And it's true that for the whole duration of that first school year, Venda did not stray from the straight and narrow, she actually went to Sunday school, and she taught her pupils how to sing all those good old-time Baptist hymns as well as the Newton County Academy song. She paid a lot of attention to Russ, as if to make up for neglecting him when he was a child, and she bought him that beautiful white stallion Marengo not just so she'd have transportation from her Jasper house to Parthenon, but so all the other kids would look up to Russ and maybe even forgive him for being such a mischievous scamp, always bent on causing trouble, maybe what we'd call a punk nowadays. Because Jossie and Venda were such good friends, Jossie went easy on Russ when he misbehaved and broke the rules, like riding Marengo around the school yard a lot faster than was safe. Russ had more demerits than anyone but Tenny, and Jossie was known to remark, more than once, that Russ and Tenny ought to make a pair, because they both had the same habit of trying to see how much they could get away with. But if Jossie was tempted more than once to expel or suspend Tenny, she wouldn't want to do that to the son of her good chum Venda.

If Venda herself had genuinely reformed, as far as her general conduct was concerned, it was only because she had outgrown the likes of lame Mulce and his belligerent brother

212

Marty, and she realized that even the late lamented Donny Kilgore had been beautiful and loads of fun in bed but scarcely worth talking to. Going off to that music school had shown her that there were men in the world who were interested in higher matters than using her vaginal muscles in lieu of their own fingers. As soon as she met Colvin Swain, on that first day of school when he'd examined her along with the rest of the teachers, and had been so pleasant and kind and genuinely interested in her as a person, she knew that this dark, mysterious man had a deep, sensitive side that could possibly respond to parts of her that no other men had ever known. Colvin was not nearly as handsome as Marty Breedlove, and he wasn't even in the same category of manhood with Donny Kilgore, but he had a certain strength, and ruggedness, and cozy down-home attractiveness about him that made him more satisfying to behold than any man she had ever laid eyes upon. Most of all, he was intelligent, even wise. Venda Breedlove felt that knowing Colvin Swain would be the best way to know herself.

The trouble was, he seemed to be preoccupied with that girl, Tennessee Tennison, who Jossie was always complaining about as a "problem pupil," even though Tenny was the top student in Venda's music class and the best soprano in the Glee Club. Although Venda was madly jealous of his constant attentions to Tenny, she understood that it was in his nature as a wise, sympathetic physician to want to help a young woman beset with problems, and she did not hold it against him. After all, he had cured the girl of cerebral palsy, deafness, blindness, and a whole bunch of other disorders. You don't blame a Samaritan for his benefaction. But Venda had been trying all year, in subtle as well as not-so-subtle ways, to let Colvin know she was available to show him undreamed-of physical pleasure, and he had not risen to the bait, and she was beginning to suspect that he was actually violating the unwritten principle that teachers should not seduce their students. That, or else he was getting all he wanted from some dumpy cow of a wife back home in Stay More.

Venda was beginning to get evil-minded again, and to itch for a man's arms and his other three extremities. She had never gone for so long, eight months, without any sex other than what could be so easily obtained in laying down with herself in fantasy or dream. As a matter of fact, it had been during one of her autoerotic dreams that she had become disgusted with herself and gone rushing out into the forest in search of any creature's actual penis, a desperate journey that had caused her accidental discovery of that magnificent four-poster with Colvin just lying alone on it with a hard-on that was beginning to droop. It was the answer to all her dreams, and fortunately she was already conveniently divested of any nightwear, since she never slept in a stitch. But when she took a flying leap onto him, he tried to push her away. And he had spoken aloud one dreadful word, *Tenny!*

Now, however, his Tenny was gone home for the summer to whatever bushwhacker shack she inhabited in the remote sticks of the county, where her folks would get her married off before she became any more sixteen than she already was, and Venda could invite Colvin to drop in and visit her in her pretty white cottage off the square in Jasper. "How about this afternoon?" she asked him.

Colvin was tempted, although he didn't particularly care for Jasper. The county seat was a place he had to visit when he needed to pick up something at Arbaugh's Rexall, or when he had to go to the courthouse, but Jasper was the private turf and battlefield of two other competing physicians, McFerrin and

Bradley, and he was not comfortable stomping around in their stomping grounds. "I better not, I reckon," he declined, and then, because it is automatic hospitality to temper any rejection with a counterinvitation, he added, "You'd better jist come go home with me."

Venda raised her eyebrows. "What about your wife?" she asked.

"Oh, I din't mean it like that," he said, wondering why Venda didn't understand that such invitations are just formalities, tendered in courtesy, not meant to be taken literally. "I just meant, if ye ever happen to be in Stay More, stop in and say howdy."

"So that's it?" Venda demanded. "I throw myself at ye, and that's all I git?" When he did not comment, she said, "You aint a-comin back here to work in the fall, so I might not never even see ye again. Except maybe in my dreams. Do ye suppose we could git together once in a while in our dreams? I'll furnish the four-poster."

Colvin could only smile as pleasantly as he could and say, "I'm sure it would be a right purty bed, but, to tell ye the honest truth, I think I'm going to have to give up dreamin. It's too risky." He raised his coach whip and gave a cluck to Nessus, and the buggy began to move.

"You haven't seen the last of me, Colvin Swain!" Venda hollered after him. He would not stop. He kept on going, down the hill, away from Newton County Academy, out of her life. "But you've seen the last of Tenny!" she screamed.

He stopped. He turned. He stared at her, and asked, "Jist what do ye mean by that?"

"You know she's supposed to git herself married, now that she's sixteen," Venda said.

"Yeah, that's right, I reckon," he said, and drove on. But as the summer progressed, Colvin began to wonder if Venda was right, that he never would see his Tenny again.

For a while, Colvin kept on trying to meet Tenny in his dreams. Every night he would find the spot in the enchanted forest where their bower had been, and it was still there. He would sit down atop that beautiful Garden Butterfly-pattern quilt of Tenny's, and just wait for as long as he could stand it. Sometimes he would call for her, softly. She never showed up, and so he just started sleeping in that four-poster. It was a mattress that Tenny had stuffed with the down of a hundred geese, and even a few swans thrown in for good measure, and it was the best sleeping that Colvin had ever had. Whenever he woke up, he was always back in his own bed beside Piney, but he was so rested that even his arthritis stopped bothering him.

Life went on. Piney was glad that he wasn't leaving three times a week to go to Parthenon, and she started showing her appreciation in several ways, cooking his favorite dinners with a lot of special pies and cakes for dessert, refraining from arguing with him whenever she was right and he was wrong about anything, and totally satisfying his libido before he dropped off to sleep and went searching for that four-poster, which he no longer sought in expectation of consummating the unfinished love with Tenny but only in hopes of finding her and talking to her and explaining to her what had happened before.

One night when he went to the four-poster, he was surprised to discover that there was another, larger four-poster right beside it, with an even more beautiful quilt in a Cottage Tulip pattern, atop which was reclining the naked, wriggling, perfumed body of Venda Breedlove. She was a sight such as no man could resist . . . except a man who had just been disbur-

216

dened of all his semen by his wife. *Sorry, chickabiddy,* he had to say to her, *but I'm all fucked out.*

Then what did ye come here for? she demanded. He explained to her that he just wanted to talk to Tenny, that he'd been coming here every night hoping to find her. He said he hoped that Venda hadn't done anything to her. *She's gone to Brushy Mountain, and probably already married,* Venda declared. *You might jist as well climb in here with me, and I'll bet ye a hunerd dollars I know something that will rise up yore pecker again.* Colvin said that he had no doubt that Venda could do it if anybody could but he just wasn't of a mind to try it, right now. Then he asked her if she knew where Brushy Mountain was. *Do you think I'd tell ye, even if I knew?* she said. *But I honestly don't have any idee whar it is. Jist some'ers at the ends of the airth.*

All that summer, Colvin had been in the habit of asking people if they might know the location of Brushy Mountain. His dad, old Alonzo Swain, had been all over the whole county and knew the name of every mountain, hill, and rise, but he'd never heard of Brushy Mountain. Colvin asked several oldtimers, patients of his who'd lived in Newton County all their long lives and done some traveling all over the county's back brush, and one very old man said that he'd been there, many years ago, but had been drunk at the time, so he couldn't even draw a map, and all he knew was that it was somewhere east of Stay More, east of Spunkwater too, up toward Mount Judea. Colvin checked with Postmaster Willis Ingledew on the possibility that there might even be a post office of that name, "Brushy Mountain," but there wasn't. Finally Colvin overcame his prejudice against Jasper to venture into the county seat and inquire at the tax assessor's office. B. E. Greenhaw, the assessor, consulted his maps and his plats and his rolls and his records, and found a Dry Brush Fork and a Bushart Holler, but no Brushy Mountain. Driving his buggy away from the courthouse, Colvin passed the pretty little white cottage where Venda lived, and there she was, sitting on her porch swing, and she saw him, and began beckoning like mad, trying to get him to come join her, but he just lowered his head and drove on.

One day Colvin got a postcard from Tenny. All it said was a question: "Dear Colvin. What do you call the disease of being unable to dream? Your Tenny." There was no return address. The postmark was Mount Judea, so Colvin decided to just send a letter addressed to her General Delivery at Mount Judea, and he wrote and rewrote it five or six times before he was satisfied with it. He told her there was no word in the medical dictionary for such a condition, so he would have to coin a word, *oneiresia,* loss of the power to dream, a word just for her and her temporary (he hoped) condition. He told her that he was awfully sorry that their romantic rendezvous in that dream had been trespassed upon by an uninvited interloper, Venda Breedlove. He explained that even though Mrs. Breedlove had been as naked as the day she was born, there had not been any actual intercourse between them. He suggested that Tenny ought to try drinking some butterfly weed tea before bedtime to help her relax, and allow herself to dream again, and if she could do that, Colvin would be glad to join her, and they could pick up where they'd left off before they'd been so rudely interrupted. He said that if she still couldn't dream, just send him some kind of little map to show how to get to her house, and he'd rush right up there and handle all her problems in person in broad daylight. He said that he sure did care for her more than he'd ever cared for anybody, and he thought she was the most wonderful person who ever lived. He mailed this off, and waited,

218

unable to do anything else for five days, until his letter was returned to the Stay More Post Office marked in a postmaster's crude scrawl "ADRESSY ONKNOWEN," and Piney, picking up the day's mail, asked him who Tennessee Tennison was. He took his letter, tossed it into a pile of papers on his desk, and said it was just some student who'd tried to get her grade changed.

The summer was almost gone before it eventually dawned on Colvin that we don't need to know the exact location of a place to reach it in our dreams. All those years he'd been obliged to practice the dream cure, when patients were no longer actually coming to his clinic, nor even sending messengers there to summon him to their homes, he had been venturing to all sorts of locations to treat the various dream patients. He had delivered babies on rooftops and tree limbs, and removed tonsils in streambeds and caves. He had performed cystoscopies while riding backwards on a galloping horse, and had set more than one broken bone while floating in the air. Seldom if ever would he have been able to say, "I'm two miles eastwards on Banty Creek" or "I'm about to enter Jesse Dinsmore's place." Locations don't matter in dreams.

So one night at bedtime he decided he'd have more energy for the journey ahead if he refrained from sex, and he gently told Piney to keep her nightdress down because he had a headache. Instead of mounting him, she stroked his temples with her fingertips, which made him feel guilty for lying but also put him right to sleep. The way was dark, and long, and bent with many strange turnings. He didn't even try to heed forks in the road, nor look for any signs or landmarks. All he had to go by was Tenny's talk about the place during her lollipop sessions: the cabin faced westward, high on Brushy Mountain, and it had tomato crates stacked in the front yard to make crude pews for the Pentecostal services. After a long arduous climb

219

through the mist, Colvin eventually came to such a place, on the western bench of a lofty mountain covered with the brush of red cedar and blackjack oak, and he was accosted by an old hound dog who might have been the one Tenny had told him about, but the dog wasn't wearing pants. His male organ was clearly visible. As dogs are supposed to do, the hound barked to alert the occupants of the house, and a man appeared.

From Tenny's description, Colvin realized the man, in his late fifties, had to be Wayne Don Tennison, but Colvin politely inquired anyway if this was the Tennison place. The man nodded. *I'm Colvin Swain, from over to Stay More,* he said, *and I'd like a word with yore darter, who was my pupil at the Newton County Academy.*

The man made a gesture toward the very top of the mountain, a lofty crag, and said, *Passel akimbo gondola armadillo bodacious oregano now, also enchilada asafetida lally-gaggin mezzo-soprano worryword.*

Colvin stared in the direction the man was pointing but couldn't see anything except the peak, obscured by clouds. Colvin gave his head a shake, to clear his hearing, and said, *I shore am sorry, but I din't catch a word ye said. Wal, maybe one or two words, but they didn't make ary bit of sense.*

Yes, violincello hacienda cabala guano jillikens, the man said, *incunabula zero formula cicada antihero sang root lashins and lavins armada lambda pagoda missingmyth.*

Colvin realized two things at once: the man was not speaking English, nor, despite certain Spanish and other Latinate words, any understandable language; and the man was not now pointing at the mountain peak but was motioning for Colvin to go. *I jist wanted to see Tenny for a minute,* Colvin pled, *to explain something to her and find out if she's all right.*

But the man more dramatically motioned for Colvin to depart the premises, and angrily intoned, *Memoranda dobbers cymlin gigolo, corrigenda lolliper adagio hoopla!*

Tenny came rushing out of the house and grabbed her father's arm, saying, *Daddy, let me talk to him!* But Tenny had aged something terrible! She looked like she was pushing forty, and her beautiful long hair was cut short, and Colvin wanted to cry, "My God! What have they done to you?" but she took his arm and led him away from the house, and out of earshot of her father. She said, *The old fart is jist talkin in tongues and he don't even know what he's sayin.* Then she looked him up and down, saying, *So you're Colvin Swain, air ye? I've heared tell the most marvelous things about ye. But also the most horrible things.* She offered him her hand. *I'm Oriole Eubanks, Tenny's older sister. One of 'em, anyhow. Redbird's coming soon—she lives way off up to Kansas City now, though she din't marry the least bit better than I did, 'cause Jerry Bob Eubanks owns the biggest insurance agency in northwest Arkansas, I'll have ye to know. He couldn't come with me. Too busy. I done been here two weeks, tryin my best to help baby sister, but I done all I could and I'm a-hankerin to git on back to Springdale.*

What's wrong with her? Colvin demanded.

Oh, jist real bad heartsick, I reckon, Oriole said. *Of course she had a bunch of ailments that Maw and Granny helped her with, nothing too serious—summer cold, costiveness, vapors, hip-swinney. But mainly she's jist reached the age where it's time for her to git married, and the only feller in this whole wide world that she wants to marry is* you, *and if we're not mistaken, you've already got a wife. So there. That's it. Pure and simple.* Oriole paused for breath, then examined him more critically, and asked, *You aint by any chance thinkin about leavin yore wife, air ye?*

What could Colvin say? Sure, he had given it some thought, but could not admit, even to himself, that he had been thinking about it. So all he could say was, *Not any time soon. I was sort of hoping to give Tenny a chance to git grown up, and finish school, and all.*

Git growed up? Oriole snorted. *Aint she growed enough fer ye already? I tell ye, if I'd had her face and figure when I was sixteen, I'd of had ever man in the state of Arkansas tryin to lead me to the altar. Well, I din't do so bad, with Jerry Bob, but many's the time I've thought it wasn't fair that God would give such good looks to jist one gal without spreadin it around! And caint none of us understand why a girl as beautiful as her hasn't already had gobs and mobs of fellers proposin to her. Is there somethin wrong with her we don't know about? You're her doctor. Does she have some fatal disease that we don't know about that's scared off all of the fellers that might want her for a wife?*

All Colvin could think to say was, *Tenny's a goddess, I reckon, and all men are afraid of divinity.*

Huh? Oriole said. *Well, it aint funny. Maw and Daddy has even went to see this fortune-tellin woman, Cassie Whitter, who lives way back up on yon mountain, to ask her how to find a man for Tenny.*

Well? Colvin said impatiently, for he knew Cassie Whitter. *What did she have to say?*

Oriole took his arm and directed his attention to the mountain peak, rising up from one end of Brushy Mountain, that Wayne Don had been gesturing at. *See that crag yonder?* Oriole said. *Wal, Tenny's jist a-sittin up there in a black dress, and I'll tell ye why.* The fortune-teller Cassie Whitter, Oriole explained, had done her "reading" of Tenny's future and had at first refused to tell Wayne Don and Jonette what she had discovered. Wayne Don would not leave Cassie's cabin until she told him; Wayne Don promised he would "camp out" there forever and speak in tongues all day long until Cassie told him. She finally gave in. "Hit wouldn't do no good," Cassie said, "to hope for her to have a ordinary husband. You mought as well dress her in a black wedding gown with a black veil and leave her alone on some mountaintop, to see who would come along and take her. Whatever bridegroom she gits is bound to be a freak, maybe a double-headed monster, a pale rider on a pale horse." That's all they could get out of Cassie, and they came back home sorely perplexed, because they didn't know any neighbors who had pale horses, let alone any freakish neighbors, except Clint McCutcheon, who was an albino, which made him pale all right, but his horse was a spotted Appaloosa, not white. And they'd never heard of black wedding gowns, or any other color for that matter, because both Jonette and her mother, Tennessee, had been married in ordinary dresses—fancy dresses, to be sure, but not gowns. The only black garment for women in the household was a sateen wrapper that Tennessee McArtor had ordered from Sears Roebuck to wear to the funeral of her husband, Ray. But it was black, and it could be made to fit Tenny. So Tenny had been up there all day on that mountaintop in that black dress, waiting to see what pale rider would come along on a pale horse, maybe with two heads, the rider, that is, not the horse, but come to think of it, maybe the horse would have two heads too.

Colvin began running toward the mountaintop. *You aint got no pale horse!* Oriole called after him, but he kept running, wishing he had any color of horse, so he could get there faster. That mountain peak was a long way up there, and mostly obscured by mist. He was tired out, and had to slow to a walk and even sit down and rest a bit during the steepest parts of the climb.

At last he heard singing. He recognized, coming from far away, Tenny's lovely soprano voice. He stood still and tried to make out the words, identify the song. But there were no words. It was not even like her father's babble. It was just pure notes, rising and falling, not meant to say anything but only to chant, or to carol, some wordless expression of a feeling he could recognize from having read Robert Burton: kindly melancholy, a mixture of yearning, wanting, hoping, desire, with maybe a tinge of loss and bewilderment. It was an incredibly beautiful song, and it made Colvin's skin break out in goose bumps, and an enormous shiver to run up his spine.

The singing gave him the strength to make one last determined effort to climb the mountain, and finally he came in sight of her, standing on the foggy peak with her arms wrapped around herself and her face lifted to the sky, singing that heartbreaking chant. Black did not become her, and he wanted to grab her and take her home and put her into a pretty dress, and marry her himself if he had to. *Tenny!* he called to her so that she would look down at him.

"Who's Tenny?" Piney asked.

He stared into his wife's eyes until he knew that he had lost his way out of the dream. For a moment he was tempted to answer Piney's question, to confess his love for his student, to express to someone who could understand (and Piney understood everything) his love and his concern and his great uneasiness and even fear over that prophecy of Cassie Whitter's. He knew who the Pale Rider was, and the meaning of the Pale Horse. He was surprised that Wayne Don Tennison, a minister of the Gospel, even if a Holy Roller, was not familiar with the sixth chapter of Revelation. Was Tenny still, at this moment, on that mountain crag? Colvin became more desperate than ever to reach her, but Piney would not let him go back into his dream again. "Aw, I was jist dreamin of buying you a pianer," he said. "We was gone plumb to Little Rock to shop for pianers, and I kept turnin down one or another, this'un sounded too scratchy, and that'un was too twangy, or tinny. I was jist rejectin that tinny pianer when you woke me up."

Maybe Piney didn't believe that, but it was the best he could do. He got up, dressed, had breakfast, and told her it was time he paid his respects on old Kie Raney. He wasn't lying, either. But instead of hitching Nessus to the buggy, he went down the road to Ingledew's Livery and asked Willis Ingledew if he had any pale horses. There was a kind of off-white or dirty-white palfrey named Lampon, and Colvin rented her and rode her as fast as she would go to the cave where he had grown up, in the woods above Spunkwater. Nothing had changed. It was almost as if he were sixteen again, Tenny's age, the age he "graduated" from Kie's preceptorship. And Kie hadn't changed a bit either. He bashfully shook hands with his former foster son and protégé and invited him to sit down and tell his whole life story since he'd left the cave at sixteen. But Colvin apologized, saying he was really in a terrible hurry, and he'd stop back later on to explain, but right now all he wanted was to know if by any chance Kie Raney might know the location of Brushy Mountain. Kie had to scratch what remained of his hair for a long time. "I aint been on Brushy Mountain since I helped a granny woman deliver a breech baby, oh, nigh on to sixty year ago. McArtors they were." Colvin begged Kie Raney to try and remember where Brushy Mountain was and tell him how to get there.

The directions that Kie gave him were similar to those he

had followed in his dream, and he recognized some of the boulders and lightning-struck trees and waterfalls that he had seen in his dream journey. But real journeys are always longer and harder than dream ones, and poor Lampon was tired and worn out by the time Colvin finally reached Brushy Mountain, and he realized he might have to dismount in order to climb up to the crag where Tenny was . . . if she was. He thought he'd best stop at the house to say howdy and ask if Tenny was still up there.

"Now that shore is a kind of a pale horse," Oriole said, smiling. "But you aint very pale yoreself, and you got only one head."

"Howdy," Colvin said. "How's ever little thing? Everbody feelin okay?"

"Maw's got some bad chest pains," Oriole said, "if you'd care to look her over."

"Later, maybe. I got to git on up to the mountaintop to see about Tenny."

"She aint there no more. That real pale horse and that real pale rider done come and got her."

Colvin was stricken. "You don't mean to tell me. You don't mean she . . . she didn't *depart,* did she?"

"She departed down to Jasper, which is where the feller finally took her. She knew him, of course, or we wouldn't've asked him to spend the night, and Daddy wouldn't've allowed her to ride off with him this morning. She knew the pale horse too. Named Malengro or Menargo or something."

"Marengo," Colvin said. Then he said, "Russ Breedlove!"

"You know the feller? Aint he a sight to behold? Maw and Granny is still swoonin over what a looker he is, and I tell ye, I'm tempted to up and leave Jerry Bob myself and see if I caint git Russ to notice me!"

Colvin was a mite perplexed. "You folks just allowed the boy to swoop down and git her and take her off like that?"

"He *was* wearin a white shirt," Oriole declared. "And when he spent the night with us, I talked Tenny into spying on him while he slept, and sure enough, he is a kind of a freak, if not a monster. But despite filling the bill all we could hope for, he claimed he wasn't comin to git her for hisself. Naw. His momma had sent him. That's Tenny's music teacher, Miz Breedlove, and she tole her boy Russ to say that she wanted to give Tenny some private lessons for her voice if Tenny would care to just come stay with her in Jasper, until school started. So Tenny just packed up her school clothes and her books and all, and off they went."

"Voice lessons?" Colvin said, more to himself than to Oriole.

Wayne Don Tennison came out of the house, and said to Colvin, "Kimono ambeer pudenda? Albino chaunk rotunda? Halo silo solo!"

"I think he wants to show you his snake collection," Oriole translated. "Or else he's inviting you to stay to dinner, one."

Colvin stayed to dinner, the womenfolk not sitting down at the table until after he and Wayne Don had finished eating, as was the custom. Then Wayne Don took Colvin to look at his collection of rattlesnakes, copperheads, and water moccasins, and Colvin petted the reptiles and made appreciative remarks. Jonette Tennison, Tenny's momma, hoped the doctor would take a quick look at her chest pains, and Colvin examined her and determined she had heartburn, which, he attempted to explain, could not be helped by the Dr. Potter's Heart Tonic she was dosing herself with, because it had nothing to do with the heart but was caused by a hiatus hernia, for which he prescribed rest, six meals a day rather than three, and the avoidance of coffee, tea, and Heart Tonic.

Throughout this business, Colvin was asking himself if he'd want to have Wayne Don and Jonette as his father- and mother-in-law. He decided they weren't any worse than Piney's folks, and he kind of liked Oriole. She was okay. Finally taking his leave, and asking how to find the road to Jasper, he said he expected he would be seeing all of them again.

But Lampon, he discovered, was in no condition to carry him the long way into Jasper, so, impatient as he was, he reluctantly decided to return the palfrey to Ingledew's Livery, wait until the next day, and take Nessus with the buggy into Jasper.

"Hon," Piney asked, "are you feeling all right? You don't seem to have been yourself lately." Colvin tried to assure her that he was "jist fine," which was his favorite expression for everything in the world. "Well, I've been thinking," she said, "about what you dreamt. You know, getting me a piano. I think it would be very nice to have a good piano, if we can find one that isn't tinny."

Colvin coughed. "I don't know if we could afford one," he said. "To pay for a good piano, I'd most likely have to teach another year at Parthenon."

"Wouldn't you want to do that?" she said, in such a way that he knew she knew that he'd been thinking about it.

"Wal, I reckon I'd best run up there and see if they still want me," he said.

So he would use that as an excuse to leave for Jasper the next day at dawn. That night he had a dream in which it seemed that Tenny was calling for him; she was somewhere out of sight trying to contact him, so he went out looking for her. He went to Venda's house, and Venda was sprawled out sound asleep and naked and inviting on her bed, but the other bed in the house had neither Tenny nor Russ in it. He tried the Academy, drifting around through the girls' dormitory and the classroom building, but she wasn't there. Next, he visited their enchanted-forest trysting place, and the four-poster was still there, although covered with dust and pine needles, and some birds, tufted titmice, had built their nest on the Garden Butterfly quilt, but there was no sign that Tenny had been there for quite some time. Yet he could clearly hear her calling his name, and he called back, "Where are you, Tenny?" Piney asked him if he was still shopping for pianos.

The next day, he left ostensibly for Parthenon but he didn't stop at the Newton County Academy. He drove his buggy on to Jasper, and pulled up in front of the little white cottage off the square where Venda Breedlove lived. He just sat there for a while, studying the house and wondering if his darling were actually inside. If so, which room?

Venda stepped out onto her porch, dressed in her house robe, with her hair up in curlers, and holding a cup of coffee. "Good mornin, precious," she said. "I've been expectin ye. Climb down and have you a cup of coffee with me."

Following her to her kitchen, he saw that there were only two bedrooms, and both were empty. "My first question is," he said, sitting down at her kitchen table with the cup of coffee she poured for him, "not where is she, but how did you find out the whereabouts of Brushy Mountain? You tole me you didn't know."

"There are some men in this town who can tell you anything if you ask 'em right," she said, and winked at him.

"Okay, then, my second question is: where is she?"

"It's Saturday, did you notice?" she said. "On weekends, Russ has to go and stay with his daddy, over on the other side of town."

"So what's that got to do with Tenny?"

"So Russ took her to meet his daddy. My ex, you know,

Mulciber, is a fine, upstandin, solid citzen, not only the best blacksmith in the country but also the Jasper Fire Chief. Even if he was a son of a bitch to me, he don't deserve to live all by hisself, and he's been kind of lonesome ever since he threw me out. Russ and me figured that maybe Tenny could cheer him up or something. Who knows? Her folks want to git her married off, and Mulciber's jist about the most eligible bachelor in town."

"Ding blast it!" Colvin exclaimed, outraged. "Why, the way I heared it, Mulce is the ugliest old galoot in the country, and so crippled he can hardly walk. What would Tenny want with a gimpy freak like that?"

Venda touched him under his chin to make their eyes meet, and said, "Women don't always git what they want, in this world."

Her double meaning wasn't lost on him. "Did you jist cook up this scheme so you could git me away from her?" he demanded. She only smiled, and began taking the curlers out of her hair. "You didn't really bring her to Jasper to give her voice lessons, now did ye?" he insisted, but she wouldn't deny it or confirm it. "But didn't it occur to you," he wanted to know, "that you'd be a-punishing that pore gal to fix her up with the likes of Mulciber Breedlove?" Venda just went on smiling and removing the rest of the curlers from her hair. "What has Tenny done to you, that you'd want to punish her?" he asked. Venda took a hairbrush and began to brush her golden hair. "Has she offended you because she's so young and fine and sweet to behold?" he asked, standing to confront her and setting down his coffee cup. Venda opened her house robe, revealing that she had nothing beneath it. He could not take his eyes off her mons veneris, and it was almost as if he were addressing his next question to it: "What I'd like to know is: if she must've hated you for jumping into her four-poster with me like ye done, and thought of you as her rival or enemy, how did you make friends with her so fast? What did you get Russ to say to her to persuade her to come here?" Venda came to him and gave him one of those kisses where the tongue too comes into play. He hadn't ever had one of those kind before, and his *corpora cavernosa* nearly hemorrhaged. He tried to push her away, but she dropped to her knees and clawed at his fly until she had it open and could get her hands inside. She brought him out and swallowed him. Then she very slowly unswallowed him, and he forgot the next question he was going to ask her. He wasn't getting any answers to his questions, anyway. But he began to remember this question, because it was an important one: "Did you trouble yourself to explain to Tenny that you hadn't been invited to that four-poster of hers, and that you and me weren't really fucking?" Venda couldn't answer, because her mouth was full, but she gave her head a vigorous shake, which bent his *cavernosa* ever which way. Colvin had never felt sexual excitement like this before, and while he knew that the busy activity of her lips and tongue and whole mouth was the main cause of it, he knew that there had to be another reason, and he asked her, "Did you put something into my coffee?" She could only nod her head energetically, which pained his pecker somewhat, because it was so stiff it wouldn't bend down. "What?" he wanted to know. She managed to mutter some syllables which, for all he could tell, were cream and sugar. "Spanish fly?" he asked. She shook her head, which wobbled his pecker. "Ginseng?" he asked. Another shake and wobble. "A drop of menstrual blood?" he asked. She giggled while shaking her head; the giggles tickled his frenulum. "Snakeroot? Mandrake? Yarrow? Mistletoe? Dodder? Wasp nests? Coon bone? Horse spleen? Powdered heart of roasted hummingbird?" He ran through the whole catalog of known aphrodisiac substances, but she just kept on shaking her head, in between thrusting it forward and drawing it back. He had never realized that the muscles of a woman's neck would allow such a variety of lively movements. He was determined to remain true to Tenny, but there is no resistance against whatever chemical substance Venda had concocted for him, and he was in her power. He could only follow eagerly when she wrapped her hand around his pecker to make it into a leash, and led him off to her bedroom. The bed wasn't a four-poster, but that was okay.

For the rest of the morning, Venda allowed Colvin to exist without a single thought of Tenny. At noon he had no physical appetite remaining but he was hungry, so she fed him dinner, pork chops and corn on the cob and a big glass of buttermilk, into which she probably put another ten or twenty micrograms of whatever private stock love potion she was using, so that without even waiting for him to digest his meal she took him back to bed for the rest of the afternoon. Again he had no thought of Tenny, and his only thought of Piney was a reflection upon those times, years before, when Piney in her eagerness to conceive again had depleted entirely Colvin's reserves of "seed-juice," but it had taken her several days and nights to do it, and now Venda had drained him empty in just a matter of hours. He was bone-dry, and tried to call this fact to Venda's attention, but she said, "You can still explode even if ye caint shoot off, cain't you?" And she was right; if anything, each successive orgasm was more paroxysmal than the one before, and he was beginning to amaze himself at the way his whole body shook and shuddered at the moment of unproductive ejaculation. "Thirty-seven," Venda remarked after one particularly violent explosion had left him so limp that he could only lie there as if in a coma. He thought she was revealing her age to him, and he wanted to assure her that even though that was a year older than he was, he didn't mind. But then she explained, "You've done come thirty-seven times," and she smiled beatifically, adding, "but I've come seventy-one, myself." He allowed as how he didn't think mortal human beings were capable of that many, and therefore they must be either inhuman or immortal, one. He told Venda that if she would reveal to him the ingredients of whatever love potion she had used on him, they could both get rich bottling the stuff and putting it on the market. She just laughed and said, "And then any hussy could use it. Do you think I'd let any woman other than me ever git a-holt of it?"

"Wal, you'd better pour me another little drap of it," he suggested.

"How about some good whiskey for a chaser?" she offered, and jumped out of bed long enough to mix him a drink.

It was real fine whiskey, better than Chism's Dew, and possibly even bottled in the bond. And she must have been generous in lacing it, because his tired, sore, scrubbed old jemmison, which looked as if it had leprosy, commenced to unbend and rise yet again, and Venda helped it along with some more of her mouth music, saying, "I bet ye didn't know I could yodel." If that's what you call it, her yodeling gave his *corpora cavernosa* a transfusion. Pretty soon, they were at it again, plunging and bucking, grunting and squealing, lifting and floating, galloping and trotting, you never saw anything like it, nor had they. Colvin realized that not only were his testicles empty but so were his lungs; he had used up all his breath, and didn't have enough of it to keep going. Venda herself was nearly all out of breath too, but she had at least enough to get on top and keep bouncing her bottom, and she still had some strength left in those powerful vaginal muscles of hers that were milking his jemmison, and he hoped that she could keep going just another minute, which was all he needed to have the biggest burst he'd ever had . . .

He happened to glance over and notice that there was a couple of folks sitting in straight-backed chairs beside the doorway, watching them. One of them was this woman's very own offspring, a young man name of Russ. The other one was Colvin's very own true love, a young lady name of Tenny. Such a situation had all the earmarks of a dream, or perhaps even a nightmare, but it was still unclabbered broad daylight. Russ had a big grin on his face like he was really having fun watching his naked mother squatting atop a chemically elongated pecker. Tenny's mouth had formed itself into that perfect O which was the envy of all her O-named classmates, and she was resting the fingers of one hand, on which she wore that amethyst gold ring, alongside her cheek, as if in astonishment. But both of them were just sitting there, watching. Venda hadn't noticed, she was trying so hard to reach number seventy-two. After recovering from the first reflex jerk of surprise, Colvin realized that it was simply too late to make any pretense. It was clear to even a blind and deaf person who still retained a sense of smell that some real fucking was going on in this room. And to a person, or two of them, like Russ and Tenny, who could see and hear as well as smell, there was no fooling whatsoever. Colvin was so close to number thirty-eight that he figured he might as well just keep on keeping on, so he did, but he closed his eyes out of some sort of politeness, as if by shutting her out of his vision he might be sparing her a little of spectacle. Venda went wild as she arrived within reach of her climax, and she reached mightily for it, and got it, and commenced yodeling again, but in a different key from when she'd had a mouthful.

Colvin didn't even have enough breath to sigh, let alone utter anything, but he used the last of his strength to thrust so hard into her that when he came back down the bed slats busted and the whole bed came crashing to the floor.

Have I made up for yesterday? Yesterday I sent you away frustrated with the interrupted telling of the first attempt of Colvin and Tenny to make love. Today I've just managed to tell you the single most intense, sustained, and repeated bout of sex that I've ever collected, as if to atone for yesterday's shortcoming. I ought to wait until tomorrow to say what happened next, but I expect you'll be coming back again anyhow. And tomorrow we're going to have to get real serious.

So let's clean up here, first: Venda and Colvin just lay there on the mattress where it had crashed to the floor, and it took both of them a long time to recover their breathing abilities. During that time, Colvin could only stare woefully at Tenny and shrug his shoulders and spread his hands as if trying to communicate by sign language that he wasn't responsible for whatever he'd just been doing. Finally Venda sucked in a big draught of air and got her eyes working, and discovered that they had an audience, and cried her son's name. The audience, both of them, began to clap, first Russ and then Tenny timidly followed his example.

Then Russ and Tenny exchanged the merest of glances before getting up from their chairs and rushing out. The courthouse was conveniently just down the street, and they went in and got a marriage license and found a justice of the peace and had themselves declared man and wife before sundown.

Eight

Is it raining out? I can't see it but I think I can hear it. Mary Celestia, because her bed's yonder by the window, is the self-appointed Regulator of the Blinds, an irony that won't be lost on you, and she prefers to keep 'em closed because even though she's blind the light hurts her eyes. So I can't watch the rain, if that's what's falling out there. I shall never again see the dogwood bloom nor watch the redhorse shoal. But I can still see and hear and smell all the Ozark rains that ever fell in my life, and I can *feel* the ones that fell on me, and I could tell you the difference between an early summer rain, such as what's falling out there now, and a late summer rain, which was what commenced deluging the village of Jasper before Tenny and Russ left that courthouse where they got married. You know of course that in the Ozarks it was considered the best possible omen for a good downpour to fall on a funeral, since it meant that the dead man's soul was at rest, and even a few drops of rain at a funeral were more comfort to the bereaved family than anything the preacher man could say. Every Ozarker knew the little verse:

> Happy is the bride that the sun shines on;
> Blessed are the dead that the rain falls on.

And it was felt, therefore, that rainy weather on a wedding day is nothing short of calamitous. Russ and Tenny had planned to get on Marengo and ride back up to Brushy Mountain for the first night of their honeymoon, and the shivaree and infare and all, and so Tenny could say to her folks, "Well, I went ahead and got myself hitched like y'uns wanted me to. Are you happy now?" But they could only huddle miserably in the doorway of the courthouse and watch that toad-strangling pourdown. Leastways that old courthouse, plain and simple as it was, built in the first years of the century out of humble rough limestone, somehow had a little classical pediment over that doorway, and that was what Colvin noticed when he went out in his buggy looking for them. He just sat there in the open buggy with his clothes already soaked plumb through and through, and the lightning crashing down too close for comfort, and the thunder reverberating from wall to wall of those mountains that surround the little town, and he observed how the young couple had that Greek pediment over their heads as if the triangle was protecting them from the storm. They didn't wave at him, and he didn't wave at them, but he began to understand what they had done, going to that courthouse. Why else would a young couple go to the courthouse? Not to pay their taxes, nor to serve on a jury.

Now I suppose some day if you'll try to turn all of this into a novel, you'll want to know some of the facts about the situation that I haven't yet offered. So maybe you need to know Russ Breedlove a little better, not that it would change your opinion of him, but it would help you understand why he and Tenny done what they did, or did what they done. What little we know about him so far is that he was seventeen years old and was about to be a sophomore at Newton County Academy, where he was considered the best-looking boy. We know that the principal, Jossie, had remarked that Russ and Tenny ought to make a pair, because they both had the same habit of trying to see how much they could get away with. He was mischievous, audacious, even bodacious. Tenny herself was known to refer to him as "an eternal boy," and while she might just have meant he'd always be a male or masculine, she could've also meant that he'd never grow up. He was charming but cruel, with maybe a sadistic streak in him: one of his favorite pastimes was catching butterflies and striking sulfur matches to hold beneath them and watch them burn, the slower the better. The biggest difference between him and Tenny was that she had the highest grades at the Academy, and he had the lowest, not because he was stupid but because he just didn't give a damn about school.

He was from a broken home, which was a rare situation in the Ozarks, where divorce was practically unknown. We've seen that his mother, all the years he was growing up, was too busy fooling around with men to give him much attention, although she really did adore him. That time she first seduced young Donny Kilgore and left little Russ alone to play with his bow and arrow, she didn't know that Russ followed her and spied on them and that was the first of many "primal scenes" he witnessed between his momma and different men, culminating in the one with Colvin. And during that first primal scene he made an astonishing discovery: Donny Kilgore had only one pecker. For quite some time thereafter, until Venda took up with another man and Russ could spy on that man and discover that he too had only one pecker, Russ considered Donny Kilgore a freak or a cripple, one. Russ wanted to ask his mother if maybe Donny had got one of his peckers cut off in an accident or something, but to do that would be to admit to his mother that he had been spying. Russ had reached puberty himself when he discovered that all those years, even while she was having her torrid affair with Donny Kilgore, his mother had been screwing Uncle Marty Breedlove, Mulciber's brother, and that possibly even Uncle Marty was his real father, or at least his co-father, along with Mulciber. Russ began to wonder—and would continue to wonder, until he had a chance to ask his hygiene teacher, Doc Swain, about it—if it were possible that his having two fathers was the reason he had two peckers, and that Mulciber was the progenitor of one of his peckers and Uncle Marty of the other one.

When his mother was fooling around with Uncle Marty, Russ liked to put on the army uniform that Marty had taken off and dress up with it, pistol and all, while he watched his momma and Uncle Marty move through every possible coital position and commit every conceivable sexual act. When eventually Russ considered his visual education complete, and was growing bored with both watching their behavior and dressing up in the captain's uniform, he told his mother that he knew about her and Marty and would tell Mulciber about it unless she would do with him what she had done with Marty and Donny and everybody else. Venda tried to explain to him that mothers aren't supposed to do it with their own boys, and therefore she simply couldn't, not that she didn't want to, because she adored Russ, and if he weren't her son she would screw him blind. Her refusal made Russ tell his father, or co-father, Mulciber, that his uncle, or other co-father, Marty, was screwing his wife, and, as we've already seen, Mulciber caught them and beat them up and put a stop to all that, and threw Venda out of the house.

When Venda went away to that Shenandoah Music School and took Russ with her, in her loneliness she listened more sympathetically to Russ's constant requests to be permitted to sleep with her or at least have her get rid of his virginity. He talked of practically nothing else, unless it was to express lewd desires about any other female who came within his line of sight. She jokingly told him that he was practically the embodiment of carnal lust, but she still hadn't said a word to him about the exceptional circumstance of his having two peckers. He pestered her so much that finally she agreed to let him feel her breasts. This of course gave him an erection, or rather a pair of them, which, she told him, were called "hard-ons," and she allowed as how it might not be too awfully wicked if she just used her two hands to make him come, and thereby started the practice, or the arrangement, that continued through the first year at Newton County Academy. She never did tell him that he was abnormal for having two peckers; she acted as if using her two hands to bring him off was just a natural thing that she did every day just as every day he helped her with her grooming and dressing, her hair and makeup and all. She just assumed that he would want both of his peckers to shoot off simultaneously, and that was her goal, although occasionally, since she was left-handed, his right pecker sometimes got off before the left one did. Ever so often, about once a week on the average, he would beg her to let him stick his peckers into her, but she would just tell him that was something that wasn't permitted. She never tried to explain to him that it was anatomically unlikely, or anything like that; she just said it wasn't "allowed" or "approved" or "permitted."

Although he hated his classes at Newton County Academy, and would flunk Latin and barely pass English and math, he would achieve a C in hygiene because the subject interested him and because he liked his teacher, Doc Swain, and would never forget the little talk he'd had with Doc Swain on the first day of school, when the doctor was examining everybody and Doc Swain did not act surprised to discover that Russ had two penises. Doc Swain admitted that it was exceptional, quite rare in fact, but he didn't tell Russ that he was abnormal, let alone a freak. "They call it diphallus," Doc Swain had told him, making it sound not like a disease but a way of life, and said that some ignorant scientists refer to these cases as *diphallic terata,* implying that they are monstrosities, but, while they are certainly curiosities, they are nothing to be ashamed of. Doc Swain told of some other known diphallic young men in faraway places with names like Cuba and Scotland and New Jersey, and he said that the prevalence of the condition was about one case in five million, meaning that there were at least twenty other fellers in the United States with the same condition. Russ was thrilled to learn this. Doc Swain asked him several questions of a personal nature, such as whether he was able to urinate through both (he was), and whether erections occurred simultaneously (they did), and if there was bilateral ejaculation (Russ didn't understand what this meant, but after Doc Swain rephrased it in plain English, without implicating Russ's mother, Russ admitted that, yes, generally he bilaterally ejaculated). Doc Swain clapped him on the shoulder and said, "Wal, son, I wouldn't worry about having an extry one, if I was you, but if it ever causes you too much trouble I could always cut one of 'em off fer ye." Doc had laughed to let him know that he might've been just kidding, but Russ wasn't too sure, and every time he saw Doc Swain in hygiene class, he remembered the suggestion and brooded about the possibility of having himself unilaterally emasculated. He kept wondering why it might be necessary, especially after they got to the chapter on reproduction and the pictures including some poor girl's whole cut-away bottom end with all those tunnels and tubes and cavities up in there, making it clear that there were plenty of places he could stick both of his peckers.

He wasn't the only one who liked Doc Swain. Russ's momma talked about Doc Swain all the time. Russ had to listen to her, during the daily ride to and from school on Marengo, and at the supper table, and even at bedtime. If Russ had begun to bore his mother with his constant talk about wanting to stick his peckers into her, she had begun to bore him with her constant hints that the only pecker she ever again wanted into her was Doc Swain's, and Russ thought Doc Swain must have a colossal pecker or an awfully handsome one, because Doc Swain himself wasn't especially good-looking. To hear his mother tell it, Doc Swain was the greatest man who ever lived, and if his momma had her way about it—and she usually had her way about everything—Doc Swain was going to become her next lover, if not her husband for life, the latter possibility hampered by the fact that Doc Swain already had a wife somewhere, not that he ever mentioned her. It embarrassed Russ to watch his momma flirting with Doc Swain, more even than he had been embarrassed watching her fucking with various other men. And his momma was becoming so preoccupied with Doc Swain that she was beginning to neglect Russ again. Sometimes she might go for a whole week before remembering that he had not one but two hard-ons that needed attention.

His mother's unrequited absorption with Doc Swain became matched eventually by the vehemence of her jealousy toward Tenny Tennison, the prettiest of all Russ's classmates and the one girl whose very presence, even from a distance of a hundred yards, would give Russ hard-ons. It took Russ a while to realize that his mother was so madly jealous of Tenny not because Tenny gave Russ hard-ons but because Tenny was somehow preventing Doc Swain from reciprocating his mother's lust for him. Russ didn't understand why Doc Swain would want Tenny, who was probably a virgin and didn't know anything, when Doc could have the beautiful, experienced, and most desirable Venda just for the asking, and this gave Russ an ambivalent feeling toward his much-admired physician/teacher: while he couldn't help envying Doc Swain because of his mother's lust for him, he also resented Doc Swain because Doc was not making Russ's mother happy.

Even after school had let out for the summer, his mother got worse instead of better. "You and me have got to find us some way to ruin that gal Tenny," she told him one summer's day. "And I mean *ruin* her." She studied Russ's face intently while an idea slowly crept into her mind, and then she grabbed Russ and gave him a kiss on the mouth. Russ had succeeded in achieving mouth-kisses with Olga and Orva and Orlena and Ohio, but those Baptist girls had always kept their lips tight together and considered the kiss finished in not more than three seconds. Now Russ's momma parted her lips and brought her tongue out and stuck it into his mouth and wrapped it around his own tongue, and his two peckers swole so much they commenced bumping into each other. After a long while, she broke the kiss and said, "Do ye like that? Russ honey dearest, if you really like me and want a bunch more kisses like that, I want you to go up to Brushy Mountain and git Tenny Tennison and bring her down to meet your father, and I want you to git 'em together and *keep* 'em together. Git the idee?" Russ said he knew his father wasn't much of a looker, in fact, he didn't mind saying that Mulciber was the ugliest wretch he'd ever laid eyes on, and he wasn't very confident that such a pretty young thing like Tenny would want to take up with him. His mother gave him another, longer one of those open-mouthed kisses, and whispered in his ear, "I promise I'll let you have what you've always wanted. If you will do this thing for me, I'll let you stick *both* of your hard-ons in me." That was a proposition that Russ couldn't refuse, but he wanted her to promise that she wouldn't let anybody else stick any peckers into her before he got his chance to do it, and she promised. And he wanted to know if the offer would be null and void if by chance Tenny and his father weren't attracted to each other, which didn't seem likely anyhow. So his mother pressed into his hand a little purple vial with a cork stopper in it, and gave him an eyedropper to go along with it, and explained that it was a love potion, and to put not more than six drops into Tenny's drink, and, if needed, not more than four drops into Mulciber's. That way, they'd be irresistible to each other. Who-ever touched a drop of that special love potion would fall madly in love with the first person they laid eyes on. Russ had just one more question: how was he supposed to persuade Tenny to go off with him, and to let her folks know that it was above-board and all? "Just tell 'em," Venda said, "that because she has such a sweet singing voice and lots of possibilities for being a great singer, I am offering to put her up here at my house and give her free voice lessons."

His mother had a little map, that she had acquired somehow from the county judge, Frank Criner, showing how to get up to Brushy Mountain, and she gave it to Russ and told him to wear his Sunday-school shirt, and comb his hair good, and all. Then he climbed atop Marengo and took off. Even with the help of the map, it was hard to find and took him nearly all day, and when he got there Tenny wasn't at home. Her folks, her mother and granny and a couple of older sisters named Oriole and Redbird, fell upon him like he was the first male creature they'd been able to lay hands on in ages, and they made a big fuss over his horse and even over his Sunday-school shirt, as if they'd never seen a white shirt before. Oriole kept saying, "Why, you aint no monster, after all!" and Redbird kept saying, "Couldn't no horse git no paler than that'un," and Russ began to get the notion that somehow he had been expected. It was a right peculiar family. The father didn't get a chance to say much, and when he did, Russ couldn't make out exactly what he was trying to say.

Finally they told him that Tenny was waiting for him, but she was waiting up on the top of the mountain. He didn't understand. He didn't know how she knew he was coming, and he didn't know why she was waiting in an inconvenient place like the mountaintop. But he followed their directions and went on up there. It was a hard climb, and he had to leave Marengo tethered to a tree while he made the last part of the climb. When he got up there, she was just sitting on a rock with her head in her hands, and she was dressed all in black, which made her look somehow a lot older, although the black was a fine background for her long light-brown hair. As usual, whenever he so much as glimpsed her, both of his peckers expanded to their full size and caused a pair of great bulges in his britches, which he had to cover with his hat as best he could. He stood there with his hat over his groin, realizing that he didn't have the nerve to ask her if she'd like to fuck, and he said bashfully, "Howdy, Tenny."

She raised her face and gazed at him without surprise. The blue sky of her eyes was rainy. "Howdy, Russ," she said. Then she observed, "That's a purty white shirt." She asked, "Did you bring Marengo with you?" and when he nodded, she said, "I guessed it might be you. But you've got only one head." He didn't know what she was talking about, so she had to back up and tell him all about the prophecy of Cassie Whitter.

He was embarrassed. "Wal, heck, I shore wouldn't mind being yore bridegroom, but it aint me. It's my daddy. I mean, I wasn't supposed to tell ye until you'd had a chance to meet him, but that's who you're supposed to marry."

"Is he a freak?" Tenny asked.

"Most folks think so," Russ said. "He's in purty bad shape, what with his crippled legs and all. But he's a good man, and he'd treat you real nice and keep you happy."

"Nothing will ever keep me happy again," Tenny said, sadly. Then she stood up. "Well, if I caint marry Colvin Swain, I might as well marry yore daddy or anybody. Let's go." Russ helped her down off the mountaintop. The west wind was beginning to blow real hard, and it was getting a mite too airish up there, and was turning dark, too. He helped her climb up on Marengo, sidesaddle the way his momma had ridden to school with him so often, and he explained to her that they could tell her family that she was going to Jasper to live with Venda Breedlove and take voice lessons, until school started. "But that aint true, is it?" Tenny said. "I don't want to live with your momma. I hate her guts." Russ assured her that he himself sometimes hated Venda's guts, and that it was just an excuse to persuade Tenny's folks to allow her to come to Jasper.

It was dark by the time they reached the cabin, and of course the Tennisons insisted that Russ spend the night. They gave him a big supper, with five kinds of dessert, and treated him like he really had proposed to Tenny and was planning the nuptials. It wasn't a big cabin, and both beds was all full up, what with the sisters visiting, so they had to fix Russ a pallet on the kitchen floor, and that's where he slept. It was a real hot August night, without any kitchen windows to let in the night air, and Russ stripped down to his underpants to keep cool, and, once everybody else had gone to bed, he left the sheet off, although just the thought of sleeping in the same house with Tenny gave him a pair of all-night erections, and he realized he'd better try to wake up in the morning before the women came in to fix breakfast.

Way along in the night, he was awakened by something like a bee sting on his thigh, and looking up from his pallet, he beheld Tenny standing over him with a candle. A drop of the hot candle wax had fallen on his leg and stung him. Tenny's mouth was open in that O which distinguished her from all the O-girls at school, and she was staring transfixed at his peckers, both of which had escaped through the fly of his underpants. Nobody except his momma and Doc Swain had ever seen his peckers before, and he was somewhat embarrassed, and grabbed the sheet to cover himself. It occurred to him that Tenny had been meaning to slip into bed with him, but why did she have the candle? Now she blew the candle out and said to him in the dark, "So you are the one, after all. My sisters said you were, and they told me to come in here and look at you to find out if maybe you are a freak, but I didn't believe them." He waited breathlessly for her to lie down beside him, and he waited, and waited, and after a while he realized that she was no longer in the room.

At the crack of dawn, he dressed and went out to sit on the front porch and think about what had happened. He felt somewhat humiliated, that she had discovered his secret and thought of him as a freak, and that she hadn't been attracted enough to want to get in bed with him. He was tempted to saddle Marengo and go on back to Jasper without her, but if he did that his mother would be angry and wouldn't keep her promise, and he could hardly wait for his mother to keep her promise. After a while, Tenny came out and sat on the porch too, but she didn't say a word to him, so he didn't speak to her. They just sat there together silently, as if they both understood something that didn't need any discussion. At breakfast, the Tennisons and the grandmother and the two older sisters all talked about the wedding and the shivaree and the infare dinner as if it was all set, and they wanted to discuss who to invite and what cakes and pies to make, and all that. Russ tried to remind them that his job was only to transport Tenny into Jasper so his mother could give her voice lessons, and that they'd both be going back to school in the fall at N.C.A. But Tenny's family just smiled and winked at each other, and went on making a big fuss over him.

Finally Tenny got her gunnysack with her clothes and stuff, and they climbed up on Marengo and said their good-byes. Tenny's sisters kept saying to Russ that if he changed his mind about Tenny, either one of them, Oriole or Redbird, would be awfully glad to have him, but Russ figured that was just insincere politeness, like when you ask somebody to come go home with you but you don't really mean it. Besides, there was no question of changing his mind about Tenny, because his mind was not his own, but his mother's; if it had been left up to him, he would have gladly made the Tennisons happy by becoming Tenny's man.

In Jasper, Tenny reminded him that she didn't want to have to see his momma because she despised her for ruining things with Doc Swain, so Russ took her straight on over to Mulciber Breedlove's house on the other side of town. It was a fairly nice place, big two-storied house, as befits an upstanding citizen, and had some modern conveniences, including one of the first "enclosed horn" Victrolas in Newton County, which Russ had persuaded his father to buy. The house was right next to the big Breedlove Smithy, where Mulciber spent his days shoeing horses and mules and fixing wagons and tools. Russ belatedly realized, as he dismounted and led Tenny to meet his father, that nobody had said a word in advance to Mulciber about this "arrangement," let alone thought to get his approval. When Tenny got her first look at Mulciber, her intended, she blanched and looked as if she were about to puke. Russ had to allow that he would have had the same reaction himself if he didn't already know the man.

And for his part, Mulciber was civil, even hospitable, but his eyes didn't light up at the sight of Tenny. "Paw, she's come to stay," Russ declared. Mulciber just allowed as how that was pretty nice, he reckoned, and he hoped she was a good cook.

"Well, I'll show her around and maybe play the Victrola for her," Russ suggested. He took Tenny into the big house and showed her the big kitchen and a room actually called "living room," meant to contain just a big sofa and assorted chairs and the big Victrola which, he revealed, had an enclosed horn. He cranked up the machine and put on a platter of a jazz band playing "I'm Always Chasing Rainbows." It was the first jazz that Tenny had ever heard, and he explained to her what jazz was, how the black folks had started it, and how the word itself, and especially the sound of the music, were suggestive of the motions that men and women are impelled to make in doing what was found in Chapter 34 from the hygiene textbook, Reproduction. Then he left her to listen to another platter called "Arkansas Blues" while he ran back out to the blacksmith shop and said, "Paw! You don't understand! I've brung her for *you!* She's all your'n, Paw!" Old Mulciber just looked kind of pensive and replied that he shorely appreciated the thought, but that he'd taken a vow when he got rid of Russ's momma that if he ever took up with a woman again, she'd have to be as homely as a stump fence because he'd had all he wanted of well-favored women, and that there Tenny gal was near about as sightly as Russ's momma, blast her hide.

There was nothing to do but dope their drinks at suppertime. Russ used the eyedropper to measure out six drops of the love philter his momma had given him, and slipped it into Tenny's glass of milk. Then he slipped four drops into his father's coffee. Next, because he knew that the stuff would make you fall madly in love with the first person you laid eyes on, he found an excuse to get himself out of their line of sight long enough for them to take a drink and look at each other. He said he had to go to the privy, and he actually did, and sat there and waited for a good long while, long enough for them to have taken a drink and then laid eyes on each other. But when he returned to the house, Tenny was just sitting there with her milk untouched and Mulciber had finished his coffee and gone. Tenny said that some customer in one of those Model T automobiles had come honking up to the blacksmith shop and Mulciber had to go see about 'em. As for herself, she was relieved he was gone, because the very sight of him had made her become so nauseated that she couldn't touch her food. "But aint you at least *thirsty?*" Russ insisted. "Don't you want a little sip of that there milk?" Tenny just held her stomach as if she were about to puke. Russ went to the window and looked out at the blacksmith shop, and there was Mulciber flat on his back up underneath an auto, some furriner's out-of-state vehicle, no top, owned by some lady in one of those newfangled skinny-tube dresses, and her hair bobbed. "Uh-oh" was all Russ could say. Then he tried unsuccessfully to get Tenny to drink her milk. She said not only was she sick to her stomach but also

251

had one foot in the grave, with a runny nose and all-over miseries and maybe a touch of the flu. She was coughing a lot. Russ commenced to get agitated, that his plans were going awry, and in his nervousness he decided he might as well have a little snort of that milk himself, just to keep it from going to waste. So he told Tenny that as long as she didn't want it, he'd just drink her milk.

There wasn't anything to do but play the Victrola some more and wait to see what had happened to Mulciber. But Mulciber never did come back. At one point in the course of his long and desperate pursuit of Tenny, Russ paused to get his breath and went down to the blacksmith shop, but there wasn't any sign of Mulciber or of that lady in the auto, and Mulciber had hung his CLOZED sign on the door. He never came back, neither, and Russ ceased to care, because he had only one thing on his mind. It was the same thing he always had on his mind, but this time it was not only on his mind but also on every other part of his being. The very sight of Tenny had always given him duplicate erections, but he'd never been able to do anything except have the red-comb-and-stone ache. Now, he was emboldened by the love potion to make overtures. He tried every good jazz record in his collection, even including "I'll Say She Does," which was supposed to incite lust in old maids. But I'll say she didn't, not Tenny. He kept asking her if he couldn't get her *some*thing to drink. "Maybe jist a glass of water, maybe?" he suggested. But she didn't think she'd be able to "keep it down." He offered to show her how to dance, how to do the new rages called the Charleston, the shimmy, and the black-bottom. It was difficult for him to demonstrate these dances holding his hat over his groin, so finally he just said, "The heck with it," and tossed his hat away and didn't mind that she could see the two great bulges making a **V** across the front of his pants. She didn't seem to pay much attention; after all, the night before, she'd already seen them without any coverings. Further emboldened by her nonchalance, he offered to show her the fox-trot, which involved some bodily contact, and gave him a chance to demonstrate that his V could fit into the V of her pelvis. This feeling so mightily emboldened him that, since she kept shaking her head whenever he asked, "Aint you thirsty yet?" and "Caint I git you nothin to drink?" and "Would ye keer fer maybe some real lemonade?" he was moved to improvise and to offer to show her the latest craze in dancing, called, he said, "the business," which would require them to lie down on the floor and for him to get on top of her.

But she looked at him sidelong, and said, "Russ, I aint *that* scatterbrained." When she saw the expression of frantic desperation on his face, she added gently, "Besides, what would your daddy think, if you was to shag his bride-to-be?"

"Tell you the honest truth, Ten," Russ said. "I don't believe my daddy wants you. He told me you are jist way too purty for him, and his next wife has to look like a stump fence."

Tenny gave him another sidelong look and declared, "I figured that was jist a trick, you saying you wanted me to take up with your paw. You really jist wanted me for yourself, now didn't you?"

Russ realized he was going to catch holy hell from his mother, but it was too late for that. "Yeah, Tenny, that's the truth. I really truly jist want you all for myself. And boy, do I *want* you!"

"Then say it," she said.

"I jist did," he said. "Boy howdy, do I want want *want* ye!"

"No, I mean, say you want me to marry you. *Ask* me to."

"Tenny, babe, would you keer to be my wife?"

"Cassie Whitter said my husband would be a two-headed

monstrosity. I reckon she must've been thinkin about *them*."
And she reached out and touched one of the prongs of his V.
Her touch drove him wild, although he was already as wild as
he'd ever been in his life. "So I reckon if I caint never marry
Colvin Swain, then you are *it*. Have you got a four-poster in
this house?" Mulciber's house had some fancy headboards and
footboards on the beds, but none of them was a four-poster.
Russ took her upstairs to the bedrooms and showed her what
they had. "Any extry quilts?" she asked. "Have you got a Garden
Butterfly pattern?" They looked through the quilt chests, but
the best they could find was a kind of homely Double Chain.
"Have you got any slow music for the Victrola?" she asked. They
searched through the platters, and tried out a few, but the only
thing even fairly slow was something called "The Sheik of Ar-
aby," with some suggestive words about "At night when you're
asleep, into your tent I'll creep." Russ began to wonder if he
was going to have to wait until she was asleep before he could
try to creep his peckers into her.

But since Mulciber never did come home that night, they
had the house to themselves and went to bed together. He asked
her if she wouldn't at least care to try a swallow of some cough
syrup or at least a glass of water for her cough, but she still
wasn't thirsty. She asked him if he had any white nightshirts
with flouncy sleeves such as swashbucklers wear, but he'd never
heard of them. She said, "There's a couple of things you ought
to know," and she began to sound like a schoolteacher, telling
him how what they were fixing to do would cause the rupture
of something called the hymenal membrane, and it would get
blood on the sheets. She took his hand and guided his finger
to feel the thing she was talking about, and the touch of her
down there excited him so much that his peckers started doing
the Charleston together. Then she raised his finger to another

254

place, and he could have sworn it was Doc Swain talking, instructing him in the existence of a tubercle at the top of her vulvar groove which was homologous with the penis(es) and ought to be respected as the seat of the woman's pleasure just as the penis(es) was/were the man's, and she asked him if he remembered page 620 of their hygiene textbook, wherein the clitoris is identified. He'd made a better grade in hygiene than any of his other courses, and like everybody else had been fascinated with that chapter on reproduction, but had been so intent on finding the word *diphallus* that he had not noticed *clitoris,* and so disappointed in not finding the former that he didn't really care about the latter, which seemed useless anyhow.

He tried to pay attention to Tenny's little lecture, but he wasn't sure how it was supposed to help him in any way. He was going to have to get blood on the sheets and that was all there was to it, so he might as well get started. Rather clumsily he got her to lie on her back and spread her legs, and he took his two dancing peckers in his hand and held them tight together to make them quit dancing, and then he tried to get them to go into Tenny's hole and rip that hymenal membrane. It wasn't much of a fit. He gave a shove, but they wouldn't go in, and Tenny said, "Ow!" like he was hurting her. He attempted to put just one at a time into her, but with both of them so stiff he couldn't get one to go in without bending and hurting the other one. He attempted several different positions, atop her, beside her, and even behind her, and raising her two legs one way or another, and finally lifting both of her legs to put over his shoulders. Nothing worked. He decided the only thing to do was see if he couldn't get one of his peckers to use that other tunnel while the other pecker went where it was supposed to, a kind of complicated position that required him to lie perpendicular to her from behind, and he tried that, using both of his hands to try to guide his peckers into their respective holes, until finally it dawned on him that there just wasn't enough lubrication. Her parts were all dry, and his parts were each oozing just a drop or two, not enough. " 'Scuse me," he said, getting up. "I'll be right back." And he ran downstairs and looked for something oily or greasy, finally finding a bottle of his father's Wildroot cream hair oil, and he grabbed that and took it back upstairs. Tenny was sound asleep. She had a smile on her face like she was only pretending, but he shook her and discovered she really was in deep sleep, and maybe having a lovely dream which accounted for the smile on her face. The Victrola was playing ". . . at night when you're asleep, into your tent I'll creep . . ." so he took advantage of her sleeping to smear some of the Wildroot over both of her holes and both of his poles, and then he tried to make entry into her sleeping body. He tried and he tried, and wore himself plumb out, and had just enough strength left before falling asleep himself to smear some of the Wildroot on his two hands and make love to himself.

The next day, he could think of only two things: one was that he was going to catch holy hell from his mother, who was going to have a conniption fit, see red and sizzle, hit the ceiling, and jump down his throat. The other thing, a more disturbing thing, was that even though the love potion had sort of worn off, he was still in love with Tenny. It must be true that whoever touched a drop of that love potion would fall madly in love with the first person they laid eyes on, but Russ hadn't realized that it meant you had to love them forever. He sure didn't mind being in love with Tenny, because she was not only the most well-favored and sightly person in the world, next to his mother, but she was also the nicest, possibly even nicer than his mother, who wasn't going to be very nice at all, from now on.

The sheriff, Sam Hudson, knocked at the door and told Russ that his daddy was being held at the jail and Russ could come and get him and take him home. Charges had not been pressed, but Mulciber was jailed for disorderly conduct, trying to molest a tourist-lady staying at the Commercial Hotel, where Mulciber had spent most of the night and was arrested in the wee hours. So Russ told Tenny to make herself at home, eat anything she took a notion to, and play the Victrola, and he'd be right back. He brought his father home, and then was obliged to work with his father in the blacksmith shop and make sure Mulciber didn't try to go back to the Commercial Hotel. All of this activity gave Russ time to think about what he was going to say to his mother.

That afternoon, he asked Tenny if she would go with him to his mother's house and tell his mother the "truth": that the sight of gruesome Mulciber had made her so pukey that she couldn't possibly marry the old geezer.

"I tole you, I don't want to see your momma," Tenny said. "That would make me even pukier."

"But you don't need to hate her no more for coming between you and Doc Swain, since it's *me* you're gonna marry, and when me and you git married, she'll be your mother-in-law, so you'll have to see her."

Tenny seemed to be thinking about that, and whatever thoughts she was having were making her very sad. Russ wondered if she really did want to marry him, and, even if she did marry him, would she always be carrying a torch for Doc Swain?

Neither Russ nor Tenny had the slightest notion that they'd find Doc Swain at Venda's house. When they went in the door, and heard the sounds coming from the bedroom, it took Russ awhile to remember that such sounds are the cries and grunts not of people being hurt but of people enjoying that supreme act which he himself had never yet known. Just as he had done so many times in his childhood when his mother was entertaining a lover, he crept silently toward the noise. Tenny followed. When they saw who was in bed with Venda, Tenny gasped, but her sound was drowned beneath those coming from the bed. The couple in the bed were having such a splendid time of it that they did not notice Russ arranging a couple of chairs so that he and Tenny could take a load off their feet while they studied the spectacle. Russ had seen this sort of thing many times before, but Tenny hadn't, so he figured it might further her sex education and maybe put her in the mood for it. She was obviously awestruck, and her mouth was fixed into that almost holy O. The bed partners switched positions, with Russ's mother on top, allowing her freedom of movements which, Russ hoped, would suggest to Tenny that perhaps she and Russ could more successfully manage their hookup if Tenny was on top doing the connecting.

Russ hoped that whatever feeling Tenny still had for Doc Swain would be wiped out by watching this. As for himself, he had all the proof he needed that his mother was dishonest and hateful: she had promised him that she wouldn't let any other man stick his pecker into her until Russ had a chance to reap his reward for fixing up Tenny with Mulciber, and even though that effort had failed, Venda was going ahead and breaking her promise without even waiting to find out the results of the attempt.

Now Doc Swain had turned his head and detected that Russ and Tenny were watching, but that didn't stop him. He just kept on. Russ thought that was funny, and he grinned at the doctor, and the doctor grinned back at him and kept on thrusting beneath the wild bounces of Venda. All those times that Russ had spied on his momma with her lovers, he had never actually seen a simultaneous coming, but now he was watching one, and not only that but the bed was coming apart too, and when it did and they and the mattress crashed to the floor, his mother looked over and saw him and cried, "Russ!" in such a way that he knew she knew that he had been spying on her all those years.

He was so impressed with the performance that he spontaneously began to applaud, the same way he'd clapped his hands in joy when his mother had brought him a present as a little boy, only it wasn't joy now, but a kind of sarcastic admiration. Tenny caught the spirit of his applause and did some herself. Then he and she looked at each other, and her eyes said to him, "I've done seen enough to make me hate him and her both for the rest of my life," and his eyes replied to her eyes, "So you and me don't have nobody in this whole world excepting each other, and we might as well git out of here and go live happy ever after."

They got out of there, and rode Marengo straight to the courthouse. It all happened so fast that he couldn't even remember afterwards if he and Tenny had actually said anything, until they were both standing there saying, "I do," and then the man said, "I now pernounce y'uns man'n wife and you kids air shore gonna git wet as dogs if you try to go out in *that!*" and he indicated through the window the growing thunderstorm.

Now it was drowning geese and strangling toads. He and his bride could only huddle in the doorway of the courthouse and wait for it to stop. "Are you okay?" he thought to ask her.

" 'Happy is the bride the sun shines on,' " she said.

"But the sun aint shining," he observed.

"And I aint too awful happy," she said.

Well, here come Doc Swain in his buggy, acting as if he hadn't just been caught bare-assed with his red hand in the cookie jar. Now the fool was just sitting there in the deluge, sobby as a dog, and liable to get hit by a thunderbolt any second now. He just sat there with all that water running down his sad wistful face and he didn't wave howdy or nothing. Tenny just glared at him. Russ didn't personally have anything against Doc Swain, and still greatly admired him, even though he had once been the chief object of his bride's affections, and therefore a rival. But Russ had never forgotten how kind Doc Swain had been to him, and how Doc had even offered to excise his extra pecker if necessary, and Russ was beginning to wonder if it might not be necessary.

"I reckon I'd better have a word with him," Russ told Tenny.

"Don't you dare!" she said. "Just ignore him, and maybe he'll go away."

But Doc did not go away. Even the horse looked miserable. The thunder was slamming back and forth all down the mountainsides, and the wind was blowing the hard rain into the courthouse doorway so that Russ and Tenny were getting wet anyway.

"Maybe you ought to go have a word with him," Russ suggested.

"*Huh?*" Tenny said indignantly. "Have you taken leave of your senses? I don't have ary thing to say to him!"

So they just waited for him to go away or for the rain to go away, but neither Doc nor the rain would leave. It commenced getting on to dark, and they both knew that it was too late to make it back up to Brushy Mountain for the shivaree and infare and all. Russ decided there was nothing to do but go on back to Mulciber's house for their wedding night. "Let's make a dash for it!" he said, and they ran out into the rain and hopped on Marengo and headed for Mulciber's. Russ looked over his shoulder at one point and saw that Doc was following in his buggy, and Russ spurred Marengo to try to outrun him.

They arrived at Mulciber's. Russ didn't know the concept of déjà vu, but he thought there was something awfully familiar about walking in and discovering a naked couple fucking, only in this case it was not the bedroom but the living room, on the sofa. Russ's Victrola was up as loud as it would go, and Russ's jazz music was playing, and there was Mulciber a-humping some stranger-lady, who, Russ recognized by her bobbed hair, was the same lady who'd stopped at the blacksmith shop yesterday. Once again Russ and Tenny pulled up some chairs and sat watching, although Russ couldn't help noticing that this couple weren't nearly so spectacular as Venda and Doc had been. Nor did they come simultaneously. When they were all done, Russ didn't feel like applauding. He told them that all in all, he'd seen much better, but they'd done tolerable. Then he told his father that he and Tenny had just gotten theirselves married down at the courthouse. His father and the lady were hastily putting their clothes back on, and his father said the lady's name was Edna. Although Russ didn't think that Edna looked very much like a stump fence, Mulciber declared that Edna was "going to stay awhile," so he'd appreciate it if Russ and Tenny would get lost. "But where can we *go?*" Russ whined.

"I was you, I'd jist take her to your mother's," Mulciber suggested.

Russ counted his money. He had once had six quarters, but he'd paid two of them for the marriage license, and two more to the justice of the peace, leaving him with only two, not enough for even a cheap hotel room. Tenny didn't have a cent. So the only way to avoid sleeping somewheres out in the rain was for them to go on back to his mother's and throw themselves at her mercy, and maybe if he told her how sorry he was and all, she might even forgive him.

On the way to Venda's, they couldn't help noticing that they were still being followed by Doc in his buggy. Tenny was still determined not to see Venda, but she was tired, and soaked through by the rain, and a bit chilled, and her cough was getting worse, and she told Russ she hoped maybe there was some way she could have a bed at Venda's without having to face the woman.

"Wait on the porch while I talk to her," he told her, and then he boldly stepped into the house to face the music, make the best of a bad job, pay the fiddler, and lay down and roll over. But he could stand up and take it. "Maw," he said, "I shore am the sorriest feller on airth, and I don't know how to tell ye this, but I've done went and fell in love with Tenny myself, and we're fresh-married."

"Sweetheart, that's only fair-to-middlin funny," Venda said. "I've had a real hard day, and if you're trying to cheer me up with some jokes, you laid an egg."

"It's the honest to gosh truth," he said. "Paw didn't want her, and she didn't want him, and I accidental-like drank some of that love potion myself, and then we seen you and Doc a-fuckin like a pair of minks, so we jist skipped on over to the courthouse and got ourselfs hitched."

Venda didn't say anything for a while, but she didn't get red in the face or clench her fists or start steaming out the ears. Finally she just said, "Go to your room." He tried to protest, but she made it clear that she was still boss, so he did like he always did when she told him to go to his room. He went to his room. He sat on his bed and put on his baseball glove and slammed his fist into it, and he felt twelve years old. By-and-by, she came into the room and closed the door behind her. First, she asked him a question: "Do you honestly think that I could tolerate my competition as a daughter-in-law?" He figured it was one of those questions that are just said for the sake of making a point, and didn't have any answer to them, so he didn't try to make one. Then she asked him another question: "Don't you think it's bad enough that I have to watch Colvin falling for her without watching my own son doing it too?" He decided this was another unanswerable question made for show, so he didn't try to answer it either. "Do you know what you are?" she asked, and it must've been the same kind of question, because she answered it herself: "You're a motherfucker!" He winced because that was truly an awful word, even though it described exactly what he aspired to be. "You're not only a motherfucker but a motherkiller, and you're killing me with what you've done!" Her face turned red, her fists clenched, and steam came out of her ears. "Oh Jesus H. Fucking Christ! I guess I didn't bring you up proper. You never learned to tell right from wrong, or even up from down, and you never learned to obey me! You stupid wretch, I sent you out to *ruin* Tennessee Tennison, I mean totally wreck her life, I mean make her so miserable that she would be sorry she was ever born, let alone was such a knockout and built like a brick shithouse! I wanted you to dilapidate her to where she'd think she was a corncrib made of corncobs! And what did you *do?* Not only did you fail to destroy her, you led her down the *aisle!*"

"Hit weren't no aisle," he protested feebly. "Hit was jist the hallway at the courthouse." But that cut no ice with his mother, who begin to pick things up and throw them against the walls. "Maw, look at it this way," he tried to reason with her. "I've done went and removed your competition. You don't need to worry about her stealin Doc's heart away from you, because now she's a married woman and Doc has to leave her alone."

Venda stopped throwing things against the wall. She stared at Russ in such a way that he realized he'd made a good point. She thought about that, and then she said, "Now, why didn't I think of that?" It was one more of those questions that don't have any answers, so he didn't tell her why she didn't think of that. Then she finally asked a question that was answerable: "Speakin of whom, jist where is this blushin bride of your'n?"

"She's out yonder a-settin in the porch swing," he said.

"Well, maybe me and her ought to have a heart-to-heart women's talk," his mother said, and started to leave the room.

"But she still hates your guts on account of what ye done with Doc Swain, and she don't want to see you. Me, I don't hate your guts but you shore let me down, breakin your promise and all."

"We'll talk about that later. I think maybe I will give Tenny some voice lessons after all, and maybe even teach her how to yodel. I'll fix you some supper in a little while. You're still grounded."

His mother left him, and he felt both relieved that he had managed to cool her off a bit, and unhappy that she had grounded him. Dang it all, she couldn't ground him, because he was a married man, and married men don't get grounded— they don't even have to obey their mothers anymore. He scarcely had time to brood about this before his mother returned and just stood in the doorway staring at him for a while, until she said:

"Okay, I get it. You really did fix her up with Mulciber, didn't you? And you've just been pretending you didn't, just to tease me, or just to git even with me for breakin my promise not to fool around with any other man until I gave you your reward for fixin her up with Mulciber. Oh, you naughty boy, you! That's just the kind of stunt you'd pull, isn't it? So all this time you've just been waiting to collect that big reward! Well, come to Momma!"

She held out her arms to him, but he didn't understand. "Where's Tenny?" he asked.

"She shore aint on no porch of mine," Venda declared.

Even though he was grounded, Russ rushed past his mother and out of the house to the front porch, but Tenny wasn't there. There was no sign of Tenny, up nor down any of the streets. The rain had stopped, completely. The last vestiges of the sunset were visible to the west, clouds the same color as that pretty ring that Tenny wore. Russ stood there a long while, watching the sunset and thinking. His mother came and joined him. It was his turn to ask one of those questions that are meant just for show. "Do you know what I think?" And since his mother made no attempt to answer it, he told her, "I think Tenny must've rode off with Doc Swain." Then he told his mother how Doc had come to the courthouse and followed them to Mulciber's and then kept on following them, all the way to Venda's, and he must've somehow talked Tenny into going off with him. That was terrible. The thought greatly pained Russ. If everything had gone the way it ought to have gone, with clear skies and all, he and Tenny would be enjoying the beginnings of the shivaree along about now, up on Brushy Mountain, with folks making stupendous noises shooting off guns and banging pans and scaring the daylights out of him and his bride. Instead, the wedding night was plumb flummoxed and shot to hell! Russ felt so sorry for himself that he began to cry, and his mother began to cry also, feeling sorry not for him but for herself because she had her own problems dealing with the situation.

Mother and son held each other and bawled their hearts out.

Nine

Tenny, as we are about to discover, no longer had hypochondria, but ironically just at the time that she was cured of it I seem to be coming down with it myself. Leastways, Dr. Bittner this morning said he couldn't find any reason why I should be having this cough. You've noticed it, I'm sure. It started somewhere along in there about when I had Tenny up on that mountaintop. Dr. Bittner didn't give me a very thorough look-see; he just had me open my mouth for a second, and then he said it was possible I had a bit of gastric reflux that was causing a backup to irritate my throat, and he gave me some pills for it, but what I probably need is just some old-fashioned cough drops, so if you can remember, next time you come, could you pick me up a package of Smith Brothers?

How did Colvin persuade Tenny to get into his buggy and

go off with him? Of this entire story, that was the part that Doc was most stingy in telling me about, as if modesty prevented him from bragging about the accomplishment. After all, she was mad as hell at him and never wanted to see him again. So I personally don't know everything that passed between them while she was sitting in that porch swing of Venda's and he was sitting in his buggy. I know only a few details, that he started off by asking her to confirm his suspicion that she had actually had a dream the night before. At first, she wouldn't even talk to him, but she finally admitted that, yes, for the first time all summer she had had a dream. He told her he had tried to reach her in her dream, but couldn't find her, and she admitted that she'd been looking for him but couldn't find him either. "Sometimes," he said to her gently, "other folks keep us from doing what we want to do, don't ye know?" Then he got her to listen while he tried to explain what had happened last May to spoil that beautiful dream they were having together, that Venda had intruded into that beautiful enchanted forest and four-poster they had created, that Colvin had not wanted or welcomed her, and that they were certainly not making love *then*, but yes, they were making love earlier this afternoon because Venda had doped his coffee with a powerful love potion. The thing was, that love potion was supposed to make a feller fall madly in love forever with the first person he saw, and although it had robbed Colvin of his willpower and allowed Venda to seduce him, he definitely had not fallen in love with Venda.

"I still love *you*, Tenny," he said. "I reckon I didn't need ary love potion the first day I laid eyes on ye, up at the school. I fell in love with you that day, and if love is a disease, as you once thought, then mine has been progressive, chronic, insidious, and terminal. I will love you all the days of my life."

Like I say, I don't know what else he said, but maybe he

didn't need to say anything else, because the next thing she knew, Tenny was standing up from that porch swing. "I love thee, Colvin Swain," she said aloud, "and you don't know how long I've waited to say it."

"I will make the rain stop for you," he said, and he believed it himself, that he could do it, and he goddamn did it. The rain just quit. It didn't taper off or fade away, it just all of a heap stopped, and the sky cleared up and the sunset was visible, and by god if he didn't also arrange for the sunset to be in all the possible variations of her favorite color, amethyst.

She got into that buggy with him, and they had a real long, powerful, thrilling kiss. They didn't care whether anybody saw them, or whether Russ or Venda came out of the house. No, it wasn't that they didn't *care;* they didn't even think of it. It never crossed their minds that there was anybody else in the world except themselves. Finally Colvin broke the kiss long enough just to cluck his tongue and say, "Gidyup, ole Ness." The buggy began to move, and Colvin wrapped his arm around her, and she lay her head against his shoulder.

If he'd had his druthers, he'd have taken her straight to Stay More. But two mighty things kept him from it: one, of course, was that there was already a woman in Stay More who loved him very much and whom he still loved right considerably; and two, it had rained so hard that the roads were quagmires, and even if the buggy didn't get badly bogged, Hogshead Creek wouldn't even be fordable. He had stopped the rain, but he couldn't dry up the route. And night was coming on.

Did I mention that the owner of the Commercial Hotel at that time was Bob Swain, Doc's own cousin? No? Well, I thought I had. Maybe I hadn't even mentioned that Bob was one of the few fellers in Jasper that Doc considered a friend. Anyway, it was no problem for Colvin to take Tenny to the

Commercial and ask Bob to keep it quiet. Colvin asked Bob, "Have any of your rooms got four-poster beds in 'em?" Bob said that only the bridal suite did, and it would cost him a bit extra, and Colvin said money didn't matter. The Commercial was a fairly large white house, two stories, rambling all over creation with porches or verandas upstairs and down hither and yon, and the bridal suite was up on the second floor, with a good view of the main road through town and the mountains to the west. You wouldn't believe me if I told you that the quilt on the bed was Garden Butterfly, so I won't, although you must believe that it was a Gingham-and-Calico Butterfly, a kind of cousin to the Garden variety. There wasn't any Victrola to play soft music, but Tenny could hum and sing both, if need be, and in the course of the evening she did. One thing bothered her: there was a toilet in the bridal suite. It was the first indoor running-water toilet Tenny had ever seen, and when Colvin explained to her what it was, she said that was too bad, and would bring other folks running in and out all night, invading their privacy. Colvin convinced her that it was their own personal toilet and nobody else would use it. The first thing they had to do was get out of their soppy clothes, and Colvin borrowed some of Bob Swain's clothes for himself, and one of Bob's wife's dresses for Tenny; it was several sizes too big, but it was a cotton-print dress with orange butterflies all over it. Even in their borrowed clothes, Colvin didn't think it was a good idea for them to have their supper at the communal tables downstairs with everybody else, so he got Bob's wife to bring a tray with some supper up to the room. Tenny's appetite had returned, but she was still coughing. Knowing her as he did, Colvin knew that she could have all the symptoms of bronchitis or even pneumonia—it was a short, dry, unproductive cough, like this one I've got—without actually having those diseases, or anything else. He felt her cheek, which was neither hot nor cold, and he took her pulse, which was normal. He asked her routine questions such as what kind of headache she might have, but she didn't have a headache, she didn't have a stomachache, she didn't have any trouble eating or breathing, she didn't have anything wrong with her except that little cough. He was surprised to find her so asymptomatic, and he wondered what had happened to make her *want* to stop being ill . . . or to replace all of her usual symptoms with just that cough. How long had she been on that mountain crag? Had she actually been made to wear a black dress? He wanted her to talk, not simply to tell him what had been happening to her, but because he was still at a loss for words himself, and needed her to do most of the talking.

So, coughing now and again, she told him everything that had happened to her recently, including the night before, when she was the guest of Russ and his daddy, Mulciber Breedlove, and Russ had been under orders from his mother to play Cupid and fix Tenny up with Mulciber, but Tenny had been sickened by the very sight of the ugly old blacksmith, who was indeed the sorriest-looking specimen of humanity Tenny had ever seen. It was a good thing she was so sick she couldn't even drink her milk, because she suspected that Russ had doped her milk to make her fall in love with Mulciber. Then she knew that he had, when he drank the milk himself and became "over-frisky" and "a-rollixin." He was so fired with lust that he had proposed to Tenny. She hadn't exactly said yes, but she'd gone to bed with him.

Doc raised his eyebrows. "So you're not a virgin anymore," he said, and was surprised that he felt no intense dismay or jealousy. Well, after all, he told himself, virginity is just a state of mind, anyway.

But she said, "I guess maybe I still am. He couldn't get it in. I mean, he couldn't get *them* in. Colvin, did you know that Russ has got *two* of them?"

Colvin nodded, although the nod itself was a violation of the oath to Kie Raney never to discuss a patient's condition with anybody else. "It's uncommonly rare," he said. "But that don't make him a freak."

"Still, Cassie Whitter prophesied that I'd marry a freak, and I don't know how to tell you this, but me and Russ got married this afternoon."

"I figured you did," he said.

"You don't hate me for it?" she asked. "Can you forgive me for it?"

"Can you forgive me for already being married?" he asked.

"I reckon I can," she said. "I guess—I guess the main thing that made me marry him wasn't because Cassie Whitter augured it but the thought I was getting even with you. I thought it wasn't fair for you to be married, and me not."

They talked until way past bedtime. Colvin of course realized that the moment might come eventually when he would be required to demonstrate his manly vigor, which was totally sapped from his day-long romp with Venda, so he wanted to postpone bedtime as long as possible. Past midnight, he began really to fret, and he wasn't sure he could explain to Tenny's satisfaction that a man who has made love thirty-eight times in one day simply cannot hope for another erection without whatever drug Venda had been supplying. So he kept talking to Tenny about everything, and eventually a subject that both of them had been avoiding reared its ugly head: what were they going to do with themselves? The sun was going to rise the next day, and the day after, and how were they going to face it and live with it, enwrapped in their great but illicit love for each other? "We have got to find a way," he said, and they spent the next hour thinking and talking about finding a way. Colvin concocted some whimsical schemes, but rejected each one of them. He could take her to live in Stay More and tell Piney that she was just a student who needed a place to live because the dormitory was all filled up. No, he couldn't. He could take her away to some distant place and start all over, like perhaps belatedly accepting that offer to teach and practice in St. Louis. No, he couldn't. He could offer Piney half of all his worldly goods and what little cash-on-hand he owned to leave him, to move out of his house. No, he couldn't. He could put Tenny back for her sophomore year at Newton County Academy, and go on teaching there himself, to give both of them time to see if they couldn't work something out. Yes, he could.

Colvin had no trouble at all persuading Tenny that she ought to return to school, because she had been intending to do that anyway, and had not even considered that her marriage would interfere with continuing her education. There were a couple of other girls at N.C.A., Olivia and Oralie, who were married, although of course they were not permitted to stay in the dormitory and had to live off-campus with or without their husbands. "Tenny," Colvin declared solemnly, "I am going to have to go on living with my wife. Do you want to go on living with your husband?"

"Do you think he would let me, after tonight?"

"What's 'tonight'?" he asked.

"You and me are really going to become lovers," she declared. She gestured toward the bed. "It's a four-poster, all right," she observed, "but it's a sorry substitute for that one we had in our dream." She lifted Bob's wife's butterfly dress over her head, and the sight of her naked body gave him such twitchings in the Kobelt bulb of his *corpus cavernosum* and the fundiform ligaments at the root of his penis that he felt his equipment was desperately trying to put itself into order. But as he got out of Bob's clothes, he realized there was just no way the blood sinuses would engorge. Tenny had never seen a limp pecker before. Colvin's in that dream as well as with Venda, both of Russ's at all times, and Mulciber's—a total of four peckers she had seen, and all of them had been hard and upright and just a little scary, especially the double-barreled job of Russ's. Now as Colvin stood there looking abashed and uncertain, her smart mind did some quick thinking and determined the reason for his dangling doodle, and she requested, "Colvin, what if we just hold each other until we're asleep? Sleep is where you go to be all alone. And dreams are where you go to get away from the loneliness of sleep. Maybe we could even find that forest again."

Which is what they did. They entangled their naked bodies beneath the Gingham-and-Calico Butterflies, and after a long good-night kiss they fell asleep and were soon meeting at the old four-poster in the enchanted forest. The bigger four-poster that Venda had dragged in beside it was still there, but Colvin found an ax and chopped it up into firewood, which he ignited to take the chill off the first signs of autumn. Once that bed was burnt, all was just as it had been before, with the moonlight exactly right and a canopy hung with long chiffon curtains a-wafting gently in the breeze to the tune of slow violins on the Victrola. And once again Tenny was dressed in a royal purple silk nightgown, and Colvin was dressed in a loose-fitting flouncy-sleeved white shirt such as swashbucklers wear to do their duels and adventures in. Tenny had made just two changes from the previous dream: she had added "Arkansas Blues" to the stack of platters the Victrola was going to play, and she had added a flush toilet identical to the one in their Commercial Hotel bridal suite, just in case she had to go, and wouldn't have to suffer the sort of run-to-the-bushes which had spoiled the previous dream. So they were able to pick up exactly where they'd left off before they'd been so rudely interrupted. Colvin was able to finish his little lecture about the location and function of the clitoris, and he did something that Russ had not even tried to do in his fumblings and probings the night previous: he actually caressed her clitoris, and with the help of his fingers and his voice and the Victrola and the moonlight and the firelight from Venda's burning bed, she was lifted to a mountaintop much higher than that she'd had to stand upon in black to await her bridegroom, and from *this* mountaintop she soared free on zephyrs that seized her and carried her all over the world. Only afterwards did she know, because Colvin told her, that she had begun to sing the same chant she'd sung on the crag above Brushy Mountain: the pure notes, rising and falling, of kindly melancholy, a mixture of yearning, wanting, hoping, desire, with maybe a tinge of loss and bewilderment. Colvin realized, however, that it was the kind of song you had to hear from a distance, not up close, and hearing it up close somehow took the haunting holiness off of it. So Colvin asked if she couldn't turn that into a song of joy, and she tried, and while singing it she realized that he was inside of her, that he had entered her painlessly, joyfully, and that she really was not a virgin anymore.

The next morning when he awoke Colvin discovered that there was some blood on the sheet. He would have to pay Cousin Bob some extra for that. He did not wake her, but took the liberty to examine her and determine that *carunculae hymenales* were all that remained of her hymen. As we are all able to do, sometimes, he sought to recapture the dream, and remembered it, and was astonished by its authenticity. Now in the light of the rising sun, he saw that the lovely landscape of her body was beaded with sweat like the morning earth beaded with dew, as if the exertions in their dream had made her perspire. He decided to take a towel and blot up the sweat and if that didn't wake her, he would leave her be.

But she woke. "Dreams are where you go to get away from the loneliness of sleep," he repeated her words to her. "But daylight comes to reveal all the other people in the world that we have to deal with." He had her get dressed, and he put her in his buggy and took her to Parthenon. "You've got to have a place to live, and I've got to see if I caint work out some kind of future for me and you."

Jossie Conklin just happened to be in her office, the only person on campus. Colvin had Tenny wait in the buggy while he went up to talk with Jossie. Jossie was thrilled to learn that Colvin had reconsidered and might want to return to N.C.A. for another year, but she had to inform him that the Baptists had sent from Baylor a new man, Tim James, with a master's degree, to teach Bible and Science with explicit instructions to teach the hygiene course without any reference to reproduction. Jossie was awfully sorry, but there just wasn't any way Colvin could teach hygiene. "I don't suppose you could teach Psychology, could you?" Jossie asked. "And coach basketball?"

Colvin lied. He knew as much about psychology as he did about basketball, which is to say that both were inexact sciences, that throwing that thing up in the air might or might not get it through the hole, you couldn't never tell, you could only use your mind to hope that it would go through the hole, but if you missed the hole you might or might not get a chance to try again. Neither psychology nor basketball was like medi-

276

cine, in which you can at least count on some things to happen. But Colvin supposed that both psychology and basketball had something that medicine lacked: entertainment value, since they were sports and had the power to divert and even to amuse. "Yes ma'am, I reckon I can handle both," he said. "But I shore hope you don't have to wait until jist before class starts to let me see the textbook."

Jossie laughed, and handed him a copy of his textbooks for Psychology. There was no textbook for basketball. He was amazed at the little coincidence that the author of *Human Behavior* was named Stephen Sheldon Colvin, Professor of Educational Psychology at Brown University. Our Colvin had never heard of anybody else with the name Colvin, and he felt a little as Russ must have felt when he learned that he wasn't the only person in the world with diphallus. Right away Colvin believed that Professor Colvin was his spiritual kin, or at least psychological kin, and could probably teach him a few things, which he in turn would attempt to teach his students. Thumbing through the book, Colvin noticed that there was a section on the nervous system, which he already had in his head. No, he wouldn't have any trouble teaching psychology.

They shook hands over the deal and agreed upon a salary of thirty dollars a month, including his duties as school physician. Then Colvin said, "Jossie, hon, I wonder if it might be possible for one of the girl students, my best pupil from last year, you remember Tennessee Tennison, well, as you may know she comes from a dirt-poor family way back up in the jillikens, and they threw her out, and she don't have nowhere to stay, and I was just wondering if she could go ahead and move into the dormitory, and live there by herself until school starts."

Jossie studied Colvin as if she might be guessing at things that weren't within her realm of understanding. Then she smiled a knowing smile and said, "Thelma Villines, the house-keeper, has already moved in, so if it's okay with her, it's okay with me."

Colvin installed Tenny in the dormitory with the help of Mrs. Villines, who reckoned she could find some work to keep Tenny busy and earn her room and board. Then Colvin had a private moment alone with Tenny to say good-bye to her and tell her he'd try to get back this way whenever he could. They kissed.

"Thank you so much for everything," Tenny said, and she walked alongside him and his buggy to the edge of the campus, but, in the superstition of the Ozarks, turned aside to avoid watching him disappear from sight.

Colvin's dealing with Jossie had been like falling off a log compared with dealing with Piney. The road to Stay More was still more liquid than solid, and several times he got mired, and both he and Nessus were covered with mud and exhausted by late afternoon, when they reached home. He had concocted a dozen good excuses, but Piney, who knew everything, knew that he must have been "carrying on" with Jossie Conklin, and she accused him of it. "Strike me dead if I never even touched her!" Colvin protested. "Except to shake her hand when we agreed on my salary . . . which, you'll be happy to know, means that now we'll be able to get for you that pianer."

"Goody," she said. "Let's go."

And sure enough, Piney insisted that Colvin take her to Little Rock to shop for a piano. It wasn't easy. First he had to scare up some kind of loan of the money, and since the Swains Creek Bank and Trust Company had been robbed and was out of business he couldn't apply for a loan, all he could do was hatch a kind of health insurance scheme which the American Medical Association wouldn't have endorsed. He examined his ledgers and made a list of all the patients who had ever paid

278

him in cash money instead of livestock, produce, working-it-off, or other form of barter, and he went around to each of them, a total of only thirty-nine, and with his hat in hand he offered to treat them in perpetuity regardless of the severity of their condition in return for a modest advance premium of only twenty dollars. Eleven of the patients claimed that they didn't see how they could possibly raise that much cash money, although seven of these admitted that it sounded like a real bargain. Five patients told him he was out of his mind. But from twenty-three patients he collected twenty dollars each, and with this money he was able to take Piney to Little Rock. Instead of using Nessus and the buggy, inadequate to freight the piano back to Stay More, he hired a team of mules and a wagon from Ingledew's livery, and with Piney sitting on the buckboard beside him, he drove to Russellville, reaching it in two days, and took a Missouri Pacific train from there to Little Rock, and spent two nights in the capital city, where he had never been before, nor had Piney, and they were able to enjoy the sights of the city, including the enormous state capitol which imitates the U.S. Capitol; the state's tallest edifice, the Donaghey Building, towering fourteen floors above the street; and the recently opened Broadway Bridge spanning the Arkansas River, the largest and most expensive bridge in Arkansas. Both Colvin and Piney, walking across it on the pedestrian skirt, found it incredible that anything in the world could cost a million dollars. At the Hollenberg Music Company, a high-pressure salesman who was himself a piano virtuoso demonstrated that the affordable pianos indeed sounded tinny. They found one baby grand that did not sound tinny but was far out of their price range, and the salesman by playing Liszt on it convinced Piney that she'd never learn how to play a piano and had better play it safe and stick with one of these here player pianos that used rolls of perforated paper to do all the work for you. Of course player pianos cost a good bit more than ordinary instruments where you have to do the fingering, and then also of course you have to get yourself a supply of the rolls of the perforated paper to make the thing go, and the transaction left Colvin flat broke except for just their return train tickets, but Hollenberg Music Company paid the freight for taking the piano back with them on the same train to Russellville, where they loaded it into their wagon.

Piney had needed a whole day just to pick out her rolls, at forty cents each for those that had words, and thirty cents for the wordless ones. Piney's selections included "Red Pepper," a rag; "Woodland Echoes," a reverie; "Barcarole," a descriptive piece from *The Tales of Hoffman;* "Baby Won't You Please Come Home?"—a jazzy blues number; "Frolic of the Frogs," a concert waltz; "Nights of Gladness," a dance waltz; and "Humoreske," a light classic. All these were wordless. The wordy pieces were: "Arkansas Blues," a blues piece that sounded familiar to Colvin; "When I'm Gone You'll Soon Forget," a ballad; "Tonight You Belong to Me," a waltz; and the following fox-trots: "All I Want Is You," "I Wish You Were Jealous of Me," "Roses of Picardy," and "Then I'll Be Happy." How do I with my imperfect memory recall all these titles? Because I played all of them on Piney's piano in the days I dwelt in Stay More and, hell, I still know the words of most of 'em, and if you and Mary would excuse me, I'll see if I can't still croak one of 'em for you:

Blues ——————— have overtaken me ———————,
I'm so weary, days are full o' gloom ———————,
Homesickness has got me down in mind ———————
'Way ——————— down in old Arkansas ———————.

I know a lot more of "Arkansas Blues" than that, but I'll interrupt it the same way Colvin interrupted me when I tried to put it on the player piano and sing it. "Doc, that was Piney's roll," he said, "but it was Tenny's song, so I'druther you'd play something else, if it's all the same to you . . ."

Piney's player piano immediately became the sensation of Stay More, and folks would come from all over to loaf around the porch of the Swain Clinic and listen to Piney a-pumpin the pedals and singing the tunes that had words to them, and even the tunes that didn't have words inspired all the listeners to make up their own lyrics. The Stay Morons invented a dozen different versions of the lyrics to "Red Pepper Rag," and they even concocted a respectable chorus for that concert waltz, "Frolic of the Frogs," as well as a four-part contrapuntal harmony for "Barcarole." But everybody's favorite was "Roses of Picardy," even though nobody had the least notion where Picardy was, and Colvin himself, who never could sing worth a damn, usually joined in when there were a hundred people out in front of his house crooning about the hush of the silvery dew and there's never a rose like you.

Of course the problem with all of this music was that it made everybody neglect the old-time folk songs and ballits that had been family heirlooms all the way back to the seventeenth century in old England and Scotch Ireland. When I was collecting the thousand titles for my four-volume *Ozark Folksongs,* published in the late forties, I had the devil's own time culling out the new stuff from the old, because so much of the repertoire of the best old singers and pluckers had been "contaminated" by what they'd learned from their Victrolas and from piano rolls.

But the Jazz Age was creeping into the Ozarks, and there was no stopping it. When the Newton County Academy opened its doors for the fall semester of its second year, Colvin immediately noticed that the dresses of many of the girls had hemlines scarcely below the knee, and some of them had painted faces (although for the first day only, because a strict N.C.A. rule would forbid the use of rouge and lipstick), and nearly all of the girls had cut their hair short, and were wearing it in what was called "bobs." He held his breath, waiting to see if Tenny might've cut short her waist-length hair.

But he couldn't find Tenny. She wasn't in the dormitory. He accosted Thelma Villines, the housekeeper, who only said, accusingly, "Didn't you never know that married gals aint allowed to live in the dormitory?"

He went to Jossie's office. The principal laughed and said, "I heard all about how you eloped with Tenny on her wedding night!"

Colvin recalled, much belatedly, that Jossie and Venda were practically best friends. "Where is she?" he asked.

"Well, as you should have known," Jossie said, "married girls are not allowed to live in the dormitories, and we had to evict her. She had nowhere to go. Her husband and her mother-in-law very graciously gave her a place to live in Jasper."

Colvin was greatly chagrined at the thought. "But she's coming back to school?" he asked.

"We shall have to see," Jossie said.

This was an October Friday, his school day changed from Monday of the previous year because the basketball teams would be playing their games on Friday afternoons. He had also promised Piney that he would not be traveling to Parthenon extra days each week if it could be avoided. So each Friday he would receive and examine pupil-patients in his office, teach a class in psychology, and coach basketball, a full day that would leave him, he had been hoping, a few moments in the company of his hopeless but not impossible love. Just as he had done on the first day of the semester the October before, he spent the morning examining everybody, faculty and students alike, for evaluative diagnosis, and finding the usual gamut of maladies, malformations, malnutrition, malignancies, and malaise, as well as malingering. It was more time-consuming this year because the student enrollment had increased by forty, to 184, and that was forty more smallpox vaccinations to give.

Doing the faculty first, he was surprised to find a friendly Venda eager to see him and be examined. Venda was the proud new owner of a Ford automobile, and drew Colvin to the window to look out at the parking lot, where it sat right alongside another Ford owned by Tim James, the new Bible and science teacher who had taken Colvin's hygiene class. Colvin didn't understand how these people could afford to buy autos on the trifling salaries they earned, but he supposed they didn't spend their money on things like player pianos. Venda didn't have any complaints, but she took her dress off anyway just to see if it might give Colvin any sort of reaction. He was trying hard to remain professional on Doctor's Day, and he kept his clipboard covering the rising in his pants. Venda said one reason she got the auto was because there wasn't room on Marengo for all three of them, and Tenny had usurped her position on Russ's horse if not on his heart.

"Where is she?" Colvin asked.

"Oh, I reckon she'll be coming in to see you for her checkup like everbody else," Venda said. "Anyhow, she can tell you that we've been good to her. She has done what she was told, and has been real handy around the house. And you may not believe this, but I really truly have been giving her voice lessons, although her voice aint in none too good a shape, with this sore throat she's got and her cough that won't never go away."

Before leaving his office, Venda took Colvin's chin in her fingertips to get his full attention while she declared, "I hope you won't let that gal come between us this year."

One of the first pupils waiting to see Colvin was Tenny's husband. Like his mother, he surprised Colvin by being friendly. Russ announced to Colvin that he intended to "go out for" the basketball team, and he hoped that "Coach," as he would now begin to call the man who was also "Doc," "Teacher," and "Wife's Lover," would find a place for him on the team. But also he was thinking about signing up for Psychology. Could Teacher tell him anything about what the subject involved? "Is psychology anything like apology?" Russ wondered.

"Well, I reckon you could say so," Colvin allowed. "We'll study regrets. We'll study why we feel the way we do, and why we think the way we do, and maybe even why we do what we do. How's your wife?"

"Oh, she caint complain," Russ said. "That cough of hers comes and goes, and she's kinder moody most of the time, but she caint really complain, so she don't." Russ explained that Tenny at the moment was over visiting her friend Zarky in the dormitory but would probably be coming in to see Doc Swain pretty soon. Then Russ said a strange thing. "Coach, there aint no use pretendin that you aint still the only feller in this world that Tenny cares about. She don't hardly talk about nothin else, and I reckon I ought to be jealous but there don't seem to be nothin I could do about it. Except maybe . . . do you recollect you once offered to hack off my extry pecker for me? I've wondered a lot if she would like me more if I had only one of 'em."

Awkwardly Colvin tried to determine if the diphallic condition rendered intercourse difficult or impossible, but Russ blushed and hemmed and hawed and managed to say only that "We aint been able to work out a good fit." And then he said,

"Heck, Doc, I don't *need* the extry one. Will you slice it off for me? Of course, I don't mean right *now,* but sometime soon?"

"Let me think about it some," Colvin requested, and pointed out that he had no experience with that particular operation and would have to study up on it.

Strange to relate, not very long after Russ had left, Colvin had a visit from one of the forty new students, a pretty girl named Oona Owens, whose file indicated that she had come from a remote village in Madison County to the west. When Colvin asked his conventional opening question, "Has anything been a-troublin ye?" Oona giggled and declared:

"I aint never been to a doctor afore."

"Don't be bashful," he said. "Jist let me check a few things. If you'll open wide and say 'Ah' . . ." Colvin put a tongue depressor into her mouth and looked around, and then he stuck an otoscope into each of her ears, and a nasoscope into each nostril. Apart from slight adenoids, her head was negative. She giggled again when he stethoscoped her chest, and also when he hit her knees with his reflex hammer. He performed all his little tests, but she didn't seem to have anything wrong with her except for the adenoids. "You're okay," he said. "I'll see you in Psych class."

"But Doc," she said, "there's one little thing a-troublin me. I caint show it to ye, though."

"Well, can you tell me where it's at?"

She quickly touched her crotch and instantly drew her hand away. "Down here," she said. "My pu*** . . . ," her voice fell to a whisper.

"Is it itchy? Have you got a rash or sores or anything on it?" he asked.

"Nope, nothing like that. Only there's *two* of 'em."

Colvin studied her, and kept his face impassively benign.

Then he said that of course he couldn't tell for sure without examining her but it sounded as if she had what was known as duplex vagina, which, although it was exceptional, quite rare in fact, didn't mean she was a freak or anything, and there was nothing to be ashamed of. Colvin told her of some other known cases of duplex vaginae in faraway places like Rhode Island and North Dakota, and that while offhand he didn't know of another case of it in Arkansas, there was bound to be a few he didn't know about. He said he hoped that after she got to know him better, as her teacher for Psychology as well as the school physician, she might feel comfortable enough to permit him to have a look and determine if she had a true duplex vagina, that is, two of them, or only a septate vagina, that is, one of them with a kind of partition dividing it into two parts. The latter condition was fairly common, and even more common was the condition of having a double uterus. Colvin felt it was premature to discuss with her her sexual life, if any, or the possibility that when she became a mother she might have to have a Caesarean, so he did not mention these things. He simply said, "I'm right sorry there aint nothin I could do to help your condition." *Except,* he said to himself, *introduce ye to a feller who's probably dyin to meet ye.*

"I aint worried," Oona said. "They don't pain me none. But will they keep me from being on the basketball team?"

"Only in the sense that they mean you're a female, and the basketball team is for males."

"Huh?" she said. "But there's a girls' team too, aint they?"

Sure enough, he discovered after checking with Jossie Conklin on the matter, there were going to be teams for both boys and girls, and he was expected to coach both. "I thought you knew that," Jossie said. While he was at it, he asked Jossie, since she was supposedly a math expert or at least the math teacher, to calculate the odds against a person with X condition, one out of five million, being found in the same place and same time as a person with Y condition, one of three million. Jossie did a lot of figuring, and even used her adding machine, but finally announced that the odds were incalculable. In other words, it was impossible.

It was almost time for noon dinner before Tenny finally came to see him. He was thrilled to see that she had not cut her hair, nor was she wearing face paint, and her dress, which obviously was a cast-off of Venda's, still came down to her ankles. She seemed kind of pale, though, and thin. "Tenny!" he said.

"Colvin!" she said, closing the door behind her, then she leapt into his arms. "I've missed ye so!" They had a long kiss, and she commenced rubbing her body all over his, especially in the areas where the legs end, then she tried to pull him down to the sofa. He resisted, protesting that there were other students outside the door waiting for his attention. "I'm a-perishin for ye!" she exclaimed. "I've got to have you inside me, right now!"

"But Tenny," he said. That was all he knew to say, which perhaps was enough, the way he said it, to try to let her know that although he himself had an enormous erection at this moment which he would dearly enjoy sliding into her, they were going to have to learn restraint and discretion and patience if they were successfully to manage their romance. "Later maybe we can steal a moment," he tried to console her, "but right now all I'm supposed to do is examine ye. Has anything been a-troublin ye?" He automatically asked his routine question, then said, "I wish we could talk for hours, but this is a real busy day for me. So why don't ye jist talk and tell me everything while I do an examination on ye?"

So Tenny talked constantly while he gave her as thorough a physical examination as his instruments would permit. She said she had nothing whatever wrong with her. He found that hard to swallow in view of her long-standing hypochondria. She said that she was so happy that school was starting up again, so she would not only get to see Colvin in his office, like now, but also she was going to take Psychology! "Do ye think I'd have any aptitude for that subject?" she asked.

"Tenny, the subject of psychology ort to have been named after you," he said truthfully, not meaning to imply that there was anything wrong with her mental processes or her motives or her behavior.

She was also going to "go out" for the girls' basketball team, so she could be with Colvin during even more of the precious Fridays, and she hoped that when they took long trips to the places where they would play games against distant teams, she could ride beside him in whatever conveyance was used. Possibly even, if any of those games involved going to other towns that could not be returned from in the same day, and they had to spend the night, they might even contrive some way to spend the whole night together, ever now and then, because she had thought about this quite a lot with both her heart and her head as well as her twitchet, and she had decided that they were going to have to find a way to hook up their sexual links not just once but many, many times repeatedly in the same night . . . or day, or whenever. "Remember," she said, " 'we have got to find a way.' That's our motto." It might even be possible for them to sneak off sometimes to Venda's house in Jasper, when Venda and Russ were at the school. Yes, Tenny was doing all right, living at Venda's house. At least she didn't mind it too much. It was a roof over her head. From the beginning, Tenny had been required to do most of the cooking and housecleaning, but she didn't mind. One of the first big jobs Venda had given her involved sorting and straightening the pantry. Venda's pantry had been a terrible mess, everything all jumbled together as if any time Venda had been to the store she had just thrown her groceries all of a heap into the pantry. There were bags of dried beans that had got all mixed up with bags of dried corn, and Tenny had been required practically to sort all those seeds, one by one, and it had taken forever, and the only thing that preserved her sanity was the memory of the time she had watched a bunch of ants carrying little grains of sand diligently and patiently to build their ant heap, and she had sought to do her sorting with the same mindless persistence. Tenny wondered if Venda had just given her such a tough job in an effort to part her from her senses, and, having failed, had given her the *next* tough job, which involved . . . But Tenny understood that Colvin had other students waiting for their medical examinations, and she had better save the rest of the story for later.

Colvin was greatly disturbed. Not over the tasks that Venda had been giving Tenny, although that was disturbing enough. What was more disturbing, for now, was what his examination of Tenny revealed. At first, he couldn't believe it, because he'd so thoroughly examined Tenny in the past without ever finding anything whatever wrong with her that it was hard now to accept that there might actually be something wrong with her. He wondered at the irony of the transposition: as long as she was a chronic complaining hypochondriac, she was safe, invulnerable, and absolutely healthy; but once she abandoned her hypochondria and claimed to be "just fine," she was actually sick. His hand on her chest detected fremitus. His stethoscope found a vesicular murmur. Her pulse was rapid. Her skin was not dry, but clammy, beaded with sweat as it had been that morning in the Commercial Hotel. He asked her to cough, and collected on the end of a tongue depressor an expectoration that was greenish, muco-purulent. He debated with himself whether to tell Tenny of his suspicions, and decided against it. "Tenny," he said, "I'll see you in Psych class, and again at Basketball, but right after that I'd like you to come back here to my office for just a minute so I can give you another test."

"Could we take more than just a minute?" she asked. "Couldn't we take long enough to see if that sofa is good for anything besides lying on with lollipops?"

He laughed, as if that might dispel his anxiety. "We'll see," he said, and kissed her again and sent her on her way, asking her to take it easy.

Then he visited Jossie's office yet again and inquired into the possibility of having a student-messenger with a horse ride into Jasper and pick up some stuff at Arbaugh's Rexall, and he wrote and signed and sealed into an envelope a note from his prescription pad to R. C. Arbaugh, requesting a vial of tuberculin. The note said that just in case they were out of stock, kindly send somebody to Harrison to get it right away, and hang the expense.

His mind was not on the subject as he went to face his Psychology class. He had read enough of the Colvin textbook, and he had a fair idea of what he wanted to say, but his concern over Tenny's condition seized his mind and would not let him think of anything else. He had distracting problems finding the meeting place of the Psych class: for some reason it had been scheduled to meet in the gym, the new, long, low barnlike building of fieldstone that completed the triangle of main buildings on the campus. The pupils were not sitting at desks but just around on the floor. At least he had been provided with a portable blackboard, and he wrote his name on it, as if there were anybody (there wasn't) who didn't know it. Jossie Conklin had not yet arrived with an armload of the textbooks.

"Wal, my friends," he started off, "I hope we're gonna have a heap of fun in here. But I ort to tell ye, right off, that what we learn in here aint really necessary. You can live without it. It won't make you rich, and it likely won't make you happy neither. So what's the point in messin around with it? Unlike other subjects you're taking, it caint be put to much practical use. It won't teach ye how to speak proper. It won't help ye to do sums. Some of y'uns remember I taught a course last year in hygiene, which at least showed everbody how to take care of theirselfs and keep healthy. Wal, this here that we're gonna do might or might not give ye some sort of mental comfort, but I wouldn't guarantee it. It might help ye understand better how your mind works. It might help ye to get along better with yore feller man. I can't guarantee none of that. But I can guarantee that if you pay attention, and put your heart into it, it will shore enough give ye somethin to think about!"

He plunged right in, with Prof. Colvin's first subject, Consciousness, and managed to keep them paying attention for half an hour's worth of talk about how imagination is necessary to consciousness, and the different levels of consciousness (which he diagrammed on the blackboard) and how each of them affects our conduct. His lecture was hampered by his thoughts of Tenny and her condition. She was right there on the floor, not next to her husband but not far from him, and she was looking up at him with adoration, and also with a look of expectation, as if he might be about to explain the meaning of life.

Seeking to demonstrate the distinction between consciousness in full control and consciousness when it is reflexive or instinctive, Colvin noticed that there was a basketball lying on the edge of the court. He picked it up. It was the first time he had ever handled one. He bounced it. It sprang free from his control, but he chased it down and recaptured it. "Now if I was to try to make this thing go through that hoop," he declared, "trying with all my might to *make* it go in, the chances are I'd shorely miss." He propelled the ball upward, and, sure enough, it did not even come close to reaching the hoop, falling short by a couple of feet or more. "See?" he said, chasing down the bouncing ball again. "But if I had learned not to let my consciousness interfere with my *instinctive* tossing of the ball toward the hoop, there's a fair chance I might get it in." He shut off his mind and tossed the ball again, and it rose in a long smooth arc and went cleanly through the net. It may have been an accident, or beginner's luck, but the students gasped, and then applauded, and several of them hollered things like, "Dandy shot, Coach!"

"Now you may be wondering, aint it a contradiction to try to consciously be instinctive? That will be the subject of our next meeting, and here's your homework." He wrote on the blackboard a list of questions he had made up for them to answer, such as, "List several examples of instinctive behavior you've observed in yourself." He wrote down the page numbers, 1–23, for them to study in the Colvin text.

Finally, he asked, "Any questions?"

One boy raised his hand and said, "Yeah, Coach. When is our first game?"

"Game?" Colvin said. He glanced at Tenny, as if her facial expression might give him some clue, but she seemed merely to be awaiting his answer to the question. He realized that perhaps the students expected him to enliven the dull classes with some games. It oughtn't to be too awfully hard for him to make up a few, although Prof. Colvin didn't really get into the matter of play and Hall's theory of games until the second chapter. "Wal, week after next, I reckon," he said. "I ort to be able to have some games ready for y'uns by then."

A girl raised her hand and asked, "Don't we need some special shoes?"

Colvin thought that was a funny, if irrelevant question, and he laughed. "Heck, you can go barefoot for all I care!" he said. The students looked at each other, and Colvin sensed that they might have been disappointed in his answer. "I mean," he said, "wear jist whatever kind of shoe you want." He dismissed them.

Several of the students lingered after class to fool around with the basketball, trying to put it through the hoop, and he was pleased to see that they were attempting "lab sessions" with his talk about instinctive behavior. But he needed that basketball for his next hour, so he reluctantly expropriated it from them.

Most all of these students, however, were also going to be in Basketball, which, he discovered, was not meeting here in the gym where there were several hooped baskets available, but up on the second floor of the main building, where his hygiene class had met. When he got to the assigned room he discovered that every seat in the room was filled, kids were sitting on the floor and standing against the walls, and there was a big crowd outside the door who couldn't get in. This potential audience included most of the faculty as well, and Colvin was dismayed at the realization that there might be not only girls' and boys' teams but also a faculty team that he would have to coach. Jossie came up to him and asked, "Would you mind if we moved to the auditorium?" Then she added, "I didn't even try to bring the textbooks, because there simply aren't enough to go around." Feeling already dazed with his agitation over Tenny's condition, and the experience of having just conducted a class,

293

Colvin wondered if he had perhaps misunderstood Jossie previously: maybe there was supposed to be a textbook for Basketball. He certainly hoped so, because he needed one. All he had was a five-cent Little Blue Book from Haldeman-Julius, *Fundamentals and Rules of Basket Ball,* which just scratched the surface and left him uncertain about the distinction between a forward and a guard.

The group nearly filled the auditorium, which at least had a couple of basketball hoops attached to the sides of the stage, which had been the basketball court before the gym was built. He was both pleased and intimidated to see that so many people were interested in basketball. He noticed that even Venda was present, and he waved at her. He was too self-conscious to climb up on the stage where the basketball hoops were, so he decided to save that for later. He just stood in front of the first row, holding his basketball in one arm, and looked out over the crowd until he spotted Tenny, and he smiled at her, hoping the sight of her would give him encouragement, but on the contrary it simply reminded him that he was going to be distracted throughout Basketball by the thought of the results of the tuberculin test he would have to give her. He cleared his throat, and had a panicky thought that he might never again have the beginner's luck shooting the basketball that he had had in Psych class, so maybe he had better not even try. "Wal, howdy, folks," he began, and amended that to "Ladies and gentleman" to include his colleagues. He really didn't know what to say next, and a long moment of painful silence drifted by, until he thought to break the ice with a little chitchat. "Aint it a beautiful day, though? It don't look to rain anytime soon, and I kinder like this airish weather myself after that hot summer we had. How is everybody feelin? I hope you're feelin fine. I'm feelin just fine myself." All of them were smiling pleasantly as if all of them were feeling fine too except that they were a little impatient for him to get down to business.

One thing that Colvin knew for certain about Basketball was that the entire object of all of that running back and forth and trying to get the ball through the hoop and steadily piling up point after point was to win. Winning was everything. "We're going to win! This is all about winning!" he said to them suddenly, and with such enthusiasm that his audience broke into spontaneous cheering. "Aint nobody ever gonna beat us! We will be the champ-peens of the whole country!"

Now there were two things that had to be talked about in the very beginning, and he might as well get them out of the way as quickly as possible. The first one was a bit of a problem. He had hoped that he might be meeting the boys' teams and the girls' teams separately, because this was a matter that couldn't comfortably be discussed in mixed company, but since everybody was here together, he might as well try to make the best of it. He needed to discuss the absolute necessity, from the physician's point of view as well as simply a matter of personal well-being, that each of the boys—including the two males on the faculty—obtain and always wear a good-fitting athletic supporter. "Call 'em jock straps or whatever," he said, "they serve an important function which it ort not be too difficult for you to figure out. So I expect to see each of you fellers with one the next time we meet. As for you gals . . ." and he went on to discuss the need for them each to own and wear a good-fitting brassiere. It ought not be necessary to call attention to the fact that all the running and jumping of basketball would make their bosoms bounce up and down like mad if they didn't have a good brassiere to hold 'em down. These here new Jazz Age fads, with boyish high-hemmed dresses and bobbed hair and what-all, might be okay just to be *seen* in, but apparently there was a new fad to de-emphasize the bosom by not wearing no brassiere at all, and that simply would not do, as far as we here are concerned.

"Okay? So the next important item we have to discuss is: what are we going to call ourselves? We need a mascot name. And it ought to be original and distinctive, not just something commonplace like Tigers or Lions or Bears or Bulldogs or whatever. Any suggestions?"

The members of the audience exchanged looks with one another, and Colvin hoped that they were actually thinking about the matter. Jossie Conklin raised her hand and said, "Perhaps in view of the subject, we ought to be the Butterflies!" and she laughed and looked around to see if any others had grasped the significance of her remark, but only Nick Rainbird, who taught history, was also laughing.

Tim James, the new man (Bible and Hygiene, and destined shortly to become Jossie's lover), said, "Since we're the Newton County Academy, what say let's call ourselves the Academi-cians?" and he fell out of his seat with his own laughter but few of the faculty and none of the students joined in.

"Let's let the students be heard from," Colvin suggested, and they listened to several suggestions, some of them good ones based upon the local fauna, such as Hellbenders, which, however, was thought a little too naughty for a Christian school.

Russ Breedlove suggested, "If it's the Newton County Academy, how about we call ourselves the Counts?"

"And call the girls the Countesses?" Colvin asked. He rather liked the idea although he wasn't wild about it. He proposed to write the various suggestions on the blackboard and let them vote on a winner. He wrote down all those suggested, and waited to see if any others were proposed.

Tenny raised her hand and rather quietly offered, "As far as that matter goes, how about the Newts?"

There was a lot of laughter. Colvin allowed as how that might be appropriate if they had to travel distances through rough country, because newts were amphibious salamanders. "Of course, newts is tiny little critters, but they're elusive and slippery and they can go ever which way," he pointed out. "Yeah, that might be an appropriate name for us. I'm all for it. Thank you, Tenny."

"Excuse me," Jossie Conklin said to him, "but what does all of this have to do with psychology?"

Colvin wasn't sure he understood her question. "Wal, I reckon if we had a mascot name, it would give us a sense of identity, you know. If we think of ourselfs as newts, even though they're slinky and no-account, we can play our games better as a team." He was proud of his answer, but he also was beginning to have a growing sense of uneasiness that something was amiss.

"A team?" said Jossie Conklin. "I should think we're perhaps a class, not a team. I facetiously suggested that if we have to adopt a mascot for Psychology class, it might be the butterfly, but I don't suppose even you, Dr. Swain, realize the connection between Psyche and the butterfly, do you?"

Colvin stared at her. Slowly he began to understand his great mistake, and as it dawned on him, he grew very red in the face and could hardly breathe. He could only stand there, thinking that it was bad enough he had mistakenly lectured to his basketball teams on Consciousness and Instinct, but it was unforgivable that he had urged his Psychology class to wear jock straps and bras. He sought some consolation from the excuse that Tenny's problem had distracted and rattled him. And indeed, that was all he could think about. His eyes sought hers in the crowd, and he tried to communicate to her by his eyes alone his misery. His real misery, he understood, was not over his embarrassing mistake but over the possibility that this lovely girl, who had captured his heart, who meant everything in the world to him, and who had even, just now, by a stroke of her original mind, given a name to the official mascot of the Newton County Academy, had fallen victim to the Great White Plague.

"Friends," he said to the filled auditorium in a voice quiet and abashed, "doggone if I aint done went and made a boo-boo. The sorriest kettle of fish I ever mommixed. I'm supposed to handle two things, Psychology and Basketball, but I've done got 'em all confused one with the othern, and I've preached to the Basketball folks as if it was Psychology, and here I've been talkin to y'uns as if this was Basketball. So I do humbly beg yore pardon. Some way we'll git this all straightened out.

"But, you know," he went on, "come to think of it, it don't make all that much difference. If you stop to think about it, in the scheme of things, in the coming and going of the seasons, in the times for laughter and the times for crying, the times for building up and the times for tearing down, and all those other times the Preacher spoke of, trying to tell us about vanity and how everthing don't matter all that much anyhow, whether we are studying Basketball or playing Psychology, or the other way around, don't really amount to a whole heck of a lot of hills of beans, nohow. There are more important things, like love and staying alive. So if y'uns will excuse me, that's all I can tell y'uns today."

Ten

A couple more afternoons is all it will take. I have enjoyed your company so much that I've been tempted to drag this story out as long as I can just to keep you here, but I think you realize yourself that we're getting toward the end of it.

Push that little red button on that thing, will you? And I hope you don't mind. My young friend Mike Luster, who aspires to be a folklorist and comes to visit me just about as often as you do, has left his tape recorder here with the request that we preserve the remainder of whatever words I have to say in this story. Not that he mistrusts your ability to remember, let alone to hear, any of this, but he just wants to be sure that the end of the story is permanently recorded. You don't need to worry that he might ever try to make a novel out of it himself.

I suppose there's a possibility that the tape recorder could intimidate me somewhat, hold me back, slow me down, whatever. For, although I insist that I've always told you the exact and honest truth without any embellishment, I've never had to be constrained by any thought of what *permanent* reception my words may have. In this regard, I've been like the old-time Ozark storyteller himself: my words have been only for the occasion, only for the present audience; I've known that my words might get repeated by my audience to some future listeners, but as far as the story goes, it begins and ends right here and now. I never had much luck trying to use a tape recorder myself, not for stories. I collected hundreds of folk songs with my recording machines, but those songs were things already known and rehearsed and possessed of some permanence to begin with. Whenever I tried to tape a good story, it somehow inhibited the storyteller.

Maybe the only differences you'll notice are these: the rest of this story aint so comical. Assuming you've been amused by a lot of what I've told you—even though you don't laugh much, I can tell when I've tickled you—you may find the rest of this story somewhat downbeat, certainly minor key. And also I'm fixing to switch it into the present tense. Why? Well, why do *you* do it your own self? In all your novels, you downshift (or upshift, is it?) from the past to the present tense toward the end, and then finally into the future tense. I've studied what you've done. I've considered that in my own collections of tales, there is often a kind of indiscriminate shifting from one tense to another, because that's simply the way those old folk stories got told, perhaps without any rhyme or reason as far as tenses are concerned.

But if you'll pardon the analogy, there exists between storyteller and listener a kind of romance, and the progress of it parallels the stages of courtship: holding hands, hugging, and finally fucking, or some kind of consummation. All that past tense business is just holding hands, making contact, nothing truly intimate. But when you shift to present tense, you're drawing the listener into more intimate contact, as if to make sure that the listener becomes a part of the story, not just an audience to it. And then, through the ultimate intimacy of the future tense, you make sure that the listener is *always* a permanent part of the story. Am I right? Thank you for bringing me the Smith Brothers cough drops. I need them.

Hug Tenny: she definitely has TB. When Colvin leaves that auditorium and goes downstairs, first to the principal's office to see if the vial of tuberculin has been delivered (it has), and then to his own office, Tenny follows him, and they lock the door. At once they use the sofa, out of similar as well as different reasons, both out of love, but Tenny out of overwhelming desire and Colvin not so much from desire as out of solace for his miseries, including his continuing embarrassment over the mix-up. He wants to ask Tenny if she herself, being in both Basketball and Psych, had not realized his error, and, if so, why in heaven's name hadn't she told him? But she will not let him ask. Her hands are all over him. Her mouth is all over him. The ferocity of her ardor almost scares him, for he has never known a woman to *want* it so much. The building is emptied now of people, the school grounds are likewise evacuated, but still there must be someone around who can hear the sounds that Colvin and Tenny are making. Somewhere out there, surely, is Russ Breedlove, waiting to take Tenny home atop Marengo. He will just have to wait.

He will just have to wait even longer, for Colvin and Tenny, when they have finished, do not rise from that sofa but lie there in each other's arms for a long time, not simply because it feels good to hold each other like that, nor simply because they are

301

all worn out from a busy day and a strenuous turn at sex, but because it is postponing as long as possible the test.

But finally he must get up and administer it. He keeps his back to her while he dilutes the tuberculin and draws into the hypodermic syringe a tiny amount, 0.1 mg., and then he takes her arm and promises that it will not hurt very much, and it does not.

"What's it supposed to do?" she asks. "What do you think might be wrong with me?"

Colvin Swain surprises himself by not telling her the truth. "Likely there aint nothing wrong with you," he says, "but this here is just a little test to make sure. We'll keep a close watch on your arm there where I stuck ye, and see if it has any kind of reaction. Now if you want a ride home, you'd better run and see if you caint find your husband." He kisses her one more time, asks her to contrive to meet him here about this same time tomorrow, and she is gone.

He has no microscope in this office. He takes home with him to Stay More the specimen of her sputum he had collected earlier, and uses his microscope to examine it, after an acid-fast stain. Long after he has finally and positively identified a bacillum, *Mycobacterium tuberculosis humanis,* he continues to stare into the microscope, watching the goddamned critter. "Know your enemy," he says to himself, and he wants to study every curve of this tiny, evil rod until he can almost predict what it is trying to do. He knows what its brothers and sisters are already doing inside Tenny's lungs. Thriving on oxygen, they are seeking out the parts of her lungs where they can get plenty of air. They are hunting for her alveoli, the tiny air sacs of her lungs, private chambers, where they can have their orgies and reproduce.

But her strong young body has not welcomed them, and it

has sent platoons of white blood cells to interrupt those orgies in those alveoli, and rout them out, swallow them up, and ideally kill them. Yet in swallowing them, the white blood cells might not be killing them but only giving them protection by enwrapping them in pockets, spinning caseous cocoons around them. These shells are the tubercles. Tenny's body becomes hypersensitive not only to the bacilli but to those tubercles, and this is what will cause her skin to become inflamed where Colvin injected the tuberculin.

Maybe, just maybe, her disease will not progress beyond this point; the bacilli will spread no farther, and any of them remaining in her alveoli, instead of having further orgies, will go to sleep and remain dormant, sealed off in those tubercles, and she will have a normal life.

That is what he hopes for. After supper, though the night grows chilly and dark, he sits on the front porch, wearing his favorite cardigan sweater. He needs to think. His dog Galen comes up and slobbers on his shoe, and nuzzles his leg, and gets a pat or two on the head for his pains, then curls asleep at Colvin's feet. Colvin is moved to think of the dog's namesake, and he remembers that Galen, the last of the great Greek physicians, quite possibly suffered from tuberculosis himself. Galen established the first institution for the treatment of TB and sent his patients to recuperate on the most beautiful beach in the world, in a place where the special herbs eaten by the cows produced the magical therapeutic milk that Galen prescribed for his patients. There is no record of the rate of cure of all those milk-drinking patients of Galen.

Colvin thinks of all the names that the disease has been called since Galen's time, when it was known as phthisis, pronounced not as bad as it looks, thigh-sis, inherited into old-time parts of the Ozarks as "tis-sis" or "tis-sick" as in the legendary tissick weevil, who was thought to cause it. But most people in the Ozarks still knew it by its nineteenth-century name, consumption, because that is what it does, it consumes the body, starting with the lungs. Colvin had enough experience with it—from patients of his who thought they had catarrh, asthma, bronchitis, weak heart, stomach trouble, scrofula, or just the common cold, and succumbed to it, despite his ministrations (there are no really effective ministrations)—to think of it as the Great White Plague. During the years of his medical education, with Kie Raney or by himself, it was the Number One Killer in the country, and he had learned to fear it more than any other disease. Like any good physician, Colvin takes pride in his ability to manage and conquer his patients' ailments, and he can stare arteriosclerosis in the face and say, "Arteriosclerosis, I am your better!" but he cannot face up to the Great White Plague with the same fearlessness and confidence. It is the one disease that is better than he.

Colvin broods on his porch for so long that finally his wife, Piney, comes out of the house and sits beside him, and, because she knows everything, she knows that something is profoundly disturbing him. All she says is, "Do you think you could talk to me about it?"

Because she knows everything, he asks her, "Is there any cure against the Great White Plague?"

Although she knows everything, she does not know that one, nor does anyone else, at that time. "You would surely know if there was," she admits. After a while she asks, "Who has it?"

"A girl named Tenny," he divulges.

"Yes," she says. "Tenny." As if it's someone she's known all her life.

Colvin wants to say more. He wants to confess his great inner conflict: he had first permitted himself to become so involved with Tenny because he knew for certain that, hypochondriacal as she was, she would never have anything actually wrong with her, she would never need him as her doctor, and therefore it was not a breach of doctor-patient ethics for him to fall madly in love with her. But now that he has discovered that Tenny does indeed have a great need of his attentions as her physician, will he have to violate ethics (not to mention Kie Raney's Oath) in order to go on loving her?

Because he cannot voice this torment, his wife at length speaks up, saying, "You'd best come in the house, Colvin. It's getting cold. Real cold. And I suppose you won't be waiting until next Friday to be going back to Parthenon, will you?"

No, he cannot wait another week. Reactions to the tuberculin test begin to show up within twenty-four hours, and he goes back to his Academy office the next day, Saturday, to meet her. She has escaped from Jasper, from her husband and her domineering mother-in-law, on the excuse that there is an important meeting of the Erisophean Society, the Academy's literary club.

Although Colvin hardly needs to see the results of the tuberculin test to confirm his diagnosis, he has to punish himself, or make himself share the ordeal that lies ahead for Tenny, by seeing it anyway: the swelling and the redness on Tenny's arm, the positive reaction declaring, "This pore gal is infected, infested with the Great White Plague. So now what, Doc?" He cannot answer.

Tenny wants so eagerly to make love again, without even waiting for him to explain what the redness and swelling from her tuberculin test signify. Colvin knows, from his vast knowledge of the enemy, that the Great White Plague is rumored to increase the sexual urge, that perhaps if it doesn't directly heighten the libido, it causes some kind of mysterious chemical effect in the body which stirs the glands, or at least it raises the temperature of the body in such a way that the heat is perceived as sexual heat. He is not certain that he can believe any of this. He wants to believe, and he has every right to believe, that Tenny desires him so ardently not because of her fever but because she loves him as much as he loves her. And when he obliges her and himself, and marvels yet again at the intensity and abandon and joy that she expresses in the act, he does not permit any thoughts of fever or chemistry to diminish his own pleasure.

They are still lying in each other's arms, in the Saturday sunlight coming through the window that is almost enough to take the October chill out of the air, when she at last requests, "Okay, my dearest dear, it's time maybe you tell me how come my arm has turned red and swole up where you stuck me."

Colvin, as I think we have seen, is a good liar but not a great one. He knows he cannot indefinitely postpone letting her know the truth. She will have to learn it all somehow, sometime. But he can be as gentle as possible without lying. "Do you recollect," he says, fully aware that they are lying on the very sofa where she had reclined to tell him about it, "that time when you was a child and your good old Grampaw McArtor lay sick abed and you spent so much time with him, and even sent your best friend 'See down inside of his lungs to see if she couldn't cure him?"

"Sure I remember all that," Tenny says.

"Well, there's just a possibility that you might have caught what he had, although catching the disease didn't mean that you'd show any sign of it for many a year. The little bacilli that cause it could have been asleep in your system all this time, just waiting for a reason to wake up and start doing their dirty work again."

306

"Colvin Swain!" she says, and sits up abruptly. "Are you tellin me that I might have *consumption?*"

He sits up too. "It appears so," he admits. He explains how the tuberculin test works. He also confesses to having taken the sputum specimen home with him and examined it under the microscope and seen the curvy rod in its acid-fast stain. Does she remember from Hygiene class, he asks, what bacilli are, and how they behave?

"I reckon I learnt the practical reason," she says, then smiles and adds, "but I never learnt the pretty one. If there is one."

"Awfully pretty from the bacterium's way of lookin at it," he says. "If I was a bacterium, I'd be mighty proud to cavort around in one of yore lungs."

"But you'd be a-killin me," she points out, rightly.

"I wouldn't know I was," he avows, rightly. "Like all other critters in this world, including humans too, I'd just be doing my job, to git along in the world, competing with my fellow critters as well as with my host or hostess for my share of being able to breathe and to eat and to—"

"To shit," Tenny says. She shudders, and clutches her chest. "So now my lungs are filling up with bacteria shit and I caint even cough hard enough to git it out." Involuntarily, but as if she wants to do it, she coughs violently, and Colvin reaches for a handkerchief for her sputum, which does not yet, he is glad to see, contain any blood. Whether it contains any bacteria shit he might not even be able to determine with a microscope, but Tenny has given him a thought: if the tuberculosis bacilli are creatures, what happens to their excrement? He realizes that science has spent much time determining that they must breathe, but not that they must eat and shit.

She clutches his sleeve and asks in the same child's voice she first asked him, a year before, "I'm like to die, aint I?"

But a year before it had been almost as if she were seeking constantly to find something that would kill her, and Colvin had to assure her continuously that she was not going to die. Now she has everything to live for, and earnestly wants to, but he is going to have to remind her that, as the textbook had concluded, we should not live to die, but live prepared to die. "Not everybody who catches the Great White Plague dies from it," he declares. "Lots of 'em live forever. Or, I mean, at least a natural lifetime."

"Can you give me anything for it?" she asks, forlornly, as if she knows the answer: there is no medicine for tuberculosis.

"I'm givin ye some creosote for your cough," he says. "And some cod-liver oil to give ye vitamins A and B. You need all the vitamins you can git. You need to keep on eating good and don't lose any more weight. You've done already lost too much." He seizes her arms and gazes earnestly into her eyes and says, "Look at it this way, Tenny. It's a mighty fracas. On one side, there's them bacilli a-trying to break ye down and consume ye. On the other side, there's you and your body, with me doing my best to help ye, fightin back at the bacilli. We don't have any medicine that can kill 'em. Caint nothin kill 'em exceptin yore own white blood cells. Remember leucocytes, in Hygiene? In the battlefield of your lungs, there's going to be a powerful fight a-raging, and you can win it!"

His pep talk about winning reminded him of what he had said to the Psychology class under the assumption they were the basketball teams. Perhaps it reminded her as well, because she asked, "Will I have to quit school?"

"Maybe not," he says. "Jist don't go around coughing in nobody's face, and let's hope you don't start a-sneezing. Sorry to say, but I caint let ye be on the girls' basketball team. It would be too strenuous for you, and you need to rest ever chance you git. But you can be the team manager and come to all the games."

In the weeks ahead, Tenny has to make a number of adjustments. She has to give up her job working in the kitchen and dining room. Colvin does not tell anyone that Tenny is tuberculous, but he thinks it advisable that she not have to handle the chores she had done to help pay her tuition, not alone because she needs to rest but also because it reduces the risk of her spreading her disease. She proposes to work in the laundry instead. The laundry is a creek bank down the hill from the school, and the laundress's job is just to maintain the big black iron kettle in which water is heated and the clothes are thrown. "So long as you didn't spit in the pot," Colvin teases her, "that would be acceptable." But he doesn't want her working, at all. He persuades her to allow him to pay her tuition, and, optimistically, he pays it for the full year, $28. She can devote what energy she has to her classes.

What she mostly needs, to prepare her for the fight against the disease, is rest. Colvin gives her a key to his office so that she can go there at all times of the day when she doesn't have classes, and rest on the sofa. Officially he uses the office only one day a week himself, but now, because of Tenny, he comes to school two, three, sometimes four times a week. Piney smiles and says nothing, because she knows everything and people who know everything are inclined to smile and say nothing.

But there are many hours, every day, when Colvin is not in his office, and Tenny comes to let herself into it and rest on the sofa. Lying on the sofa reminds her of all those sessions with giant lollipops, and it is a comfortable memory. Now, though, she is alone, and only occasionally has Colvin to talk to. Colvin wants her to open the window beside the sofa to let in as much fresh air as possible, although the air is cold and

Tenny must keep her winter coat on. He tells her the fresh air will help stop her cough, but she does not quite understand why, if the tuberculosis bacilli are such lovers of air and seekers of oxygen, this exposure to the fresh air isn't aiding and abetting the enemy. And indeed, medical science itself is confused on this matter, but Colvin is inclined to side with those who believe that fresh air is beneficial.

Lying there for hours on the office sofa, Tenny is bored. If she can fall asleep and take a nap, fine, and she often does, but more often she just lies there. She begins to stop by the library upstairs to get whatever reading matter she can find, a magazine or a newspaper or a book. The library has a few novels that might keep her in sustained thrall, by Gene Stratton Porter, Harold Bell Wright, Rafael Sabatini, and Grace Miller White, but for some reason she is not able to read a novel. She makes an attempt to read one of them, Kathleen Norris's *Butterfly,* attracted by the title, but can only plod through a couple of chapters before losing interest. Colvin brings her to read some books that he has obtained for himself and finished: F. M. Pottenger's *Tuberculosis and How to Combat It,* D. Mac-Dougall King's *The Battle with Tuberculosis and How to Win It,* A. K. Krause's *Rest and Other Things,* and Dr. E. L. Trudeau's *An Autobiography.* She finds these readable and interesting and very helpful, although they impress upon her how easily and frequently fatal the disease is. The latter book introduces her to the concept of the sanatorium, and she wonders how far it is to Saranac Lake, New York, and she begins to have daydreams of living that kind of life in a place like that, with nothing to do but rest, eat good food, get lots of sunshine and fresh air, and live forever.

"Colvin," she says wistfully one day, "I don't reckon there's any place like Saranac Lake hereabouts, is there?"

310

No, he tells her, the nearest thing to it is just the Arkansas State Tuberculosis Sanatorium at Booneville, down in Logan County on the other side of the Arkansas River, maybe a hundred miles or so away, and probably not nothing at all like Saranac Lake.

"Oughtn't I to be there?" she asks.

"Hell, it aint even in the Ozarks!" he tells her. "It would sort of be like gittin sent off to prison, and you'd be surrounded with a lot of folks in worse shape than you, and you'd feel all cooped up, and have lots of strict rules to foller." He pauses, then adds rhetorically, "and when would I ever see ye again?" When she cannot answer that, he observes, "Tenny, this here is your own private sanatorium, with your own personal doctor who loves you. And you git to stay in school besides."

She not only stays in school, but, typically, excels in all her classes. In Colvin's course in psychology—and, for the most part, he has straightened out the difference between Psychology and Basketball—Tenny is always the first among the hundred or so filling the auditorium to raise her hand with answers to his questions about Reflex, Instinct, or Sensation, and, more importantly, to *ask* pertinent questions about things he has overlooked or never even considered.

Despite his first-day error, or because of it, the Psychology class continues to refer to themselves as the Newts, and to talk about winning, and to think of themselves as a team who are out to beat the world by developing superior reflexes, instincts, and sensations.

Principal Jossie Conklin summons him to her office one day. She begins by saying how much she has been enjoying the Psychology class, and how she has learned so much in the class about Expression that she has had an easy time of approaching the new man, Tim James (Bible and Hygiene), and revealing to him her attraction to him, which he has reciprocated, even to the extent of—with some suggestions from her best friend, Venda Breedlove—the development of episodes of quite intimate contact between them. But, and this is the main reason she wants to talk to Colvin, Jossie has inadvertently discovered that Colvin is "keeping" Mrs. Tennessee Breedlove in his office, perhaps for purposes of gratification of the flesh. What happened was, Jossie had observed Tenny letting herself into Colvin's office on a day when Colvin was not there nor supposed to be there. After a while, Jossie had let herself into the office with her master key and discovered Tenny sound asleep on Colvin's sofa. Rather than wake her and ask for an explanation, Jossie had decided to keep a close watch and see what was going on, and, on another occasion, when Colvin was there and was supposed to be there, she quietly unlocked his door and peeked in to discover that he was doing something he was not supposed to be doing: he was atop Tennessee with his trousers down. Jossie had been quickly able to determine, from Tennessee's own behavior and sounds, that the student was not being taken advantage of, in fact was a willing, eager, even joyous participant in the proceedings. Indeed, Jossie has to confess, she had even learned a thing or two, by watching, about the possibility of the female's taking a less than passive role in the exchange, contrary to what she had been taught or had assumed and had followed in her relations with Tim James. Nevertheless, in any event, be that as it may, for having said all that, Jossie feels constrained to demand, "What in hell is going on?"

"Tenny and me are crazy about each other," Colvin confesses.

"Obviously," Jossie says. "But you are both married to other persons, and you are committing adultery, and you are using school property for illicit purposes, and you are violating every

312

conceivable standard of personal and professional morality, and I ought to fire you and expel Tennessee." When Colvin cannot think of a proper defense against that indictment, Jossie goes on, "But Tennessee is the top student in this school, and you are not only doing a bang-up job with Psych class but I hear that your boys' basketball team went up against the fearsome Antlers of Deer and lost by only thirty points." Colvin is humbly grateful for that "only." But it is true that the Deer team is the best in Newton County, and the Newts had been lucky they hadn't lost by a hundred points. "So," Jossie says, "I can't fire you, and I don't suppose it would do me any good to try to forbid you to keep on seeing Tennessee. But I can't allow her to have a key to your office, so that she can come and go in there any time she pleases."

"Wal, heck," Colvin protests. "Mostly she just goes in there to rest on the sofer."

"*Rest?*" Jossie says. "If you call that *rest,* I'd like a chance to watch when she's *busy.*"

"No, I mean when I'm not here, between her classes, she needs to take it easy, doctor's orders, on account of her condition."

"What's her condition?"

"You know," he says truthfully, "doctors aint supposed to tell their patients' troubles to other people."

"Okay. But is it contagious?"

Once again he decides to lie, but a little white lie about the Great White Plague. "Nope."

"That's what you said about her cerebral palsy," she reminds him. "But the whole school caught it." And he is all too aware that there is a possibility the whole school could catch Tenny's tuberculosis if they were exposed to it closely and constantly over a long period of time. He cannot promise anything.

Jossie says, "Well, you are lucky that poor Venda isn't holding this against you. Maybe because she's got another boyfriend now."

As a matter of fact, fortunately for our story, which already has such a tangled web of interpersonal relationships that it needs all the simplification it can get, Colvin has not been seeing much of Venda, outside of Psych class, where she has called attention to herself with some rather stupid answers to questions, and a general ineptitude for the subject. He has escaped her extracurricular blandishments with the lie that he is being faithful to his wife. Venda would have found this inexcusable and frustrating, but it happens that Nick Rainbird, the History and Natural Science teacher, also as a result of being in the Psych class and learning the same ideas of Expression that had helped Jossie start something with Tim James, has been liberated to express his long-secret infatuation for Venda. So passionately have Venda and Nick become involved with each other that she has even lost interest in her continual revenge upon poor Tenny. After subjecting Tenny to the three ordeals, or tasks—the sorting of the jumbled pantry, the shearing and gathering of wool from some dangerous sheep, and being sent to climb Mt. Sherman with a bucket to fetch home some water from an ice-cold spring that was jealously guarded by a cranky old man's attack dogs—Venda had planned a fourth and final, crushing task for Tenny but, becoming involved with Nick Rainbird, Venda couldn't even remember what she had planned. "Oh, the hell with her," Venda has said. "She can go to Hades for all I care." And while this may be construed as a dismissal, perhaps in its perverse way it is consigning Tenny to the fate of her fourth and final task, her descent into the Underworld of tuberculosis.

While Venda has lost interest in Tenny, her son has not.

Russ still sleeps with Tenny every night . . . except those occasions when the basketball teams must travel to such remote locations for their games, Huntsville over in Madison County, Valley Springs in Boone County, Snowball in Searcy County, that an overnight is necessary, and while Russ opts to bunk with the other guys in one room, and Tenny is presumed to be bunking with the girls in another, Coach and Manager are actually contriving and conspiring to spend the night together in a third, in each other's arms. Russ does not know this, but he knows that his wife cares more for Coach than for anyone or anything in the whole wide world. He has resigned himself to this fact. He cannot change it any more than he could change the seasons so that summer would follow autumn. Still, he is able to sleep with Tenny almost every night, kissing her goodnight and snuggling up against her and, after waiting until she is deeply asleep, experimenting with one or another positioning of his dual peckers in an effort to get one or another of them to penetrate one or another of her orifices, always, alas, without ease or success. These sessions usually leave him achy and restless. But he has made a shrewd and remarkable observation: after such a night, he always plays better in basketball, as if the frustration and pent-up jism of his efforts with Tenny are translated into his energy for the game. Russ Breedlove is the star forward of the Newts, or at least the highest scorer, and he doesn't mind admitting to himself that his shot goes through the hole more frequently and adroitly because he cannot shoot off either of his peckers into any hole.

But there are still all those days when there aren't any games to be played, and Russ would sure admire to shoot off both barrels every chance he could get. He is still convinced that if only he could get rid of his surplus pecker he would be able to poke the survivor not only into Tenny but into any gal who struck his fancy. He keeps planning to visit Doc again when the man is Doc and not Coach or Teach or Wife's Lover, and remind him once again of his standing offer to slice off the spare. He keeps putting it off, however, and eventually it is Doc who calls him in, not, as it turns out, over the matter of performing the surgery.

"Russ, son," Doc says, "has Tenny told ye anything about what her trouble is?"

Russ realizes that Tenny has many troubles, but he isn't sure which one Doc is talking about, so he shakes his head.

"She hasn't told you she has tuberculosis?" Doc asks.

"Aw, hell, Doc," Russ observes, "at one time or another'n in her life, she has had cystic fibrosis, multiple sclerosis, neurosis, diagnosis, halitosis, and just about ever other 'osis' there is."

"Those were only in her mind," Doc points out, "but she has really and truly got tuberculosis, and it can be catching if you're exposed to it long enough, and I thought I'd better warn you that it would be better for you if you didn't sleep with her."

Russ narrows his eyes at Doc. "Shitfire, Doc," he says, "you're jist a-makin that up, because you don't want me to sleep with her, because you'd rather sleep with her yourself."

Doc coughs and blushes, and Russ realizes he has hit him where he lives. But Doc tries to deny it. "No, now, I'm a-tellin ye the honest to God truth, boy. What she has got aint easy to catch, like the common cold, but if you're exposed to it night after night, month after month, the chances are you jist might come down with it yourself."

Russ thinks. At length he asks, "Is that there tuberculosis the reason she coughs so much, and is gittin right skinny, and looks so pale, and drenches the bedclothes ever night with her sweat?"

"You've noticed," Doc says, not without a little sarcasm.

"Well, then, believe me, it's serious, and it's catching, and I jist thought I'd better do what I could to keep you from gittin it too."

"Thanks, Doc," Russ says, "but there aint a extry bed in our house. I may jist have to start sleepin with my momma!" The thought greatly amuses him, and he has a fit a laughter, although the possibility privately captivates him.

"Let's keep this a secret," Doc requests. "No sense in gittin anybody alarmed about it, so I don't want nobody in this school to know about it."

Russ agrees to keep mum, and takes his leave, but comes back a moment later. "Doc," he says, "I hate to keep on reminding you, but there's still a little problem that you promised to fix." He points to his crotch.

"Yeah, I aint forgot," Doc admits. Then he asks, "What do ye think of Oona Owens?"

"Don't change the subject, Coach," Russ says, although, by changing his form of address from "Doc" to "Coach" he has already partly changed the subject himself, because if he is the star forward of the Newts, Oona is the star guard of the Lady Newts (or Newtesses, as some call them). "She's a whiz, aint she, Coach?" Russ observes. "Aint never seen a gal who can grab a ball the way she can."

Coach Swain has often, during practices, allowed the girls' team and the boys' team to scrimmage against each other, by prior agreement "playing dirty," no holds barred, the girls clawing and scratching and as often as not outrebounding and outshooting the boys. Russ has never faced a boy guard anywhere who can hamper him as effectively as Oona does. He not only admires her ball-hawking and bodychecking, but he also thinks she's an awful pretty dish for an athlete. He even adores the odor of her sweat.

"Have you ever thought of steppin out with her?" Coach asks.

"Shoot, Coach, I'm a married man," Russ reminds him.

"So am I" is all Coach says, but it is enough to remind Russ that Coach has not allowed the marriage vows to stop him from extramarital activity, including with the two women closest to Russ, his mother and his wife.

"You're jist tryin again to git me away from Tenny," Russ accuses.

"No, I'm jist tryin to git ye to find out if there might not be some other gal in this big wide world who could pleasure ye more than Tenny."

"How could Oona do that?" Russ wants to know.

Colvin Swain must do some debating with himself. As Doc Swain, he is bound by oath not to let know Russ know of Oona's "condition." But as Coach Swain, he has no oaths. No, perhaps Coach Swain is not allowed to know everything that Doc Swain knows. "There is jist no tellin," he says to Russ. "But if I was you, I'd shore keep my eye out fer a chance to play with Oona off the basketball court."

And sure enough, there eventually comes a chance, during the post-Thanksgiving tournament in Eureka Springs, which requires two nights on the road, and possibly three if the Newts can advance into the semifinals. For once, the teams are staying in an actual hotel, albeit a small and very cheap hotel, but one in which there are several rooms at their disposal, three for the boys' team, so that they'll only have to sleep two to a bed, three for the girls' team, ditto, one for Coach (and clandestinely Manager too), and even a spare room which happens to be the place where Russ Breedlove and Oona Owens discover that they have an anatomical affinity which affords many possibilities and delights. Coach Swain is supposed to chaperone his players on these overnight trips, but he is preoccupied and does not seem to know or notice that Russ and Oona are spending the night together. He is somewhat troubled, or disappointed, the next day in the tournament, when both the Newts and the Lady Newts are embarrassingly blown away by their opponents, principally because their star players, Russ and Oona respectively, are not giving it their all. Although eliminated from the tournament, they have one more night in their hotel before the long trip home, and once again Russ and Oona conspire to seclude themselves together in the spare room.

In his own room, with Tenny, late in the night after they have exhausted themselves with sexual doings, Colvin cannot resist telling Tenny what may be happening nearby between Russ and Oona. He is violating his oath, but he feels that Tenny ought to know. The disclosure renders Tenny speechless. Colvin wonders about this, because she has already told him that Russ is no longer sleeping with her, that Venda has consigned Tenny to sleeping on a pallet in the pantry, and that Russ has even told her that as far as he's concerned they might as well not consider themselves man and wife anymore. Finally, Colvin has to ask her, "Well? Does it make ye mad that your husband is cheatin on ye?"

"Oh, no," Tenny says. "I jist feel kind of jealous, as if she's able to do somethin that I could never do."

Colvin laughs. "Would you want an extra vagina if you could have one?"

"I'd like to have a dozen of 'em," she says, "if you could have a dozen penises."

He laughs again. "Where would you put all of 'em?"

"Here," she says. "And here. And one of 'em around here. And one up here."

Playfully they re-create their anatomies so that they could

be joined together all over their bodies. Almost by accident, Tenny gives herself a vagina in her left lung, her bad lung, and at the moment of realization of what she has done, she begins coughing, and for the first time spits up blood.

Hemoptysis. He has hoped that this would not happen. He realizes that it is spontaneous and inevitable, but that sexual activity can bring it on. There is less than a teaspoon of blood. This hemoptysis does not alter the prognosis, except that it may spread the disease to other parts of the lungs, and it can also increase the risk of pneumonia.

" 'See?" she says. He thinks at first she is saying it accusingly, as if she knows that their act of love has caused it. But then he realizes that she is calling out to her old playmate or other self. He hopes that verily 'See will return and help in the battle. He knows that Tenny must remain in bed for seven to ten days until the bleeding has stopped, but he can't keep her in *this* bed.

"We've got to git you home so you can rest in bed for a week or so," he declares.

"Home?" Tenny says, and laughs. "Where's that?"

"Don't laugh," he says. "Try to stay as still as you can. Don't even talk unless you have to. Talking and laughing can make it worse."

As soon as he had learned that Tenny has been sleeping on a crude pallet in Venda's pantry, an airless room reeking with smells of foodstuffs—vinegar and onions and spices and moldy cheeses—Colvin has been putting his mind to the problem of a better place for her. She cannot return to the dormitory. There are a couple of spare rooms in the gymnasium, but they are not heated at night. Likewise his office is unheated.

Now he decides bravely to take her to Stay More. Of course he cannot put her up in his own house, not with Piney there,

320

but he can put her up in the hotel. Not too long before, the old woman living in the big Jacob Ingledew house on Main Street, the woman you have chosen to call Whom We Cannot Name in your architecture novel, died, and the house was inherited by Willis Ingledew, the bachelor storekeeper, who moved into it with his spinster sister, Drussie Ingledew, who realized that a house of a dozen rooms was too big for the two of them and decided to turn it into a hotel, the only hotel that Stay More ever had, and not a very successful one. In fact, when Colvin installs Tenny in one of the upstairs guest rooms, a south-facing one (Colvin's own house is on the north side of the hotel), she is the only guest there. Both Drussie and Willis are greatly in Doc Swain's debt for various medical services that he has rendered for both of them, and they welcome the chance to barter Tenny's hotel bill in return for their medical bills, and they are even amenable to Doc's request that they not tell a soul that a young lady is confined to one of their upstairs rooms. Colvin explains to them simply that she is a student at N.C.A. who has come down with a disease—medical ethics prohibits his revealing to the Ingledews just what the disease is— which requires confinement to bed for as long as ten days, and the N.C.A. itself simply does not have the facilities for such infirmary care. The reason for secrecy, he says, is so that word will not leak back to the student body of N.C.A. and possibly bring a horde of other students wanting to be treated likewise in the Stay More Hotel.

Tenny loves Stay More, as all of us who have seen it are bound to do, even if she can only see south and west from her room—enough, at least, to see the big general store, the old gristmill, pretty Banty Creek, the schoolhouse, and the looming rise of Ingledew Mountain. She is, however, somewhat nervous at the thought that Mrs. Swain, her lover's wife, dwells just a short distance to the unseen north. Her agitation is compounded by the fact that patients with hemoptysis usually become extremely nervous. Knowing this, Colvin gives her half a grain of codeine sulfate, and watches to see if he might need to give her morphine, but he does not. Not yet, at least. The codeine quietens her, and he hopes he can keep her quiet and resting without any more of it. Even if he could get up his nerve to sneak out on Piney in the still of the night, he makes no attempt to sleep with Tenny while she is in Stay More.

But he visits her several times a day, and in the evenings too. Drussie Ingledew is, if nothing else, an excellent cook, and she follows Colvin's dietary instructions to the letter in making sure that Tenny gets the nourishment she needs, including half a gallon a day of the same splendid well-water that helped my own recuperation at Stay More. With all of this attention, Tenny ought to be getting better.

Piney observes that Colvin isn't running off to Parthenon every chance he can get. He seems to be hanging around his office at home much more than usual. Or he seems to be moseying down to the Ingledews' house/hotel more than once a day. She could easily ask him why, but she decides to ask Drussie Ingledew, who, being her nearest female neighbor, is also the closest thing on this earth to what might be called a "best friend," other than Colvin himself. At least Drussie and Piney are on good speaking and gossiping terms, and Piney has permitted Drussie to come and pedal her player piano any time she feels like it. But when she asks Drussie why Colvin is spending so much time at the Ingledews', all Drussie can say is to stammer that it appears Willis and Colvin have got a lot to talk about. Piney, knowing everything, knows this is not true: she knows that Colvin doesn't talk to Willis at all except to exchange howdies. Drussie knows that Colvin is spending most of his time upstairs just talking to the girl. Or listening to her. Once, Drussie eavesdrops, curious to see what on earth could possibly be the subject matter that can keep them talking for hours on end, but all that she can make out is that the girl is talking about how "it looks as if I have always had this need to suffer, so now I'm really and truly doing it," and Doc Colvin is trying to tell her that although he is sure sorry about her suffering, he feels he ought to try to get her to see that if people didn't suffer they wouldn't appreciate all of the many things that bring on the opposite of suffering, namely, pleasure and joy and happiness. If it didn't rain so hard, we wouldn't appreciate sunshine. Et cetera. Drussie thinks Doc would have made a good church preacher.

Piney is so happy to have Colvin staying in Stay More so much more these days that she makes a mistake: early one morning, even before putting the breakfast coffee on to boil, she sits herself down at her piano and puts in the roll of "Roses of Picardy" and plays it, singing all the words about the hush of the silvery dew, et cetera. It is only when she is all the way through, all the way down to "there's never a rose like you," that she realizes her grievous error, and announces loudly to the house, "Any fool knows, *Sing before breakfast, Cry before supper,*" which, although Piney knows too much to be superstitious, is the one superstition which she does not consider a superstition because it is so unfailingly true. All day long she waits to see what is going to make her cry.

This is the day that Colvin has to make an important decision. Tenny's hemorrhaging has not stopped. If she loses much more blood, he will have to give her a transfusion. He knows that the next step in the treatment, if the bleeding continues, is artificial pneumothorax. This involves injecting gas into the pleural cavity in order to collapse her lung and keep it from working. He has induced pneumothorax with other patients, and knows how to do it, and he possesses in his clinic the Floyd-Robinson apparatus for properly doing it, although he realizes the Floyd-Robinson is not without its faults: the manometer is too short, and sometimes if the patient coughs it can blow out the entire contents.

After giving her a sixth of a grain of morphine to relax her, he explains to Tenny what he is going to do, and asks her to try very hard not to cough during the procedure. He has made sure the room is warm enough that he can remove her gown, and he has her lie on the side of her "good" lung. She cannot quite understand why he wants to make one of her lungs stop working, and is uncertain about how well she can breathe with only one lung. He tries to assure her that she can breathe just fine with one lung, and that stopping the bad lung will force it to rest, just as she is forcing her body to rest, and rest is really the only cure for her condition at this stage.

The very sight of the Floyd-Robinson needle with its trocar and tubing attached would be enough to throw any patient into shock, so he must be very careful that she does not see it. He gives her novocaine, taking care to infiltrate the pleura. He is going in behind her armpit, and he uses a small cataract knife to make an incision to allow the needle to penetrate more smoothly. Very slowly and gently he inserts the long needle, wishing he had a third hand to place on her forehead, a fourth hand to hold her hand, and a fifth hand to wipe the sweat off his brow. Tenny whimpers. The sound is so childlike that he realizes just how young she is. Now he begins frequently to pull out the trocar on the back end of the needle, and take readings from the manometer. The manometer now begins to fluctuate, and shows a negative respiration, and he realizes that the needle has reached the desired space between two layers of pleura. He can now inject the gas. As the gas goes in, he keeps a steady eye on the manometer, as it begins to register positive pressure, and he slowly injects about 15 cc of gas every minute or so, until he has injected 250 cc, which has taken him nearly half an hour.

"Tell me when I can cough," Tenny pleads. "I need to cough, real bad."

"Shhh," he hushes her. Her voice is causing the manometer to fluctuate, but he realizes he has injected enough gas, and he slowly pulls the needle out, and seals the wound with collodion. "Okay," he says. "Cough, but not too hard." And she does.

Immediately afterwards she feels fine, and even wants to get out of bed, but he wants her to lie still. He takes a washrag, dips it into the washbasin on the stand beside the bed, and wipes the sweat from her face and body. He takes a hairbrush and smooths out her long, long hair, which he then arranges nicely on either side of her head on the pillow, and down over her bare breasts. She is a vision, and he bends down and gives her a long kiss. He is not unmindful that you should never kiss anyone with TB, but this is not just anyone; this is Tenny.

She breaks the kiss, and whispers, "There's somebody standing in the door."

He turns. It is Piney. He is mortified, more even than he had been that time that he and Venda were caught in sexual labor by Russ and Tenny. That time, at least, he had had the excuse of being under the influence of both a love potion and whiskey, and not responsible for his behavior. Now he has no excuse for being a mature, conscientious, respected physician, sober and ethical, who is keeping his mistress as a patient in the Stay More Hotel and is discovered by his beloved wife giving his mistress a kiss which is passionate enough to show any but a blind person or an idiot that he is deeply in love with her.

For her part, Piney, who knows everything, does not know what to say. She does not need an explanation, nor an introduction. She knows that this is Tenny, of whom her husband spoke often in his sleep and finally in his wakefulness in telling Piney that the girl has the Great White Plague. Piney knows that Tenny is not simply Colvin's patient, not simply his student, certainly not simply his friend, but his true love. Piney knows, without even observing the Floyd-Robinson apparatus beside the bed, that her husband is doing his level best to cure the girl of the Great White Plague, and she knows that if anybody can cure the girl, Colvin can do it. But the kiss she has witnessed confirms her in her knowledge that some kind of bond exists between Colvin and Tenny that transcends both conventional morality and "reality," whatever that is, and is a bond that can never be broken. This is the thought, and the knowledge, that brings tears to Piney's eyes, and validates the supposed superstition, *Sing before breakfast, Cry before supper.* So in a sense she has brought this great sadness upon herself by foolishly neglecting to remember that venerable axiom. Her own sense of blame does nothing to diminish her tears, but increases them, until she is standing there weeping so hard she cannot stand it, and, being unable to stand it, turns and flees.

It is the last that Colvin will see of her. Much later, he will hear a rumor that she is living with her sister Sycamoria on the other side of Demijohn, and, later still, he will hear that she has moved into Harrison, the biggest town in that part of the Ozarks, and is working there in a grocery store. And later still, he will attempt to locate her, at least to offer to convey to her the player piano, if she still wants it, but he will not be able to find her in Harrison. Years later, and even at the time I was a patient in Doc Swain's house, some of the folks of Stay More will still be speculating that Colvin is still waiting for Piney to return, but if that is true, and I have reason to doubt it, it is a futile expectation.

Three or four more treatments with the Floyd-Robinson apparatus are necessary in order to complete the collapse of Tenny's lung, but Colvin is able to carry out only a couple of these before Tenny is evicted from the hotel. Drussie, with Willis backing her up, comes to Colvin to tell him that, one, since Piney has moved out he might as well move Tenny into his own house, and, two, there is such a scandal attendant upon the rumors of why Piney has left town that the Ingledews don't want to contribute to it any further by harboring a love nest under their roof.

Reluctantly, because he still thinks there's a chance that Piney might come home any minute as soon as she recovers from her shock or grief or jealousy or whatever emotion she is having, Colvin moves Tenny into his own house, but puts her to bed not in the big bed that was his and Piney's. He puts her in the selfsame cot that I was to use during my convalescence there, and I have to confess that when I learned that fact it gave me the same sense of immediacy and actuality that I am trying to achieve with this present tense. One reason he will not put her in the big bed, apart from its being Piney's, is to minimize the temptation for further sexual activity. For although Tenny despite her illness continues to be as hungry for him as ever, if not more so, he doesn't think it's wise to risk further hemoptysis brought on by the labor of love.

When finally her lung is collapsed, and the hemorrhaging has stopped, her disposition and outlook have improved so much that he allows her to get dressed and get out of bed. She even wants to fix meals for the two of them, but he doesn't think she's strong enough yet for that. He does allow her to sit at the marvel of the player piano and pedal it, asking her not to play "Roses of Picardy" but willingly listening to her play "Arkansas Blues" over and over again.

She is not well enough to return to school. During his day-long trips to Parthenon each Friday, during which he does his job as quickly and perfunctorily as possible (and the Newts, both girls and boys, have yet to taste their first victory), he canvasses Tenny's other teachers for her lessons, so that she can try to keep up. And of course he gives her special tutoring in Psychology.

Then the Christmas season comes, and school shuts down.

Colvin cuts down a scraggly cedar tree, eschewing a more attractive pine, and Tenny helps him trim it with popcorn strings and gilded walnuts and strips of colored paper glued into chains.

"What would you like for a Christmas present?" he asks her, being not very good at shopping, or surprises.

"I just want to be fucked!" she exclaims. It is the first time he has heard her use that word, and he is both somewhat shocked and aroused. He dearly wishes he could oblige her, and he attempts to explain why it is not advisable. She pouts, and sulks, and continues to brood until finally she announces, "I want to go home for Christmas. I mean, really *home*. Brushy Mountain."

When he has determined that she will not have it otherwise, he decides that it will be good to get her out of this house, which is still haunted by Piney's spirit if not her presence. And almost without his noticing, his practice has collapsed as much as Tenny's lung, on account of the scandal. Despite the increase in illnesses that are provoked by the stress and guilt of the holiday season, people have stopped coming to Doc Swain's or calling for him to come to them, even as a last resort. Unbeknownst to him, he has become an outcast in his own community, and it will take him some time to overcome it.

So he hitches Nessus to the buggy, and takes Tenny home to Brushy Mountain. Snow has fallen and accumulated in the upper reaches, and the going is difficult, but he gets her there, wrapped snugly in furs. Her family, having heard not a word from her since Russ took her away on his white horse, are overjoyed to see her, but they can see at once that something is wrong with her, and she tells them right off that she is being consumed by the Great White Plague, and that Doc Swain has had to collapse one of her lungs.

She turns to him. "I never did bother to ask ye. How long has my lung got to stay collapsed?"

"Two years, at least," he admits. "Maybe three or four."

"*What?!*" she says. "How come you never told me? I thought it would only be for a few weeks or so." She pounds her fists on his chest until he can seize her wrists and stop her. And she may be heard, at other times of that day, saying to him such things as "What have you done to me?" and "How could you do something like that?" and she begins to realize that she is losing her temper, and that she is very angry at the world, or at life, for having allowed her to come down with a real disease, and she is taking out her anger on her dear sweet Colvin. But this knowledge doesn't stop her from doing so. The Tennisons and her Grandma McArtor cannot help but notice it, and they wonder what she is doing in the first place with this man she hates so much, since it was Russ Breedlove that she was supposed to have taken up with.

Angry Tenny wants to take over the rest of this story, and we may soon have to let her. She wants to assert herself, to stop being the passive dupe of artificial pneumothoraces and the helpless victim of dreadful diseases and the passive, fragile heroine of a novel and to see if she can't take control of her own life. So she decides to send Colvin away. He is permitted to spend this one night, sleeping on a pallet on the kitchen floor, but he must go back to Stay More after breakfast. In her own bed, thinking of him sleeping on the pallet on the kitchen floor, she remembers that that is the same way and the same place that Russ had slept, and, dwelling upon this, she cannot sleep. Insomnia has rarely been a problem for her, but eventually she rises and lights a candle, and remembering how she had accidentally dripped hot candle wax on Russ, sets the candle at a distance from Colvin's body. She gives him a little shake, and then a less gentle shake, but he is deep asleep. She whispers his name without succeeding in waking him. She speaks his name aloud without waking him. She slips under the covers and embraces him without waking him. Now she notices that his penis is fully erect, making a tent in the bedcovers, and she marvels at this, wondering what kind of dream he could be having. Fondling it, she remembers all the incidents of pleasure it has given her, and she decides that she would like one more. She hikes the hem of her nightgown and sits atop him, and gets it into her very easily, and sighs and moans so loudly it ought surely to waken him, but it does not. Taking charge now, wanting to keep this moment of joining as a sensation to be experienced forevermore, even through eternity, she will permit time for her, and thereby for us, to slip into the future tense. She will rise and settle, lift and ease down, again and again and again. Not only will she create enough buffing and smoothing to throw her into her own mighty climax, but she will also generate enough sliding of his penis's skin to force his testicles to erupt their contents upward into her. She will only briefly reflect that it will be perhaps the wrong time of the month, two weeks since her last period, the only time in her heavy affair with Colvin that she has not observed the calendar or taken precautions.

The next morning she will be tempted, before sending him on his way, to ask if he will not have been at all aware of what she will have done. But she will still be maintaining her attitude of anger, or at least vexation, and she will not even bring herself to be properly appreciative of the gift he will give her upon his departure, which will be the only Christmas gift he will have been able to think of that might be useful to her: a year's supply of the roots of butterfly weed, which he has dug up from the very patch that Lora Dinsmore had turned into when Alonzo pursued her, roots which Colvin has reduced to a powder with his mortar and pestle. "It won't do ye no harm," he will say. "And maybe it's all that can help." She will not want her folks to see her kissing him good-bye, so she will not kiss him.

At least the tea made with the powder from the butterfly weed will be more soothing, and therefore helpful, than the various remedies and nostrums that her family will begin to employ upon her. Throughout the holiday season, one after another of these will be tried, beginning with Grandma McArtor's old-time, surefire cures which Grandma will regret she will never have been able to use on Grampaw McArtor until it was too late. One of these she will remember from back home in Tennessee will involve a rattlesnake, and Wayne Don Tennison will sacrifice one of his prize pets so the snake's skin can be pickled with whiskey, and Tenny will drink the whiskey. But this will only make her drunk, so more radical cures will be tried:

As an inhalant, it will have been known that pulmonary disorders can be relieved by constant exposure to the unpleasant but beneficial fumes of feces, so Tenny will be instructed to spend as much time as she can stand, hour upon hour, sitting in the privy, taking deep breaths. But it will be so cold out there that this will come close to giving her pneumonia, and the odor will cling to her whole body and will make her offensive company.

Also from an excretory perspective, it will have been widely known that urine is a specific for pulmonary tuberculosis, and Tenny will be urged, and then required, and then compelled, to imbibe her first water upon arising, morning after morning, until she will be tempted to try to get back out of the future tense because she will no longer feel in control of what will be happening to her. The butterfly weed tea will help to remove the taste.

She will tell this to Colvin on a postcard, belatedly thanking him for the butterfly weed, and she will conclude, "Between shit and piss, I am fed up with all the old-time superstitions, and I wont have nothing more to do with none of them. But I will keep on drinking your tea."

Tenny's momma, noting that the grandmother's traditional albeit radical remedies will not seem to be working, will decide to dose Tenny with Tuberclecide, Prof. Hoff's Consumption Cure, Yonkerman's Tuberculozyne, and Nature's Creation. None of these, however, will produce any noticeable effect, since the essential ingredient of most of these is simply a combination of turpentine and kerosene.

Tenny's much-older sister Oriole will come home for a visit, mainly to show off the new automobile which her rich husband will have given her for Christmas, a Climber Six Roadster—"The Car Made in Arkansas by Arkansawyers."

Like her fancy Climber auto, Oriole will be progressive and modern, and when she will find out that baby sister has the TB and will be doing nothing for it except fooling around with the stuff that Gran and Momma will have been trying on her, Oriole will decide to take matters into her own hands. She will put Tenny in the Climber and drive her to the Booneville Sanatorium.

Tenny will hope that their route might take them through Stay More, so that she might see Colvin once again. She will have forgiven him for the artificial pneumothorax, which probably has done her a lot more good than the shit and piss and kerosene, and also the butterfly weed has kept her calm and helped her cough and made her feel generally good.

But the route will not go to Stay More. To get from Brushy Mountain to Booneville, Oriole will drive the Climber on some terrible roads westwards only until she can reach the state highway, which will be graded and fairly smooth and will get them to Russellville, and thence across the Arkansas River, out of the Ozarks, up into the Ouachitas, and finally to Booneville.

So the best that Tenny will be able to do is to send Colvin a postcard, once she will have settled at "San."

Colvin will crush the postcard in his fist, and will be heard to say to nobody in particular, or to all of the postal patrons of Stay More, most of whom will have forgiven him his scandal, because he will now be living alone and paying the awful price of his loneliness for it, "The soul has gone out of the Ozarks!"

Eleven

Bless your heart, you've brought me a bouquet of butterfly weed! Mary, lookee here at what Harington has done! Oh, goddamn me, I not only forget that Mary can't see these flowers, more importantly I forget that today Mary aint even there! Is she? No, last night Dr. Bittner decided to move her to City Hospital for a while. Nothing too serious, I hope, and just in case you're looking for synchronicities as you usually do, it don't have anything to do with Mary's lungs. It certainly aint TB. Something wrong with her gallbladder. She can't eat. Dr. Bittner says it could be cancer of the gallbladder, maybe not, but he wants to be sure. Anyway, I'm sure sorry she's not here to listen to my telling of the end of my long tale, but I reckon she can make it up, hearing it on Mike Luster's tape recorder, if you'll kindly push that little red button there.

No, wait, first I just want to say another thing about Mary and then I want to say something about these lovely butterfly weed flowers you've brought me. I don't want you to take this as any sort of criticism or blame of any kind, but do you recall that Mary was your instructor for freshman English, for all of two weeks, back in the early fifties? Mary hasn't forgotten it, how you came to her and told her you were transferring out of her class because, one, you'd spent all your high school years with women teachers and you were hoping to have men teachers in college, and two, damned if you were going to read the Holy Bible as your first assignment in the course. You were kind of an arrogant sonofabitch, weren't you? With a typical freshman attitude. You didn't know who Mary was, that she was the only expert on Ozark folklore at the University. You thought she was just some homely looking spinster teacher like all those you'd had in high school, and you thought the worst part of it was that she was so all-fired religious she was going to make you read the Bible. Well, let me say two things: just as you didn't know who Mary was, she had no idea of course who you were, that you were going to become, many years later, one of her favorite novelists. Anyway, you didn't hurt her feelings dropping her course. It happened all the time to her. But it made her a little sad that she hadn't been able to make clear to you, maybe on account of your poor hearing, that she was assigning some of the Bible to read not because she was the least bit religious, which she aint, but because it contains some of the finest fiction in the history of literature.

I reckon I bring this up, on this very last day that I may see you, just to remind you that the story I've been telling you, no less than the Bible, can be taken either as the exact history of some people, of the love between a doctor and a young girl in a remote part of the Ozark Mountains, or it can be taken as a clever yarn. The point is, what difference does it make? Would you have enjoyed it any more if I could verify everything in it? I have here at the foot of my bed a stack of photocopies which our mutual friend Bob Besom—special agent in Special Collections at the University, last heard from when he showed us parts of Doc's journals to indicate how Doc was involved in the dream cure with Lorraine Dinsmore—has taken the trouble to copy from various issues of *Sanatorium Outlook,* a newspaper written and published by the inmates—I mean, the patients— at the Booneville Sanatorium between 1923 until the year 1970, when tuberculosis had been so largely eradicated, partly, as we'll see, because of what Doc Swain did, that the sanatorium had to shut down and become a ghost town. Anyway, there are a few references to a Tennessee Breedlove, or a Mrs. Breedlove, or "our sweetheart Tenny" in these issues, if you'd care to look at them.

But before we join Tenny at the sanatorium, let me just thank you from the bottom of my heart for these lovely orange flowers, which, I take it, are your parting gift to me just as the roots of this plant were Doc's parting gift to Tenny.

The plant goes by more names than tuberculosis does: in addition to butterfly weed, it has been called white root, silkweed, pleurisy root, orange milkweed, orange root, canada root, witchweed, swallowwort, wind root, chigger weed, archangel, agerajum, and, one of my favorites, Indian paintbrush, because, as you can see, it looks as if each flower, compounded of dozens of these little umbels, each one of which resembles, if you look closely, a ballerina in bright orange tutu, could be the head of a brush that an Indian might have smeared with orange pigment in order to paint a picture.

I won't ask you where you picked these, because I think I know: the roadside, or waste places, spots where even other weeds can't grow, because the butterfly weed can stand the most severe drought and the worst possible soil. It can grow anywhere. And even though the monarch butterflies, after getting drunk on the nectar of the flowers, lay their eggs on the leaves, and the caterpillars strip the foliage bare, it doesn't kill the plant. The plant keeps on growing, and seems to grow forever.

Will we find a metaphor here for Tenny? I doubt it. Much as I'd like to draw parallels between the bacilli consuming Tenny and the caterpillars consuming the butterfly weed, there really isn't any connection. The caterpillar eats in order to metamorphose into a gorgeous butterfly. What possible beauty is there in what the bacilli do, other than propagate their awful species?

And since we are not concerned with the butterflies and the caterpillars so much as the big white roots of the plant, which are used to make that miraculous tea, we might conclude that the only connection, if there is one, is in the botanical name of our plant, *Asclepias tuberosa,* and its double allusion, to both the great Greek physician and to tuberculosis. But I'll have to leave you to explore that. I am running out of time.

As far as butterfly weed is concerned, one of the first things that will happen to Tenny, when she will be checked into the sanatorium, will be that a gruff nurse, Mrs. Hull, searching Tenny's belongings, will discover the year's supply of powdered butterfly weed root that Colvin will have given her, and will confiscate it, on the grounds that it violates a regulation: patients are permitted to have only those medicines that the sanatorium doctors prescribe for them.

"But it makes me feel so much better!" Tenny will protest. "And it aint really a medicine, just a harmless stuff for making tea."

"There's another rule you better learn fast," Nurse Hull will snap. "Don't *never* talk back to me."

Tenny will quickly discover that Booneville will not be Saranac Lake, nor will it be Davos-Platz, which she will not have known about, because this will be the same year that Thomas Mann will first publish *The Magic Mountain*. Tenny's magic mountain will be twelve miles away but will seem to loom closer, Mt. Magazine, at 2,800 feet the highest point between the Appalachians and the Rockies. The sanatorium itself will be at a high elevation, over a thousand feet. It will have its own farms and dairies and gardens for the raising and growing of all of the food consumed in the sanatorium.

"They set a real scrumptious table here," Tenny will write to Colvin, "and I am trying to get my weight back up, although many a morning I just can't keep my breakfast down."

She will be installed in Hemingway Hall. This certainly will carry no allusion to the novelist, who will not have published his first novel yet, in fact will still be proofreading his first collection of stories, *In Our Time*. Judge Hemingway of Little Rock (no known relation) will have been one of the founders of the institution, which will have been one of the very first state sanatoriums in the South, and will eventually become the largest in the nation.

Hemingway Hall will have a very long veranda running the whole length of it, upstairs and down, and Tenny will be taken to the upstairs veranda her first afternoon. As far as her eye can see, women and girls are wrapped in identical blankets, reclining on identical white wooden lounge chairs, all of them wearing identical expressions of wakefulness but obliviousness. There will be almost a military aspect to it, the uniformity of it, the endlessness of it. Tenny will not know just what she will have expected, but she will not have expected to conform to the identical poses and blankets and sickly demeanor of all these dozens of females lined in ranks off into the distance. Mrs. Hull will place Tenny in an empty lounge chair and wrap her in blankets, saying, "You will stay here until the bell rings at three o'clock. You are a lunger, is what you are, like all these other ladies. Some of them are chasers, but you may not become a chaser until you've proved that you can abide by all the rules and handle yourself properly. There will be two hours of absolute rest each morning, and two hours of absolute rest each afternoon. You must rest four hours each day, in addition to ten hours sleep at night. The reason you need so much rest is because—" Tenny will want to interrupt and tell Mrs. Hull that she has already had quite a lot of experience at resting, on Doc Swain's orders, and she knows how to do it, and doesn't need any explanations of the need for it. But Mrs. Hull will consider that talking back, and will reprimand her for it. So Tenny will wait patiently, stretched out on her wooden lounge, until Mrs. Hull will finish her long lecture on the need for rest, and leave her alone.

Tenny will ask the woman reclining next to her, "Aint there nothing to read around here? No magazines or nothing?"

The woman will look at Tenny in shock, and then will look at the woman on the other side of her, as if to confirm that the other woman will have heard Tenny. Then she will say, in just a whisper, "Hush! We aint allowed to talk during Rest, ever, and we shore aint allowed to read nothing during Rest."

Tenny will lie there, taking in the view of Mt. Magazine, but her eyes will be hurting from the bright sky, until finally the bell will ring, and all of the women will get up identically, rising in the same motions, unwrapping their blankets in the same motions, and folding the blankets neatly in the same motions to leave on their identical wooden lounge chairs.

The woman next to Tenny will inform her, "Rest is over. It's Our Own Hours now." Our Own Hours is a kind of free spell, nothing required, and the residents of Hemingway Hall will want to meet the new girl, give her the once-over, and give Tenny all of the "inside dope" on the way of life here. Introducing themselves, they will reveal to Tenny something which will confirm her impression of the sameness, the uniformity of the place: every last one of them will have a given name or a nickname starting with P: there will be Pinkie, and Peeny, and Paula, and Petra, and Polly, and Portia, and so on: there are even some with very unusual names like Philadelphia and Phronsye and Persephone.

Giving her the lowdown on what's what, they will want to warn her that while visiting between the sexes is permitted in certain supervised areas during Our Own Hours (and a number of them will have already gone off to visit men and boys), the one rule that is the most hidebound rule at the sanatorium is that no "pairing off" is permitted between men and women. You may think of one of the fellows as your boyfriend, but you cannot go off alone with him, anywhere, anytime. Why, just last week two of the patients were caught trying to do some heavy wooing out in the woods behind Echols Hall, and both of them were "fired," that is, sent home to their families.

One thing that will be permitted, or at least will be overlooked or even not known to the authorities, will be communicating with your boyfriend at night by flashing him messages in Morse code with a flashlight, if his cottage or dormitory is within sight of yours. There will be a canteen in the main building, carrying all kinds of wonderful things and goodies, where you will be able to buy a flashlight. Will Tenny know the Morse code? No? Well, Pippa or Prunella or Poppy will be glad to teach it to her. First, of course, she will have to find herself a boyfriend to "correspond" with, and the best time to do that will be during the Monday night and Thursday night picture shows, when the men and women will be allowed to sit together.

Tenny will find some things to like about the place, such as those picture shows (even if she will never sit with a male, she will never have seen a picture show before, and will be spellbound, and will become almost addicted to the magical screen), some things that will leave her indifferent or just annoyed, such as the required religious worship services four times a week, and some things that she will not like at first but will come to appreciate, such as the daily shower. She will never have had a shower bath before, and, if you can imagine, her first experience with this new ablution will greatly discomfit her.

She will enjoy seeing her name in the newspaper. Hand me the top sheet from that stack. Just a few days after her arrival, she will get this issue of *Sanatorium Outlook,* and just as the picture show and the shower will be totally novel experiences for her, so will be the experience of seeing her name in print, set in type, somehow permanized. Here it is: "Let us welcome the new arrivals this week: Mrs. Petunia Butterfield, Gardiner Evans, Miss Patricia Brewer, Harry Dunlap, Mrs. Tennessee Breedlove," et al., et alia, two dozen names in all, but there is our Tenny big as life among them.

Here directly below the list of new arrivals is another column of names, beneath the headline ARRESTED THIS WEEK. Tenny will study the names, equally divided between males and females, not finding anyone she knows, and wondering what crimes they will have committed. She will have noticed, particularly among the men patients of the population, a number of shady-looking characters, almost thugs, whose very appearance will frighten her. But some of the women too, sickly and morbid and mean-looking, will have looked as if they were capable of

342

felonies or at least misdemeanors. Tenny will suppose that it will be possible to get yourself arrested just by violating any of the two dozen rules which she will have been required to memorize, and she will wonder if the sanatorium has its own jail where those arrested are locked up. Reading this house-organ newspaper, she will also learn that there are thirty thousand cases of tuberculosis in the state of Arkansas. She will wonder, since the population of the sanatorium is just a fraction of that, if all the others are just dying at home. She will learn that one of those thousands does indeed die every two and half hours, around the clock. And she will learn that the motto of *Sanatorium Outlook,* indeed the motto of the sanatorium itself, is "Better, Thank You."

Tenny will wait a long time for someone to ask her, "How are you today?" so that she will be able to say, "Better, thank you." But the chance will never come—not because nobody will ever ask her that, but because if they did she will only be able to reply, "Not any better, I'm sorry to say."

She will not be able to avoid the feeling that day by day she will be growing worse. The simple mirror will tell her that. She will visit the sanatorium's doctor for women, Dr. Baker, a handsome and friendly young man, more often than she will be required to. He will have given her X rays and fluoroscopes and a bunch of other tests. He will ask her who performed the artificial pneumothorax and she will tell him about Colvin. "Good job" will be his only comment. She will ask him if she cannot please, please have returned to her the harmless butterfly weed that Nurse Hull took away from her, and he will ask her where she got it, and she will tell him that Doc Swain gave it to her. "I suppose we might as well let you have it back," he will say, "but let me have it tested chemically first, just to make sure it can't do you any harm."

On her most recent visit to Dr. Baker, she will remind him that she will still not have got the butterfly weed back. Then, after he will have spent long minutes listening to her chest with his stethoscope, she will ask, "Will I ever be able to say 'Better, thank you,' when somebody asks how I am?"

His face will be full of sympathy. "I wish I could encourage you," he will say. "I wish so much that I could give you some hope. I wish so much that I could make you into a chaser." She will wait to hear him add, "But I cannot." He will not. His face will seem to say it.

She will write to Colvin, plaintively, "If I could only live long enough, I might learn how to live." But she will not be learning anything about how to live in that sanatorium. Paradoxically, she will be a prisoner of the clock and the bell which rings to signal the end of one period and the beginning of the next, but at the same time she will have no sense of time at all, so that after two whole months she will think that she will have been there only a month, and she will have to depend upon her one close friend, Penny (who will rhyme with her and even agree with her in many ways, including the nature and extent of her condition), to remind her that it is Monday or Thursday, the day of a picture show.

"I hate to ask you for anything, dear Colvin," she will write to him. "But the sunlight on the veranda hurts my eyes so, and some of the other women have smoked glasses which they wear to shade their eyes. I could buy some in the canteen, for only 78 cents, but I don't have a penny to my name."

In return Colvin will send her ten dollars, and a birthday card for her seventeenth birthday, on which he will write: "I wish this was more. But I am trying to save up my money so I can come and visit you, which would cost me hotels and food and all. Do you want me to come and see you?"

Tenny will be very happy that Colvin wants to come and visit her. Most of the other patients will have visitors from time to time, but she will not have. She will be worried that the very sight of Colvin will make her want to violate all sorts of rules with him. She will have heard the rumor that there is a certain place, in the basement of the main building, where patients who are married may take their visiting spouses for brief sessions of supposedly conjugal recreation, but Tenny, not married, or at least not to the man who will be visiting her, will not be able to apply for the use of that facility.

On a lovely day in March, with signs of spring in full flourish, Colvin will arrive during morning Rest and will wait patiently for morning Our Own Hour, when Tenny will come downstairs and into his arms. After they will have kissed, Tenny will tell him that one of the rules forbids all kissing. "I'll probably be arrested," she will declare. "Every week, a passel of folks gits arrested, for all kinds of things."

"I wish you could be," he will say, chuckling, and when she will look peeved he will take the trouble to explain to her something that nobody else has troubled to explain. "Arrested" in sanatorium parlance has nothing to do with the detainment of violators but refers to the checking of the disease. If your tuberculosis is arrested, you are well enough to go home, hence the *Sanatorium Outlook*'s regular list of those arrested is a list of those released from the sanatorium. "It would be so wonderful if your disease could be arrested," he will say to her. "But I reckon you know the chances are pretty slim for that."

She will have to wait, nervously, while Colvin will go off to confer with the sanatorium doctors, with Dr. Stewart and Dr. Baker. Our Own Hour will be expired before he returns, but he will have received permission to remain with her the rest of the day. "I aint too darn certain your doctors and me saw eye to eye on a lot of things," he will declare. "Leastways, they let me look at your X rays, and I managed to reclaim your butterfly weed. Also, I got permission to examine you myself. Come on."

Colvin will take Tenny out to his buggy, still drawn by good old Nessus, and will drive her the four miles into the town of Booneville, where he has a room at Herod's Hotel, not fancy but comfortable. Along the way, Tenny will want to know all of the news he knows from home. He will tell her that he will not be teaching at the Academy this term, although he will still be visiting once a week as the physician. Tenny's husband, Russ, and his girlfriend, Oona Owens, will be inseparable, and it will be assumed that since Tenny will never return that Russ and Oona will become permanently connected. Venda and Nick Rainbird will be talking of getting hitched. Jossie Conklin and Tim James will be doing likewise, and Tim will have been hired by the Mission Board to replace Jossie as principal. The basketball teams will be dissolved, but Russ himself will be teaching archery, and quite a lot of the student body will be taking lessons in the sport. Tenny will not ask Colvin if by any chance Piney has returned home; she will assume that Colvin will have told her if Piney had.

Finding herself alone with Colvin in his hotel room will be almost too much for Tenny. She will beg him to take her to bed. She will complain that it has been so long, months now, since she will have had him inside her—not even informing him of that last time, which he probably didn't know about—and she will miss it so, will dream of it so, will want it so.

"Dr. Baker told me you had morning sickness for two or three weeks," Colvin will say to her.

"Hell's bells, Colvin, I've had morning sickness, afternoon sickness, evening and night sickness too, day in and day out, but all I've got right now is heartsickness and lust. Take off your doctor's face if not your clothes and come to bed with me."

But he will keep his doctor's face, frowning, and will say, "Throwing up in the mornings is not a symptom of tuberculosis. It's usually a symptom of pregnancy."

She will think about that, and will declare, "It's true I aint flown the red flag the last few times I was supposed to."

"So," he will say. "It sure didn't take you very long to find yourself a boyfriend." His voice will express anger, so unlike him, and he will add with bitterness, "You know, I've been persuading myself it's just a superstition, or leastways just a faulty observation, that folks with TB are prone to get horny. But you seem to be a living example!"

She will laugh. "I never heard that. But I can tell you there are some gals in Hemingway Hall who don't never talk about nothing else! I can also tell you, though, that it's practically impossible for any couples in that sanatorium to find any way to get together for that purpose."

"So how did you manage to do it?"

"Colvin, even if I had a boyfriend, which I don't, the only way he could've knocked me up, with all the rules they've got in that place, would've been to slip me his sputum cup—we've all got these sputum cups we have to turn in twice a day—he could've slipped me his cup filled with his jism instead. Yeah. That must've been what happened." Saying this wryly, mockingly, she will have hoped to bring a grin to Colvin's face, but he will still look as all-fired solemn as ever.

"Then who was it?" Colvin will want to know. "When and where?"

She will take his hand. "Dear Colvin, I have never had any man inside me but you."

He will withdraw his hand. "The last time we did it was that Eureka hotel in November! That wouldn't give you morning sickness in February!"

"No, the last time we did it, or maybe I ort to jist say the last time I did it to you, was on the kitchen floor of my house on Brushy Mountain, in the middle of a night before Christmas."

He will stare at her, and will abruptly sit on the bed. She will sit beside him. "That's pretty hard to believe," he will say.

"I reckon there's a lot about me and you that's pretty hard to believe," she will observe, smiling. "But I did it to you without ever waking you up, and got your jism inside me at just the best time of the month, so now me and you are going to become Mommy and Daddy."

He will shake his head. "Having a baby will kill you."

"If it does, then the baby—and maybe it will be a girl—will keep you company in your loneliness, and maybe sometimes remind you of me."

Colvin's eyes will fill with tears. "Tenny, I won't never need nothing to remind me of you. I will remember you every day of my life, all the days of my life. But listen to me, sweetheart. It takes *nine* months to make a baby, and even if you could hold out that long, and the baby could be born, the baby would be infected with tuberculosis too. Even if you could do it, would you want to bring into this world a baby as sick as yourself?"

Tenny will think about that. Instead of answering his question, she will ask, "You don't think I can last nine months?"

"I brought you here to look at you," he will say. "Now we'd best get on with it."

He will have her undress. He will spend a long time with his stethoscope pressed to her chest, her back, her sides, even her shoulders, having her take deep breaths, shallow breaths, and coughs. He will look into every one of the openings of her body, including the one through which she will have hoped to pass the baby. "Hmmm" is all he will say, then or throughout his hour-long examination.

At length, he will ask, "Did Dr. Baker ever tell you how long he thought you might last?"

"No, only that I don't have much of a chance."

"There's something you've got to think about, Tenny, and I won't beat around the bush. Trying to carry that baby in your womb is going to shorten your life, which, Lord knows, aint going to be very long anyhow. My advice is: terminate the pregnancy. Now."

"You mean take it out of me? Aint that illegal?"

"Yeah, abortion is illegal, not only according to the laws of the state of Arkansas, which strictly forbid it, but also the policy of the sanatorium, which will not allow it."

Tenny will burst into tears, letting out a lot that she's been holding back. "I wanted so much to have your baby," she will say between her sobs. Colvin will keep his arm around her for a long time, until she will be able to stop crying. At length, when she will be in control again, she will ask, "So how can I git it taken outen me if nobody will allow it?"

He will tell her about Doc Kie Raney, and the oath that Kie had made him swear as a young doctor just starting out. "I've been practicing medicine now for many a year, but I've never performed an abortion. That don't necessarily mean that I don't know *how* to do it, though. I think I can do it. Would you trust yourself to me, knowing that all I want to do, all I could possibly do, is make you live just a little bit longer?" At these words, Colvin will burst into tears again himself, which will prompt Tenny to begin crying all over again, and they will just hold each other and have a good long cry for a good long time.

The rest of Colvin's visit will be a blur in her mind. Much of the rest of her short life will be a blur in her mind. She will recall asking Colvin if the abortion will hurt and he will assure her that it will not hurt nearly as much as the artificial pneumothorax, but it will hurt none the less, and produce blood. He will refuse her request to have a glimpse of the fetus. Will Colvin stay two more nights at Herod's? Or only one? She will not be able to tell. She will know that they will never be able to sleep together, and he will take her back to Hemingway each night, and then eventually he will be gone. She will not even be able to recall the details of their parting. There will not have been anything dramatic or sentimental about it that will furnish her memory something to dwell upon. Her memory, like her vision, will withdraw into blur.

When Dr. Baker will find out that she has had an abortion (which his very next examination will uncover), he will pretend at first to be sternly disapproving, because of sanatorium policy, but then he will say, "You know, if it weren't for the damned policy, I would have done it for you myself. Your Colvin Swain is a very wise man, and an incredible physician, with a vast knowledge of tuberculosis. Did he tell you that Dr. Stewart offered him Dr. Schroeder's job? Schroeder is leaving, and we need a men's physician, and Dr. Stewart made your Colvin a very good offer, with the added inducement that he'd be able to keep a close watch on *you,* who are apparently his all-time favorite patient. But apparently that wasn't enough to persuade him to give up his practice in Stay More. Tell me about this Stay More. What's it like?"

So Tenny, growing increasingly nostalgic herself, will attempt to give Dr. Baker a picture of Stay More, what little she knows of it. She will be haunted by the "what-if" of the possibility that Colvin could have become a permanent fixture around the sanatorium, and she will wonder why Colvin will have never mentioned the offer to her, but she will understand something she will not say to Dr. Baker: Colvin will have turned down the offer not because of his love for Stay More (although certainly that will be a strong consideration) but because he will have known that if he took the sanatorium job he might not hold it very long before his "all-time favorite patient" will no longer be there, because she will have gone to that Other Place where people no longer have to breathe or try to breathe or eat or try to eat or shit or try to shit.

She will be moved, eventually, from Hemingway to Hospital. The latter will not require long stretches of sitting on the porch in Rest. In fact, the schedule in Hospital will not even be the same as elsewhere in the sanatorium. No one in Hospital will be allowed out of bed.

One day Dr. Baker will announce to her, "We would like to try a thoracoplasty on you." The very name, which rhymes with nasty, will terrify her, and none of Dr. Baker's efforts to explain the need for the operation or what it involves will do anything to lessen her horror. She will realize why so often the rest of her short life will be becoming a blur: because a clear view of it will be too much to take, and she will not be able to accept the idea of a thoracoplasty, which will involve the removal of all of the ribs on one side of her chest, leaving her deformed and with long hideous scars. All she will be able to see in the blur is her body as a misshapen blob.

"If I've got just a short time on this earth anyhow," she will say, "I'd much rather that Colvin laid my pore body to rest with it still looking mostly like it ought to."

"But possibly the thoracoplasty will buy you some time to enjoy life a little longer," Dr. Baker will argue.

" 'Enjoy' aint the word," she will say.

"Wouldn't you rather get out of Hospital and go back to Hemingway?" he will attempt to tempt her.

She will realize that she misses the long Rests on the veranda, especially now that spring is here and everything is blooming and the air is so fine. But to pay eleven of her ribs for it? "Could I write to Colvin and ask him what he thinks of the thoracoplasty?" she will request.

Dr. Baker will look annoyed. "The operation ought to be done at once. I've scheduled it for tomorrow morning. By the time your letter got to Stay More and you received a reply, it would be too late."

She will attempt to write Colvin anyway, that last evening before the operation, but will discover that she cannot properly apply a pencil, let alone a fountain pen, to a sheet a paper. The effort will resemble a first-grader's letters, and, dismayed at her handiwork, she will allow all the letters to become a blur. She will ask the nurse to write a letter for her, but dictating a letter, something she will have never done before, will deprive it of its privacy and she will not be able to tell Colvin that she thinks Dr. Baker is some kind of mean rascal. "I guess by the time you get this, I won't be your Tenny anymore," she will say.

She will have hoped that the operation will be one of those where they put you to sleep and when you wake up it's all over and you don't feel a lot of pain. But she will discover that the operation will be performed under local anesthesia. She will be made to lie on her good side, with sandbags holding her flexed body in place, and most of what happens will happen behind her, on her back. If it will not have been for the newly acquired power of her mind to make a dull blur out of everything, she will have been able, if she desired, to count the removal of the ribs, one by one, with a big pair of shears that makes one cut on one end and another cut on the other end, and then she will have been able to hear the sound of each cast-off rib clattering into a bucket. But she will blur all this out and will think instead of Colvin's Hygiene class, that first day when they studied bones and she had made her comparison between the skeleton and the timbers holding up a building. What now will hold her up? Will she be able to stand? To walk?

Dr. Baker will assure her that with the help of a chest support she will be able to stand and to walk but that she ought to spend as much time as possible at Rest, on the Hemingway veranda. He will tell her that all the bandages will have to remain in place for a week, and that she will have to resist the temptation to look beneath the bandages to see if her body is still there.

After several days, she will ask him, "Was that operation supposed to make me *feel* any better?"

Maybe it will be a question that he will have never given any thought, because he will not be able to answer it. "Thoracoplasty has often been thought of as a lifesaving last resort," he will tell her. "We didn't do it to make you feel better."

By cruel coincidence, the day that the bandages will be removed will also be the day that Colvin will return.

"I wouldn't advise you to look in a mirror," Dr. Baker will caution her. But of course that will not stop her, although her mind will shift automatically into blur as she approaches the mirror, and she will not be able to notice the length or the shape or the configuration of the scar, nor even how it has made her lopsided. Being in blur, her mind will not even be able to notice that her face will still be Tenny, her hair will still be Tenny, her breasts—albeit one of them will be droopy on one side—will still be Tenny.

Being in blur, her mind will not even recognize Colvin when he will appear. "Tenny, sweetheart, it's me, Colvin," he will attempt to get her to see him. "I've come to take you home."

"Colvin?" she will say, trying to see him through the blur. "Why are you here? Have you come to take that job?"

"No, hon, I've come to take you home. Let's get all your stuff together and get out of here."

Dr. Baker will appear, and Tenny will recognize him. He will begin talking to Colvin, and Colvin will begin answering him, the two doctors talking simultaneously in rising animosity. Their contention and their noise and their gestures, which seem to be threatening each other with bodily harm, will upset Tenny and force her further into blur. She will be too blurred to notice that Dr. Stewart will have arrived also, and that the three doctors will have gone into another room, closing the door so that Tenny cannot hear their quarrel. For a long time they will leave Tenny alone in the cocoon of her blur.

"Tenny. Tenny." The caller of her name will be Colvin, and she will attempt to fight her way up out of the blur so that she can see him. "Tenny, sweetheart, listen to me careful, and see if you caint answer. Do you want to go home?"

"Not to Brushy Mountain," she will say.

"No, no, no. I reckon I had in mind Stay More. I ort never have let you leave it in the first place."

"Okay," she will say, and will manage a smile.

"Well, I aim to take ye there. The confounded problem is, this goddamn institution has got a policy which says a patient caint be discharged just on the signature of a physician. A family member has to sign the discharge papers."

Tenny's mind will be coming out of its blur enough for her to understand what this means, and she will wonder how they could possibly get the discharge papers up to Brushy Mountain for Momma or Daddy to sign them.

"There aint but one thing to do," Colvin will say, "and that's for me to become a family member. Tenny, will you marry me?"

Tenny will be simply thrilled, and will come entirely out of her blur. "Colvin Swain, how could you want to marry me, looking the way I do?" And she will turn to show him the hideous scar running down her back.

He will put his fingers beneath her drooping chin and lift it up. "You are just as beautiful as you ever was, and always will be," he will declare.

"But aint me and you both already married to somebody else?" she will want to know.

"Not as far as we're concerned," he will say. "As far as we're concerned we've done already been married to each other for quite a spell. But we've got to make it official. So I've got to run out and see if I caint find us a preacher. You just go up to your room and put on your best dress, and pack your suitcase, and I'll be back before you know it."

But Colvin will take a long time to return, and Tenny will begin to worry. She will have another worry too: just as her mind has a way of drifting into its blur, maybe she's also beginning to imagine things. Maybe Colvin will never have been here at all.

Nurse Hull will insist that Tenny take her afternoon Rest, even if she will be wearing her wedding dress. Tenny, still largely in control of the future tense, will determine that it will be the very last Rest she will ever have to endure.

Rest will not have ended when Colvin will return, with a man, dressed in gray and with one of those funny collars. Tenny will whisper to Colvin, "He aint a Catholic, is he?"

"No," Colvin will say. "He's an Episcopalian. I presented our situation, in honesty and truth, to several preachers, but they all turned me down, except this feller."

Where would they like to be married? Right there on the Hemingway veranda, in full view of all the other patients? No, they will go downstairs to a private room, the same room that Dr. Baker and Dr. Stewart will have used for their fight with Colvin. Tenny's friend Penny will serve as a witness and sort of the maid of honor. Colvin will reject the idea of either Dr. Baker or Dr. Stewart as the other witness and best man. He will recruit a simple man, a groundskeeper nicknamed by the patients "Grasshopper."

Tenny will be greatly moved by the beauty of the ceremony, so rich in contrast to the simple words that the courthouse justice had used to marry her and Russ.

She will be especially delighted that the ceremony, like this narrative, will appear to be in the future tense:

> Tennessee, will you have this man to be your husband; to live together in the covenant of marriage? Will you love him, comfort him, honor and keep him, in sickness and in health; and, forsaking all others, be faithful to him as long as you both shall live?

She will be about to answer in the future tense, "I will," but her poor body will collapse, and only the quickness of Colvin and the preacher will prevent her from falling to the floor. A chair will be drawn up into the gathering, and she will remain seated for the remainder of the ceremony. As soon as her body is propped into the chair, she will say, determinedly, "I will."

> Colvin, will you have this woman to be your wife; to live together in the covenant of marriage? Will you love her,

comfort her, honor and keep her, in sickness and in health; and, forsaking all others, be faithful to her as long as you both shall live?

Colvin will say, "I will."

The preacher will read from his Bible. "And they twain shall be one flesh; so then they are no more twain but one flesh."

Then Colvin will take her hand and say, "In the Name of God, I, Colvin, take you, Tenny, to be my wife, to have and to hold from this day forward, for better for worse, for richer for poorer, in sickness and in health, to love and to cherish, until death do us part."

She will reach for his hand and will repeat the words after him, "In the Name of God, I, Tenny, take you, Colvin, to be my husband, to have and to hold from this day forward, for better for worse, for richer for poorer, in sickness and in health, to love and to cherish, until death do us part." Then she will add, on her own, "Except that we won't be parted by death."

"That's for sure," Colvin will agree.

The minister will cast a disapproving eye upon this improvisation, then he will announce, "Now that Colvin and Tennessee have given themselves to each other by solemn vows, with the joining of hands, I pronounce that they are husband and wife, in the Name of the Father, and of the Son, and of the Holy Spirit. Those whom God has joined together let no one put asunder."

Tenny's husband will bend down and give her a long kiss. And over the next few days, he will kiss her so frequently and so passionately that she will be moved to ask, "Are you trying to give yourself my disease?"

"Yeah," he will admit. "I reckon I am."

Tenny's last memory of the sanatorium will be not so much a memory as an awareness of the need for her last blur: Dr.

Baker and Dr. Stewart, and another doctor too, whom she will not have recognized, still arguing with Colvin, continuing their controversy all the way out to the buggy, as Colvin will place her in it, and will climb into it himself and will say some final angry words at the doctors, and will cluck at Nessus and drive off.

She will never know just what the doctors were fighting about. Once the sanatorium is behind her, the blur will dissolve, and she will be able to see everything, to hear everything, to smell everything, all the way home to Stay More. Or almost.

Right away she will need to put on the smoked glasses she will have bought at the canteen with the money Colvin will have sent her.

When they reach the open highway, Colvin will say, "Now Tenny, I want you to tell me if the buggy's bouncing hurts you at all. I want you to let me know whenever we're going too fast, and I'll take Nessus down from a trot to a walk."

And when she will never complain about any discomfort of the buggy, he will say, "I want you to tell me any time you feel any pain, anywhere, and I'll give you something for it."

But she never will. Her only requests, infrequently, will be when she will need to "go," not just to make water but to defecate, an awkward and embarrassing situation, and the only truly unpleasant aspect of the journey.

They will need to spend three nights to reach home. The first night, their honeymoon night, will be in Paris, and Colvin will not be able to avoid making a few jokes about the great romantic city of Europe and what an ideal place for a honeymoon it would be. He will have very little money; they will stay in a very cheap hotel. She will not expect, nor ask, that he do on the honeymoon night what husbands are supposed to do. She will remind him that in a way they'd already had their

358

honeymoon night, that time in the Commercial Hotel in Jasper when she'd got married to Russ. She will be happy enough to go to sleep in his arms, although she will wake more than once to find him hooked up to her chest with his stethoscope. "Put that thing away and go to sleep," she will say, and will realize how bossy, how wifely, it sounds, and she will think, *Tenny Swain.*

Their second night, in a hotel in Clarksville, she will have thought for a long time about having control of the future tense and what it implies, and how it's something both powerful and dangerous, like dynamite: it can help build or it can help destroy. It will be easy, with the future tense, to get little things you want; for instance, she will ask Colvin, since he will be trying to go to sleep with his ear up against her chest anyway, if he would mind sucking on her breasts, and he will gladly oblige. Since she will never have been able to have a baby, she will want to know what it feels like, and Colvin will not mind, although he will admit he will never have done it before. She will discover that it will make her very horny, and she will wish that they were able to make love, because obviously it will have made Colvin somewhat horny too. The exquisiteness of the sensation will be something that she will be able to take with her, wherever it is that she is soon going, that Other Place perhaps. In the past tense, "He sucked her breasts," and regardless of how well he did it, it was done, and all she had left was the memory of it. In the present tense, "He sucks her breasts," and it is driving her wild, for the whole duration of the present moment, but the moment does not last. In the future tense, "He will suck her breasts," and it will be a feeling that she will be able to have any time she will want it. For eternity.

Their third day on the road, she will begin to think a lot about dear old Grampaw McArtor and that Other Place that he

359

talked about going to when he died, that place where every bird and bug went when their time was over, and the birds and bugs as well as the people didn't have to breathe anymore, nor eat, nor take a shit. She will wonder what sort of place it really is, because Grampaw didn't give her a very good description of it, and just suggested that perhaps folks could go fishing or fiddle and dance and sing even if they didn't breathe nor eat nor take shits. Tenny will wonder if the place will look anything like *this*, for they will have reached the Ozarks now—"Not much further to the Newton County line," Colvin will say—and she will want that Other Place to look as much as possible like this place. She will recall those old jests about how Ozarkers gone to Heaven break down and cry every springtime out of homesickness.

Fortunately for her husband, who will be broke, the proprietor of the tiny hotel in Fallsville will know Colvin, and will agree to let them have on credit the room for their last night. Tenny will not touch her supper. "You aren't eating," Colvin will observe.

"One out of three," she will say.

And later, in bed, when he will do his thing with the stethoscope, and pressing his ear to her chest, he will observe, "You don't seem to be breathing."

"Two out of three," she will take enough breath to say.

And all the next day, as they will drive the last miles over the hills and mountains toward Stay More, not once will she ask him to stop so that she can relieve herself. She will say to herself, "If all three of them things have done come to pass, I must already be *there,* but I sure caint tell that it's no different." She will so pleased and comforted to know that it does not look any different that she will snuggle up against Colvin and put her head on his shoulder.

"Thank you for bringing me home," she will say to him.

"Thank ye for coming home," he will say, and then, in the future tense, "We will soon be there."

And in the future tense, they will always soon be there.

From that vantage point, with her corporeal head on his shoulder, she will cross forever from the world of eating and breathing and shitting to the world of . . . but we will have to let her, who will always remain in charge of this tense, to tell what she can.

She will be glad to discover that although she has surrendered heartbeat and breath and digestion and elimination and all that bodily business, she will not have surrendered her control of the future tense. They will pass a fisherman sitting on the bank of the creek, and she will be so certain that it will be Grampaw McArtor she will try to call this to Colvin's attention, but will discover that she will have surrendered voice as well. She shall never again be able to "speak" to him. She will have surrendered all her senses: hearing, sight, touch, everything. So how then will she be able to perceive? Only she will be able to tell, but she will be able to tell this much: that all senses will be replaced by a single pervasive sense of *tell*, as in "How can you tell?" or "Can you tell what that thing is?" or "You can't even tell the difference"—none of these implying speaking, informing, or narrating, but only perception, not necessarily visual. Tenny will find herself able to tell anything. She can tell the time of day without a watch, but will have no desire to. She can tell what Colvin is thinking, but will never be able to tell him that she can tell. She can tell that she will never again feel any pain nor hunger nor be required to toil. She can tell at once the answer to a question which has always bothered her about this Other Place: "Do people—or souls or whatever they become—ever go to sleep and have dreams?" She can tell that both sleeping and dreaming are parts of the living body's functions, and thus she no longer will need them, nor have any further thought of them. Even if she will have wanted them, she will be too busy telling ever to have time for them.

She will become almost like a child with a new toy, discovering what-all she can tell, what-all she will be able to do: she will so easily rise and soar a thousand feet above the buggy and can tell its movements in relation to the winding road and landscape; she will be able to leap on ahead to Stay More and can tell that the town will be waiting there for their soon arrival. She can tell that the sense of humor will be the most powerful of all "living" qualities retained by the "dead," and her playful sense of humor will think that it would be funny if she could just stand there on Colvin's front porch waiting to welcome him. But while that impossible image will amuse her, she realizes that a much more serious moment will be occurring as soon as Colvin brings the buggy to a halt and discovers that his bride apparently asleep on his shoulder will no longer be alive.

She can tell there will be nothing she will be able to do about it. She will be able to *be* there, but she will not be able to make her presence known or felt or heard. But she can tell that just being there will make it much easier on Colvin. That, and his own knowledge that the duration of her life on earth could only be numbered in hours.

Still, he will be wracked with grief. He will simply remain in the buggy for a long time holding her body. Then he will carry her into his house and place her on a bed, her hands folded together over her stomach. He will go into his office and write the death certificate, and she can tell what he has written under "Cause of death:" *Fibrocavernous pulmonary tuberculosis.*

362

Later he will take her to E. H. Ingledew, who is both the town's dentist and its mortician. E. H. will embalm the body and prepare a casket for it.

Colvin will have to speak with several people about the matter of burying her in the Stay More cemetery. By ancient tradition, only native Stay Morons can be buried there. As you pointed out in the architecture novel, not even the great Eli Willard, the perennially returning peddler, who had spent enough of his very long life visiting Stay More to be considered at least an honorary Stay Moron, was permitted to be buried in Stay More cemetery. One had to be born in Stay More to be buried there. (Strictly speaking, as we recall, Colvin himself was not born in Stay More and thus had no right to be buried there, but all the dead Swains had always been buried there, so it was his right by default.)

After much deliberation and heated argument, the men of Stay More will agree upon one solution: if a double headstone would be erected, Tenny on one side waiting for Colvin's eventual interment on the other side, that would be acceptable. And that will be what will happen. There will be few attending the graveside service, in a downpour, scarcely enough people to make up the four singing parts of the four-part harmony for "Farther Along"; indeed, there will be no soprano, but Tenny will provide it herself, delighted to note that the words of that old funeral hymn are in the future tense: "Farther along we'll know all about it, farther along we'll understand why . . ." But she will already understand why.

Tenny will always like to visit the spot, anytime she can tell, not that she will necessarily approve of the barbaric custom of sticking dead bodies into the earth. She will like that double headstone, an ultimate expression of bigeminality, if you will, even though it will be many years before Tenny will get a chance to tell your architecture novel. Once, years or so later, while she will be admiring the double headstone and dusting some debris off of it (for the one power of moving things which the dead retain is a certain control over the breezes), an automobile will drive up, and a woman will get out of it and stand for several long moments over the grave, which will not yet have received Colvin. Tenny can tell that it will be Piney. She can tell that Piney will be feeling some sadness, and just a tinge of jealousy, to be reading the name "Tennessee Tennison Swain" carved into the same block as "Colvin U Swain." Piney will not remain long, and will visit nothing else, no one else.

Well, sir, you yourself will go back to that cemetery yourself the next chance you will get, tomorrow maybe, so that you will be able to confirm that it will be there like Tenny has been telling you. Tenny will be there when you will arrive, and although she will possibly not manifest her presence to you in any way, not even in the breeze, she will let you know that she will be fully in control of the future tense, and will never relinquish it. But if you will stand at that grave long enough, which now contains both of them, and if you will listen hard enough, with your hearing aid turned up as high as it will go, you might even be able to hear the lovely soprano voice singing that aria of pure notes, rising and falling, not meant to say anything but only to chant, or to carol, some wordless expression of that feeling of kindly melancholy, a mixture of yearning, wanting, hoping, desire, with maybe a tinge of loss and bewilderment. You will think you are being haunted by the last fading notes of the Ozarks.

She will never have haunted Colvin, let alone have appeared to him. But, having waited a decent, seemly length of time after the funeral, she will begin regularly to "do something" about his nocturnal erections. She will recall that information he'd given her about incubus and succubus, and she will even recall (she can tell anything that she ever said or was ever said to her) her exact words in proposing what they'd originally tried to do: "I'll be your concubine and succubate you?" And of course she will recall as if it were only a moment ago (in fact it was) the night on Brushy Mountain she caused the sleeping Colvin to impregnate her. So it will be easy for her to begin the practice that she will continue for the rest of his life: entering his dream and giving his erection enough attention to detonate and defuse it.

Alas, it will be my mention of this which will lead to some ultimate ill-feeling between Colvin and myself, and to my departure from Stay More. Colvin will have been continuing, on a daily basis, to sit with me on his porch and relate the end, painful though it be, of the long story he will have been telling me. Almost by unspoken consent, I would cease being his houseguest as soon as his story will have ended. My typhoid fever will have been totally cleared up, I will have been fit as a fiddle, and there will have been no excuse, really, for me to stay more at Stay More except my love for the place and my desire to hear of what will have happened to him in the years after Tenny's death.

But there is so much of what you have been learning that Colvin could not possibly have known: all the things that happened to Tenny on Brushy Mountain and in the sanatorium, all her thoughts and feelings that have come to us under her own point of view in the future tense. If I didn't get any of this from Colvin, and I'm not just making it up, where does it come from? I wish I could give some "valid" explanation, such as that Tenny's spirit visited me as I lay on that cot which had been her bed. Or that she will have told me all of this during the "visitations" when she comes to me if I close my eyes right.

But the truth will be that Tenny can not only tell, she can also tell.

At whatever point Tenny will have taken over the telling, and the "telling," she will not only have made herself immortal but also have made her story not something which happened, or is happening, but will be happening, as long as she is still "around." And believe me—or you know it, don't you?—she's very much around. Remember I told you how I can close my eyes to make someone disappear and be replaced by someone else? Don't be offended, but I will be replacing *you* with Tenny, all the time. I will see her *now*.

One afternoon Colvin and I will be sitting on the porch, and Rowena will be quitting for the day. As Rowena will walk down the porch steps and out into the road, she'll give her fine hips a jauntier swing than usual, and when she'll be out of earshot, I'll banter with Doc, "Did you ever git any of that?"

Doc will chuckle, and will blurt, "Never had no need of it."

"Oh?" I will say, and before I can stop myself will ask, "Because Tenny takes care of you every night?"

Doc's mouth will fall open, and he will stare at me, and then his face will grow very red. I will not be able to "tell" if the red is embarrassment or anger. Maybe some of both. Then he will demand, "How'd you know that?"

"It's part of the story," I will observe.

"But goshdang ye, it aint no story that I ever tole ye!" he'll declare. "Where'd you hear it?"

"Did you ever tell it to anyone?" I will challenge him. "Even Latha?" He will shake his head. "Then how could I have heard it anywhere?"

"Have you been sneaking into my diary?" he will demand.

"You never told me you kept a diary," I will say.

"I don't," he will admit. "But where in blazes did you learn about what Tenny does at night . . . unless you're just making a wild guess?"

Well sir, we will have gotten ourselves into quite a flap or row over this matter, and, as such things will, it will escalate until we're hurling epithets at each other which we will both regret the next day. Quite possibly I will have known that my time at Stay More will have come to an end and unconsciously I will have been picking a quarrel with him in order to make the parting easier. But as it will turn out, we will even argue over his bill. He will refuse to present me a bill, and will accept nothing. I will insist upon paying at least for the medical care if not for all the room and board or "hospitalization," but he will act as if my money is tainted and won't touch it.

I will not even be able to recall my last words to him, as I will be putting on my hat and lifting up my knapsack. But I will think they were: "Don't you see, Doc? She will still be telling all of it, and always will."

We will keep in touch, sporadically, over the years, with postcards. Doc will never have been much of a letter-writer. I will learn over the years how he will continue his obsession with the Great White Plague. Not from him will I learn the story of how, during the Second World War, one day in the heat of August, Colvin will discover some of his free-ranging chickens acting sick, having trouble breathing. Still being a veterinarian himself from way back, he will take cultures from the chicken's throats and after incubating the plates for several days he will observe cultures of actinomycetes developing. He will excavate the soil in which the chickens will have been scratching, and will find that the organisms are resident in the soil, and he will continue working with these cultures until he feels he has discovered enough to send them off to other scientists who are working on the problem, one of whom, named Selman

Waksman, will convert Colvin's cultures into a powerful anti-biotic called streptomycin, and will receive the credit for having discovered it. Colvin will not have been interested in any credit, anyway. He will simply have wanted, with all his heart, to wipe out the Great White Plague. And his streptomycin will have done it.

Will it be time for you to leave, now? Yes, soon; I will have only two things essentially left to say: how Colvin himself will have gone to join his beloved Tenny in the Land of Telling, which you will possibly already have known. I will forget the year; perhaps it will have been as late as 1957. They will say, as they will never tire of saying wondrous things about Colvin U Swain, that he will have had an opportunity to have done something that he had not quite been permitted to do that day on those rounds in the St. Louis hospital so many, many years before: he will restore a dead man to life. You will wonder, anyone will wonder: if he will have been capable of it, why will he not have done it to Tenny thirty some years before? We will never know. We will know only that this man, who will be clinically dead, and will have been so for a great number of hours, will be resurrected by Colvin. We will not even bother with the man's name. The man will have meant nothing personally to Colvin; just one more Stay Moron with a terminal disease. But Colvin will have always believed: *The patient need not mean anything whatsoever personally in order to receive the physician's most devoted attention.*

Anyway, the gods or Whoever will have been angry with Colvin for restoring life, because one day not long after, while he will have been walking fast to get out of a rainstorm, he will have been hit by a thunderbolt and reduced to a pile of ashes, just enough ashes to be placed in a cannister and interred beside Tenny at that double tombstone.

So much for Colvin. Recently, I will have written this simple note to Mary:

"Dear Mary Celestia: The VA people will attend to all the details of my burial—undertakers, coffin, grave diggers, etc. Even the flag on the coffin, the chaplain, and a government marker for a tombstone. *ALL FREE*. If anybody asks you for money, call your lawyer. Wommack, isn't it? You don't have to do *ANYTHING*. If you don't feel like going out to the National Cemetery, *Don't Go*. I am sorry I have no money to leave you, Mary Celestia. I love you, as always. Vance."

I will not know, of course, how much more time Tenny will grant me in this future tense of hers. I might well be able to stick around for a few more years, but I'd just as soon get on over to the Fiddler's Green in the Land of Telling as soon as they will be able to make room for me on the Liar's Bench. I tell you, when I reach the Land of Telling, I intend to tell 'em a thing or two!

But all that telling, whether we mean knowing or narrating, is as immaterial and fugitive as those breezes bearing Tenny's song, or the imagined choiring of trees. Her future tense may never come to an end, but it will pause for now, with the realization that the only way she will ever be able to give shape and substance and heart to it will be to transmit it to me in such a way that I will be able to pass it along to you, and you will be able, one of these years, to turn it into novel, giving the reader two whole handsful of Tenny's future tense.

Which is exactly what I will have done, for Tenny no less than for you. Good-bye, my boy. Godspeed.